Two Souls

Two Souls

Book 1

By
David Davila

ARPress
ILLUMINATING IDEAS.
EMPOWERING VOICES

Copyright © 2022 by David Davila

All rights reserved. No part of this publication may be reproduced, distributed, or transmitted in any form or by any means, including photocopying, recording, or other electronic or mechanical methods, without the prior written permission of the copyright owner and the publisher, except in the case of brief quotations embodied in critical reviews and certain other noncommercial uses permitted by copyright law. For permission requests, write to the publisher, addressed "Attention: Permissions Coordinator," at the address below.

ARPress
45 Dan Road Suite 5
Canton MA 02021

Hotline: 1(888) 821-0229
Fax: 1(508) 545-7580

Ordering Information:
Quantity sales. Special discounts are available on quantity purchases by corporations, associations, and others. For details, contact the publisher at the address above.

Printed in the United States of America.

ISBN-13:   Softcover   979-8-89356-291-0
                eBook   979-8-89356-290-3

Library of Congress Control Number: 2024903323

Table Of Contents

CHAPTER 1

"Two Souls," Juanita the old woman said out loud firmly. She spoke out the name of the evil Witch doctor that she would soon speak of. She looked at the children sitting several feet away from her waiting in anticipation. The village children that had gathered to listen to the story of Two Souls. She smiled then waved her hand to quite the children down. She put her right hand to her ear until there was a complete silence. After a moment pause, she brought her hand down to her lap and took a deep breath. It was as if to inhale the piece of her surroundings before she began. She looked up into the sky. She saw an eagle flying above this to Juanita was a sign that the "Great One" was watching and giving her the sign to continue.

The old woman said out loud and firmly as she spoke the name of Two Souls once again. She looked at the children sitting several feet away from her. The village children that had gathered to listen to the story of Two Souls. She smiled then waved her hand from left to right to quite the children down. She put her right hand to her ear once more until there was a complete silence.

She took in another deep breath.

"Ah," she sighed then says, "It is a good day."

She looked at the children then placed a wooden box on the small bench then sat down next to it. She began the story of "Two Souls."

The old woman used her legs to scooted back on the bench. She starts to lean back as she did the front legs of the bench lifted off the floor. She leaned back against the wooden shack that was her home.

The shack seemed as if it would topple over on its own from the old age. Juanita was wrinkle with age and time as well. The shack creaked the paint was peeling. Time had taken its toll on both of them. Both had seen there better days in this life. The old boards squeaked as she leaned back against the shack. She studied the look on the children's faces. All the children had the expression of anxiousness written on them. Juanita smiled a big smile at them. She took out an eagle feather from her pocket. In the old language she began to say a prey to protect them from evil. She paused for a moment then spoke.

"Children listen to my words carefully for this story that I am about to tell you is true. A story that in time has become only a folktale to most. A tale that the old ones which that had never happen. Listen carefully!"

Juanita waited another moment for her words to sink in. "Children it is said that Two Souls climbed up that mountain."

She pointed in the direction of the mountain in back of them she then continued on with the story.

"There. There Two Souls climbed up the mountain to the place of the seven guardians. The seven guardians carved into the seven pylons that rest against the walls of the crater. Seven small knolls in the center of this crater. The pylons in front of these small hills guarded or sealed in what is behind the carved demons. Yes! Demons where carved into them. These pylons circle around the inside of that mountain. I will explain how this was possible. Long time ago a crater the size of a football field had been created by a meteor. I should say that whatever it was that landed had life and had created the crater. They had placed the stone carvings around the inside of the crater. No, one really knows how they got there. It was not a U.F.O. This world has many magical thing, angles, ghost, and demons. All that we know is that they are there. If you stand in the middle of this crater and follow the pylons from the ground up. It will seem, as if the pylons touched the sky. From where you stand it appears that they are looking down on you. From these pylons seven hideous creatures from the underworld reach out. Yes! They seemed as if somehow, they are alive. You can feel their evil presents children. It is as if their eye followed your every movement.

Though they are all hideous creatures the seventh? The seventh is the most horrifying of them all. It faces to the west. It is a serpent. But not like the serpents we know as being a snake, or dragon. The seventh one was more like a cross between a dragon and snake of sorts. It is a two headed serpent. One of the serpent's head was that of a man with snake eyes. The other head was that of a "Diamondback Rattler," with human eyes. This thing was not sent from heaven it was sent by the evil God below."

The old woman stopped for a moment as several of the children shifted to get comfortable. She waited, knowing the ground was hard on the back end. She began to speak again. She looked at the children with their hands on their laps looking up at her listening earnestly to what she had to say. She leaned forward and the bench front legs thumped dully on the wood planks that formed the porch. She stood the planks squeaked as well. She walked up to the wood brace that held a small roof that gave shade to the porch.

"Here amongst our people, it is said children. It is said that Two Souls worked around a fire. A fire he had lit in front of these two headed demons. Here he chanted the Devil's chant. A chant that he sang as he danced around the fire. Two Souls vowed to return and take his place in the present world. Here he would become the prince of evil. I know that some of it sounds as if it were made up. But believe me it was not children. The remaining Aztec off springs like me tell of this story. They want to keep it alive for it needs to be kept alive and never forgotten. Many believe that it is made up and that it is just a folktale as I said before. They believe that the serpent demon did not exist. I tell you straight out that they are wrong children. They are very wrong. Two Souls did live, and he will do as he promised. One day he will return. Several of the boys laughed and waved their hands as if swatting a fly in front of them in disbelief. One of the girls looked at the boys angrily tilting her nose up at them then turned back around. One of the mothers dressed in a green dress and a Mexican scarf wrapped around her shoulders stepped up to her son. She tapped him on the shoulder letting him know she did not care for his disrespect to the old woman. As the boy looked up at her she slapped him in back of the head.

"Laugh again Pedro."

The boy gave his mother an angry look. His mother stepped forward again and as she did, she raised her hand. He looked at her and his face change from the angry look he had given to her to that of that of an angel smiling back at her. He smiled and blinked at her. Though the slap in back of the head really did not hurt him. He did not feel like getting swatted again. The old woman waited for the boy to turn back around. She nodded to the boy's mother and continued.

"Unbelievable or not I have a son who did not believe in the ways of the old ones. Yes, he was of the new age. He decided to leave. He packed up and went to the United States. He left his beliefs behind here in this land and his people. He got married and had a son.
He has never returned. They did send my grandson to live with me in his infant years. I taught him everything. The rituals to protect himself from the evil one. I told him of Two Souls and that one day he would have to do battle with the evil one. He wanted to believe in the old ways of our people. But when he got older, he decided to go to the United States to find his father. He was torn from this world to his father's world. He was confused and he did not know what to do. So, he joined the Marine Corps. He fought well in this war, the Viet- Nam war. He was given the Medal of Honor. The last time I saw him was many years passed.   Once I was told that they had seen him and that he was living on the streets of Austin, Texas as a homeless bum. I can say this broke my heart.

"Do you think he will ever come back?"

"I don't really know Dolores, only time will tell," she told the little girl in the front then sighed and continued, "let me give you some background to this story. Maybe you'll be able to understand it a little better. They say that Montezuma had a sacred serpent. It was a giant rattler. They say that if this serpent appears to you. You should kiss its tongue. The belief is that it will bring you great wisdom and powers Dolores," she tells the little girl then continues, "but children there is a bad side to this story. A side that you most heed to. You see this serpent could be a demon. It could be the Devil so one has to be very careful. Now, Two Souls on the other hand he was evil from the day of his birth. The old ones say that their where no stars in the sky and that the night was darker than it should have been. They say that the wolves howled that night as never before. Animals know, they can sense when evil is near. If he was not of the dark side, it did not matter for the evil presents was there on that night. His mother's labor was all most done.

He was to be born at midnight and it waited for it wanted him. When Two Souls got older, he went up into the hill. It was as if it had been preordained. This is where Two Souls met with the Devil Serpent. This is when he sold his soul to it. He sold his soul for power. For power from the underworld. It is said that "Two Souls" was quite a good looking man when he climbed up that mountain. But when he returned from the mountain he had changed. He had returned with two faces.

"How grandma?" Pedro asked.

"I do not know but he did come back with two faces. Half of his face was still that of a handsome young man. The other half was that of what seemed to be scaled reptilian. A hideous deformed creature. More of a snake than that of a man. He was given the highest of all evil powers. From that day on he had become the most horrifying and the most powerful Witch doctor ever known to man. The old ones say that he could turn people into horrible things. If they did not live up to their bargain with him. In a way I guess they had made a pact with the devil himself. I as a small child as you heard this story for the first time when I was five." My grandmother would say to me.

Juanita my grandmother lived to be a hundred and twenty-seven years old. I was your age when I heard the story. My grandmother told me that Two Souls was in his early thirties. Many of the men and women from our village differ on the age. All I can tell you Juanita she said. I was ten years old when he climbed up into that mountain. Many years past and Two Souls remained young. His body remain that of a twenty-year-old. But his heart that was another matter. His heart was tiring, and it would soon stop as all do. Two Souls was given a ritual that would restore his heart. It gave a new meaning to the phrase. "TO LIVE IS TO DIE, AND TO DIE IS TO LIVE." Two Souls had lived over four hundred years. This was before he sold his soul. He knew it was time for his journey to hell. To hell where he would invoke the powers of the great demon once again. He dressed in his old Aztec head dress and feathers. He climbed up the mountain to the crater. To the seven small hill that circled around inside it like fingers forming a hand cradling it. It was a slow climb with an occasional stop for him to catch his breath. Climbing the mountain, he now stood in front of the two headed serpent. He stood in silence just looking at the demon. It was as if he were speaking to it telepathically. He stood mumbling words in a deep tone. The six guardians carved into the other six pylons were there as if to protect him.He knelt in front of the demon. He placed his ritual tools on the ground. He prayed the Devils prayer for immortality."

"Old woman, prayers are for the Great one?"

"Yes, Gilbert, but the "Evil One" has prayers for his bidding as well."

The wind blew softly caressing their bodies sending a chill up their spine. Suddenly it was as if they could fill the evil circling around them. The small dirt swirls moved about then vanished into thin air. The children shifted and turned away from the dust. They then got comfortable as the dust and wind died down.

"Two Souls," she said out loud then soften her voice as she continued, Two Souls lit a fire at the base of these two headed serpents. The fire grew with tremendous energy. Its luster in the night gave life to the serpent.It made it appear as if it were alive. Its shadow seemed too swayed back and forth. It looked as if it swayed back and forth as all snakes do before they strike. The serpent's eyes followed Two Souls as he moved about and chanted. As the fire grew it took life of its own. It as well seemed that the serpents shadow behind it had come to life. The shadow swaying as a separate entity. Abruptly a strong stench of sulfur fills the night air. It lingered heavily over the crater. The sulfur smell was a hint that the dark one was coming. Two Souls continued to chant as he looked at the serpent statue. His eyes moved up following the statue upward.

The demon towered over him. He believed the demon statue welcomed him. He could see fog rolling in over the ground. The clouds move above like a cattle drive that caused a dust storm as they rushed along up above. The clouds slowly covered the crater above forming a dome overhead sealing the place in below. It was as if it were a barrier of sorts. A barrier that kept everything in and allowed nothing out. Two Souls stood he turned to look at the other creatures carved into the pylons along the inside of the hill. Each pylon with its own unique creature. As the fog lower down, it was as if Two Souls could see the demons trying to escape from their captivity. Each trying to get out of the pylons. The carvings trying to escape but contained by the prayer imprinted over their heads. Prayer the only thing that held them captive. Midnight the witching hour had come. Two Souls turned back around and then knelt down before the two headed serpent.

He began the ritual that would bring hell amongst the human race with a vengeance. Immortality and powers that would let the devil live within him. He stood and from a pouch that he had picked up off the ground he began to make a circle around the serpent. A green powder first then with a yellow powder. He made another circle around the two headed serpent. He continued to chant as he completed the circle around the serpent enclosing the area around him. No, matter what came out of this night. May it be human, or beast, he was protected.

He was protected as long as he did not break this circle. As long as he did not, nothing could get in or out. Nothing could harm him. He began to dance. The fire bringing the beautiful headdress and the green quetzal, the blue cotinga feathers, and gold disk's tail to life. His shadow behind him dance following his every move. In Two Souls left hand he held a scepter. He held it high as he danced and chanted. The scepter held a head of a rattler. A diamond as big as a golf ball that was clutched in its teeth reflected the fire light. Its reflection like small flashes of fire blinking on and off sparkling. The scepter was at least seven feet. In the middle dead center the diamond sat with all its brilliants. He took the scepter placed it at the right side of the serpent. He chanted to the demons of the night. He danced the dance of the dead. He stopped looked at the two headed serpent. He then took a dagger from his side. He cut twice across his right cheek then twice across his left forearm.

"We are now blood brother's spirits of the underworld," Two Souls said as he lifted his head up to look at the sky. He stretched his arms out wide as he said the words out loud. Stars twinkled in the distance around a full moon. A moon that was hidden from his view by the fog. He continued his ritual then a hole began to form in the clouds up above. He looked up and could see twinkling stars above. He saw two shooting stars shoot across the sky from two different directions. A tail of fire follows their path. The stars seemed to be on a collision course of destruction heading towards each other. Suddenly at the last minute. The last second to impact they shifted. Each shot off in different directions. They circle high then joined then shot up even higher into the heavens. It had been a sign for Two Souls.

He took the same green and yellow powders from the small leather pouch. He walked up to the left side of the statue. He tossed the powder into the fire at the base of the serpent demon. The fire rose with enormous power and radiance. Two Souls knelt down in front of the serpent. From another large leather pouch at his side, he withdrew a clay pot, a chalice, and a small wooden mold. He reached for the dagger at his side. This dagger magnificent in its own rite. It had a pearl handle and on the hilt of the knife. A large silver rattlers head with red rubies for its eyes peered back. On the ground yet there was another pouch. But this pouch had life of its own. Something squirmed inside it. It wiggled with life. Two Souls placed the clay pot into the fire. He placed the raw gold into it. Before placing the pieces of gold into the clay pot. It is believed that he carved three sixes on each of the three pieces of gold. He knelt down again in front of the serpent demon. He lay the chalice in front of him then the dagger to his left. He reached over retrieved two small pouches. He took a pinch of the two different powders into his fingers. He stretched his arms out wide as he said the words out loud. Stars twinkled in the distance around a full moon. He continued his ritual then the hole in the clouds above began to grow.

"Let us become one tonight dark brother," he chanted. He tossed the powders into the fire at the base of the Demon serpent. Again, the flames shot up with a brilliance of colors then fused. They formed a rainbow of light around the circle he had made on the ground. The time had come. Death would soon come upon him like a ghost in the night. Suddenly the serpent demon began to glow with an illustrious green aura. The aura surrounds the statue. Two Souls took more powder and toss it into the flames making the rainbow of colors more magnificent. The flames shot up and danced like newfound demons themselves. Two Souls reached down grabbed the pouch that had life of its own. He opened the pouch placed his hand into the opening. He then slowly retrieved a pinkish brown "Diamondback Rattler." The snake hissed as it came to life. It coiled around Two Souls arm coiling around it like a coiled spring. The Diamondback rattled its tail frantically with hate. The dark brown patches with a tint of black around the edges hinted of the danger and the ability it had to kill man. Two Souls lifted the snake eye level to his. He stared into the snakes' eyes as if hypnotizing the snake.

The snake mouth opened exposing the two huge fangs on the inside of its mouth. Two Souls slapped the top of the snake's head then chanted several words. These words put the snake into a deep trance. He took what appeared to be a small pear like fruit form his side. He bit into it. He began to chew the substance in his mouth. He spit the residue out of his mouth and began to chant. He took the remainder of the fruit and placed it into the chalice on the ground. He looked at the demon statue chanted more words. He placed the chalice down in front of him. He took the dagger chanted and lifted his left arm. He said several words then cut twice across his wrist. He let his blood fall into the chalice. He placed the dagger down. He lifted the cup high over his head. He chanted then placed it back on the ground. He placed the head of the rattler over the chalice. He squeezed the side of the snakes' head, and drained its venom into the cup. Again, he lifted the chalice high above his head.

"Like church grandma?"

"That is right Rudy just like church.

The old woman waited for a moment then continued.

"Two Souls stood and walked up to the fire. He reached into the fire with his bare hands. He retrieved the clay pot that now held molten gold. His hands sizzled as the heat burned through his flesh. He walked back turned around then stared at the demon for a moment and knelt back down before it. He poured the molten gold into the mold he had placed on his right side for this precise moment. He lifted it high. He chanted for several minute the ritual of the Devil. He spoke out loud.

"This is our brother from below the earth its soul is of pure darkness. For it knows no light. Its evil is strong for it can make a man kill another man for its worthless contribution to man. I ask of you to accept this offering. Give me immortality to live. To live for you Dark One." By this time the gold had harden. Two Souls tapped the mold with his dagger several times until it released its hold on the gold. From the mold it felt free. It was released and before him was a coin with a two headed serpent with human eyes on one side. On the other side a man with snake eyes. He raised the chalice over his head.

"Elixir of life give me power to live beyond this meaningless world. Evil powers of hell give me life to live. Bring me back from hell the world of the dead. Give me the demon's soul of all darkness. I summon you to make us as one Dark One." Then suddenly out of nowhere an explosion of flames at the base of the demon. The statue began to glow brighter and brighter as time passed. It seemed that it would burst from the enormous amount of power being generated through it. An eerie quietness surrounds the place. Abruptly like a giant spear in the night the green energy around the demon shot up into the sky. It came back circled around the serpent dove into the fire below. The fire exploded sparks flew out like possessed drunken fireflies encompassing the night air. They shot off in all directions. Two Souls drank the liquid drinking the potion that would prolong his life long enough to fulfill his rebirth. He placed the chalice down then lifted the rattler off the ground.

In his left hand he took the dagger. He cut deep into his chest with the accuracy of a surgeon exposing his heart. He dropped the dagger to the ground. With his right hand he reached in grabbed his rib gage. He pulled with all his remaining strength. The bones cracked echoing out like a tree limb being snapped. Barely alive now he slapped the snake on the top of its head. He chanted then again, he slapped the snake on top of its head. The snake hissed the pupils of its eyes seemed to widen. Its rattlers sang out the death tone. Out of thin air children an image began to form above the serpent. It took shape to that of a serpent man. He chanted then again, he slapped the snake on top of its head. The snake hissed the pupils of its eyes seemed to widen. Its rattlers sang out. Out of thin air children an image began to form above the serpent. It took shape to that of the demon Two Souls.

"My dark brother of the underworld I see you before me. I know the moment is near. Make us as one."

His words were slow with weakness as he stumbled. He mustarded up the last of his strength. He took the snake thrust its head deep into the open cavity. The "Diamondback Rattler" lashed out violently striking out its rage against Two Souls heart. It injected him with its venom. For a few second Two Souls remained standing. The snake latched on to the heart. Like an oak tree he then plummeted to the ground. Dust scattered in the air as his body fell with a dull thump."

"He died?" Frances a little girl of about eight years old asked.

"No, Frances this is when it got worse." "How! Grandma."

"At this precise moment the fire exploded shooting molten lava straight up into the sky. Where did this lava come from I do not know. I just know what was told to me and what was written. It shot the molten lava up like a water fountain. The lava separated and formed into hands. They circled down and reached under Two Souls body lifting him off the ground. Two Souls body was now suspended in midair. The wind whirled around the statues whistling the cry of the dead. In the distance you could hear the baying of coyotes in unison like banshees coming to claim a soul. The hands of molten lava began to change. First fire then it began to separate into small specks of green light. These specks of energy circled Two Souls body like hungry parasites twirling around him moving faster and faster. The small specks of light began to turn different colors eating away at his body slowly disintegrating it. When Two Souls was no more abruptly the specks of energy shot up circled then shot down into the amulet cupped in the serpent's hands.

At this moment the amulet glowed with evil. A raven circled above. Its head pointed down as it shot down like a missile. It tucked in its wing to its side and began its descent. Swooping down it descended rapidly with its claw stretched out. With perfection and accuracy, it grasps the amulet in its claws. It lifted its head flapped its wing and took flight up into the night sky. It is said that whoever finds this amulet its very soul it will possess. Two Souls will take them over. He will live again amongst the living. Not, as man, but as the Demon Serpent. He will bring a living hell to us literally. If Two Souls is not sent back to hell before his powers are complete. He will then release the rest of the creatures carved into the pylons in the crater.

"You just want to scar us old woman."

"No, Pedro this is a true story. Two Souls went up to the hills and did not return. Remember this Pedro. You might think someone is not watching you but there is usually someone out there seeing what you are up to. In Two Souls case the Great one was watching. Several month later one of the men from our village went into his dwelling. He found a leather scroll that explained the ritual. The story is true children I have the dagger that belongs to Two Souls. The year this all happen was right at the 1519 when Hernando Cortez had arrived in our land. How my great grandmother wound up with the dagger is yet another story."

The old woman picked up the small cigar box next to the bench that the children had been scrutinizing from the beginning of the story. The old woman reached down lifted the box. Opened the lid and pulled out the dagger. The children looked on in awe. On the pearl hilt of the dagger was a rattler made of silver, and red ruby eyes that sparkled. She moved the dagger from one side of her to the other showing the children.

"How do you know that is the dagger he used?"

"I know this to be the dagger because Two Souls was my great grandmother's husband. No, one wanted the dagger for they were scared of it. They believed that it would bring evil upon them. But, there is always a, but children. In this case the, but was that since my grandmother was his wife that it would only be right that she kept the dagger. Before my mother died, she handed over the dagger and the story. For now, I am the keeper of the dagger. But I feel that my grandson will need this dagger soon. He will know what to do with it. He knows the story of Two Souls," the old woman finished.

She then walked down the steps and walked back to the back of the shack vanishing from sight.

CHAPTER 2

In Austin Texas, a few days later what Juanita had predicted to the children had commenced. The evil began to bloom like a flower. Death rose and the immoral acts grew. Several police officers rushed in through the emergency doors of the hospital. Two paramedics rushed Detective Pete Rodriquez down the corridor to the I. C. U.

"Get out of the way," police officer Garza shouted out urgently as he made his way ahead of the gurney.

Several nurses and pedestrians moved out of the way. Their eyes remained on the gurney pondering what had happen to the man being rushed to the I.C.U. Chief Golds trailed behind the gurney as the paramedics rushed down the corridor with Pete. Doctor Jack Samuel stepped out of the E. R.as they approached the double doors. He stopped the gurney looked at Pete then at Chief Golds. He firmly ordered the paramedics to take Pete into the emergency room a.s.a.p. at the double doors Samuel stopped and faced Chief Golds.

"Sorry Chief, I can't let you come in."

"Hold up doc.," Golds says.

He then looks at Sgt. Garza, then at Blendez, "Check the room out." Garza went into the E.R. first the Blendez.

"Sorry Doc., someone knew the detective would be there. If they knew that then someone set him up. Meaning the same person could tip them off that we were on our way with him here doc."

"Understood."

"Damn, it to hell I told him he was getting too close to something. It just did not feel right Doc. The call was from a girl. When they arrived she was found dead. She had overdose. Probably murder to get to her father. It is possible he is involved in money flow of many businesses."

Garza stepped out of the E. R. Sgt. Blendez then walked up to Chief Golds.

"It's clear. Clear except for the medical staff that is in there now getting things ready Chief."

"Look to put your mind at ease Chief if I do not step out of the E.R., means I know all the people in the room," Jack tells him.

"Okay! Doc., take care of the man."

The doctor turns around and walks inside.

"Blendez get three other officers. Make sure he is well guarded."

"Got it Chief," Blendez says and begins to walk down the corridor.

Doctor Samuels conversed with one of the nurses as she pours a disinfectant over his hands as he scrubbed and prepared for surgery. The nurses and the anesthesiologist prepared Pete. Jack studied the wounds then spoke out loud so everyone in the E. R. could hear him.

"Let's go to work."

Bullet holes, but barely any blood he thought.

"Must have missed the vitals," he whispered to himself.

He paused for a moment then told the nurses to turn Pete onto his stomach.

"Doc.," said one of the nurses in surprise. "Yes! I can see the bullets.

Doctor Samuels could see three bullets protruding about a quarter of inch out of Pete's skin. Three bullets that surrounded Pete's heart in a triangle.

"This one is one for the books," he said.

Jack began to retrieve the bullets from Pete's back. Each bullet made a twanging sound as they hit the metal tray on the crash cart. Jack sighed then took off his gloves and tossed then on to the crash cart. It had been a perfect procedure. The bullets went clean through not damaging any of his organs. The miracle was the fact that the bullets had missed his heart. Missing it by a fraction of an inch. One bullet lay next to it barely scrapping the surface of the heart. They would now wait. Wait to see if the bullets damaged something internal. Hopefully they had not missed something with the human eye. Jack took off his face mask. He walked out into the corridor. Chief Golds and several officers approached him as he stepped out of the E.R.

"Well doc.! Golds says.

"You men can rest easy. Everything came out just fine. Go home and get some rest. "

"How long doctor? Asked Sgt. Blendez.

"Pete will stay three or four days in intensive care before he is moved to a room."

"Thanks doc."

"Chief one thing for certain the detective is one lucky cuss."

 "What do you mean doc.?"

"I think the man had an intervention. All three bullets missed his heart. And their seemed to be no internal damage."

 "Sound like Pete, doc."

"Go home, get some rest," Jack said and walked down the corridor turned the corner into another hallway and was gone.

One month later in room 418, Pete joked around with Dr. Samuels. Jack pulled off the bandages around Pete's torso.

"Watch it doc. That causes me serious pain you know." "You know Pete you are one lucky person. Hell, you're lucky you can feel any pain at all. You're lucky the bullets did not pierce your heart. In its own rite that in itself is amazing. The tree bullet holes made a perfect triangle. Reminded me of a pyramid. Like something guarding the heart."

"So, you think because the bullets lodged the way they did that is what kept me alive. The magical powers of the pyramids," Pete exclaimed.

"No, Pete! What kept you alive is that you are one nut case," Jack says and both men began to laugh.

Sgt. Blendez knocked on the door. He waited for Pete to tell him to come in.

"Come in." Blendez stepped into the room. "Pete."

"Blendez how's it hanging?" Pete quipped.

"I'm doing Pete. Pete there is a Karen outside. She says she wants to speak to you. "

"Tell her to come in Blendez," Pete said then faced Dr. Samuels and said, "Doc., if you don't mind I think I need time alone. And thanks Jack. I hope I am doing the right thing.

"You are in the hospital what can you do wrong."

"I am going to ask her to marry me Jack. I just hope I'm doing the right thing."

"That sound like a good ideal Pete. Maybe she can keep you out of trouble."

Dr. Samuels stood up from the chair and was about to walk out when Pete caught him off guard with his next words.

"Jack one more thing before you leave." "Yeah!

"I like for you to be my best man Jack?" "I don't know what to say Pete."

"How about I'll do it."

"I will be honored Pete, Yes, I'll do it." "Good! And thanks again Jack."

Karen walked in as Jack walked out. Seeing Karen saunter up to him in a slow walk he reflected back on how the two of them met. He recalled that he had just gotten out of the Marine Corps and his truck was acting up on him. It was just a couple of years he had gotten out of the Corps. He had a few bucks and was moving up to detective. He thought perhaps if he fixed the truck himself, he could save a few dollars. He met Karen by pure luck. No, it was their destiny. Either way he did not care. They had met and that was the operative word, "Met." He recalled driving up to the library parking his truck out front. He had cut the engine off. The truck coughed then cut off. He climbed out closed the door behind him. He began to whistle as he walked up the stairs. "I'm in heaven. He smiled to himself as her remembered. Yes, he was in heaven especially when he sees her for the first time. He had not seen her when he had walked in. He had gone directly to the repair books. He looked at the huge thick repair manuals. "Chilton," in bold letter on the center of the binder the top part read," auto 1952-1969. His truck was a sixty-five Chevy straight six. He took the repair manual in hand walked up to the desk where he would check the book out. He placed the book down on the countertop not looking up. He paused for a moment as if to think if he should take the task on by himself. Besides what did he know about being a repairing a vehicle. He lifted his head up and saw her for the very first time. His throat got tight, and he became tongue tied. Her beauty had caught him off guard. In the floral pattern dress she wore, she was breath taking literally he thought to himself. She had auburn hair on an oval face with full lips. She had the cutest pug nose he had seen with big brown eyes that melted Pete's heart like butter with their softness.

"Can I help you," she asked.

"Ah! Ah," he stammered then somehow managed to get the words out. "I need to check this book out.

"I need to see your library card."

"I don't have a card will my driver license do?"

Pete felt a little dumb for he should have known about the card. Time passes and he had just forgot with all he had in his head. With the war and just being back for two years. Karen reached into a drawer she took out a form and handed it to Pete.

"Fill this out for the next time. But you will not be able to take that book home anyway. These auto manuals stay here. If you need information out of them there is a copy machine by the entrance."

After several month and a lot of trips to the library he finally said the right words to her. The simplest of word, "Do you want to go out with me?"

Karen smiled at Pete then said, "That was all you had to do, was to ask."

Three months later someone had set him to take a fall. They shot him in the back three times. Karen had visited him every day as he recovered Pete recalled. Seeing her his thoughts retuned back to the present. He waited until she had approached the bed and stood at his side. She bent forward and hugged him tightly.

"Ouch! Pete grunted.

"Oh, I'm sorry. I did not mean to hurt you."

"It's all right I was just faking," Pete said then took her hand in his.

She studied Pete wondering why he was holding her hand. He smiled and remained silent for a moment then asked her bluntly.

"Will you marry me?" "Yes!"

 "Don't have to think about it?"

"Nope! I love you Pete," she told him and hugged him tightly.

She then lay her head softly against his shoulder. The sun began its slow ascent into the morning sky awakening the souls below. Bringing life to the city of Austin, Texas. The sun rose on the horizon where night met day. It was like seeing an eyelid open up for the first time. Jesse Gonzales, young man nineteen years old. A true Texas born and raised in the good city of Austin. Jesse grew up in the so-called ghetto, with dreams, and hopes of getting out of the place he lived. He was not like some of the others that just wanted to hang around and get stoned. He wanted more out of life. Jesse wanted a life with substance. He wanted a wife, children, and a nice home. Jesse spirit was more of that of an old wise man. Jesse liked to think thing out. He was not impulsive like the young and restless one. He was tired, tired of fighting every day with life. No! He did not contemplate death besides that was the coward's way out. Even though on occasions he felt as if it were futile. Futile was just a word he thought to himself every time he got in that kind of mood. The defeatist mood is what he called it. It might seem futile at the moment he thought to himself. But he would not let society's bull shit bring him down. There was more out there. He just knew there had to be. There had to be. It was America the land of the free. A land where a man could be a pauper one moment and filthy rich the next. He deeply believed in the American way. He believed in the creed that all men are created equal. He felt it calling out to him like a voice in the wind. Calling him constantly calling out his name. He could hear it. Jesse did not want much. He had one true ambition in life that meant the most to him. That was to become an Austin police officer. A cop a protector of life not a destroyer. He wanted others to be proud of him as well as himself. The most important person in his life was his mother. Perhaps maybe if the young men in the hood as they call it. Saw him climb out of society's bull and become something people respected then maybe others would follow. Growing up in the hood he had seen his mother work too hard to make ends meet. He saw her go to work just to come home to cook. To slave over a hot stove, then just too plop down exhausted in the recliner he had bought for her for her birthday. She would plop down exhausted and fall fast asleep only to repeat the same thing over the next day. Jesse life was not an easy one, but he had no real problem with life in general. In his short life span he had managed to see more than most would see their entire lives. Death, he saw often. Disease, depression he had seen all the elements of the dark force at work. Jesse's mind wondered far into the past as he tried to recollect some of his memories of the past. He began to recall his father. It was hard for him to do for he did not have many memories of him. He did recall one moment. He remembered grabbing his father's hand as they both walked quietly to the corner store. He pictured the day as if it were just happening. He remembered looking up at him thinking that his father was a giant. At six years of age his father was a giant too him. He remembered the texture of his father's hands. His hands where rough like sandpaper. They stopped next to a man. His father began to converse with him. After several minutes he tugged on his father's hand. Jesse figured the man was taking too much of his time with his father. His father looked down at him. Jesse turned his father's hand over and ran his small finger across several of the thick flesh bumps on the palm of his hand. His hands where rough like sandpaper.

"Dad, what are those things?" "They are called calluses." "Do, they hurt you?"

The man talking to his father laughed out loud in amusement at his innocent words. His father looked at him smiled then answered.

"No, Jesse, one gets them from working. From working hard like a man should," his father said in a heavy Mexican accent.

"They look like they hurt."

"Just remember one thing Jesse, get an education."

Out of nowhere a surge of anger flooded his mind like a cloud It seized his thoughts. He began to ask himself question. Why had his father left them all alone? Why? From the time his father left them He had known he was to become a man. To Jesse his father had been taken away overnight at least this is what he thought. At six what did he really know about death? The understanding of death was his father. He felt cheated he loved his father.

Again, the thought of why crossed his thoughts? He recalled what his brothers would tell him when they caught him crying.

"Jesse sucks it up crying is not going to bring him back.

It won't do any good."

A quiet calmness filled the room as he recalled the past, and as quickly as the anger had flooded his mind it had vanished. Jesse wondered how it was possible that his mother somehow managed the shores of a father. She fed them and clothed them. She had managed to feed him and two brothers by herself and with her minute weekly pay. She would tell him it did not matter when he would bring it up.

"Mother's do what they have to son."

Though it did not matter to her Jesse felt he owed her a lot. He was determined to pay her back and somehow, he would. Jesse walked into the closet reached in and took a red and yellow plaid shirt and put it on. He was about to walk out of his room when he caught a glimpse of one of the pictures on his dresser. He stopped and took a few steps back. He reached for the picture in the wood eight by five frame. He studied it for a moment then began to reminisce. It was a picture of the past. A smile broke on the right corner of his mouth. In the picture he had to be at least two years old. He remembered that they had gone for a picnic at the park. He was still in diapers cradled in his father arms. In the background his mother stood next to a picnic table. Roy the second oldest of the boys stood on the concrete bench. He leaned back against his mother. She held him tightly around the waist their faces pressed together cheek to cheek.

Beside them was John the oldest of the three who sat on the tabletop. His feet are planted firmly on the bench, and he is frowning into the camera. Frowning as his sister the oldest took the picture. Jesse smiled thinking what had made his older brother frown like that in the picture. Who knew? In the distance in the pool to their left the youngest and second oldest of the sisters swam in the shallow part. Jesse's thoughts jump a few years into the future. He was sixteen he could hear his mother call out to him and his brothers.

"Stop your fighting and get dressed before you make yourselves late for school," she shouted out in her heavy Mexican ascent that filled the house.

Jesse chuckled softly as he recalled this moment. He remember that he and his brothers would laugh. Then they would begin to kid with her which made her even madder. Or maybe that is what they thought. He remained looking at the picture for a moment longer. He placed it back on the dresser then picked up the other picture. It was an eight by five as well in a wooden frame. In this picture it was only his mother. The nostalgia for the past brought a sadness, and a lump to his throat. His mother had aged in the passing years. She was a small, framed woman, petite with a full face, and black hair that seemed to shine as the sun reflected off of it in the first picture. In the picture in his hand his mother had gray hair with a few black strays. Her face was wrinkled from time, and of just being tired. To him his mother remained an angel sent from heaven.

Jesse would always remember what she had done for them. He placed the picture back next to the others. He made a vow, and he would keep it. He had vowed to his mother that he would one day make enough money to take care of her. His mission in life was to buy her a house she could call her own. It was the only way he could ever repay her back and have his soul at ease. Jesse's mind snapped back to the present as he heard his mother's voice.

"Jesse you come and eat your breakfast before it gets cold." room

"Okay Ma," he answered back and began to walk out of his He entered the kitchen where she was turning over a tortilla. He walked up to her kissed her on the cheek then sat down at the table. His plate, his brother's plate, bean, sausage, in the center of the table. They did not have much, but his mother could set a table no matter what. And she made it look good. She turned faced the doorway and called out.

"John, Roy, you boys hurry up before your breakfast gets cold and you make yourselves late for work."

"Okay Ma! Roy shouted from his room. "Okay Ma! John shouted from the hallway. "Okay hell! She shouted back.

All three of them began to laugh at her attempt to be stern with them. Through the laughter they managed to answer back.

"Coming," Roy shouted back.

"On our way Ma," John said as he stepped into the kitchen.

He walked up to her and kissed her softly on the forehead and took his seat at the table.

"On our way Ma," she mimicked him sarcastically as she flipped over a tortilla on the burner.

She walked up with a plate of warm tortillas and placed them in the center of the table. She walked around the table and sat down across from Jesse. Jesse watched her, and studied the seriousness to her face. That only meant one thing he thought to himself. She was going to push the issue of the police academy again. She looked at him for a moment then spoke.

"Jesse, I want you to listen to what I have to say without saying a word until I have finished."

"Okay Ma."

"I heard they were taking applications for new cadets for the academy."

"How Ma, and from whom?" Jesse asked as he looked up at her and took a bite of his food.

"I said to wait until I was done then you could ask questions. For now, just listen. Please!"

"Okay! I'll listen," he said and took another bite of his food.

"A friend of mine has a son who is going to apply she told me. I know how much this means to you Jesse."

"Ma!   We have talked about this before," Jesse says as he looks into her eyes.

"Oh! Don't Ma me you came to me when you were in high school.

Ma, I want to play football. Do you remember? I said I wished that you wouldn't play football, but you insisted and insisted. I signed the permission slip against my better judgment. I was afraid that you would break your neck. Jesse I am giving you my blessing to go after your dream."

"Yeah, go for it," John says as he reaches for a tortilla. He sat down and took his place at the table.

"Yeah, butt hole! Go for it," Roy said as he entered the room then added, "I wish I would have followed my dream."

"What dream was that to sleep all day," John quipped. "Up yours asshole," Roy said quickly back as he took his place at the table.

"Testy aren't we," John retorted back.

"Why don't you mind your business by shutting up?"

Jesse looked at his brothers then at his mother. He remained silent for a while contemplating everything carefully then spoke.

"Okay Ma, I'll go and register."

"All right! Now can we eat," John said then picked up his plate and looked at it. Their mother's eyebrow furrowed up as she looked at him as he smiled back at her. She scowled then walked up to the stove, and returned with his eggs, and placed the eggs in front of him. John looked at his plate.

"Don't look at the plate the rest of the food is on the table like always. Now, just serve yourself."

"Beans, eggs, and bacon again."

"No! John, blue eggs and pink bacon," their mother quipped back.

"Ma you mean green eggs and ham," Roy corrected.

"You say it the way you want I say it the way I want." "Ma, can I have a tortilla?" John asked.

"You have bad legs," she snapped the words then added, "better learn to get your own now. Because when you get married."

"Ma, when I get married here in one month all I will have to say is bring me a tortilla woman."

His mother gave him a stern look then said, "You go ahead and dream big mister big shot. Shit! I have talked to your fiancée she is a woman of the ninety's. You tell her to get you a something your better do it on your knees. And besides I don't think she knows how to make tortillas.

"Okay maybe she doesn't."

They all laughed. She looked at them then began to laugh as well.

"That's all right Ma, that's miner. I will just come down here to eat, okay Ma."

"Okay Ma," their mother mimicked sarcastically.

"Mom, I am not leaving for a while. Maybe I will never leave," Roy says. He smiles at her.

"Ah si hijo," she answers back and kisses him on top of the forehead then caresses his hair back.

She turned and walked up to the stove and reheated a tortilla. They watched her as she returned and reached for Roy's plate and went back to the stove. She reheated his food and then placed it in front of him. The tortilla to one side still had steam rising from it. Roy looked at his brothers and smiled.

"What about me Ma?"

"What about me Ma," she mimicked John again.

She looked at him then reached over and grabbed a tortilla from the plate in the center of the table. She returned to the stove reheated the tortilla. She placed it in front of John then looked at him and said, "You better cherish these moments," then shook her head. She sat down and they conversed and laughed as all family's do.

CHAPTER 3

Jesse applied for the academy as he had promised. Two weeks later he received the letter to take the test. Four weeks later he was walking on needles and pins. Jesse's mother waited as well anxiously for some kind of reply. She checked the mailbox everyday while Jesse was away driving a semi for one of the local trucking outfits. Jesse came home one day about noon. He walked into the house only to find his mother sound asleep on the recliner while the television talked about a disaster somewhere in the world. At first, he was taken aback. Why was his mother at home? He pondered it for a moment then remembered it was Saturday. He walked over to her reached down and pulled the blanket up over his mother. He kissed her softly on the forehead. He turned sharply as the sound of the mailbox startled him. He heard the mailbox lid rattle shut. He went to the screen door. He opened it catching a glimpse of the mailman as he walked down the sidewalk to another house.

"Thanks Fred," Jesse called out to him.

The mailman turned around smiled waved then continued on to the next house. Jesse's heart began to pound. He could feel every thump of his heartbeat. He reached up opened the lid. He reached into the mailbox and retrieved the letters inside. He looked at them for a moment then began to go through each piece of mail. There it was the one with the official Austin, Police logo. His hands seemed to freeze as he picked it out from the group of letters. Again, he looked at the official letterhead then nervously he opened it. He began to read what it said inside. He nodded his head in agreement. It was confirmed he was accepted into the police academy. He was to report there in three weeks. Short notice but it gave him enough time to give his two weeks notice at work. He turned back around and began to enter back into the house.

"Ma! Ma!" he shouted excitedly.

"What is it Jesse?" His mother called out startled. She sat up in the recliner and wiped the sleep from her eyes.

"I've been accepted Ma. I will be going to the academy." "Good, it is about time they let you know something," she said then hugged him tightly.

Her eyes filled with tears she knew he would be leaving home This saddened her. But yet still she was happy for him at the same time. It was what he wanted for a long time. Now his dream was coming true. She stepped back to look at Jesses then spoke.

"So, when do you have to be at the school Jesse?" "It says that I have to report to the academy in two weeks."

Jesse looked at his mother's sadden eyes peering back at him.

"You, know I can still withdraw my name from the list Ma? It is not too late to do so."

"No, Jesse I am not sad. I am crying because I am happy for you. This is what you always wanted. It makes me happy for you. Just promise me that you will visit once in a while."

"You don't have to worry about that Ma," he said then hugged her as if she would vanish into thin air at that precise moment.

Six months later in the corridor of the Austin City Auditorium Jesse's mind wandered back. All the cadets waited excitedly in the hallway for the doors to be open so they could be seated. The months had passed quickly he thought to himself. He was just happy he was done with the hard part. It had been an arduous task but somehow, they had managed to survive the worst.

He had managed to come out on top. As they say top dog in his class. He had passed successfully. It was the happiest moment of his life. He began to wander back to the time at the academy. Why the thought? And why the thought of something was not right. Something was happening to him he could feel it. He had felt something wrong within himself. But what? What in God's name what could be wrong? To make things even more bizarre he had gained about twenty pounds of solid muscle. And this was without having to work out. He recalled as they waited that someone had asked him if he had a sun burn. He had asked why? They had asked the question because his skin was peeling. If he did not know better, he would have said it was the sudden growth. Not to mention the pains. The God awful pains that had started up at the academy. And now they were becoming more frequent. There had been one more puzzling thing. Maybe puzzling was an understatement. What was strange was that when it got cold. It was as if his muscle did not listen to his motor impulses. The colder it got the harder it was for him to move. But then when it warmed up, he found movement easy. He found a new strength within. His thoughts were brought back as the double doors clank then opened.

"We made it Jesse. We fucking made it," one of the other cadets fervently told him as the doors swung open.

Jesse smiled and nodded his head several times in agreement. They all shuffled into the auditorium in a military manner. They did as they had been instructed. Jesse felt a queasiness to his stomach. He hoped it was not the beginning of the awful pains that would cause him to throw up. He hoped it was just nerves of excitement overwhelming him. The day they all had waited had at last come. The anxiousness in all of them built up as if they were ready to explode for inside. Each one of the cadets took their seat quickly filling up the first three rows in front. They waited patiently. Ten minutes passed seeming like an hour an hour seeming like four. People of all races began to enter and began to take their seats. Their voices echoed out with their emotions. The excitement in their voice carried out through the air. After a few minutes several men walked up on to the stage. They took their places. The auditorium began to quiet down. The three men that had walked up on stage was the Chief of Police, the Mayor, and detective Pete Rodriquez.

The Mayor stood and walked up to the podium first. He slowly waved his hand to the right the place became immensely quiet. So quiet one could have literally heard a pin drop. He wore a gray pinstripe suit that seemed to bring out his tan. His hair was almost completely gray except for a few strands of black hair that intertwined with the gray. His chick bones strong. His blue eyes piercing, and his face set with a stern look. All the cadets shouted out their greeting in unison. The Mayor lifted his hand again and the room became silent. He waited for a moment then began his speech.

"I want to welcome each and every one of you aboard. I want you all to know that you are now Austin's finest. I am honored to have you start protecting the streets of this fine city. People of Austin are proud to have you on the force. That is all I have to say for now. Now let me introduce the next speaker a good friend of mine. Let's welcome Chief Golds."

Everyone focused their eyes on the Chief as he walked up to the podium and took his place. His hair was styled in a crew cut fashion kind of like the Marine Corps cut. His uniform was pressed neatly in a military manner. Every crease in the proper place which made him look more like a soldier than a cop. He was five seven stoutly built. He had a four-inch scar on his left cheek that gave his square jaw and face a profound look. Golds was not new to death or crime. Golds had spent two tours in Vietnam where he had received the scar. He had received it on one of the night maneuvers. The Mayor reached out his hand and shook Golds hand then silently said.

"It's all your Chief."

Golds waited until the Mayor had taken his seat then began.

"Police officers some of you already know who I am. And some of you will soon have the honor of meeting with me. For now, I will not bore you with a speech. I just want to reiterate what the Mayor said. I wish you all good luck and God's blessing. I know you are all eager to go on your way. But we have one more speaker Detective Rodriquez."

They all clapped their hands acknowledging the detective. He greeted the Chief at the podium. The Chief nodded his head and walked to his seat. Pete grabbed the edge of the podium with both hands. He looked around into the crowd. He waited a moment then began. He wore a brown suit with a light tan shirt and no tie. He stood at five eleven and weighed two hundred thirty pounds of solid muscle. His hair was black which appeared to be almost a blue as it reflected off the lights from above. He had strong features that resembled those of the Mexican Indian. His eyes were pitch black like the night without ending. If you looked into his eyes, it was as if he could see right through you. If there was such a thing as a perfect officer of the law, then detective Rodriquez was that man.

"He looks as mean as a junkyard dog ready to bite but he's really as kind as a pit-bull," Pete said in humor.

Laughter filled the auditorium. Detective Rodriquez scrutinized the audience then lifted his hand. He waited for the place to quiet down. The place was quiet except for a few squeaks of the chairs as people shifted to make themselves more comfortable.

"I welcome each one of you aboard. I will only say a few words of wisdom, Rodriquez said strongly and continued, "I will announce the top dog in his class. Then the rest of the names in order of their standing. First, I want you all to know that there are high risks out there. It will be like walking out into a war zone at times. You will have to use your judgment as well as milieu and intuitiveness. I spent two tours in Vietnam with the Chief. He can tell you as well as I can that it is not going to be a picnic out there. When I was discharged from the Marine Corps. I joined the police force I hand many a close call in the Nam, the bush as they call it. But not once was I ever wounded, nor did I receive a direct hit. Not once. But out here I have been shot at and hit several times. I have been cut twice and have come close to being beaten to death by a mob. I just want you to know from experience we know the dangers you all will face in the coming years. Now enough said. I know you want to go and celebrate. Now to get down to business to the more serious of matter.

"Cadet Gonzales Jesse," he called out the first name and continued," Mets Molly, Jones Freddy, Gilbert William,"

Pete stepped back from the podium and stood at attention. "Attention," he bellowed out the word.

The new officers quickly jumped to attention. Pete waited for a moment then shouted.

"Dismissed." Pete did an about face and walked up to the Mayor and Chief Golds.

"Mayor," Pete said and reached out his hand.

He shook the Mayors hand then nodded his head at the Chief and disappeared through the curtains at the back of the stage. The new officers and visitors mingled giving their congratulations to one another. Jesse stared at the detective as he was walking towards the curtains.

"Jesse, you all right?" Molly asked. "Yeah, I'm fine."

"Impressed by the detective?"

"Yeah, hope I will be as good as him. I heard some of the officers talking about the detective. He has one hell of a rep."

"I heard it as well," Molly told him as they watched Pete vanish from sight.

One month later the sun began its ascent upward as it usually did. The heat increased as it climbed higher. Claiming the sky above as its mate. Jesse stirred in his bed the temperature inside his room was already extremely warm. Or at least this is what he thought for that particular time of day. He brushed the thought away. It was warmer than it should be he said softly to himself. Heat vapors outside rose up from the concrete sidewalks saying back and forth like angry snakes moving upward, sideways, dissipating into the atmosphere. Jesse stirred again in his bed in discomfort. The sheets clinging to his body from his own sweat. He lazily tossed the bed sheets off to one side. He stretched out like a cat wakening up from his sleep.

The fan on the windowsill turned from side to side. It blew air just a few degrees cooler than the temperature inside his room. Jesse blinked his eyes several times. His eyelids seemed to scrape his eyeball from being too dry. It was as if the lubricant of his eyes had dried up. It had been a restless night for Jesse. He attributed the dryness to the heat. It had to be what else could it be? There was no other explanation he thought to himself. Then all of a sudden. It was as if his thoughts had been interrupted by some unknown evil. The thought that bombarded his head at the moment. The evil thoughts that tormented his own sanity. The images he saw in his head. One could not ever or even begin to explain. Or even be able to talk about it without someone thinking him crazy. Jesse grabbed his head wishing the images would leave at that moment and leave him alone. But the worst feeling within him was a new hate that he could not explain. A new hate that was growing stronger every day inside. A hate for humans. It was as if he were becoming something else. It was as if he was becoming a crazed animal.

His facial muscles tightened up abruptly imprinting the hate in a scowl. Just the word or thought of man raged him. And the other thing he now hated was the coming of night fall. The nights became more restless as the month passed. Every night for the past two months. He dreamed of ripping someone apart with his bare hands then feasting upon their very flesh like a wild creature. The piquant taste of blood lingered on his tongue as if he had just tasted it. As if he had just ravished sweet human flesh and had enjoyed its very unique taste. The thoughts sent new feeling of tremendous power through his limbs. It was an exhilarating feeling that tingled through his nervous system bring him to life. Jesse tried to force his thoughts to the back of his head. He hope that it was just a crazy nightmares.

"Yeah," he said out loud then added, "That has to be it, nightmares."

But he was awake? Or was he, and if he was awake then why did they seem so real at the time? Still the thoughts scared Jesse. Nothing made sense to him any longer. Sometimes it was as if he were walking a fine line between the realm of reality and the threshold into another world. The world of insanity with no return to the present world. Jesse shakes his head then stared out into space. He slowly began to relax then suddenly an image of death appeared before him. He grabbed his head. He began to cry out for the images to go away. He fought back with memories of his mother and his childhood. It was all he had to fight this evil. Every day was harder than the next. Each day he yields more and more to this new power. The evil tormenting his soul. Oppressed and confuse he turned over onto his side. He lay his head upon the top of his hands and brought his knees up close to his chest into a fetal position. Jesse lay quietly letting the warm air from the fan blow on him caressing his body. Why? Why was all this happening he question himself. Why? He had been a good son. He had tried his best to be good. He had done his best to stay out of trouble. Why? Tears rolled out from the corner of his eyes and down his face onto the bed. Sweat began to bead up fusing together streaming down his body. He felt a slight dull pain in his lower abdomen.

"Oh God! It is starting up again," he said out loud.

His stomach churned at that instant. A knot formed in his throat as he felt an urge to vomit. Jesse swallowed hard but his mouth had become too dry. Dry as if the water had been drained form his system. It was like waking up with a hangover. Jesse knew this was no hangover for there was more to come. He had no control over it. Suddenly a sharp searing pain shot up from his navel to his sternum. It shot though him like a bolt of hot fire. Jesse screamed out in agonizing pain.

"Oh! God," his words trailed off.

The pains were coming in stronger now. He could feel his stomach muscle trembling. All of a sudden, they contracted and they began to move in and out like that of a belly dancer. He could not stop it. He had no control over it. Abruptly his stomach lurched in violently. He opened his mouth, and he began to purge out the poison in his belly. Rapidly he climbed out of the bed and made his way into the bathroom. He cradled his stomach in his arms. After a few moments the pain vanished subsiding. Jesse sat down on the toilet seat placing his head into the palms of his hands as he bent forward. He began to rock back and forth. He moaned in despair. Whatever had him in its power? Whatever it was? What was its purpose? He could not figure it out. All Jesse knew was that it felt as if his insides would explode out of his body. After the attacks he could feel his intestines shift inside him as if they had a mind of their own. As if they were being altered inside of him. More thoughts of enormous hate flooded his mind. Again he fought with the images in his head. He began to talk out loud to himself in hope that it would help.

"I'm going to be twenty-one years old. I have never heard of anything. Or can I recall any stories of some kind of stage one went through like that of adolescence. A stage to enter adult hood? Jesse spoke out loud questioning the occurring episodes.

"Perhaps it was just the damn flu?" he said to himself.

Tears of fear and pain rolled down the side of his face and down his cheeks. At that precise moment out of the blue his stomach lurched in violently. Jesse's eyes open wide, and he looked. Again, a flash of hot searing pain shot through his body causing him to fall to the floor like a log onto his knees. His eyes quickly clouded up with tears. The tears blurring his vision. He began to crawl on the bathroom floor. He waved his hands out as instruments of sight like a blind person. He felt the edge of the toilet with his hands. He lifted the lid and placed his head over the rim just in time. As he lifted the toilet lid his stomach lurched in causing him to expel the yellow substance from inside. Yellow thick globs shot out of his mouth hitting the water then rapidly fusing into large masses of glob. As he looked at it, it reminded him of the globs fusing together inside a lava lamp. Each glob hitting the next and fusing. He could not recall eating anything like what he saw. Not pudding, ice cream, nothing, that he could recall. Whatever it was it smelled like rotten eggs. Jesse moaned as he helped himself up on weak legs.   He used the wall for support and stood. His weak arms quivered with the remnants of his lost strength.

"Oh!   God please help me," Jesse pleaded.

Jesse's vision was blurred. He used his hands to follow along the wall to the sink. Fumbling with his hands he managed to find the towel rack. He took the towel from the rack. He blindly reached down feeling for the faucets that he knew lay below. Now he knew what a blind person had to go through every day. It was an awkward feeling having to use only his hands for sight. It was like being in a dark tunnel trying to find a dime he thought to himself. His fingers came across the faucets he turned it on. He splashed water on to his face. He tilted his head back and wiped his face. Slowly he opened his eyes. He blinked several times hoping his sight would return. After several minutes he looked into the mirror and was happy to see himself. A blur but with every second his vision was coming back. He closed his eyes for a moment then opened them back up. He looked into the mirror again. He was happy to see himself looking back at him. The reflection in the mirror was that of a ghostly man peering back at him. Looking at him through bloodshot eyes. Yet it was a clear vision. He had sight. He stared at himself in disbelief for a second then cleaned up the mess. He threw the towel into the waste basket. He walked out of the bathroom and walked back into the bedroom. Without stopping he went straight to the closet reached up to the overhead shelf as if nothing had happened. He grabbed his cap and shoes off the shelf. He placed them on the bed then returned to the closet. He took a freshly pressed uniform placed it next to his cap and shoes. He moaned once then quickly got dress.

Jesse walked up to his dresser looked into the mirror and nodded in approval. He put on his belt and looked down at the brass belt buckle. It appeared it had been accidentally touched and smudged. The oil on one's hand quickly smudges the brass. He tilted the buckle upward in an angle where he could reach it with his shirt sleeve. He wiped off the smudge looked back into the mirror. He reached up and picked off an imaginary bit of lint off the brim of his cap. He straightened his collar as he stared at the reflection of himself. Out of the blue as he straightened up his collar a dullness swept over his brain. This dullness brought a strange feeling upon him. It was as if he were standing beside himself watching himself staring into the mirror. Staring at his own reflection. Creepy he thought. He brought his hands down from the shirt collar as he watched his hands come down. It was as if it were moving in slow motion. He felt a tingle down his spine. A tingle of fear then the thought creepy. He put it all in back of his head besides he did not know what it was. He looked down at the alarm clock on the dresser. So many things were happening. The feeling of him being able to watch himself in a second party. The creepy feeling and now it seemed the clicking of the second hand on the clock as they ticked away was causing him to lose his mind. It reached his ears like drums pounding away, pounding away. As he looked down at the clock the second hand jumped forward. It stops on the next mark. The ticking sounded becoming louder. Again and again, the sound was getting louder bombarding his ears. Jesse began to think but could not remember. The clock jump to another mark and it came to him. The alarm. He remembers the alarm would go off in just a minute. Jesse wanted to cover his ears from the bombardment sounds echoing to the back recesses of his ears. He knew that if the alarm went off it would be more devastating than what he could withstand. Without wasting a second, he picked up the clock into his hand. But he had waited too long. The alarm cried out with its ringing. The pain shot from his eardrums up to his brain. The searing pain shot through him causing blood to flow from his ears and eyes. Yet, somehow Jesse had managed to cut off the alarm. The ticking continued.

"No!"

He shouted at the top of his lungs and flung the clock against the far wall. The room turned into a blurred red color. A savage rage began to take control of his mind. Like a wildfire out of control Jesse's face contorted. The hate of a rabid animal ran through him. With this uncontrollable hatred he struck out at the mirror with a closed fist. As his fist hit the glass it shattered under the tremendous force of the impact. A large spider web formed under it instantly. Blood smeared on the glass where a glass shard had entered his flesh. In a daze Jesse pulled back his hand and looked at it. His knuckles bleeding and a small cut underneath the small finger. He pulled out the shard protruding out from his flesh. Blood ran down the mirror streaking the glass as it moved downward. His cries of agonizing pain echoed out through the room. The God awful pains. How do I stop them? He grabbed his head in his hands the pain quickly shifted to his abdomen. The pain seemed to explode out from his navel. His intestine shifted causing the room to flash as if a bolt of lightning had just struck in front of him. He grabbed his stomach hunched over. He fell to the floor onto his knees. Crouching over he tilted his head up forcing himself to look up.

"Oh my God what is happening to me? What is happening to me?" He said out in despair.

His intestines shifted violently and again Jesse gasped for air as his stomach wrenched in. It was as if someone had hit him with a baseball bat knocking all the air out of him depleting his oxygen. Jesse felt his heart was about to burst. His facial muscles tightened up as he strained to take in air. Then as quickly as it had sprung upon him it left leaving him in the middle of the floor gasping for air like a fish out of water. He tilted his head back his lungs slowly filled up with oxygen. He inhaled deeply several times until he had regained his composure. He reached up with one hand. He grabbed the edge of the dresser for support. He pulled himself off the floor. He brushed himself off bent down and grabbed his cap off the floor. He placed it back on his head then opened the dressers top drawer and retrieved his keys. As he pulled his hand back out of the drawer, he saw the blood.

"Shit! Shit, this is all I need now," he said out loud to himself.

He quickly walked back into the bathroom and up to the medicine cabinet. He pulled out some iodine and bandages then bandaged his hand. He lifted his hand up to his face.

"Looks as good as new," he told himself.

Jesse chuckled at his own remark. He then walked to the front door opened it. He stepped out onto the porch. He took in a deep breath as he looked around. He sighed then thought.

There is no time to dwell on the strange occurrences for right now. Jesse put everything that had happen out of his mind.

"It never happen," he said softly to himself.

He turned around inserted the key in the lock and turned it until he heard the tumblers lock into place. He turned back around walked up to the edge of the top step and looked out at the kids playing a game of street football. Their field was the street. Pads were for sissy.

"Danny over here," one of the other players yelled out for the ball.

"Got him he's down the clown," Ernesto bellowed out.

Jesse listened carefully to a chirping bird in the distance. He could hear a dog as well barking a few houses down. Scanning the surrounding brought back memories. He wished that he was still a kid himself at that moment. A 1969 avocado green Firebird with a white vinyl top passed down the road and blew its horn. One of the passengers waved her hand out of the window and shouted.

"Going to work Jesse?"

He just smiled and waved back. The kids playing their game moved scrambling to the side of the road. Some seemed a little miffed at the interruption of their game. Others whistled and called out to the girls.

"Baby I'm your little taco come and take a bite out of me."

"In your dreams fool," one of the other girls in the car yelled back at him.

"I'm your dream come true," another of the boys shouted as they passed him.

"Yeah, you're a dream Rudy. You're a fucking nightmare," Ernesto tells him.

The other boys began to laugh. Moments after the laughter had died down they started up the football game again from where they had left off.

CHAPTER 4

Jesse slowly walked down the steps. The sun beamed down on him. But the sun seemed stronger. It seemed as if the sun would burn through his clothing. As he looked up at the sky his eyes began to turn red. Then a pain shout through his eyes up to his brain. Jesse quickly placed his hand over his eyes like a visor using his hands to reflect the sun away. Out of the blue without warning of what was coming next. The flesh on Jesse's face began to bubble up in swells as if being burned. The flesh seemed to bubble up and then vanish. Then bubble up again as if he were in a big pot boiling. It was awful whatever it was it was awful. This awful burning sensation what was happening to him? His vision became blurred. He tried to focus hoping it would clear up but to no avail. Again, he tried to focus his eyes to clear his vision and again it was useless. Then something else occurred. His whole body began to sweat profusely as if he had stepped into a sauna. All his cloth were drenched in his sweat. He suddenly felt an urge for meat, raw red meat. What purpose did it serve? What in God's name did it all mean? Jesse felt he was going insane. He knew that if he told just one living soul they would not believe him. But maybe now they would. His memory went back to all the struggles he had endured. It was tuff just trying to survive in his neighborhood. A task in itself to stay alive he would not let these attacks scare him. But the fact was that they were scaring him. It wasn't normal. It was not a way of life. He tried to think of something to take his mind off what was happening. Maybe just maybe if he relaxed it would stop. Then he heard his mother's voice.

"Never give up, Jesse always give all you've have," her voice ran through his head.

Abruptly he was startled by a voice. "Good morning, Jesse."

"Grandma," he said surprised.

Jesse lowered his hand. His grandmother could see the swells bubbling on his flesh as if his skin was burning.

"Oh, my God!" his grandmother shouted out frightened.

Without warning Jesse toppled over and plummeted to the ground like a giant oak tree. Jesse hit with a dull thump. He felt a sharp excruciating pain shoot through him as his head hit against the concrete sidewalk. A soft moan escaped his lips then he became still.

"What's wrong Jesse? What is wrong with you?" His grandmother cried out.

She yelled out then rushed up to him as quickly as her old legs allowed her to. She knelt down beside her grandson. She lifted his head up from the concrete. Seeing the blood on his forehead she began to scream out for help.

"Someone, anyone, please help me please someone help me."

The kids playing football in the street realized that something was wrong. They stopped in the mist of their game and ran up to the old lady. One of the boys seeing Jesse's condition ran as fast as he could to his house to tell his father. The boy's father rushed out of the house and up to give aid to the old woman. He stopped and looked at Jesse then asked her what was wrong. She removed her hand from his forehead. The man eyes open wide as he saw the blood-stained forehead and the grandmother's bloody hand. She looked at the man with tears in her eyes. Tears ran down the side of her face and down her cheeks. The man rushed off not saying a word. He entered his house and quickly made the phone call to 911 and requested an ambulance. Jesse's grandmother worked his body onto her lap. She cradled him next to her and began to rock him back and forth singing softly to him.

"Oh! Please don't let my grandson die lord. Please don't let him die."

The man rushed out of his house and returned to her side and spoke.

"Senora the ambulance is on its way."

Jesse's eyes opened suddenly as if his eyes would pop out of his head. His body wrenched up violently. His back bowing up then with force slammed back down onto his grandmother's lap. His eyes began to bulge out of their sockets as if he were straining for oxygen. The small capillaries in his eyes swelled up. They began to pulsate as the blood rushed through them. The small vessels straining from bursting at that moment. They swelled even more in just the few seconds that had pasted. The blood vessels pulsated as blood was being pumped through them at a high velocity. Jesse clenched his hands into a fist digging his fingernails into the palm of his hand. His knuckles turned white from the strain. He let out a scream as if he were summoning up demons. He was screaming out names, words, in a different language. The cries of the underworld were begging to be released from inside of him. The man jumped back startled. His eyes opened wide with fear and confusion. The voices he heard or thought he heard escaping from Jesse's mouth was not human. The man blessed himself and then told his boy to bless himself as well.

"Go home Ernesto right now," the man said then added, "Senora this isn't natural this boy has a demon inside of him. I'm sorry Senora I am telling you he has a demon inside of him," he repeated then looked at his son, Ernesto.

The boy looked confused, but he knew enough to know what was happening. It was not something that happened every day.

"Don't have to tell me twice dad," the boy said and they both rushed home.

People from the neighborhood not knowing what happen began to gather in hope of finding something out. Something that would feed their curiosity like flies on an afternoon hunt for food. Each one wanting to know what affliction was brought down upon this young man. Sirens echoed out in the distance as they made their way to their destination. Jesse's grandmother looked down at him.

"Help is coming," she whispered softy.

Her mind jumped back to the past. She recalled back as if it were just yesterday. It would be her sixth grandson it was noon when she had gotten the call. Several days later she had gone to see him. She remembered that all the infants were all crying, all crying except Jesse. The sound of the ambulance siren and the screeching of its tires grabbing at the pavement as they turned the corner brought her back to the present. Looking at Jesse she felt helpless. She wanted to do something for him anything. She caressed his hair as she looked into his eyes. The once brown eyes that lit up with life luster now were sunken into their sockets. She turned as she heard the door to the ambulance open. She could see a woman rushing towards them. She looked back down at Jesse.

"Help is here you are going to be all right," she assured him.

A woman paramedic with brown hair and the body of a bodybuilder knelt down beside them. She quickly reached into a black bag she was carrying and withdrew a stethoscope.

"Senora," she called out to the grandmother," she noticed the confused look on the old woman's face.

"Please don't let nothing happen to him. Don't let him die."

"We will do everything in our power, everything possible to keep him alive," she told her and quickly checked his vital signs.

The other paramedic a thin man with a pencil mustache rushed up to them with a gurney.

"How is he Spanks?" Garza asked. "Not good," Spanks replied back.

"Senora we are going to have to put him onto the stretcher," Garza says.

Jesse's grandmother remained incoherent for a few seconds.

"Senora we are going to need you to fill out the information on these medical papers. But we cannot waste any more time. We need you to come with us to the hospital to fill out the paperwork."

"He will be all right," Spanks assured her.

Confused and dazed the grandmother bent down and grabbed her purse from the ground. She began to walk after the gurney to the ambulance. Her movements were like that of a robot in serious need of oil. Oil on the stiffened joints now fragile rusted by time. Spanks and Garza placed Jesse into the ambulance. Spanks jumped into the back of the ambulance and inserted the I.V., into Jesse's arm. Garza climbed back out of the ambulance closed the double doors behind him. He stopped and looked at the old woman wondering if she would soon break. Break like a piece of brittle glass right in front of his eyes. Garza walked up to her grabbed her by the arm and helped her into the passenger side of the ambulance. Securely buckling her in the seat he then ran around the truck and climbed in. He turned the vehicle on and switched on the siren. It bellowed out its cry of emergency. As they drove away the old woman just stared out of the windshield without saying a word. Garza floored the gas pedal. The siren catching the oncoming traffics attention as it cried out the message to get out of the way. Crying out for the passenger in this vehicle that was riding with death. All vehicles but one seemed to obey the warning. The driver of the sixty-nine El Camino continue to cross the intersection even though the light was red. He shot down the road barely missing them. Garza blasted away with the horn warning the driver. As the man in the El Camino passed, he stuck his head slightly out the window then extended his arm out. He flipped them off and slurred several raw words of obscenities to them. This indicated the man was under the influence of alcohol or drugs.

"You crazy son-of-a-bitch," Garza said under his breath so the old lady would not be able to hear.

Garza took another corner as the ambulance swerved around Spanks called out in concern. Not for his driving but for what was occurring in back with Jesse.

"Something bad is happening Garza hit the pedal to the metal and I mean like today," Spanks exclaimed urgently.

Suddenly, Jesse's eyes bulged out of their sockets as if to pop out. Small blood vessels surrounding the eyeball began to swell protruding above the surface of the white of the eye. The vessels seeming more like small red worms pulsating with life.

Then abruptly several exploded as the blood rushed through them splattering onto Spanks' uniform. The old woman turned just as the blood vessels ruptured. She quickly covered her mouth and abstained a scream.

"Hurry Garza," Spanks yelled out to him.

"Hold on we're almost there. Just a few more blocks Spanks."

"Oh! Shit he's going into some kind of convulsion."

"All most there," Garza says out loud more to himself than to Spanks.

Jesse's body arched up and slammed back down onto the stretcher hard then began to shake. The white of his eyes began to darken at the corners then slowly glazed over with a black covering like a blanket. Chills ran down Spanks' back as the evil from Jesse's eyes penetrated into her mind. Jesse clenched his hands tight forming them into fist. Sinking his fingernails into the flesh of his palms. A crimson of red appeared around the edges where his fingernails bit into the palm. A numbness took over Jesse's brain easing the pains. It was as if his brain was floating alone in space. It was as if his brain and skull where now two separate items. He had to fight this evil. Even if the fight within his mind would wind up being futile. It did not matter for he was losing to this evil whatever it was that was taking him over. He began to fall deeper, and deeper into the abyss of darkness. He became unconscious to this monster. This monster that was too strong in his being now. In a matter of seconds, he would become oblivious to the world around him.

"Were losing him Garza step on it."

"We're here!" Garza answered back as he took the corner.

The tires grabbed the pavement. The ambulance screeched to a halt in front of the emergency entrance to the Hospital.

Garza cut the ambulance off and ran to the back of the ambulance. Spanks jumped out of the back. Both of the paramedics helped the gurney down to the ground. Rapidly they rushed Jesse through the corridors of the hospital. They could see the double swinging doors up ahead that lead into the E. R. on a white background in bold red letters the word emergency was written on the wall. They wheeled the gurney through the double doors into room where a medical staff was already waiting. One of the nurses checked the I. V., in his arm while another took his vital signs. Garza stepped back turned and returned to the ambulance where he had left the old woman. He opened the door and took the woman's right hand and helped her down form the ambulance.

"Come with me Senora."

"My grandson. Where is my grandson?" she asked.

"He will be fine senora. He is with the best medical staff of the ER," he says then walks her into a room and sat her down at a table.

"Senora I will be right back do not leave this place."

"Where are you going?"

"I am going to get the paperwork you need for Jesse." "Please do not let anything happen to my grandson." Garza placed his hand on her shoulder.

"It is going to be all right. Your grandson is going to be taken care of," he told her then pointed at the chair, "Please sit down I will be right back," he said then left for a moment. †He said then left for a moment.

He returned with a clipboard with papers. He handed it to her and told her to fill out the information on the medical forms.

"When you are done with them return them to the receptionist."

"If you need someone to come and pick you up Senora, just tell the receptionist to make the call for you."

Inside the emergency room Jesse's body again wrenched upward arching his back up like a bow. His stomach stretched out as he strained. His torso then relaxed it was as if one were seeing the dead trying to revive themselves. His skin had become blistered as if he had been in a fire. The doctors and staff did all then could. After two hours they had managed to get his vital signs stable.

"There is nothing more we can do except wait," Doctor Samuel said.

He removed his latex glove then his face mask. He then throwing them into a trash basket to one side. Nurse Gamble move the patient into the holding ward meaning the intensive care unit. She got several of the nurses to help her with the gurney and the I.V., as they moved Jesse. Moans escaped from several patients in the intensive care unit as they wheeled Jesse to a spot that had just been vacated by another patient. They lined up the gurney with the hospital bed. They transferred him out of the gurney into the bed. Jesse lay in bed wrapped up in bandages from his head to his toes except for two slits left around his eyes for him to see out of. Jesse lay in bed wrapped up in bandages from his head to his toes except for two slits left around his eyes for him to see out of. Jesse's eyes peered through the openings like two black abysses. The bright lights above penetrating down. Penetrating deep to the back recesses of his eyes like a blazing meter heading directly at him. Burning, hurting him and all Jesse could do was to close his eyes. The intensity of the lights burned through his eyelids. But why?

Jesse hoped the pain would go away then suddenly as if his pray had been answered the light began to change. With his eye lids closed he could see a prism of lights with all different colors. It was like seeing the colors of a rainbow before him. The colors spreading out as they ate away at the world before him. The effect was like a fire starting at the corner of a paper. Eating away at it burning until it was all gone. Jesse did not know what was occurring, but it was strange. Suddenly in a blink of an eye the colors were gone, and the dark void of space returned. He had entered into another universe a universe within his mind. Maybe he was asleep and that was why he could see himself floating in this black abyss. Was it possible that he could permeate the barriers of his own mind perhaps? Either way it was incredible all the same he thought to himself? It was as if he were seeing an actor on stage playing out his role in life. But in this stage, he was the actor yet unconscious to the present world. How was it possible that he could see himself? Strange is the only word that ran through his thoughts. Jesse's body jerked up bowing in the center. It seemed as it were about to break in half right at the waist. A sharp pain, a flash of white light, then his body fell flat onto the bed. Jesse found himself in a void. In this void of space Jesse felt a gust of wind shoot past him. It was like two hands reaching under him. It lifted his body upward.

He felt alone now in the dark abyss. In this universe he was in. In this world his back was not bowed in the center. He was just suspended in the center of darkness. In the distance he could see a funnel growing twirling round, and round underneath him. With each twirl it was becoming larger and larger. He floated like a piece of debris in the eye of this tornado like funnel. Why was this funnel shape growing and taking him into its belly. Why? The faster this funnel twirl and blew its violence grew with intensity. The tornado shaped object began to move upward quickly engulfing his body taking him deeper into the eye.

In the I. C. U. Jesse's mouth opened as if to scream but here was no scream.   No sound just a yellow substance that purged from within him his belly, and out of his mouth.

In the void of space electrical charges began to shoot out from all directions. First a soft crack then moments later each charge shot out with a louder crack. The electrical spear of lightning shot out. Shot in and over the funnel as if to give the tornado life. Turbulence grew as the wind grew. Moments later there was no more of Jesse. This thing had finally taken Jesse deep into its belly. A burst of a green light, and Jesse had suddenly entered another world. It was a new world of bright orange. In this world his body was surrounded in a blue aura. A loud crack and another bolt of lightning. He had entered into another world. At the four corners of this universe were waterfalls. How many worlds how many dimensions of his mind was there. How many did he have to enter before he found piece. He could see his body moving into a vertical position. His mind relaxed. Jesse felt like going to sleep then from up top from out of this dimension eating away at the waterfalls from the bottom up.

A wave of red blood began to roll upward eating away at the waterfalls. His body lay on top of the red mass motionless like a canoe floating alone in an ocean. Then the blood appeared. It began to boil around him. One by one bubbles of blood shot up and exploding.

The fire balls shooting out like missiles. The flaming globs of blood rocketed across in every direction horizontal, vertical, perpendicular. They splattered as they hit each other in motion. It was like a firework display. The flaming globs of blood changed colors, red, yellow, green, and blue. Abruptly a flash of light and he had returned to the dark void. Jesse could hear voices, voices like that of a small child. A face began to focus in and out of view. This face he knew he had seen it before. But where he thought to himself. The boys' face faded back in to view and he was smiling at him. The boy faded away slowly. Who was it? The thought hurt his head. The need to know who it was gnawed at his brain. Who was it?

Back in the present time Jesse began to spew more of the yellow substance from his mouth. Nurse Gamble rushed out of the I. C. U., and moments later returned with Doctor Samuels. The doctor approached the hospital bed. He scrutinized Jesse's condition then took out a pen light from his smock pocket and leaned forward. He turned Jesse's head to one side. He flashed the light into Jesse's ear then moved his head back. He shone the light at Jesse's eyes looking into the pupils.

"Hum! Doctor Samuels moaned then said under his breath, "that is strange, very strange," he then spoke out loud to the nurse, "nurse Gamble give him a sedative. At least we can take away some of his pain."

Jesse's mind blocked out the present and returned to the void.

"Take my hand please," the child requested of Jesse. Jesse reached out his hand grabbing the boys' hand.

Instantly he vanished through the void passing through a set of curtains into the past. He felt his heart speed up with excitement. The excitement of the unknown. Suddenly he saw trees, a houses, and children playing. Instantly like a hammer between his eyes he realized who the child was and where they had gone. The boy was himself and he had entered the past into his childhood. He could see his two brothers making their way between two houses making their way up to the railroad tracks.

Jesse returned his attention to his house for the time being. The large peach tree next to the garage bloomed with peach blossoms as it did when he was six. He then noticed the tall Arizona ash at the edge of the yard by the street. He remembered playing in the dirt below its branches for hours on certain days. He stared for a few seconds at the white house that he had loved so. To him there would never be a house as the one he had grown up in. The child pulled at him tugging at his hand. Instantly, he vanished through the void passing through a set of curtains into the past.

"Follow me," he said.

As soon as Jesse touched his hand there was a flash and he was at the railroad tracks. His brothers played laughing and moving about.

"John, Roy, Jesse," he heard his mother's voice calling out to them.

"We're over here Ma. We'll be home in a little while," John the oldest of the three called out to their mother.

"Look, look," Jesse cried out excitedly pointing his finger at a lizard darting across their pass. Running over the gravel, and over the tracks making its way into the tall grass.

†Jesse cried out excitedly pointing his finger at a lizard darting across their pass.

"Follow it Jesse," Roy called out.

The lizard had been too fast for him. It quickly darted through the tall grass to safety.

"There over there," Roy shouted out as he caught glimpse of it dashing up the telephone pole.

Roy reached into his back pocket withdrew his slingshot. Without missing a beat of rhythm. He placed a rock into the leather tongue of the weapon. As he did he began to run towards the pole.

"Wait for us," John called out.

All three boys ran down the small ravine up onto the tracks then back down to the other side heading south. There was something about going down to the other side that began to frighten Jesse. The gravel sent an unexplainable fear into him. He knew now what day it was. He knew why he had been brought back to this time and date. The fear overwhelmed his brain. He wanted to cry out for help. He had put this horrible day out of his mind.   He had put it into the back of his head for many years.

In the I. C. U., tears rolled down the corner of his eyes hidden away by the bandages.

"Why did you bring me hear?" Jesse asked.

"I did not bring you here Jesse you did. You know the answer," his child image answered back.

Jesse looked at himself then returned his attention to the children as they ran after the lizard. It was amazing how they all resembled each other he thought to himself. He was wearing a blue plaid shirt and overalls. His brother Roy wore the same except he wore a red plaid shirt. Roy and Jesse looked so much alike sometimes people would ask if they were twins. Roy had a scar over his left eyebrow where a rock had found its mark by the hands of John the oldest of the brothers. John wore a yellow plaid shirt and was just a few inches taller than them.

"Where did it go?" shouted Roy.

"Quiet! It's up on the top part of the pole," John whispered.

They made their way around the pole moving quietly taking soft step not to alert the lizard. They loaded up their slingshots. The lizard scurried up even higher up on the pole. It vanished around the other side. They circled around to the other side. They aimed then pulled back on the leather tongue holding the rock in place then let loose. The rock flew out hitting the pole with a dull thump. One of the rocks hit the target cutting the lizards tail off. The lizard jumped from above into the tall grass below.

"Shit! It got away," Jesse said disappointed.

"Well follow it Jess," Roy retorted in a sarcastic tone. "It's too hot to chase it any longer," says John as he wipes sweat from his forehead.

"Come on John please," Jesse pleaded.

"No, I think, I am going to go swimming instead down at the park."??

"Yeah, that sounds good to me," Roy agreed. "How about it Jess?" John asked.

"No, I think, I want to hunt for lizards it is more fun. Besides you even said it was fun the last time."

"That is true Jess but not today it is too hot." "Swimming would be better today," Roy agreed. "No, I am going to hunt lizards."

"Ah, let's go Roy," John said impatiently then walked up to the street looked over his shoulder at Roy, "Well are we going or not."

Roy hurried to catch up to John. When he reached his brothers side he asked.

"Do you think he will be all right by himself?"

They looked over their shoulder back at Jesse, but already he was walking south bound toward the Airport Boulevard Bridge.

"Should we go back?" ask Roy. "Na, he'll be alright."

"You sure he'll be alright?"

"Sure, he will," John said then added, "I'll race you home."

"You're a fucking worry wart you know that Roy. He'll be alright. Besides by the time we fix the flats on the bikes he'll be bored. He will come home, and he will want to come with us."

"Yeah, you're probably right," Roy concedes.

CHAPTER 5

Jesse searched high and low but had no luck finding any more lizards to shoot at with his sling shot. He turned around then begins to walk up to the same spot they had seen the previous lizard that had gotten away. As soon as he reached the telephone pole, he heard a faint rustling in the grass. In his child imagination he begins to talk out loud to himself.

"I Jesse, I am the greatest hunter in all of the world."

Jesse then reaches into his pocket. He withdrew another small pebble. He decides he was low on ammunition. He walks down the small ravine to a pile of gravel left behind after the track repairs. He knelt down beside the rock pile. He searches for the small round pebbles he needs for the size of the leather tongue. He fills his pockets until they bulge out. It seems as if his pockets would burst from the amount of rocks, he had shoved into them. The weight of the rocks weighed his pants down. He grabbed his sling shot off the ground. With his other hand he held up his pants. The back of his overalls sagged down. Quickly Jesse made his way back up the ravine to the top. He made his way up to the center of the two tracks. He looked south then north.

"I am the greatest hunter. I will hunt this creature of the jungle for its trophy," he said out loud as if he were talking to a crowd of people.

Jesse thought he heard something. A shuffling coming from the tall grass. He moved over the tracks and down to the other side into the grass. He searched the grass with his hands moving his right hand up the side of a blade of grass. Its sharp cut into his flesh like a fine razor. Abruptly at that moment the lizard jumped up in the air. Its feet moved like the front wheels of a locomotive with each stride it moved faster. It made its way up to the center of the tracks running north. Jesse placed a rock into position and aimed as he ran. His hands trembled from the tension of the elastic bands. He released his grip on the leather tongue and out sailed the rock. The force of the bands hurling it out at an incredible speed. There was a thump as it found its target the lizard jumped up landed dead on its back.

Its intestines hanging out of its stomach. Jesse pulled up his pants then began to walk towards it.

"I will mount this trophy's head up on my wall for my brothers and all the world to see."

Jesse bent down on one knee. From the corner of his eyes, he caught a glimpse of something glimmering in the grass. He suddenly lost interest in the lizard. The twinkle, the sparkle of what lied just a few feet away interested him more at that moment. He climbed back down the ravine. He made his way to the sparkling object. He knelt down parted the grass with his hands. He studied the coin like object on the ground before him. It appeared to be a gold coin. He had never seen gold only in his brother Jesse bent down on one knee. From the corner of his eyes, he caught a glimpse of something glimmering in the grass. He suddenly lost interest in the lizard. The twinkle, the sparkle of what lied just a few feet away interested him more at that moment. He climbed back down the ravine made his way to the sparkling object. He knelt down parted the grass with his hands. He studied the coin like object on the ground before him. It appeared to be a gold coin. He had never seen gold only in his brother's schoolbooks. Still, he knew it was gold.

"I have found the lost treasure of the Incas," he said not knowing that indeed he had found a treasure.

He had indeed found an artifact from the time of the Aztec. Little did Jesse know that the treasure he held in his hand held something that was, evil. Something that was not of our world. Evil from the underworld. In fact, what he had found was the amulet forged and blessed by the spirit of an evil Witchdoctor. Jesse began to dig with his fingers around the object. On occasions he used the tail end of his sling shot to assist him in removing dirt. Removing the dirt that kept it hidden for so many years. Slowly he uncovered it releasing it from mother earth.

"I must be careful, for I have entered the world of monsters," his imagination raced on.

Jesse had done just that he had entered the world of a monster called Two Souls.

A raven appeared from out of the blue. It cawed out several times then landed on top of the telephone pole. It scrutinized Jesse movement below. It would watch until it was time for it to fly away. Not aware that his finger was bleeding he placed his finger on the gold object. Startled as the Raven cawed again, he looked up. He did not see the coin awake. He did not see the two small eyes open and stare at him. Nor did he see the amulet sprouted a mouth. The blood had given it life. It came to life like an infant sucking away at a bottle. It sucked away at the droplet of blood. It sprouted fangs like those on a vampire but miniature. It bit down sinking the small fangs into Jesse's finger.

"Ouch!" Jesse cried out.

It retracted its fangs as soon as it heard Jesse's voice. It then opened its mouth licking away at the blood from its teeth. Not realizing the danger Jesse ignored it and began to play once again.

"I have been bitten by the monster scorpion. I must find a cure quick before the poison takes its affect. I must find the Black Rose of death. For only its poison along with the white lotus can it counter the poison of the black scorpion, I must go to the other side of the island. It is the only thing that can save me now. I know now that this is not a coin. I know that it is an amulet left behind by the gods."

Jesse finished cleaning off the encrusted dirt on the coin. He turned it over then over again examining it carefully. One side was clear. Or it appeared to be. The encrusted dirt covered the man snake eyes. He turned the coin over. He looked at the face of the serpent with human eyes.

"Hum! Jesse said out loud to himself thinking that it looked more like something someone would wear around their neck.

He realized that it was an amulet that had been left behind by someone. What Jesse did not know was that it was an amulet and that it was forged and left behind four hundred years ago. Suddenly the image of the two headed serpent began to glow. It began to burn his flesh. He quickly dropped it to the ground. The earth below the amulet began to glow hot red from the extreme energy it was releasing. Jesse stumbled back falling on his rear. Bewildered he studied the amulet for several more minutes. He watched curiously at it. He hesitated for a moment then reached down feeling it to see if it was still hot. He picked it up in his hand. He studied it some more then looked momentarily towards his house to see if his brothers were coming back. Quickly his thoughts returned back to the amulet. His mind ran wild.

"I'll just put a hole here at the top and place a chain on it. I can wear it around my neck. I have found the lost treasure. I have survived the many monsters and the task of the gods."

Again, the amulet began to glow but before it burned his flesh as before he dropped it the ground. A thick gray smoke began to move upward from the amulet. The air smelled of sulfur. The smoke took form transforming into a large hideous serpent. Jesse's heart began to pound rapidly with unrelenting fear that only a child could experience. He could hear his heart pumping pounding away in his ears. It was horrible but, in another way, amazing. Before him the smoke was now taking form. What was before Jesse had completed its transformation. It was a huge serpent at first then as the shape became real a head began to sprout from the serpent's neck. After the completion of its transformation before him stood a creature that was half man, and half that of a diamond back rattler. All he could do was to stare frightened as never before. The thing from the side of its neck had bloomed like a flower bulb. It swayed back and forth before him. Its black forked tongue flickered in and out of its mouth. Its head darted forward closer to Jesse. It hissed just an inch away from Jesse's face. Jesse tried to scream but his attempt only came out in a muffled sound.

He tried to move his feet, but it seemed that he had become paralyzed. His feet felt as if they had been glued to the ground. It was the demon in front of him. It had put him under its spell somehow. It had taken the form of the evil witch doctor Two Souls. It opened its eyes causing Jesse's to move back. The evil penetrating from the demon's eyes reaches into the back of his mind. The deep yellow of its eyes. The red oval shape iris on the human side and the human eye on the other side glared coldly at him. The demon swayed its two heads back and forth. Each having a life of its own. It then called out in a raspy evil tone.

"Jesse."

Jesse felt his knees shaking form his fear. His fear shot through him like a pail of cold water being poured over him. Again, the demon swayed its head back and forth. It opened its mouth exposing large white fangs dripping of thick saliva. The fangs reflected the brightness of the sun making it appear as if to sparkle for a flash of a second. It flicked its black tongue in and out. Saliva fell to the grass below. Between Jesse's crying and sobbing he managed to speak out to this thing.

"What do you want with me? I did nothing wrong."

"I want you Jesse," it said moving forward again almost touching Jesse's nose.

"Why?"

"Why, because you will let me live again. I will take your soul and live. I will take your life as mine and live forever.

"No!" Jesse cried out and moved slowly backing up the incline of the ravine keeping an eye on the demon.

No, sooner had he blinked his eyes and the demon vanished in a puff of smoke. The amulet lifted off the ground and began to float towards Jesse. He stared at it in bewilderment not knowing what to do. There was nothing he could do but watch. It reached him and placed itself over his heart. It vanished through the shirt's material Jesse wore. Jesse could feel the heat from the amulet against his skin.

"No," Jesse shouted at the top of his lungs as frantically fought with the buttons of his shirt.

He opened up his shirt. The amulet begins to sprout eight legs like that of a spider. The tips of each of the legs had sharp points like that of needles. The gold legs of the amulet began to sink into Jesse's flesh. They entered his flesh, and they began to pulsate. With every beat of Jesse's heart, it went in deeper. Jesse watched on as his flesh opened up as if it had been cut by a scalpel. There was no blood just his heart pulsating with life. The red raw muscle pumping away. Jesse cried out helplessly. The gold amulet vanished into the heart. The red muscle closed over the amulet. His skin repeated the process closing and healing leaving no trace that it had even happened. Jesse felt his urine run down his legs. He ran loosing traction and he fell. He hysterically moved his hands grabbing at the ground and gravel underneath him not giving way. He fought with every ounce of his strength. He clawed at the earth and gravel until his fingers bled. The vision in Jesse's head began to break up. The boy let go of his hand and vanished into the blue void.

"No, don't leave," Jesse cried out.

"Help me," the child's voice trailed off in the distance. "No, don't leave me," the raspy voice of the demon mimicked him then it began to laugh wickedly, "Your soul at this moment is becoming part of me Jesse. When you have become twenty-one, I will have become strong in you. I will then take control of your soul then you will die, and I will live forever," said the demon then everything became silent.

Back in the I.C.JU. Jesse stared up at the ceiling through the slits cut in the bandages that covered him from head to toe for him to be able to see. In the silent void he just stared at the ceiling.

CHAPTER 6

Monday, twelve o'clock at the institution for the mentally insane. Bobby better known as the serial killer, "The Slayer." Bobby was convicted on charges for the brutal murders of fifteen men and women. His sentence was for him to be confined within the walls of the institution for the duration of his life. For the possibility of an attempt to escape the facilities was given the order to keep him confined to his bed. Here he was to be kept under heavy sedation. Heavy sedation in a vegetable state. But today was different for today Bobby was able to think, to feel, to calculate his next move. For the first time in years, he could think though his mind was still drossy from medication. He could think. Slowly he would regain control of his mind. Bobby would keep his secret for another day or two. His purpose would be to fool the male nurse that brought him his medication every day. Bobby could hear the door tumblers unfastening setting free the lock mechanism. The door opened slowly. Bobby continued to look up at the light above as if still completely in a state of limbo.

"Here you go girly girl, medication time sweetheart," the nurse says then squeezed Bobby's nose with his thumb and index finger. He opened Bobby's mouth as he always did and placed the pills into his mouth. He placed the glass of water to his lips then pour the water in. A small, muffled gurgling noise escaped form Bobby as the nurse forced the water down his throat.

"Don't choke now we wouldn't want to lose you now would we. There you go girly girl now sleep tight," the nurse says then turned and pushed the metal cart outside turns around and locked the door behind him. The nurse opened the small port door and peered back into room. Bobby waits and listens for the port door to be shut. He listens for the squeaky wheels of the cart too began to move down the corridor to the next patient.

"You will sleep soon enough asshole,"

Bobby said under his breath then flipped the man off. Three weeks passed. Every day like clockwork he began his regiment of pushups, karate forms, and meditation. Today was the day of reckoning. He opened his eyes and clapped his hands. Clapping his hands summoned the spirits of the warrior. The strong medicine that put him in a state of limbo. The medicine that put him in what he called a robotic state had now been purged from his system. Now he paced up and down his confines like a restless animal waiting to feel freedom after captivity. Today he would once again be the predator. He struck the wall with his fist, and it felt good. Not as good as it would feel in just a few minutes, but it felt good just the same. He looked around at the white walls. Oh, how he hated them.

"Soon the control will be mine," he whispered to himself.

He waited patiently estimating where the sun was as he looked out the window. The one pleasure that was not taken away from him thanks to his lawyer. His lawyer had said that even animals in captivity are allowed to see the sun rise and descend. Six p.m.

"Soon, soon asshole. You will regret what you have done to me over the years," he says softly to himself.

It was time for him to make preparations for his escape. Bobby heard the door shut close several doors up. This indicated that the male nurse would soon visit him. Bobby pulled the pillowcase off the pillow. He placed the pillow in the center of the bed then covered it with his blanket. He fluffed it up making it seem like his body lay underneath. He stopped quickly as he heard the nurse's keys rattle. He moved swiftly positioning himself against the wall next to the door. Bobby's eyes rolled up showing the white of his eyes as he leaned against the wall. It was as if he were having an orgasm. The nurse opened the port hole three quarters of the way up on the door. He looks in seeing what was to be Bobby that lay in bed.

"Good sound asleep like a baby."

The adrenalin flowed through every part of Bobby's being like a rush of a good drug. Several years in this place locked up like an animal. They could not confine the will of God. He knew that the voices in his head would set him free. And all he had to do was to listen. The voices would leave him alone for a short time. The voice now where there to free him. But soon they would give the order to kill. The door opened the nurse popped his head in.

"Wake up sleeping beauty. Wake up papa's here."

Bobby's body tensed up the veins in his arms instantly swell like cords of wire running in all directions. He wrapped the edge of the pillowcase around his hands tightly. A wicked smile grew on his face as he waited for the nurse to get into his killing range. The excitement of the kill. Oh, what pleasure his mind had missed. Bobby was a small thin sickly built man. He weighed a solid one hundred and fifteen pounds. His eyes sunken in further than normal giving him the appearance of a skull like face. A ghoulish look of the dead. The green hospital robe did not help. The robe made him look like something ready for Halloween. Yet with a feeble frame Bobby possessed an enormous amount of strength. Doctors who study the mind believe that his strength was due to abnormal brain messages to the adrenalin gland. This in hand determine the amount of adrenaline being released and giving him this unusual strength. The nurse shoved the door close with his foot. He pushed the metal cart towards the bed.

"I'm here sweetheart I'm home," he says.

He took the small cup from the metal cart filled with Bobby's medication then bent over to pull the bed sheet down over Bobby. He pulled back the sheet. Then in surprise he shouts out, "What the fuck."

He had been taken by surprise but not it was reality that set in with fear. Bobby moved in for the kill with perfection. Swiftly he wrapped the pillowcase around the nurse's neck. He turned his head and that was all he had time to do. The medicine in the small paper cup spilled to the ground. Bobby kicked the back of the nurse's leg and down went the man on to his knees.

The nurse desperately gasped for air. Wildly he reached back with both his hands hoping to grab Bobby's hands. He hopes to regain control of the situation. Bobby shifted his body placed his knee on the man's lower back and at the same time pulled back harder on the pillowcase. Bobby's muscles strained, they tremble. Bobby pulled with the rest of his remaining strength. The sound of the nurse's neck snapping several times as it broke reached his ears. It was as if one was hearing several twigs being snapped in half. The nurse went limp with death. Bobby let loose of the pillowcase and the nurse fell with a hard thump to the floor. Scrutinizing the man for a while he then abruptly kicked the man in the ribs.

"Well, how does it feel to be home papa," Bobby says sarcastically.

Bobby kicked the man one more time and it felt good. He then began to undress the male nurse taking his clothes and putting them on. Now dressed in the nurse uniform he turned around and made his way out of the room and out into the corridor. He had to go on instinct there was no time to devise an escape plan now. He took the metal cart outside the door. He began to stroll it down the corridor. He kept his head down only looking up on occasions to see where and how far the front desk was. He could see the nurse at the desk looking at him. He continued to walk thinking what he would do next if she recognized him. Freedom lay between him and the double doors several yards away. One way would be easy the other would mean he would have to fight his way out of the place. He hoped she would not talk to him.

"So far so good!" he said to himself continuing to move forward to the double glass doors.

Bobby kept silent as he began to pass the nurse. He could see the nurse eyebrows furrow up slightly in puzzlement. Bobby knew he was going to have to fight his way out at that moment.

"Ron," she called out to him twice.

Bobby faced the glass window and looked straight at the nurse. The clothes on his back sagged from being two sizes too big for his frame. Ron the nurse Bobby had just killed was a tall man with a fair build. Seeing the sagging clothes on Bobby the nurse pressed the alarm button. Bobby smiled at her then move quickly to the doors.

"Stop, stop," she cried out. "The fuck you say."

Bobby lifted the metal cart and threw it at the woman behind the glass window. It flew through the air scattering the medication in all directions on the floor. The sound of the glass breaking echoed out through the building. The woman lifted her arms up in front of her face just in the nick of time. Only allowing the corner of the metal cart to catch her nose. It sent her plummeting to the ground. Blood ran down the bridge of her nose where the edge of the cart found an opening. If her reflects had been just a little slower. The damage to her face might have been more severe. Just then a Hispanic security guard appeared at the double doors. The security guard made his way in. Bobby looked at the man wondering if he would be able to pass through the two-hundred-and-sixty-pound man. He waited silently making no attempt to escape from him at that moment.

The automatic door switch to the double doors clank shut. There was only one way out and that would be through this man. The guard rapidly rushed forward towards Bobby with a club held up high in his hand ready to strike Bobby down. Bobby hit the floor in a dive, feet first then lifted his foot and thrust out the heel of his right foot. It hit the man in the groin. The guard let out an agonizing scream as he dropped the club. He grabbed at his groin as the searing pain shot threw like fire. Like an oak tree that had been shopped down he fell to his knees.

Another guard came in through the double doors. He was as large as the first weighing just a few pounds less than the first guard. He rushed him like an angry bear protecting its cubs from danger. Bobby sidestepped and kicked out at the man's leg. At the same time hitting the man behind the head with a close fist. He used his knuckles like a hammer. The man skin broke open under the impact. The guard grabbed the back of his head then brought his hands up to his face. Anger rushed through him as he saw the red coating his fingers. Bobby wasted no further time. He immediately spun around in a spinning back kick. He hit the man square on the jaw knocking the guard out. He then rushed towards the double doors. He hit the release button. The metal lock clanked open. Bobby looked over his shoulder.

"The Slayer," cannot be kept locked up it is the will of God that I be set free," he said looking at the nurse behind the glass.

Bobby made his way through the doors. He then made his way down the corridor and out of the building. A block away at Lamar and forty fifth he walked south. Seeing a cop car, he stopped at the bus stop as if to catch the oncoming bus. The cop drove by slowly looking Bobby over ignoring the fact that the clothes on him was too. It was the way people dressed now days besides. Bobby looked the other way and mumbled under his breath.

"Make like a pig and go after someone."

The cop car passed then turned right. The car lights suddenly went on flashing blue and red. It had seemed that Bobby had gotten his request. The cop pulled over a black impala several yards up. For Bobby it was a good thing. Bobby watched as the cop got out of the car. This was a signal for him to move on. He began to walk south on Lamar making his way up town.

Sirens filled the air as they rushed to the asylum

CHAPTER 7

In the I. C. U., Jesse's eyelids began to flutter rapidly then abruptly he opened his eyes. He began to scream. Nurse Nancy Gamble rushed to his side. The nurse grabbed his arm softly just above the wrist.

"It's all right young man you are going to be all right now lay back down," she told him in a gentle tone.

She assisted him down by grabbing the back of his shoulder. She assisted him back down into the hospital bed. Jesse seemed to relax instantly trusting this kind woman. He squinted trying to focus his eyes on her face. There was only a blur image a shapeless blur. Inside he was alarmed that he could not even make out the shape of her face. Being blind after being able to see was not something to take lightly. In despair he turned his head over to one side and stared silently at the north wall. He could not remember how he had gotten to where he was at. He knew by the smell that he had to be in some kind of hospital. Or a medical establishment at least that is what he thought. He could hear whispers, voices, he turned back around. He felt as if he were losing his hearing as well. Anxiety was eating away at him now. He wanted to scream with frustration. He looked towards the shapeless figure at the edge of his bed.

"Please what is wrong with me? God why can't I see you? Why can't I hear anything the way I should? Where am I?"

"Everything is going to be all right young man. The doctor will be here soon.   He will be able to tell you everything. He will answer all your questions. Now, rest."

If everything was going to be all right, he thought to himself. Then why could he feel his insides shift at that precise moment? Every muscle in his body twitching. Jesse felt no more pain. The transformation that was taking place with in him now was all most complete. It was changing him but to what. Jesse would become twenty-one in just two days. His birthday would play the major role in what was to come. Suddenly like a tidal wave surging through his body he felt a savage rage of hate taking over him. Two souls face flashed before him. Everything in the room turned into a red haze. Something had happened to his eyes. The images were clear, but it was not like viewing through one's own eyes. It was like seeing through pink colored sunglasses. Or infrared glasses. The hate burned through his mind penetrating his whole body with pure evil. It was as if there were two separated entities lived within him. Each one fighting to take control of the other. It was tearing his brain apart. He looked at the face before him. Nothing made any sense. He needed answers. He grabbed the nurse's arm. She flinched from the pain from the tight grip on her wrist.

"Where the fuck, am I?" His voice came out in a deep growl.

She was startled from the abrupt manner. She looked at him and was about to answer him when one of the staff members yelled out urgently.

"Excuse me I will be right back," she told Jesse.

She left quickly to help where she was needed. Barely alert to his surroundings the dying sixty eight year old man lifted his arms as if clawing at the air. He stiffened as if he had become a statue. Petrified his eyes rolled back in his head. Doctor Samuel's looked at the monitor and the white fence in the center dropped becoming a flat lined.

"He's flat lining," he yelled out.

He slammed his fist into the man's chest several times. "Come you old fart give me something to work with come on," Samuel said out loud. Jack studied the man for a moment. There was no spark, no twitch, nothing. Nurse Gamble had seen this many times in her career. She rushed to his side with the crash cart.

"Nancy get the paddles ready," he says.

Nancy grabbed the defibrillator without missing a beat. She covered the defibrillator paddles with a blue gelatin that would act as a conductor. She handed them to Jack.

"Stand clear," he bellowed then repeated his words.

The old man's body lifted a couple of inches off the bed. His arms sailed up wildly like that on a puppet on a string then limply they swayed with no life back to his side.

"Come on old timer you can do this," Samuel told him.

He looked at the monitor. He hoped that the flat line would begin to dance across the monitor with a heartbeat. There was nothing only the lifeless white line that ran across the screen. He reached out his hand and it was like Nurse Gamble read his mind. She placed the syringe with a four-inch cardiac needle in it into his. He inserted the needle slowly into the man's chest until very little of the needle was showing.

Aspirating gently slowly the syringe filled with fifty cc of dark blood that had filled the sac around the heart that had kept it from being workable. Samuel worked the heart but still there was no response no life.

"That's it," Samuel said then added, "I think this man needs his rest. We have kept him from his destiny long enough."

Nurse Gamble could see the look of disappointment on the doctor's face. He had given his all. He had done everything possible to bring the man back to life. Maybe he had tried so hard to save this man because of the closeness in their ages. The man being six years younger added to his attempt to save the man. The residue of the excitement lingered in the air. From his bed Jesse could taste the adrenaline on his tongue as some of the staff rushed by him. The air was heavy with the smell only detected by him. He could almost taste, the sweetness, to it. His senses had been altered. He felt his strength increasing as if his body was feeding on what he smelled in the air. He was becoming stronger and keener than anyone could imagine. Jesse had known exactly when the old man's heart had failed. It was impossible as a human, but whatever he was becoming gave him these new abilities. It was incredible he thought to himself.

Incredible he had known the instant the heart had given its last beat. "Unbelievable," he thought then smiled. He lifted his hands close to his face then searched. He moved his hands up and down his body. He was covered in bandages. But why was this?

What had happened to him? How did he wind up here? He tilted his head to one side. He felt someone approaching weird he thought but still amazing. Fascinating, he whispered. He sniffed the air and for some reason he stuck his tongue out. It was the nurse. He could taste her body scent as well as the perfume the woman was wearing. The other thing that was strange was the fact that he could not see but yet he could. He could not hear. But yet he could hear clearer than before. He could sense the slightest movement the slightest change in temperature dropping or rising. Nurse Gamble approached the bed she let down the side guard rail. The rail clanked securing itself into place. As it clanked Jesse grabbed her by the wrist again. His voice coming out in a strong growling tone.

"Tell me where am I."

Nancy jerked away her hand barely breaking away from his strong grip. She stepped back she looked at him in bewilderment. She wondered if she had imagined the terrifying voice that had come from Jesse. She stepped back hesitated for a moment.

"Who are you?"

She stared at Jesse in disbelief. Had the horrible detestable voice come out of Jesse? Tingles like that of a million ants running up her back shot over her skin. It couldn't have she said to herself. The evil in his voice. It was just impossible maybe it was the long hours she had put in that day. That had to be it long hours were the cause of her hallucination. Sleep that is what she needed, and she would stop imagining things. She shook her head then ignored the incident.

"Lie back down I know you are confused for right. I will tell you my name." Jesse did as he was told.

"My name is nurse Gamble," she said then pulled the hospital blanket up to his chest.

"How did I get here?"

"You don't remember anything that took place?" "All I remember is pain. A God awful pain and the darkness."

"I can't really say what happen to you. I can only tell you what is written down on the report. I'll read it to you and maybe you will be able to remember."

"Yes, I need to know something, anything."

Nancy could not see his face under the bandages. But he seemed more at ease now. She looked at him then began to read off what was written on the chart. Jesse suddenly felt an urge to strike out and kill. This feeling sent new impulses to his nerves like small charges of electricity. The veins in his arms and neck swelled up pulsating as his blood rushed through them as never before. It was all new, but he was now beginning to understand some of what was taking place. Suddenly he felt the warmth generated by Nancy's hand as she placed it on top of his. Jesse clenched his hand into a fist grabbing at the edges of the hospital bed. He did not want to kill her but whatever it was that was controlling his thoughts. The thoughts that where to kill to kill her now.

"No, I can't," Jesse fought with his own mind. "Did you say something," Nancy asked him.

"No! I just felt a sharp pain in my side."

Nancy noticed that he was grabbing on to the edge of the hospital bed. He must be in pain. She placed her hand again over his and squeezed softly.

"You are going to be all right doctor Samuel's is one of the best doctors I have ever met."

His anger seemed to leave as quickly as it had come. Jesse stared up at her as she began to read again.

"Says they received a call and the paramedics arrived to what appeared to be a seizure call."

She flipped the first page over. She looked at him for a moment before she continued. She said a few words then stopped all of a sudden.

"What is wrong," Jesse asked.

"The writing is very technical I better get the doctor to read the rest to you. I'm just a nurse. Dr. Samuels will tell you the technical stuff."

Nancy knew what it said but she thought it would be better coming from the doctor. The doors open and Jack walked into the I. C. U.

"I was just going to go and get you doctor."

Samuel approached the bed and no sooner had he done so when the anger in Jesse came back. The anger in Jesse grew turning the room red. The hate for man grew instantly. He gritted his teeth. The corners of his mouth turned into a snarl like that of an angry animal. This hate for man only hidden by the cloak of bandages that covered Jesse's face.

"Doctor," Nancy said then handed him the medical chart.

Jack read the first page then flipped it to the second page. He read it then studied the patient before him for a while then spoke.

"Nurse Gamble tells me you want to know what happened to you young man. Is this true?"

"Yes."

"That is clear enough. It is a good sign. Anyone that wants to know why he is in a hospital must want to leave. He paused for a moment then continued, "Good! Says here that the paramedics received a call to what appeared to be a seizure.

When you were brought here it appeared that you must have had some kind of allergic reaction. This could have been brought on by something you ate causing the swells. It could have been an allergic reaction to the sun as well. An allergic reaction to the sun is rare, but it does occur. Something about the chemistry in the body shifts and at this point I believe that is when it happens."

Jesse took it all in. Both Nancy and Samuel's placed a hand on his arm. Jesse shifted his head to one side. Jesse scrutinized her as a pet would do when confused. Again, he managed to refrain himself from lunging out and killing them both. This evil demon in his soul was growing stronger and soon he would not be able to control it any longer. With each second that past he did not want to control the feeling. Jesse's eyelids began to flutter rapidly. The demon within was taking him undertaking him into a state of comatose. Comatose the final stage of evolution for Two Soul's to take over Jesse. Nancy looked at the doctor bewildered.

"What is happening?" She says out loud.

Samuel checked Jesse's pulse. It was to faint if it had been a pulse at all. He reached into his smock and took out a small pin light. He held open Jesse's eyelid as he examined the eye's pupil. It was like seeing through snow. A field of snow where just one drop of water had been dropped forming the pupil and in the center, there was just a black abyss. Jack stopped for a moment gathering his thoughts. He realized that there was no white to the eye. It was impossible. That could not be, but the proof was lying right there before him. One moment he had the white to the eyes. The next second, they had become totally black. Right before his eyes as he collected his thought. Now something else was happening. A coat like that of a cataract patient began to cover Jesse's eyes. Jack knew that what was happening to this young man he would not find in any medical book. Jesse's breathing had as well been altered for the hibernation period, the metamorphosis. Lumps began to pop up all over Jesse's body. Appearing then bursting oozing out body excretion.

"What in God's name," Samuel said out loud then said, "nurse Gamble get me some scissors right now."

Nancy handed the doctor the scissors he took them in his hand and began to cut away at the bandages. He began at the toes then up to Jesse's hips. He pulled away the bandages. A horrible stench hit their noses like that of decay flesh. Nancy gasped and covered her mouth and nose with both hands.

"If this is an allergic reaction to the sun? It is the worst case ever. And this stench that is emitting from him if I did not know better I would say it had to be gangrene. But these blistering swells I just don't know what or where they come from. I do know that they are rupturing at a fast pace and forming into large gashes. Fluid ran down Jesse's leg. The rotting flesh exposed a grayish skin underneath the gashes. Away from everyone's eyes as Jesse lay on his back two large claw like bones began to grow at the base of his shoulder blades. Jesse's muscular structure was growing rapidly as well. Doctor Samuel's was bewildered there was nothing he could do. He had no explanation all he could do was to put new bandages on Jesse. Jack and Nancy oblivious to the real danger that lay in the hospital bed.

"Nurse Gamble finish up here I need to make some calls. Keep a close watch on him. Let me know immediately if there is any kind of change out of the ordinary. Anything be side what just happened here and if it means staying another shift make it so. I do not want anyone that does not know what has just occurred taking your place. There has to be something in the medical records," he said as he turns and walked out of the I. C. U. Jack did not believe that anything like it existed even though he believed this he would not give up. There was that one in a millionth of chances. Call it luck, but still it was a chance and he had to give Jesse that one chance.

CHAPTER 8

The big hand struck twelve, the midnight hour. Bobby looked over his shoulder. He walked slowly with his hands in his pocket. His shoulders shrugged forward as he whistled the tune from the QZ. Further up ahead Bobby could see a stores with neon lights flickering fighting to stay lit. Bobby moved rapidly towards the store several feet ahead. He stopped and peered in through the window of the store. One of many that ran along the block. He placed his forehead next to the window. He placed his hands to the side of his head to take a better look inside.

"Costumes, hum, I like dressing up," he said to himself.

The ideal of getting a disguise entered his mind. He walked up to the glass door looked around then kicked the door in. The sound of shattering glass filled the night. The alarm wailed out that an intruder had just forcefully entered the establishment. Bobby scanned the place twice. He spotted what he was looking for. He walked up to the rack that held several monster mask. He picked one up to take a better look at it. He repeated the procedure with several mask. He took the one he like the best then threw the others on to the floor. He looked at the mask in his hand for a moment. From the corner of his eye, he spotted a cape. A black cape.

"Yes, indeed a cape is what I need to go with this mask," he said out loud.

He walked up to the Batman mannequin and retrieved its cape. He stopped he listened to the sirens. Maybe they were coming for him.

Or maybe not. But he needed to get out of there just in case. He rushed out of the store and headed for town.

"Monsters, I like monster," he said then dawned the creature mask and the cape. The night darkness cloaked him even more so than before. With the mask and cape, he became invisible in the night. He quickens his stride. He was several blocks away from the store. He heard more sirens filled the night as the cop cars rushed to their destination. Bobby whistled and twirled like a ghoul in the street. He shouted out loud not fearing his capture.

"Invisible, I am, I am invincible yes I am," he sang then twirled around then shouted out loud, "they can't catch me I'm the gingerbread man."

Bobby made his way down the side of the street then went left off Guadalupe on to thirty second to. Bobby made his way down the side of the street then went left off Guadalupe then on to thirty second. He continued to walk several blocks. He could see the highway. I.H. 35 he whispers then looks to his right. A hospital. Time to set free the voices from my head. He crossed the street and head for a small tree and three small shrubs next to the building. Behind some bushes he placed the mask and cape. He then walked up to the front of the hospital. He entered through the main entrance stopped at the elevator. He looked around smiled at the receptionist. The woman looked at him awkwardly but seeing him in the nurse's uniform she managed a smile. Inside the elevator Bobby pushed the up button to the fourth floor. He waited for the elevator to stop and the door to open. Ding! The bell announcing its arrival on to the fourth floor. People began to climb in instantly as well as to get out. One of the men entering the elevator was to close for comfort for Bobby. He hit the man with his shoulder. He then gave the man a cold look. The man moved to one side sensing the malice in Bobby's cold stare.

"How about waiting for me to get out of the elevator first. What do you think I can beam myself out of this place," Bobby told the man in a rude tone.

"Sorry mister," Bobby repeated the man's words and walked out onto the floor.

He look down the corridor scrutinizing ever thing that led down the hallway. He began to walk down the corridor. Bobby looked over his shoulder once. It did not matter any longer he thought for there was no way they would take him alive. There was just no way he would return to the asylum. Several of the nurses passing him looked at him curiously. Again, they ignored him for the fact that he had on nurse uniform on. They saw the name tag on his uniform and continued on. Though his clothe sagged on him two sizes to big anyone that saw him just thought he was part of the hospital staff. Though weird looking it was the way kids dress now days. Bobby stopped at the double doors of the I.C.U. He looked inside. Bobby saw Jack talking to one of the nurses. He heard him telling her that he would be right back. He turned and began to walk out of the unit. One of the doors to the I. C. U. began to open. Automatically Bobby moved in the way he had adopted to elude his adversaries over the past years. He stopped in front of a door on his right. He read the number 421. He looked over his shoulder as the doctor stepped out into the corridor. He grabbed the doorknob opened the door and darted into the room. To Bobby, it was more of a game he was playing. Samuel stopped abruptly as he caught a glimpse of Bobby's back.

Samuel stopped abruptly as he caught a glimpse of Bobby's back. Something hit Jack as not being right. There was something about the frame of the man. Jack knew something about him but could not put his finger on it. What was it that caught his interest? Something was just not right he thought. He would have to investigate. Jack made his way up to room 421. He reached down for the doorknob and was about to turn it when he was stopped by one of the nurses.

"Doctor Samuel you have an urgent phone call," the nurse tells him.

Bobby waited against the wall for the doctor to enter. He waited like a predator. Like a wild cat waiting to lunge on its prey. Waiting to kill the doctor that was the detective's friend. Jack let go of the door knob and moved down the corridor. The phone call saved the doctor for now Bobby's mind raced.

Suddenly Jesse opened his eyes. He could taste the adrenaline in the air. He stared into space through new eyes. The dark deep pits that had become his eyes during his metamorphoses were now blood red with a yellow oval in the center for its pupil. All his senses where heighten, stronger, keener, renewed, alteration complete. He was now perfection. His muscular structure testifies to the magnificence of his transformation. There was nothing left of Jesse not the boy one knew. Jesse was now a creature that would never be forgotten.

The creature, Two Souls climb out of the hospital bed. He was about to rip the intravenous feeding tube in his arm away when it picked up a scent. It was the nurse. Its memory told him it was Nancy Gamble. It looked at the windows then contemplated its escape. He did not want to be seen for now. The creature climbed back into the hospital bed. It closed its eyes as to be asleep. Nancy walked in approached the side of his bed. Nancy looked Jesse over. She noticed the bed sheet was off which was awkward. But maybe he had awakened for a moment and had tossed them off to one side. She stared at him for a moment. She then walked out to the monitoring room to check his vital signs. His heart rate was a little slower everything else seemed okay. It opened its eyes with infrared red vision it scanned like a scope designed for night use. Nancy left the monitoring room and entered back into the, I. C. U. It closed its eyes again and lay quietly as she approached. The demon's right hand lay exposed on the bed away from Nancy's view. Its razor-sharp claws protruding from the bandages. She looked at him not detecting the demon's hand. The hand that was able to kill her without any effort. The creature moved in its hand slowly back under the hospital blanket. She looked at the crook of his left hand. The intravenous feeding tube in his arm was in place. She noticed bandages had been torn away. Must have been from the growth to Jesse's body. She could see the pinkish brown leather like flesh underneath the bandages that had torn away. She stayed in a trance for a moment.

"Well, it is not normal but at least the swells have stopped. Maybe you are starting to recover?"

She noticed the deformity to Jesse's trapeziums. The muscle growth made his neck and traps look as if they were one. She shrugged it off believing that it was perhaps the bandages that had bunched up. She knew there was something wrong. She had never seen anything like this before. It was odd and confusing for her. She could not help the boy as a normal patient. She would have to wait for the doctor.

"I hope you get better. I'll be back to change these soiled bandages," she says and walked out of the unit.

Back in room 421 Bobby caught sight of the patient in the room. He smiled with new interest. He walked up to the end of the patient's bed. He looked at the seventy-year-old woman. She opened her eyes still half asleep.

"I am the nurse do you need anything? Do you need your pillow fluffed up perhaps?"

"Yes, that will be nice young man," she says in a tired voice.

Bobby noticed the woman's hospital chart hanging at the foot of the bed. He grabbed it and read its contents.

"I see that you just had a heart bypass old ticker having a little failure problem? I can help you. I will fix it all up for you."

Bobby walked back around to the side of the bed lifted the old woman's head with one hand. With the other hand he fluffed up the pillow. He lay her head back down softly on to it.

"Is that better?"

"Yes. You're a God send young man." "Dream my old princess," Bonny whispers.

A wick smile grew on his face as he said the last word. She noticed the look on Bobby's face. She opened her eyes wide with fear. Her mouth flew open as if to scream. But there was no scream to be released by her larynx today. Bobby pulled the pillow back out from the old woman head. He placed it over her head and pulled down on the edges of the pillow. The woman's eyes seemed as if to pop out of her eye sockets underneath the pillow. The fear of suffocation raced through her mind. Bobby pulled down harder the woman's legs began to thrash wildly. She grabbed frantically at the pillow with her hands. Her heart to weak from the surgery she just had. There was no fight left within her. She gave in to Bobby. The struggle for life had ended. Bobby released his grasp then tossed the pillow to the floor. The old woman stared into oblivion. Bobby walked up to the small hospital dresser at the other side of the bed. Where a lamp and phone had been placed. He opened the drawer and looked inside. He began to whistle, "Whistle while you work." He stopped as soon as his hand ran across cold steel. He pulled out his hand and in them he held a pair of scissors.

"Looky, looky," he said then opened them wide.

It did not matter what he said any longer for the old woman was dead. He ran a finger down the edge of the blade. He inspected how sharp they were. Hum! He looked back at the old woman. He then bent down kissed her on the lips. He caressed her forehead with his finger. He placed the point of the scissors to her skin. He pressed down and began to carve the word, "Slayer." At the same time, he was carving the word he talked to her as if she would soon reply back.

"You know I am sent by God. This was meant to be. They could not have kept me locked up in that place for ever."

The voices in his head had stopped. All he had to do was too killed. It felt good the cloud over his soul had lifted. Yes, the voices had stopped. He had done his job for now. At least until the voice requested another victim. He rubbed his hand on the woman forehead. With his fingers he wrote the sentence on the far wall. "The Slayer is back."

Jesse, now the hideous creature Two Souls climbed out of the hospital bed. Jesse was now the past. The creature ripped the intravenous feeding tube from its arm. It lifted its hand and with its razor-sharp claws it pulled and ripped the bandages from its body. As it pulled away at the cloth. A mucus like substance stuck to each strand of material. It formed strings of sticky slime. Slime that refuses to separate from its body. The strands of slime breaking in half and falling to the floor below with a splatter. As it pulled away at another piece of cloth it made a sucking sound. It pulled away the decayed old flesh that belonged to Jesse. It reached back pulled the remainder of the bandages off its back. It threw them to the floor. It flapped its large leather like bat wings as if to examine their mobility. The mucus like substance strung across from wing to wing. The substance parted and hung from the corner of each wing. It flapped its wings sending the mucus all over in every direction. It tilted its head back, It flicked its black forked snake like tongue in and out of its mouth. With each flicker of its tongue, it collected molecules in the air. Two Souls radar sensor picked up images as well as the taste of blood of the victim Bobby had just killed in room 421. It could taste the rush of adrenaline released by Bobby into the atmosphere. It scanned the entire room then stopped and faced the large windows. Lightning cracked across the sky as a storm rolled in with its own vengeance against mother earth. Thunder roared in the distance like large war drums. Roaring out that a new evil had been born and that it would bring hell to human's below. Lightning struck out above.

The windows shook from the generated power of each electrical blast. Two Souls thirst for blood had grown. It moved swiftly accurately with the finesse of a jungle cat. It moved to a man in a coma first. It stared down at the patient for a second. Its large reptilian head swayed from side to side as if deciding which of the body parts it want from the man. It scrutinized the wires connecting the man to the monitoring unit. It swung its arm out the tips of its finger cutting off the monitor switch by accident. Without knowing it had managed from being detected.

There would be no alarm giving a distress that something was in the room or that the man was dying. It swayed its head once more. It reached down grabbed the man's arm around the bicep. With one swift movement it twisted it off completely at the shoulder. Blood spewed from the veins like water fountains squirting out in rapid gushes flooding the floor. The pungent smell of blood reached its nose making it feel alive. The man's body twitched several times. It relaxed as the red substance of life pooled out of him onto the floor. It lifted the man's arm above its head. It tilted its head back. Its jaws began to dislocate then project outward. Its large white fangs began to curl back into forty five degree angles. The dislocation of its jaw would allow its mouth to open wide enough to insert the arm into its mouth. It placed the arm in fingers first. It jagged teeth grabbed pulling the arm back with its teeth. It released its fangs then moved them back into a forty five degree inching the arm further into its throat. In moments the arm had vanished without a trace.

The only indication it existed just seconds ago was the lump in the demon's neck. The lump that slowly slid downward into its stomach. Blood ran down the side of its mouth. It tilted its head back to let the last bit of morsel slide down. It looked at the dead man again then bent forward slightly. It then thrust its hand deep into the man's chest. It pulled at the heart. A sick sucking sound filled the air. The wound fought with the demon's hand not wanting to release the man's heart from his chest. It dislocated its jaw and repeated the process as before. With its large fangs it bit down working its jaw back and forth inching the heart into its throat. The neck expanding as the heart slid down and vanished. In its throat the heart pulsated once more and then expired. The creature moved towards the windows blood dripping from its mouth. Flashes of lightning lit up the night sky. It stopped then looked back over its shoulder. It tilted its head to one side and then looked up. Abruptly it turned its head back around bringing its attention back to the windows. It began to run towards the windows.

Lightning shot in an angle across the window. One step then another and another. It pick up speed moving steadily without missing a stride. It moved faster. Then from about four feet away from the windows it pushed off with its powerful dragon like legs. It sprung off its legs and shot out crashing through one of the windows. Glass broke into a million pieces of crystal. It took flight into the night. Out in the open it stopped in midflight and just before it would start to drop. Suddenly it spread its wings and flapped then several times. It's giant bat like wings lifting it into the sky. Flashes of lightning gave it life. Thunder drummed away roaring out in the distance. It shot up and another blast of lightning cracked like a giant whip. From a distant it seemed as if the lightening had shot straight down entering Two Souls back and shooting out to the other side. It appeared as if it had exited through its stomach like a huge zigzagging illuminating spear of energy. An illusion that gave the creature a move horrible existence.

The electrical bolts of light giving its silhouette life as it suspended itself in midair. It flapped its wings again shooting through the clouds moving back and forth through them giving it the appearance of a mythical dragon. Several minutes later it shot back down through the clouds then flapped its wings. It shifted changing direction then circled around the hospital three times. It brought one wing in and slightly down and changed direction and darted back up into the night sky disappearing from sight. Nancy walked out of the elevator on to the fourth floor with a cup of coffee in her hand. She walked up to the front desk.

She walked up to April and greeted her. April, her best friend. Maybe her only friend. It had been that way sense the fifth grade as far as she could recall.

"Hey Ape," it was Nancy's abbreviated name for April. "Nance, what I tell you about calling me Ape?"

"It is just short for April you know that."

"Gee, Nance I at least just changed the y in your name." "Hi April," Nancy told her leaning on the desk with the coffee cup between her hands.

"Hi! That is much better."

"So how's my girl?" Nancy asked.

"I guess fine just a few more hours to go until morning." "How about yourself," asked April.

"Just taking a small break," Nancy said then took a sip of the coffee.

"What about the patients?"

"They are all hooked up to the monitors. If anything is to go wrong, it will sound the alarm."

"I have a date for you. I think you will hit it off with this one wonderfully."

"April, I have told you before that I will know when the right man comes along."

"Oh, come on Nancy come to the barbecue please. Do it for me. You'll enjoy yourself. If you don't at least you will get something to eat. There's going to be plenty of hot dogs April tells her.

She then makes a jester with her hand as she opens her mouth. She smiles at Nancy as she pretends that the wiener is going in and out of her mouth.

"Your fucking wicked April you know that."?? "So, is it a yes?"

"Yes, I guess so." "Seven pm on Sunday." "Seven it is."

Bobby looked around and smile again, he was pleased. He turned and walked up to the door. He waited a moment then cracked it open. He peered out into the hallway then looked in both directions. He then cautiously made his way towards the I. C. U. Reaching the double doors he entered then went into a search mode scanning the room. He made his way in and up to the metal crash cart. His fingers and eyes searched through the instruments. Instruments that sparkled with their own unique power. He lifted a surgical knife up eye level. He ran his thumb down the blade. Blood trickled onto the blade instantly. Blood droplets fell to the floor. He clinched his fist tight.

"Whoa! Fucking good knife. Just call me doctor love. Doctor I love to cut people open."

He began to sing as he walked down the center in the mist of all the patients in the I.C.U. He begins to count softly.

"One little, two little Indians, tree little, four little Indians."

He stopped for a brief moment then asked as if they would reply back.

"Okay you poor souls of your mother's. Which one of you wants to go first to the light?" ask Bobby as he moved the blade across his face.

The sucking sound of life support systems sounded out like large lungs sucking in air then expelling it out. The life support systems allowing the person in need of air to stay alive. Bobby twirled around in the center of the room. He stops abruptly pointing his finger at a patient as if he had been playing spin the bottle.

"You are the next lucky contestant."

Bobby watched as the blood from the patient being purified passed through one plastic tube from the machine then back into another. Just as Bobby was about to speak, he felt a cool moistness brush against his face. He walked in the direction in which it was coming. As he approached the windows he stopped looked down at the mutilated body of the dead man.

"Fuck, I don't want these assholes operating on me.

Quacks, that is what they are quacks," he says then ignored the body.

He turned back around and made his way up to the broken windows. Bobby looks down at the small fragments of broken glass on the floor. He follows the trail back to the windows. He walked to the window edge looked down below. Pedestrians as well as some of the staff gathered below looking up to the fourth floor. Bobby knew he would have to move fast for soon they would come to investigate what had happen. Maybe not he thought there would be no need for alarms on the fourth-floor windows. Who in the hell in his right mind would try and enter through the windows from the outside. Bobby smiled then walked back down the aisle of the sick.

"I have to cut things short. I'm glad, I'm not in this fucking hospital. Shit, what kind of management runs this place? People could freeze to death or worse," he said then laughed out loud. Bobby walked back to the dead corpse stepping into the blood.

"Shit I hate when this happens," he says then shakes his foot as if to get rid of the blood on his shoe.

Bobby sees the open chest wound were the man's heart use to be. "I guess someone got to you first ha!"

The voices in Bobby's head called out to him. Kill the weak Bobby, kill the weak. Bobby stopped again and turned around looking at the sick. It would be in the name of mercy. Mercy killing his mind raced on.

"Sorry folks did not mean to detain you people from your happiness."

"You will be first and the rest of you will follow," says out loud.

The old man looked at Bobby. The man had tubes and I.V. hooked up to his arm. Bobby smiled then went into a mission mode. He slashed out with the surgical knife he had found on one of the metal carts. He cut their feeding tubes, pulled at the monitor wires. The alarm in the monitoring room went crazy. Bobby knew they would soon come so he had to hurry up what he was doing.

"Why not," Nancy agreed then turned looked over her shoulder for a moment then added, "you're just to, bad April.

No, sooner had the words left from Nancy mouth when the alarm reached her ears.

"What the hell," Nancy exclaimed and began to run down the corridor to the intensive care unit.

She turned back and yelled out to April, "push the button and call for a code blue in the unit."

Like a snake undetected he made his way out of the I.C.U. He walked with his head held down. Halfway down the corridor Nancy passed Bobby. Bobby kept his head down and pointed towards the I. C. U. Nancy looked at him giving him a puzzled look.

Strange she thought then whispered to herself as she rushed along. There's something odd about that man. She did not have time to stop. Whatever was happening in the I.C. U., was more important. The question ran through her head at that moment whether Bobby had just come out of the I. C. U. Maybe he had come out of one of the other rooms. She put her thoughts to the back of her head. She ran into the monitoring room. She stared through the window out at the patients in disbelief. The horror paralyzed her. The ugly scenario before her could not be real. She must be dreaming she had to be. If she wasn't she hope she was. She even went as far as to pinch herself to check if she was awake. The horror of what had occurred hit her like a Mack truck ramming into her. She screamed out at the top of her lungs. Nancy's lungs seemed as if they would burst. April hearing her screams dropped what she was doing and began to run to the I. C. U. She glanced over at Bobby as he kneeled down to tie his shoelace. She stopped.

"Nurse when you finish there come to, the I. C. U. with me."

Bobby stood up slowly he lifted his head. He stared directly into April's green eyes. The ghoulish face leering at her made her blood run cold. But before she knew what had hit her it was too late. Bobby lifted the surgical knife up high.

"No, you come with me."

The elevator doors open, doctor Samuel stepped out as well as two orderlies just in time to see Bobby bring his hand down slicing across April. The elevator doors open. Doctor Samuel stepped out as well as two orderlies just in time to see Bobby bring his hand down slicing across April's jugular vein. The two orderlies rushed him in hope that there might be something they could do for April.

"Bad mistake hero," Bobby told them as one of the men grabbed him in a bear hug.

The man was twice Bobby's size but that did not matter. In one swift movement Bobby placed his leg behind the man's leg. The orderly fell to the floor releasing his grasp. The other man rushed Bobby. Bobby side stepped out of the way. He kicked out hitting the man square in the groin. He then twirled around with a round house kick to the man's face. The man fell to his knees hard. Bobby swung the blade cutting behind the neck. The man gasped then fell face first to the floor.

"Fuck, I bet that hurt," Bobby said sarcastically.

Three other security guards walked out on to the floor and rushed Bobby.

"Bobby, give yourself up," Jack tells him.

"Bobby, give yourself up," Bobby mimic him in a sarcastic tone.

One of the security guard, swung his club down trying for Bobby's head. In a cross block Bobby stopped the attack at the man's wrist. He moved his left hand and grabbed the man's wrist then twisted. The man bent forward and with his other hand Bobby reached under and placed the blade at the crook of the man's arm severing the artery. "Now you die like the pig you are," Bobby says. He grabbed the man's head in his hands then twisted breaking the man's neck. The other two guards were about to rush Bobby when Jack stepped forward.

"No, let him go there has been enough killing in here," knowing that Bobby would probably have probably kill the two remaining guards as well.

Bobby kicked the guard in the ribs then said, "Rest in peace my dear friend."

"You sick son-of-a-bitch," shouted one of the guards.

Bobby walked up to the doctor. He stared coldly into the man's eyes. He remained silent for a moment. Jack knew Bobby and he knew if he made one wrong move, or gave in to fear. Or showed weakness it would mean his demise.

"Doc, how have you been?"

Jack remained silent. The door to the elevator opened and Bobby began to twirl laughing his ghoulish laughter.

"I want to kill you so bad. But today is your lucky day doctor," he says as he steps inside the elevator.

The door began to close but Bobby stopped it. He looked at the doctor then said.

"Doc, just to let you know they can't keep an angel of mercy from doing his job."

Jack watched as the door to the elevator closed. He brought his thoughts back to the more important matter.

"Let's get these people some attention," Samuel ordered then added, "You two guards check all the rooms on this floor. If this man, you just saw was in here. He brought death with him."

Jack made sure that doctors and nurses cared for the people in the corridor and that was if they were still alive. He then made his way to the I. C. U. He knew that there would be lots more dead people but when he entered the care unit.

Entering he could not believe the massacre that had taken place. Tears rolled down the corner of his eyes. He hated Bobby and he hoped him dead. He wanted to scream out at the top of his lungs. They were all dead all of them dead. Why? Why on earth do you let things like this happen lord, Jack thought to himself? What kind of monster do you allow to bring this down upon us? Deep down inside he knew it was human error not God. The brain being the strongest part of the body but yet fragile in its own way.

No, one really quite knows what makes a person cross that fine line. Maybe it was all the polluting to our world and like a cancer it was eating away at our brains. Drugs or other materials. Or was it that one just gave up on life in general. Jack walked up to the window and stared out into the night. He stared at the incredible electrical charges being released across the sky. Some of the night staff had just entered into the I. C.U. He turned around to face them.

"Do not disturb anything in this place. Everyone go outside there is nothing we can do for these patients now. We must not touch a thing here until the police give us the okay."

Jack turns back around looks at the windows. He ask himself why had Bobby broken them. He then just stands there in silent staring out into the night.

CHAPTER 9

At the precinct detective Pete scooted back his chair. He pushed away from the desk then stood up. Pete walked up to the coat rack. Grabbed his holster then his revolver then returned to his desk. He withdrew the Springfield from its holster. He looked at the blue steel forty-five before he placed it down on the desktop. It carried an eight shot magazine with a front blade and a rear adjustable sight. Pete thought of it as his Baby Blue his good luck piece. He strapped on the shoulder holster then picked up the Springfield. He looked at it then pushed the release button to release the clip. It popped out into his hand. He examined the clip making sure he had a full magazine. He then shoved it back in place. He put the gun back into the holster. He grabbed his coat off the back of the chair. He flung it over his shoulder. So far it is a pretty boring night he thought to himself. The phone rang. He picked it up and answered it.

"Hello this is detective Rodriquez how can I help you?" "Pete."

He knew the voice on the other end instantly. It was Chief Golds.

"What's up boss?"

"Pete I just received a call from the hospital. There has been a massacre."

"What do you mean massacre chief?" I mean like in many dead Pete."

"Massacre at the hospital," Pete said in disbelief.

"All the patients in the unit. All of them, every last one in the I. C. U., dead."

"Have any clue to who or why?"

"Yes, I do Pete. That is why I called you. You're not going to like what I have to say."

"Go ahead boss." "It was Bobby."

"Bobby is the suspect?" "That's right Pete."

"Are you positive Chief?"

"It was Bobby I wanted you to hear it from me Pete." "That's fucking absurd. It is impossible Chief. It can't be. He is locked up in the asylum. He is under medication like a vegetable."

"Look, Pete I know that is where he is presumed to be.

But Doctor Samuel saw him just a few inches away from his face." "Fuck, I should have put a slug in him when I had the chance."

"Find him and bring him back in one piece Pete. Without any bullet holes. Just bring him in."

Pete hung up the phone then ran his fingers through his hair then whispered to himself.

"Bobby I should have killed you."

An officer opened the door and stuck his head in through the opening.

"Chief said you needed a team." "Blendez you know the team."

"They are ready sir. Just waiting on you."

"Get all the men into the briefing room a.s.a.p.," Pete said then became pensive.

Pete's mind took a quick detour for a moment as he flashed back to the past. He recalled the dreaded day his wife had been murdered. Murdered by the hands of Bobby. Better known as the "Slayer." Pete's heart weighed heavy in his chest. He recalled the vision of his wife lying on the ground with her neck broken. Her dress torn apart from her neck down to her waist. In the center of her torso Bobby had stripped flesh from her body. He had placed his calling card. The word "Slayer" penetrated through Pete's mind like a wrecking ball hitting the side of a building. Bobby the name bombarding Pete's mind. His hate was so strong he felt like throwing up his food at that moment.

"If it wasn't love twisting your stomach up in knots it was hate. Go figure," Pete thought out loud then walked out of the office

Jack was still looking out the windows when Pete had arrived. His mind was still disturbed by what had happen. His mind ached to scream but he knew it would not do any good. He needed to distract himself from the horror. There had to be some good something beautiful left in the world. His eyes caught one of the stray cats darting across the parking lot. He then looked up at the night sky. Lightning shot across the sky. Jack marveled at the universe. It was the one thing that nothing on earth could ever destroy. It was one of the many wonders of the world that gave him peace of mind. Peace of mind in a crazy mixed up world. Tonight he could stare at the sky for hours just to loose himself from the human race. Time passed rapidly the sound of sirens brought him back to the reality of the world. He watched as the police cars screeched to a halt surrounding the building. The officers quickly positioned themselves behind open car doors. Quickly they placed the butt of their rifles firmly into their shoulders. They wrapped the sling of the rifles around their wrist. They placed their left hand under the magazine well for extra support. They aimed at the entrance into the building. Other officers moved in with revolvers and assault weapons at the ready. Two officers rushed the entrance shifting and turning in all directions. Making sure they saw everything possible not to miss anything out of the ordinary. Sgt. Blendez moved in to disperse the men into the building in teams.

"Jicks, Smith, Gomez, Freddys, take the south entrance. Martinez, Boats, Grimes, Lopez, take the north entrance," he called out the names of the officers for the east and west entrance then added, "No one is to come out or go into this place. I don't care if it's God himself. No one leaves no one comes in. God himself no one leaves no one comes in. Now take your positions."

Pete pulled up in an unmarked vehicle. Jack watched as Pete and his partner climbed out of the car and began to walked up to the front entrance. Jack recalled the day he had met Pete for the first time. "Get out of the way," Garza shouted urgently.

He shouted to the people standing in the corridor of the hospital. As the paramedics wheeled Detective Rodriquez to the emergency unit. Chief Golds as well as several other officers trailed behind the gurney as Pete was rushed him to the I. C. U. Jack seeing the detective's back and the three bullet holes immediately ordered the paramedics to take him into the operating room A.S.A.P. He knew there was no time to waste. The foot of the gurney hit the double doors as they barged through into the E.R. Jack stopped abruptly and put his hand out stopping Chief Golds as well and the other officers.

"Doc."

"I have to stop you here Chief.

"God damn it! I told him he was getting too close to something. It just didn't feel right. Whatever the detective had found out was his death sentence."

"I understand Chief do what you have to do. I have to attend to the detective Chief. If he is to live?" said Jack. He then turned and walked into the E. R.

"Blendez get three other officers down here and make sure that Pete is protected."

"You got it sir."?

"I mean guard him like he was the fucking president Blendez."

"Done," Blendez assured him.

Blendez walked up to his team. He picked four men out of the group. Ramirez, Williams, you will be on the inside after the operation. Hanks you and Smith will be on the outside guarding the detective. For now, we are to glue our butts here at these doors. We don't move until the doc., comes out and you two move in. Nobody is to enter after the doc., leaves."

The doctor's mind retuned back to the present as soon as he saw Pete climb out of the vehicle below. Pete looked up at the fourth-floor windows. He closed the car door. He thought for a moment then spoke.

"Sgt. Blendez is everything ready?"

"Ready, the men are in position sir. The area has been secured."

"Okay, let's go see what the hell happened."

They walked through the entrance into the building.

Doctors, nurses, and patients, watched as the team made their way up to the elevators. Pete saw that several of the staff members where crying and others seemed to be gagging. Pete knew what ever had taken place. It Was not going to be pleasant. Pete withdrew his Baby Blue from its holster. He checked the magazine. He had checked it before he had left the office, but it was more of a ritual with him. A ritual, that meant the difference between getting kill and staying alive. It was a priority. He never entered any place without making sure his only true back up was functioning. He re-holstered the 45 Springfield then scanned the corridor and the people making sure he did not miss Bobby. He knew Bobby and he knew that the man was insane. He knew that he would show himself just to get under one's skin. If he knew he could get away with it without being caught. Down deep inside Pete knew there wasn't going to be any Bobby. Not yet. Not until more people died.

The question was where? Where would Bobby strike next? Where? Pete and several of the swat team moved into the elevator. Several others took the stairs. The men on the stair moved quickly for the fourth floor. The elevator doors open just about the same time that the men that had taken the stairs entered onto the floor. The swat team made their way down the corridor heading towards the I. C. U. Their boots echoed out in unison sounding out in perfection. The many hours of drills had paid off. The two lead men looked into every room as they moved up the hallway. Room 421, the officer looked at the number then opened the door slowly and stepped in.

"Fuck! Blendez said out loud to himself then added, "The detective will want to see this for himself," he then stepped out of the room in a hurry.

He made his way down the corridor up to Pete. He told Pete what he had seen in the room.

"And sir it is not a pretty sight." "It never is Blendez," Pete tells him.

"Blendez you know the procedure lock her down. No one comes in or out until I give the okay."

Pete entered the room and stopped midway. He stared at the wall for a minute. It was Bobby there was no doubt in his mind. He knew if there was one dead body the chances of another or two dead bodies was ninety-nine-point nine percent. Jicks, team leader 2, entered into the I.C.U. He paused for a moment taking everything in then he caught a glimpse of Doctor Samuels just staring out into the night. He brought his attention back to the I.C.U. then call for Pete.

"Detective you better come to the I. C. U., then added A.S.A.P."

Pete heard the urgent tone in Jicks voice. Pete stared at the wall for a few more seconds then at the old lady. Blendez no one comes in except White-Cloud.

"Done," Blendez acknowledged.

Pete made his way into the intensive care unit. The horror hit him like a baseball bat between the eyes. Could one man do such and act his mind raced. Pete saw Samuel looking out of the windows just standing there lost in his own thoughts.

Pete walked up to him and placed his hand onto the doctor's shoulder. Pete knew that being a doctor was to save lives. But for the doctor to see this. To see the loss of lives whether or not it was his fault would be devastating.

"Doc.," Pete greeted him.

Jack turned around and managed a smile. "Been a while doc?"

"Yes, it has Pete."

Again, Jack's thoughts took a leap back ten years as began to recall the past. How they had become friends. He could see Pete being rolled in on a gurney to the I. C. U. His mind jumped forward as he recalled Pete and Karen his wife to be walking down the aisle. From doctor to best man. It was strange how they met and how their friendship had flourished. He jumped back remembering Pete on the gurney. Pete had three, 38 slugs lodged deep in his back. Pete had gotten to close to something, and someone wanted him out of the way for good. Three bullets lodged symmetrically in a perfect triangle. One bullet hit him about a half inch above the heart, the second missing his spleen directly under the left side of the heart, and the third passed almost all the way through the right side. Barely breaking the skin but protruding enough to see the lump of the bullet pushed against the stomachs skin. He had told Pete how lucky he had been to still be alive. He recalled the exact words.

"Detective you have to be one of the luckiest people I know. You have to have an incredible amount of luck for the bullets to have surrounded your heart like that. What are the odds of something like this happening detective? And surviving the ordeal just fucking lucky."

"Just give me hope doc will you," Pete had replied weakly.

He had broken a small smile at the remark. After Pete's wounds heeled. Pete would tell say.

"Doc., that it was the mystic powers of the pyramids do."

Pyramids or not Pete had been one lucky man.

No, sooner he had climbed out of his car when he saw Pete and Bobby sail out through the window. Glass flew all over as they crashed through landing on the ground. Pete struck Bobby several times with his Springfield. Then forced the barrel of the gun into Bobby's mouth. Pete's eyes gleamed with hate. He pulled back on the trigger of the gun. Samuel recalled shouting out to Pete.

"Don't Pete," his voice trailing.

Pete paused, his finger still pulling back on the trigger. He stopped pulled the weapon out of Bobby's mouth slowly. Blood stained the barrel of the gun. The trigger now squeezed halfway back. He pointed the weapon at Bobby's head. He began to squeeze the trigger again. At that point just a split second before the trigger released Pete moved the gun to one side. The bullet passed through Bobby's ear and into the ground. Jack walked up to Pete and took the gun. Jack knew something horrible had to have happen.

"Are you going to be all right Pete?

"Yeah, doc. I'll be okay, he said and stood up.

"Don't move a muscle Bobby or I will kill you right here and now.

Jack gave Pete back his Springfield then turned and walked up to the house. He walked inside and scanned the surrounding.

He moved into the dining room. It did not take him long before his eye saw Karen's mutilated body. With the word "Slayer" slashed across her stomach. The word jumped out at him. Now he understood how Pete felt. Hell, he felt like going out there and finishing the job for him at that precise moment. Several cop cars pulled up with their sirens wailing. They climbed out and rushed up to Pete. Pete watched without saying a word as the officers took Bobby into custody. They handcuffed him and escorted him to one of the cop cars. As they placed him into the car Bobby kicked the door and managed to stand and lean against the door. The officer pushed him back into the car.

"They can't keep me locked up. I have been sent by a higher power to do his bidding. There is nothing you can do. There is no way anyone can stop me from doing his work," Bobby yelled out at Pete. The officer closed the door immediately drowning out Bobby's words. What Bobby had done that knight put him into the category of being a monster.

"It's been a while," Pete said again to Samuel. Jack's thoughts returned to the present.

"Yes, Pete it has."

"Looks like Bobby made a mess of things again."

"That is an understatement, but I think you are right." "Jack this time I will put him away for good."

"I thought the system put him away for life in that place."

"Jack that is what I thought as well. But somehow he managed to escape."

The forensic team arrived and instantly they began to dust for prints. They set themselves up in an automatic mode. At that moment any clue would help. One of the forensic crew walked up to the shattered window. He studied it for a moment then began to dust the jagged edges of the glass. All Pete needed was a single clue for a conviction. This conviction would be different. With this one he would prove what he had told the judge. Bobby was a danger to himself and to people. The operation was the only thing that would keep him from hearing the voices. The voices that told Bobby to kill. A lobotomy special order for Bobby. If Bobby lived? Pete's thought ran wild. Pete walked up to the windows his mind trying to work the puzzle out. Why had Bobby broken the windows in? What would be the motive in that? White Cloud the lead man for the forensic team walked up to Pete. White Cloud was one of the few remaining Apache Indians still around. He stood six five and weighed close to three hundred pounds. His black hair cut short his high cheek bones and strong frame made him look more menacing. There was no expression to his features unless he smiled.

"Pete, my friend, come over here with me."

They walked up to one of the hospital beds. The bed that Jesse had laid in just a few hours ago. White Cloud knelt down and with the tip of his pin he poked at some kind of material. He poked at it and lifted the object up. The material was stained with blood and mucus that clung to the cloth.

"What the hell is that?" Pete asked.

"Jesse, that is part of the bandages that covered the young man that laid in this bed," Jack tells them.

"Jesse, hum!" Pete sighed.

"If you think that is weird?" White Could interjects. "Go on."

"Pete the kid that occupied this bed just a few hours ago was one of ours."

"One of ours?"

"That is what the doc., said Pete."

Pete took in the words thought for a moment then spoke. "What else?"??

"Seems this invisible character left," says White Cloud.

"I don't think the young man left White Cloud. The man that occupied that bed could hardly have walked," Jack relate to them.

Yes, that's right Pete. The young man was brought to us two days ago. It appeared he had some kind of an allergic reaction to the sun. Rare but it does happen.

"So, we have a kid with an allergic reaction to the sun.

Cloth stained with blood, and mucus. A hospital bed with the same substance it appears but with a missing body. Shit this is getting better every minute."

White Cloud reached down and rubbed his finger on the bed sheet. He brings his hand up. He rubbed his finger again examining its texture.

"Stuff feels like glue. Doc. I think the young man whacked off," White Cloud quips.

Pete chuckle softly then turned and face Jack. White Cloud returned his attention back to the pink raw flesh exposed on the bandages left on the ground.

"White Cloud has jokes today doc," Pete says. "I guess he does Pete," Jack said nonchalantly.

Sgt. Blendez walked up to where Pete. White Cloud stood up and waved one of his team over. Seeing the mutilated bodies and the smell of death Blendez began to gag at the stench of human waste and blood that reached his nose.

"Welcome to the crowd," White Cloud says.

"Let's retract for a second. You say an officer lay here in this bed and this is all that is left of him now?"

"I know it does not make sense Pete but that is it." "Maybe he walked out."

"Believe me there is no way the young man could have walked out of this place on his own. There is just no way in hell."

"Blendez get on the two-way and tell Johnson to comb every inch of the area outside. Tell him to search for a young Latin male that should be naked.

"Twenty-one years of age."

"You heard the doctor, got that Blendez?"

"One more thing after you tell Johnson to comb the area. Get your team and comb the entire fourth floor," Pete said then faced White Cloud then added, "When do you think you can have something for me?"

"Chief, busy not know," he said then smiled and said, "I have to take these few specimens to the DNA people. I'll tell Joe that it is a rush job. You know he loves that. Hell he owes me a few favors anyway. I'll let you know as soon as I get the results Pete. The medical examiner will take the dead corpse back to the morgue for a better look. If anyone can find that needle in a hay stack you know old Sally can."

"I heard that White Cloud," Sally the medical examiner replied back.

"I said oh, not old."

The room filled with static as Blendez's, two-way radio came on.

"Team leader one, this team leader two over." "This is team leader one over," replied Blendez.

"The area is secure, over."

"I acknowledge that team leader two," Blendez answered back then cut down the volume on the two-way radio.

"Pete why is it that when we meet it is that something terrible has just happen?"

"Jack I wondered about that as well," Pete answered back. "I hope you get the son of a bitch this time Pete," Jack said angry.

"I caught him once, I'll catch him again."

"You'll catch him but at what cost Pete. Do not make him your life."

"Damn Doc. You sound like the department psychiatrist." "I really don't mean to Pete. But it is that I worry, and you are a good man. A good friend and you need rest from being a detective. I want Bobby caught at whatever measure. I am just saying to make it quick Pete."

"I'll do just that Jack."

"Why don't you come over Pete? It has been a while since you have come to visit Jane and me. We both know how hard it was when you lost Karen."

Pete was about to get angry but calmed down. He withdrew the retort caught in his throat. He loved Jack like a brother and he could see the real concern in his eyes.

"I know you think you know how I feel Jack. But you don't. Only the person knows how he really feels."

Pete kept his hair trigger temper at bay. There was only three people he would do it for. One was Jack, the other was White Cloud, Sally and Chief Golds. He trust his life in their hands. For others he would have snapped their head off without a second thought.

"Jack was there anyone that might have seen what happen?" "Yes, now that you mention it nurse Gamble the graveyard

RN."

"Where is she now Jack?"

"She was just taken to one of the rooms to recover from the shock. I do know that Bobby was the only one that came out of the I.C.U.

"Jack you know I need someone that saw him. I mean saw Bobby come out of the intensive care unit."

"Isn't what he did in the corridor to the guard and to April enough to put him away?"

"That is exactly what they will do just put him away.

They just put him back at the crazy farm. I need an eyewitness that saw him come out of here. There cannot be a margin for his lawyer to turn things around. I want him to get that operation. I do not want him to have any loopholes none whatsoever. I have to question the nurse, Jack. We have to stop Bobby from ever doing this again."

"She's in room 420."

Dr. Samuel and Pete walk out of the I. C. U., and down the corridor into room 420. Nancy lay with her eyes open still in disbelief. They stepped into the room. For the first time in ten years his heart seemed to come alive. He felt a lump grow in his throat. In the hospital bed was a beautiful woman by the name Karen. A woman with long blonde hair. Her face oval shaped with full lips and a slightly piggish nose that seemed to make her look younger than she was. Her sun bronzed skin complemented her blue eyes. Pete was speechless. He was breath taken away and all he could think of at that moment was, "Sleeping Beauty."

"Pete this is nurse Gamble," Jack introduced her then noticed that there was an attraction between the two of them immediately. It was about time in a way. It would bring beauty back into an ugly world for Pete.

"Nancy this is Detective Pete Rodriquez. He has to ask some questions of you. Is that all right?"

The horror of what she saw reflected form her face.

"You know you do not have to answer any question if you do not want Nancy."?

"You can take your time miss. It is, miss?" Pete said hoping that it was.

It was a hell of a time for something of this nature to be happing. But it was happening. Stranger thing do occur.

"Yes, detective it is miss," she told Pete then began to tell her story, "I took a small break I returned and walked up to April's desk up front. We talked for a while then the alarm went off. I ran to the I. C. U. On my way there I came across a peculiar looking man. A sickly looking man. But when he smiled, I thought nothing more of it. I walked up into the intensive care unit. It was horrible detective. All I could see where bodies. Bodies thrashing about, blood squirting, from severed veins onto the floor. I could not do anything for them detective" she her voice breaking.

Jack placed his hand softly on to her shoulder then told her he would send in something for her to take to calm her down so that she could fall asleep. Jack began to walk out of the room then stopped next to Pete and whispered. They stepped out of the room.

"What is it Jack?"

"She is pretty shaken up. Let's give her some time to recuperate before you question her any further Pete."

"You're the doc," Pete agreed.

"You think you have enough on him now."

"Shit! Jack she saw him in the corridor. I wish that it was that easy. But for right now what I have doc, is nothing more than a mass slaughter. I have bandages with what appears to be some kind of mucus like substance on them. I have windows that were broken outward instead of inward which does not add up."

"What, the hell do you mean."

"Did you notice the small fragments of glass on the floor?"

"Yes, but what does that have to do with all of this. I don't understand Pete."

"Okay, I'll explain. Did you see any large pieces of jagged glass on the inside of the room?"

"No, now that you've mentioned it."

"You see doc, if the windows were broken inward there would be large fragments on the floor. Numerous of them mixed with the small pieces but there are only small fragments. That means the windows were broken outward. Now the hard question to answer is why? For what reason were they broken outward?

"You make it seem as if Bobby had broken in from the outside of the building. Or that something jumped out of the building because Bobby was seen in the hallway."

"That is the gist of it."

"That is absurd. Just fucking absurd."

"I know how crazy it sounds Jack. I know nobody could have survived the drop. Unless they had repelled off the fourth floor. I'm just trying to put this fucking puzzle together without the missing parts."

Sgt. Blendez walked up to Pete, "excuse me doctor he said then told Pete what he had found out, "Seems our man has just claimed another victim down at the capital. There has been a report that it was a man wearing a monster mask fleeing the scene. A witness said it looked as if he had a large cape that flapped behind him as he left the grounds. The same witness then said he tried to see in what direction he would flee. But then said that he went around a tree, and it had vanished."

"Get enough men to cover each of the entrances and then meet me at the car. You and I are taking a trip to the capital Blendez."

"Jack one more thing before I go. This building does have surveillance cameras."

"Of course."

"Make sure White Cloud gets the tapes and no one else doc." "Okay Pete."

Pete turned and walked up to the jagged glass where White Could stood. He waited for White Cloud to pick up the fragment of glass. His job was a tedious one but that one fragment might give him a clue to help the investigation.

CHAPTER 10

It started to drizzle by the time Pete and Blendez had arrived at the state capitol. They made their way up the barricade. The yellow tape surrounding the crime scene read,

"Police line, do not cross." The officer on the other side of the tape was about to raise his hand for them to stop when he recognized Pete and Blendez. Pete pulled up the collar to his coat. He shrugged his shoulder. He liked the rain, but he hated for it to hit the back of his neck.

"Detective," he said then moved the tape aside for them to pass through.

Pete quickly caught sight of the Chief up ahead. It appeared that he was having a few words with the District Attorney while a reporter took their picture. Must be election time Pete thought as they walked up. Lightning whipped across the sky with the magnitude of thousands voltage. Thunder roared like a lion ready to do battle. It gave the night an unsettling filling. The rain began to come down harder. Pete lifted his coat collar over his neck again. The Chief pointed and Pete eyes followed in the direction he had indicated. Pete spotted the cadaver. They made their way up next to the dead man. Rose a heavy set black officer crossed their path on her way up to the dead man as well. She stopped momentarily and looked at Pete for a second then back down at the corpse then spoke.

"What brings you on to the scene flat foot?"

Pete just looked at her. Getting no response from him she smirked then moved on. She made her way up to one of the cop cars. She began to speak to Sgt. Frazier, a white stoutly built man with strong features.

"Look who's came to the crime scene," she said in a low tone.

He looked towards Pete, their eyes met. He stood and began to walk up to him. He stopped in front of Pete and stared coldly at him. There was bad blood between the two men.

"Frazier," Pete said without any concern. "Long time no see," Frazier said sarcastically.

"Let's stop the bullshit big guy," Pete replied back. "You were never known for your tact now where you." "What the fuck you want Frazier," Pete said miffed as

Blendez looked on.

"What the hell are you doing here Pete this is not your case." "I'm not here to step on anyone's toes this is your investigation Frazier. I wouldn't be here if it wasn't that Bobby has escaped from the nut house. He is loose and he is killing again. No! Frazier let me rephrase that. He is massacring innocent people like a damn butcher."

"So, you think it is Bobby who is doing the killings." "I believe so, and if he's not doing all the killings himself then he must have help this time, and that's not good." "Your nuts you know that. You're nuts he is locked up." "Look! Jack saw him two inches away from his face. We need to work on this together Frazier. He is doing the voices bidding without question."

"Okay! Pete we can settle later," Frazier says.

There was a short pause then Pete spoke, "Who, do you have working forensics."

"Well?"

"Big James, he's good."

"If you don't mind, can we get White Cloud out here as

"We'll get White Cloud out here no reason to get both men down here. Now you need to come with me Pete."

Pete and Blendez followed Frazier. Pete wondered where the hell the man was taking them. Frazier stopped then pointed down at the ground. Pete looked down at what appeared to be some kind of material almost like a thin film of rubber. Rose lifted one of the corners.

"Stretch it out Rose," Frazier tells her. "Looks like rubber," Blendez said.

"I need help here."

Blendez looks at her then grabs the other end and pulled. "Holly shit! Looks like whatever it came off of had legs and arms," Blendez exclaimed then felt a chill run down his back.

Blendez looked up at the dome lights surrounding the capitol something had caught his eye. A silhouette of something shooting across the sky. He blinked his eyes then asked himself if he actually seen a shadow shoot across the dome. The only thing that could get up that high and shoot across the dome part of the capitol would be a bird anyhow he whispers. In this case it would have had to have been a big bird. It was his imagination. He returned his attention back to the corpse that lay about seven feet away from them. The Medical Examiner approached the scene. She was a small woman about four nine one hundred and thirty pounds with graying hair. Seeing Pete standing there she greeted him. Pete greeted her back.

"What brings you out at night Pete?

"No, what brings you out here at night? What no deputy M. E.?"

"What you don't approve of me being here," Sally snapped. "Ah, no that is not what I meant Sally."

"Pete it's all right you know I like to take all the good cases myself. You know I only have two more years of this shit left. Then it's to the Bahamas for me."

"The real reason is."

"And we're short, staffed Pete.

Sally took a pair of latex gloves out of her black bag. She put them on knelt down beside the corpse. Pete looked into the open chest cavity where once there had been a pulsating heart. This was not Bobby's

M.O. His mind raced as he tried to put the pieces together as he looked on. Sally moved the cadaver's head to one side the man's head rolled without any resistance rolling over like a puppets head.

"Looks like a fresh kill maybe two hours old. No, sign of rigor mortis yet."

Sally noticed the man's neck and that it looked like a swelled balloon. Two large puncture wounds looked back at her oozing a yellow excretion. A white fragment protruded from the wounds on the victim's neck.

"Pete you better take a look-see. Pete knelt down and turned the man's head slightly so that he could see what Sally was looking at. His eyes focused on the white object protruding from the man's neck.

"Hold his head steady Pete," Sally tells him.

She tried to extract the object with her fingers at first. Whatever it was that had been lodged in the victim's neck had a tight grip. She reached back grabbed her black bag. She put it in front of her. She rummaged through it until she had and instrument that looked like giant tweezers in her hand.

"Tilt his head just a little more for me Pete."

She then grabbed the object with the large tweezers. She made sure the grasp of on the object was firm. She then pulled slowly until she had extracted it. She quickly placed the object into a plastic bag then numbered it.

"Frazier, hold this for me," she said as she handed it to him.

Each time he saw Sally reach into the black bag it reminded Pete of a magician pulling a rabbit out of a hat. Sally took a small vial placed it next to the puncture wounds.

"Hold his neck steady."

With her free hand she pushed down on the wound. Like a rupturing pimple the yellowish excretion jetted out catching Pete on his coat sleeve. Pete looked at Sally.

"Whoa! It's a gusher," she said humorously then smiled.

She grabbed another small glass vial and repeated the process. Once again, she reached into the black medical bag. She grabbed two towels the disposable kind and tossed one to Pete.

Pete stood up and wiped the yellow substance from his sleeve. Most of the excretion had soaked through his coat sleeve.

"What do you think it could be?" Blendez asked.

Pete tossed the white cloth to the ground next to the body.

"You know you can get fined for littering Pete," Sally told him.

Pete bent down picked up the towel. White Cloud approached them at that moment.

"Here you go Sally," Pete told her as he reached out and handed her towel.

"Rattler Fangs!"

"What did you say?" Frazier snaps then added, "Just tell us in simple laymen's terms."

"Fangs! "What?

"Couldn't be more laymen termed that. Fangs, Frazier. That thing that you are holding is a fang."

"Okay, smart guy what kind of fang is it?"

"I just said what it was. Listen closely. It looks like a rattler's fang."

The look of its Frazier was covered with disbelief. "Rattlesnakes fang," Frazier.

"You're, all nuts. You know how big that snake would have to be," Frazier says.

"Are you sure?" Pete asked.

"Red man does not speak with forked tongue white man does"

"Knock the comedian bit White Cloud. Are you sure?" White Cloud unbottom the first two buttons to his shirt.

He reached into his shirt and pulled out a small object that dangled on a gold chain around his neck. It was the same as the tooth Sally had just extracted but four times smaller.

"My grandfather used to catch Rattlers for a living. He would sell their venom, skins, and what he didn't sell he would make things with. All kinds of things out of them bracelets, necklaces, headbands, you name it."

Sally grabbed the plastic bag from Frazier and looked at it then said.

"You know if this wasn't four times larger than what White Cloud has around his neck. I would have to agree with him. See this right here. This orifice could be the passage way for the poison to be injected into its victims."

"It could also be what the killer wants us to believe. It could be manmade, and the killer has poison with him to inject into the victims," Frazier said then added, "Hell we don't even know if the yellow substance from the man's neck is poison."

"Looks like a dog tooth to me," Rose says.

"I'll have an answer for you in a couple of hours Pete," Sally said then added, "Pete I need some help. I need two able bodies to get the gurney down here to get this cadaver to the morgue."

"Where's the wagon at," Blendez said.

Sally pointed in its direction. Blendez left and moments later returned with the gurney.

"Rose how about giving me a hand."

As they lifted the body off the ground there was a sudden blinding flash.

"What the fuck!" Blendez said out loud. "Did I hear you right?"

The phantom voice reached their ears while they focused their eyes on him.

"Did you hear what right?" Frazier asked.

"Did I hear you say that it was a dog's tooth? Of what I saw it had to be one big ass dog."

Blendez looked towards Pete and saw the expression growing on his face. He knew that Pete hated reporters especially after his wife had been murdered. Blendez rushed the reporter like a bull and began to push him away from the scene.

"Watch the equipment asshole," shouted the reporter.

As he passed the dead corpse, he saw the open wound. The man

As he passed the dead corpse he saw the open wound. The man's chest looked as if it had been torn open.

"Looks like a big animal got hold of him. What was it a wolf? Is that it? A wolf is loose in the city. I've heard that they have been attacking people. Yeah! That is a great angle best headline yet. Werewolf stalks the city of Austin, awesome." said the reporter then rushed off.

"You know the man is right. Whatever attacked this man and ripped out his heart could not have been a man. And if it was a man he had to have some large claws. Or some kind of special extractor," Sally said then pulled a cigar out of her breast pocket.

She lit it then took a deep puff. She exhaled the smoke. She stared at it as it dissipated upward vanishing from sight. Sally then pointed at the man's chest and says.

"See these large groves in the walls of the hole where it seems as if something dug into the flesh," she said and paused.

"Go on Sally," Pete said now interested on what she had to say. †Pete said now interested on what she had to say.

"Look closely and you see where it looks like four fingers dug into the flesh."

"I see what you are getting at fingers. Or extractor just damn fantastic."

"Pete whatever it was fingers, or extractor? It clamped down around the heart extracting it perfectly. As far as I know there is no human with hands that can do such a clean job. It was a perfect extraction. The only way it could have been done is whoever did this. Or whatever did this had to have had a special tool with him. He would all so have to have had a vast knowledge in the medical field."

"Maybe a doctor," Pete said. "Possibly," Sally agreed.

"How about the puncture wounds and that object Sally?" "I do not know Pete. But this I can tell you. The man had to have been asphyxiated before the heart was removed." "What makes you think that?" asked Blendez.

"See the bluish tint to his face and neck?" Sally says. "Yeah! And?

Sally flicked the ashes off her cigar. They accidentally flew into the man's chest wound.

"Ooopse," she said jokingly.

She saw the look on Blendez face, so she continued, "whatever is in the man's neck there is enough of it to restrict an elephant's breathing.

Sally took off the latex gloves then tossed them on to the man's torso. The gloves landed in what appeared to be a perfect X underneath the open wound. The crossed gloves gave the body the look of being laid out in a casket for viewing. They all looked at Sally as she exhaled and kept the cigar in her mouth from falling out. She shrugged her shoulder then spoke.

"Okay Blendez, Rose, let us take this body up to the van."

Blendez and Rose made their way to the Medical Examiner's van. The reporter returned but this time he had brought his entire crew. Holding a microphone in his hand he approached White Cloud.

"Hey you Indian," he called out.

"Oh! This is going to be good," Pete said out loud. "The name is White Cloud asshole."

"Hold up there big fellow. White Cloud it is? So, White Cloud can you tell me what is going on and what you have found?" "How Indian, no speak English," he said then smiled then said as he pushed the camera away with his hand, "Get the fuck away you are disturbing a crime scene. And if you do not move back about six feet away. I will have you and your crew locked up you fucking turd. Got that."

"Okay, move back, move back," the reporter told the crew.

The reporter studied the man for a moment then realized he was not going to get any answers from White Cloud. The camera crew took footage of the surrounding then focused back on the reporter. Frazier and Rose left for their black and white. The body had been transported to the M. E. vehicle and was on its way to the morgue. Pete looked around taking in every branch, human, vehicle, lights, anything he could engrave into his brain for later.

"Okay, Blendez let's get out of dodge."

He waved his crew to follow him as he saw Pete. "Detective, detective," shouted the reporter.

Pete turned and began to make his way to his car.

The reported was persistent following them. Pete was just about to climb into the car when the reporter shoved the microphone just inches away from Pete's face.

"Detective," he queried then continued, "what can you tell me about this crime. Is the criminal roaming? Is the city safe?"

"I have nothing to say," Pete said.

"Is it not true that the man had two puncture wounds on his neck? Were they like that of a wild animal that had bitten him?"

"You saw the man all I can tell you is that he was murdered."

"Detective could it have been a wolf that attacked him." "Look this is Texas not the open forest of Oregon. I have nothing more to say. Your interview is over."

"I know you. There was a big story about you and your wife about ten years ago. Something about a serial killer if I am correct."

Blendez could see the anger seeding in Pete's face. He knew Pete had a short fuse with some people. He knew if he did not do something it would end up bad. The last time one of the reporters shoved a microphone in Pete's face he reacted in pure instinct. He grabbed the man's wrist and twisted his arm then struck the man's elbow with his other hand. Though he did not break the joint he had definitely put a hurt to the man's cartilage. There was only one thing to do. Blendez rushed around the car to the other side. But was too late. By the time he reached Pete. Pete's temper had exploded like a volcano. And in a swift passing second, he had hit the reporter square on the jaw. He sent the man back into the camera man. The camera fell from the man's hands to the concrete walkway. The camera lens flew off shattering. The crew scrambled for the equipment like children scrambling for candy from a piñata.

"Tell the jerk when he wakes up. That if he ever sticks the microphone in my face again, he will receive it where the sun doesn't shine. Got that," Pete told the camera man.

The man nodded his head in acknowledgement. He then spoke softly to himself, "you crazy shit."

Pete had extremely good hearing. He stopped but then decided to let it go. Blendez moved in between the two men before the camera man would wind up like the reporter.

"Don't say anything else just pick up your boss and leave," Blendez told the man.

He turned back around and made his way back up to Pete. Pete turned and made his way into their vehicle. He waited for Blendez to fasten his safety belt then turned on the vehicle. In the distance you could see forensic still combing the area and a few cops moving about. Pete looked at the capitol then at the report now standing. Pete smiled knowing the man looked straight at him. Pete backed up then stepped on the gas pedal and pulled out into traffic.

"You'll hear about this. You don't know who you hit you dumb cop," shouted the reporter as he ran down the street after them.

CHAPTER 11

Above the state capitol building Two Souls the winged predator flew high. Flying in the air circling scanning the area below like a vulture waiting for prey. Waiting for prey so it could ascend down upon it with its vengeance of death. Its radar sensors allowed it to pick up the smallest degree to the highest degree in heat fluctuation. It could detect the slightest movements. It could smell the sweet aroma of adrenaline of fear and a droplet of blood. The creature flapped its bat like wings forcefully making it shoot forward at a rapid speed. It circled the building twice. It flapped its wings twice then brought one of its wings in. Swiftly in a matter of a second it shifted direction and headed south. Though it craved for the red raw flesh that was imprinted in its head. It was not time for it to be seen. It would return and it would kill. It would let humans see it and permeate their every being with fear. It flew high above Congress Street. It passed Twelfth Street. It lowered its right wing and moved right then straighten out flying straight above an alley looking for food and continued heading south. A few moments later it sensed movement below. It scanned the alley. With the swiftness of a large bird it drew in its wings close to its side. Lightning flashed and it moved its head back and forth scanning focusing on the two bodies below. It lowered its head and began its descent. Just as it approached the pavement it lifted its head back. It rapidly flapped its wings stopping it suddenly in midair. Its descent suspended its body just inches above the ground. It then flapped its wing twice more. The force of suction and air allowed it to land on one foot then the other. Each foot hitting with a loud thump. It began a slow trot. Water ran down its wings and down its body. Rain rushed along the side of the buildings running off into the rain gutters. The two transients in the alley where oblivious to Two Souls arrival. Two Souls flapped its wings shaking off the rain then slowly approached them in a slow trot. It stopped studied both of the men. Water splashed away from its feet making a swooshing sound was made by the force of each stride. Each footstep pushed the water from under out of its way. Joseph Martinez a transient wore a gold arm band and a gold bracelet that he wore around the sleeve of his Marine Corps dress wools. The dress wools from his past indicated that he had once had a life. The bracelets were engraved with old writing. The writing of his ancestors in the lost language of the Aztecs. It had been the last thing his father had given him before he had passed away. A family heirloom of the past. His father had told him it was one of the true relics left of the Meso-Americans. Jim Smith the other transient was a white man who also wore a Marine Corps wool coat. The left arm was pinned up to the shoulder from the missing arm that he had lost from a grenade in the Vietnam War.

They stumbled over next to the dumpster sat down on the wet ground. They scooted up next to the wall. Joseph reached into his coat where he had hidden another bottle of wine. He opened it took a swallow. His face contorted to the sour taste of the liquid inside the bottle. He passed the wine to his friend. He watched him take a swallow then took the bottle back from him as the other man handed it back to him. Joseph squinted his eyes. He tried to focus on the thing that was approaching. He opened his eye, but he had drank too much wine. The alcohol he had drank blurred his vision. The rain made it even harder to see.

Slowly the image began to come to life. Joseph could not believe his eyes. He asked himself if this thing before them could be real. Or was it just the cheap wine's effect that made this illusion seem so real. The stories of the evil Witchdoctor entered his thoughts. He then question, if the stories of Two Souls could be real. Joseph recalled that he was of Two Souls blood line. There was something wrong with the wine it had to be? It could not be real? Jim turned around his mouth falling open at the sight of the creature leering down at him. The creature reached down grabbed the man by the neck. In his drunken state Jim could not react in time. Before he knew the creature lifted him up like a paper doll off the ground. Joseph dropped the bottle of wine as reality struck him deep with fear. The creature stared into the man's eyes. It sent the darkness of hell into his very soul. Its jaws began to dislocate projecting out. Its fangs dripping of venom as they moved into a forty-five degree position. The beaten weathered worn face of the transient turned pale from fright. Two Souls the name bombarded Joseph's head. The story of the old ones were true. There was no way to dispute it for the truth was before him. Again, the name Two Souls bombarded through Joseph's head as he looked on. It sunk its fangs deep into Jim's neck injecting its poison. With a swift forceful movement of its head, it snapped the man's neck like a small twig.

It bit down harder, and the sound of bone crushing reached Joseph's ears. Joseph froze looking on as it severs the man's head off. Jim's head plummeted to the ground and rolled into the water running towards the rain gutter. The pressure of the water passing the head made the head rock back and forth. Two Souls reached down lift the man's body off the ground then flung it into the air. The body hit the building wall. It seemed to stick to the wall for a moment before the lifeless body fell to the ground. Two Souls turned moved its head forward and leered at Joseph. It began to move towards him in a slow stride. Joseph lifted his arms up high to shield off the creature attack. Quickly he began an old chant his mother had taught him as an infant. It had been a small prayer. A prayer of the Virgin Mary that would ward off evil. Two Soul's stopped all of a sudden tilted his head to one side. It stared at the gold arm bracelet around Joseph's arm. It appeared as if it was reading the engraving on the bracelet. Joseph lowered his arms hoping it was just an illusion caused by the spirits of the wine.

It stared deep into his eyes as he looked up from under his arms. Two Souls moved its head forward closer to Joseph's arm. It scrutinized the bracelet. Its breath heavy just inches away from Joseph. It was as if he were looking into everything that is known to man to be evil. Everything that had been written down on the dammed was standing inches away from him.

The creature's grotesque face contorted. Its lips moved back into a snarled. A cold chill ran down his spine. The grotesqueness of this creature was made even more pronounced by the red eyes, and yellow oval in the center of its eye as the pupil. Joseph knelt down on his knees and made the sign of the cross. He knew chants thought to him by his grandmother. But still he preferred the one taught to him by his mother. If all else failed the sign of the cross would do. Two Souls shifted its head to one side then to the other as a dog would do when studying his master. It then turned and began a slow trot out of the alley. It flapped its wings its leg muscles tighten. It pushed up off its legs like pistons to a hydraulic machine. They hurled it up into the air. It took flight out of the alley then across six street. It shot into the adjacent alley on the other side of the street. It began to flap its wings quicker. It tilted its head back then pushed forcefully with its wings. It shot up out of the alley and into the night. It tucked one wing in close to its side and shifted direction and headed east. The rain fell harder as each droplet of rain hit its wings. It sounded like rain falling on to cardboard. Two Souls circled around and landed on the N. C. B. building. It perched itself on the edge and looked down at prey walking and moving about on Congress Street below. It watched, studied, and took in its surroundings. People opening up for business entered in and out of the buildings early in the morning hours. The first hint of sun penetrated through the morning clouds. It opened its wings out wide enjoying the warmth of the morning sun on them. It was time for it to find a place to hide. A place where it would not be seen for the time being. It began a quick trot and sprung into the morning air.

Frank and Mary waited for their morning bus on sixth and congress. Frank glanced up to see the stars above before they faded away by the birth of the morning sun. He focused his eyes. He was not sure but he thought he had seen something on the ledge of the N.C.B building. Eyes he thought to himself. A shadow that seemed to fly and then perch itself on the ledge and eyes. Frank was tired he thought to himself and began talking to his wife. The creature started to squat down as it prepared to leap of the edge and take flight into the air again. No, he did see something he knew he had. Though had not seen the creature he still felt a chill run up his arms.

"Did you see that Mary?" Frank said excitedly.

"See what?" Mary said nonchalantly to her husband as if not to care.

Frank looked back up and pointed across the street to the top of the N. C. B. building and pointed.

"What the hell are you pointing at Frank?"

"Looked like a pair of red eyes looking down this way at us and now they're gone."

"Eyes, Frank."

"Eyes you know the things you see with," Frank said somewhat miffed.

"Calm down what you saw was probably some cat jumping off one of the pipes up there."

Now what would a cat be doing up there he thought to himself. He could not let it go. He knew he had seen something.

"I saw a pair of red eyes. I don't care what you say. Cat or not I saw eyes looking down at us. I'm telling you and besides what would a cat be doing thirty feet above ground on the edge of that building?"

"How would I know Frank I'm just suggesting that it could have been a cat."

"Well maybe it could have been," Frank concluded to the possibility. The remaining of darkness now lifted up and slowly vanished.

The shadow he had seen was still visible. Whatever it was had vanished and was gone. In the distance above it shifted directions heading west. It was as if it knew where it was going. There was a place it knew.   Perhaps it was a place it knew as Jesse. A place where it knew it would be safe. It flew for about an hour soaring above the old power plant. A power plant that had been abandoned for several years on First St. Right next to Town Lake. It hovered over the place like a glider as it spread its wings wide. Its wing span counting both wings and its torso was twelve feet in length. The width from the claw at its shoulder to the bottom of the wing was five feet tapering off to four inches at the tip. Bones ran down the wing like ribs every two feet. The leather like wings seemed to have veins running in all directions. Abruptly it drew in both its wings.

It shot down like a missile. It flapped its wings hard. Its feet just inches away from the ground. It began to flap its wings rapidly allowing it to catch the air. It landed in a slow trot. Its huge ghoulish silhouette began to take shape as day broke. It tilted its head. Its tongue flicked in and out of its mouth. Its radar like sensors honed in on what it had been searching for. It walked near the embankment of the lake as it moved along the edge of the river the water caught its reflection. It walked towards a large drainpipe. A drainpipe that was big enough to drive a full-size car through it. The lake water rippled as the remaining droplets of rain hit it from the night lamps above. Soon everything would be dry from the sun's warmth. The sun had already began to evaporate the water from the ground. As it approached the entrance to the drainpipe it looked over its shoulder. It was as if it were making sure it had not been followed by any human. Inside the tunnel its two pit organs located between the nostril and its eyes on either side of its lower face worked like and infrared radiation sonar. With this it could detect the difference of a mere thousandth of a degree of heat. Nerve impulses from the organs crossed opposite sides of the brain allowed it to stereoscope heat images. This helped it to pinpoint any movement and enable it to strike out at any prey with perfect accuracy. Two Souls hideous body made its way through the tunnels of drainpipes. It moved deeper and deeper into the maze of tunnels underneath the city of Austin. Rain from the rain gutters ran through the pipe from every cutter above. The creatures of the night scurried in panic. Rats jumped into the water from pipes above that where fastened to the concrete pipe. Bats flew in all directions in a frenzy.

The swarm made their way out of the drainpipe. With its razor sharp claws Two Souls lashed out sending several bat to their death. The bats hit the water with plopping sounds like that when a pebble is thrown into the lake. The sound mixed with their squeals of death filled the labyrinth of tunnels. Two Souls shifted and stopped abruptly.

It honed in on three large objects making their way into the water. These objects heading towards it. As they got closer the images became clear to the creature. Three cotton mouth water moccasins. Two Souls listen for a moment then made its way in further to an intersection where smaller pipes ran into the main artery. Ahead of it one of the snakes. The largest of the three remained in the water. It lifted its head above the water several inches and hissed. The other two slithered onto the dry part of the concrete pipe. Two Souls turned its head and looked at the two smaller ones on the dry part of the pipe. It then returned its gaze back to the one in the water. It opened its mouth and let out a horrifying screeching sound as if to answer back to the hissing snake. The cotton mouth moved back as if it had understood what the demon had said. The demon spoke as if to be speaking to the world.

"This is now my domain, and I am the new ruler of this dark world," Two Souls said in a half hiss half grating voice.

The creatures stirred within the pipe as the screeching sound reached their ears. The creature reached down and lifted the water moccasin up. It's pet head like one would pet his cat. Two Souls placed the snake on its shoulder. The smoky gray cotton mouth coiled around its neck. Two Souls then made his way into the heart of the drainpipe. About a mile and a half from the entrance in the heart of the pipe was a huge dome that connected all the large drainpipes together. A light hung from the north wall next to what appeared to be steps that ran upward to the street above. Under the light there was a large platform that raised about two feet off the ground. It laid six feet by four feet wide. It had been built like a step up to reach the metal stairs that ran up to the man whole cover above. Two Souls climbed upon the platform. Here this would be his throne and he would be king. It studied the steps closer and focused on the manhole cover above. It quickly picked up a swarm of bats moving down in a military manner. Moving in a perfect formation.

Several of the bats took flight getting in range of the demons deadly claws. It caught one in its hands and crushed the life out of it. It pulled pieces of flesh off the bat and fed it to the snake around its neck like one would feed a bird. It tossed the remainder of the bat to the other two snakes waiting patiently.

"Here my children of the dark. You will not need as long as I live," it tells them.

Two Souls unwrapped the coiled snake around its neck and placed it on the platform. The snake did not move it just wait for Two Souls. It lay down next to the snakes. Here the creature would wait. It would sleep and here it will wait for night to come. Night would allow it to hunt, and it would use the night as an invisible cloak. As time moved and Two Souls slept snakes of all kinds began to find their way into the drainpipe.

Finding their way through the maze of tunnels up to their new king and ruler of the dark world. Morning was approaching quickly. With morning people woke and life began, and another day began. David and Billy woke up ready to begin the day. They had their day planed out. Today they planned to visit the old power plant and explore the drainpipe. Their father had gone to work. Billy made their breakfast. He made a couple of pop tarts with a side of milk and they ready to go. They walked out of the house locked the door and made they made their way up to the tracks. They looked both ways to see if a train might be on its way up the track. They walked down the tracks heading west towards the city.

"Okay Billy we have to make our way towards First Street."

They stopped at the bridge then walked down the small incline to the hike and bike trail below. Moving west making their way to the old power plant and the drainpipe. As Two Souls slept David and Billy reached the opening. Inside newcomers had entered and had made their way straight for the new king of the dark domain. The creatures of the night slithered over the demon's body. Rattlers, cotton mouth, garden snakes and other species.

"Over their Billy look over there," David says "Yeah!

They walked up to the huge drainpipe stopped and looked inside. Billy walked up to the pipe and yelled standing in the opening.

"Hello! The sound of a faint echoed bombarded back several times, hello, hello, hello.'

David picked up a rock off the ground. He looks at his brother for a moment the said, "Move out of the way Billy." David waited for his brother to move then threw the small rock into the pipe. The sound as it ricochet off the concrete wall abruptly awakened the demon up from its sleep. Again, David threw in another rock and the sound reached the demon. David waited for his brother to move then threw the small rock into the pipe. David picked up another rock and tossed it in. He loved seeing the rock skip across the side of one wall to the other. Two Souls tongue flickered in and out of its mouth rapidly as it collected the molecules in the air. It hone in on the intruder. There was no indication of a human or animal. All it picked up on its sensor was a small speck that bounced off the wall. It caught an image of a hand grabbing the edge of the pipe at the opening.   It leaped off the platform and began to move at a fast trot towards the intruder. Water ran from the pipe to a small man made ditch that let the water run back into the lake like a small waterfall. Meanwhile David continued to throw small pebbles into the pipe without knowing of the danger that was heading in his direction. Billy his older brother, two years older being nine years old. Meanwhile as David threw rocks into the pipe Billy threw rocks at the perches swimming below where the water rejoined the lake.

David heard something coming from the pipe something he had never heard before. Rats plopped into the water scurrying to safety getting out of the demons way. The sound of the rats falling into the running water intertwined with the demons footsteps.

"Billy did you hear that?" "No, what was it you heard?"

"I don't know but it sounded like a wild animal Billy."

 Billy tossed another rock into the lake then turned and faced his brother then walked up to him.

"Billy I heard something horrible I think we should leave."

Billy made his way up to the entrance of the pipe then took one step into the pipe. He turned back around looked at his scared brother.

"Gee what a paranoia David," Billy told his brother then turned back around and looked into the pipe."

"I do not care let's just leave."

"Okay, we will leave David but before we do. I am going to take a look inside."

"No, Billy."

Billy reached back and grabbed his brother and pretended to pull him along.

"No, Billy. Please, please Billy," David screamed frightened."

Billy looked at his scared brother for a moment then said, "all right you stay here and be the guard for me okay."

"Okay Billy but you hurry so we can leave. I know I heard something. I know if we stay something bad is going to happen." David stood on one side of the entrance looking toward the lake. He knew he had heard something, and he did not want to look in the drainpipe.

"Knock, knock who's there?" Billy said out loud then looked back trying to look calm.

He laughed then looked back at David and said, "see there is nothing in here stay right there I' am going to explore deeper inside."

"I really wish you wouldn't," David told his older brother.

A scratching sound did reach Billy's ears. Billy froze for a second and listened closely as his heart pounded rapidly. What he had heard were the claws in the center of Two Souls wings where they folded scraping along the walls of the pipe. Billy's ears suddenly picked up on the sound of splashing water as the creature's feet hit with every stride it made towards him.

"Run David," Billy shouted as if something was about to grab him, "Run David," he repeated and began to run.

He lost his footing and slipped falling face down into the water. He looked back over his shoulder. He saw what appeared to be yellow eyes. Its eyes caught a hint of the light making them seem as if they glowed. He moved his legs quickly using one side of the pipes wall to help himself stand. Standing he moved his legs as fast as they would allow him. He looked back over his shoulder as he stepped on the edge of the pipe, he saw something coming toward him fast. Missing the edge of the pipe he made a one eighty and landed on his back. He scooted back as fast as he could. After a moment he stopped and began to sit up. All of a sudden something landed on his chest. Billy began to scream. David not knowing why his brother was screaming began to scream as well. Something hit Billy in the chest. Billy waved his hands frantically swinging wildly at the black object rapidly moved up towards his face.

"A-h-h-h-h-h, a-h-h-h-h-h, a-h-h-h-h-h," Billy cried out at the top of his lungs.

David's eyes looked as if they were about ready to pop out of his eye sockets from his fright at that moment. His eyes focused on the huge black water rat scurrying over Billy's face. The rat jumped off Billy and rushed to the edge of the embankment and jumped into the water below. Billy patted his face then his arms and chest.

"Where did it go? What the hell was it?" Billy questioned confused.

"It's gone Billy it was just a rat. It swam across the lake to the other side."

Billy quickly scrambled back up on his feet then ran up to his kid brother shouting.

"Run, run David," as he grabbed for his brothers hand.

Their hearts pounded with fear, fear of the unseen. Fear of being dinner for whatever was in the pipe. After running for several yards Billy slowed down and released his brother's hand. Billy placed his hand on his brother's shoulder and pulled him to a stop.

"It is all right David we are safe. Safe away from the pipe."

Out of nowhere David turned and hugged his brother tightly as if he was about vanish. He looked up at Billy then said, "Please now can we just go home this time?"

They continued to walk down the hike and bike trail that ran along the lake side.

"I did hear something that did not sound like anything I have ever heard before. You didn't hear it?"

"It was just the rat squealing David that is all you heard."

"It was no rat Billy."

"It was a water rat and that is all it was now let it go."

Billy knew his brother was scared and so was he. Whatever it was had scared him and David. And the eyes he saw did not look like they belonged to any rat. He was just glad he did not see what was behind the eyes. He would keep that a secret from his brother. There was no way he could explain the screeching noise and the footsteps. It did not matter how big the rat had been even in the tunnel of the pipe.

It could not have magnified its footsteps that loud. There was something in there, perhaps a man?   Man or beast he did not want to find out. His mind raced on and all he knew at that moment was that it had to have been as big as a man or bigger.

"Oh, I don't know Billy."

"Shit! You want me to prove it to you. I'll go back into the pipe right now."

"No, Billy, please."?

"What a wuss. What are we today diapers are us?" "Stop it Billy."

"Whoo, whoo," he cried out as he waved his hands and pretended to run then added, "I see him it is coming run, run."

"Please Billy, please stop or I'm going to tell dad."

"Go, right a head David go right ahead and tell. You tell pops and we will both get in trouble. You know how the old man is. He gets scared when we get in trouble."

"Dad doesn't get scared Billy he gets mad," David exclaims.

They looked at each other for a moment then smiled then continued to walk slowly down the trail. David reached up and grabbed Billy's hand.

"Billy."

"Yeah! What is it David."

"Do you really think dad gets scared for us?"

"I don't really know. We are all he has since mom died and when we get into things, we shouldn't he loses it rather badly. So, in a way maybe he does get scared for us."

"Yeah! But he doesn't look scared to me."

Billy laughed at David's remark about their father then spoke, "shut up David," he tells him.

They remained silent the rest of the way home.

Two Souls reached the opening and stood at the entrance of the pipe. Its black tongue flicked in and out of its mouth rapidly like a tiny whip. It watched the two boys vanish into the distance. Two Souls turned and returned to the platform that was his throne. It would now wait for night fall to come for it to kill.

CHAPTER 12

After his visit to the morgue Pete returned home about one that afternoon. The morgue was still fresh in his thoughts. The place always reminded him more of a mad scientist laboratory from one of those horror flicks. He threw his coat onto the chair that he had placed at the right far corner next to the wall by the window. He threw himself onto the bed and moaned staring up at the ceiling. It had been a hell of a day. He needed a sleep and he needed answers. Sally was not able to tell him anything as of yet. It was the same as before. Sally had said that she had a good ideal, of what it could be. But at the moment she could not say. She had told him that when the test results returned, she would disclose what she believed. Pete began to doze off. He began to dream of Vietnam. The past tormented him. Tormented his very soul and the stress added to it. The accruing dreams were so real it was as if he still was in the mist of weapon fire. Guns rat-tatted away the projectiles crying out as they found their main directive. His thoughts went further into the god awful war. He could see men running for their lives running for safety. He could see their mouths open wide as they shouted to take cover. Their voices only to be drowned out by the mortar fire. The lives of many good men gone in an instant. The wounded lying on the ground calling out to a father, mother, or wife, like small children. Their cries not from the pain or being frightened. But for that of deep anguish. For all they asked at that final moment of judgment was closer.

All they wanted was to tell their parents or love ones that they loved them just once more. It was a strange war. It was even stranger what it could do to a man. It was as if they were repenting asking forgiveness before they departed from this world.

"Sgt. Rodriquez," Major Qin his commanding officer called out to him.

Pete got close to the ground. Enemy fire was heavy Pete crawled quickly through the small trench up to the Major.

"Sir," Pete said then waited for the man to reply. "Sgt. Rodriquez we have to move out immediately," the Major told him then tucked in his head as a mortar fell a few yards away from them. After a few seconds he spoke again, "Get the men rounded up. We have to secure the perimeter. And I mean like now. And one more thing Sgt. If I get killed, you are in charge. The platoon will be yours. Before you say something Sgt. First Sergeant Golds is getting his leg looked at. I don't know how bad it is. But you are the next man in line. Everyone else has bought it Pete," then says, "Got that?"

"Got it loud and clear sir."

The major began to move in the opposite direction through the trench. Abruptly Pete's dream shifted from the war to Karen his wife. He had just returned home and had seen her lying on the ground dead. Why? He asked she had never hurt anyone. Why? His mind raced on. The phone rang waking Pete up from his nightmare. In a way he was angry in another way he was glad for it took him away from the thoughts in his head. Especially the thought of his wife's death.

"God I feel like shit," he said in a drowsy voice.

He then looked at his alarm clock as the phone rang again.

Pete reached for the phone brought it to his ear then spoke, "hello this is detective Rodriquez. How can I help you?"

"Sorry I dialed the wrong number," said the voice on the other end then hung up.

"Sorry wrong number I just love when that happens. I just love to be woken up from my sleep in the early morning hour for the fucking wrong number," he said to himself.

He looked at the phone then hung it up. Pete rolled his tongue around inside his mouth he could taste a strong acrid irony after taste. He sat up at the edge of the bed. He stood and went into the bathroom. He grabbed a small bottle of eye medicine and placed a couple of drops of the liquid into each eye. He looked into the mirror and opened his mouth and stuck out his tongue. He looked at himself for a moment then spoke.

"I need more damn sleep, but time cannot wait. I have to find Bobby before he kills again. Just do not answer yourself and I think we can say that you are still sane," he said out loud.

He walked out of the bathroom in his briefs went to the kitchen and started a fresh pot of coffee. Pete's thoughts shifted suddenly. He caught himself thinking of the nurse. He returned to the bedroom he took a quick shower. He got dressed then returned to the kitchen. He entered the room his nose quickly picked up on the fresh aroma of freshly brewed coffee. It smells good and it was the best smell he could think of for the afternoon he thought. He poured himself a cup took a couple of sips enjoying the flavor. It regenerated his brain in away kick starting it up. It allowed his brain a quick wake up. His thoughts bombarded inside his head. I know there is something I am missing.

I just wish I knew what it was. Everything all the details of last night. The death of all those people and that was putting it mildly. It had been more like a massacre. Either way it just did not add up. There was something missing to this puzzle but what? He could not put his finger on it but soon enough he would put two and two together and he would figure out this mess. All he needed to do was to start at the very beginning. He would have to dissect every bit of information every clue he already had. Just like all riddles he thought the answer usually stares the person in the face. The answer is right in front of their very noses. These kind of riddles are the hardest to solve. He pondered the thought for a moment then poured himself another cup of coffee. The phone rang again he looked toward the phone thinking not to answer it. But after the fourth ring he placed his cup down on the counter and reached for the phone on the wall.

"Hello this is detective Rodriquez." "Pete."

"Chief my buddy what's up?"

"Quit with the buddy bit. I need you and your side kick to come to the precinct A.S.A.P," there was a click then the dead tone coming from the phone. Pete stared at the phone for a moment. What was it that was so important that the chief had to call him? Pete placed the phone back on the wall mount then finished his coffee. He stepped out into the mid-day sun. It was like walking into an oven. The humidity had come down strong. He could already feel his T- shirt sticking to his body. The weather report had said that it would be in the mid eighty's today. But standing out in the open it seemed like it was at a hundred.

With the weather and all that was running through his head it was beginning to give him a migraine. Pete walked to his car climbed in started it up. He sat for a moment thinking of his youth lately it just kept popping into his head. Maybe it was that he was realizing that he was getting older and how things where so simple when one is young he thought. But like all things one must come back to reality. He began to think of the dead people and the images attacked his mind. It had not been a natural thing. He needed answers if there where answers. He decides to make a trip to the hospital. He would take a detour and he would then deal with the chief later. First things first. Something was just not right it puzzled him. It had to do with the crime scene or was it the attraction he had instantly felt for the nurse. Nancy was her name he thought then chuckled softly then said out loud.

"That is all I fucking need now."

He put the car into gear. He backed out of the driveway he drove to the corner turned and drove for a few minutes then pulled up on to the I-35 ramp. Taking I-35 would be the fastest way to his destination. It would take him at the most he estimated about seventeen minutes. Fifteen minutes later he was getting out of his car and walking up to the entrance of the hospital. He stared up at where the shattered windows should have been on the fourth floor.

"That was fast already the windows had been replaced," though he thought the words he told himself if he answered back he would commit himself.

He reached into his coat pocket and withdrew a pack of smokes then pulled out a cigarette. He put it in his mouth lit it and took in a deep draw feeling his lungs then exhaling the smoke. There is no way anyone could survive such a drop unless he could fly. The word fuck escaped from his mouth. Why was he even thinking of it? The only way down would have been down through the elevators. The other way out would have been the stairs. One would need wings for that plunge down. The only exit out of the windows would be dead. His head began to pound from the migraine he took another deep drag of the cigarette then flung it away. He looked up at the windows once more then went into the building. He made his way up to the receptionist at the desk. There were two women the older lady slightly plump but still quite attractive tended to an outpatient. The other was in her twenty's brunette with huge breast at least D cups she was at the moment giving a visitor directions back to I-35 highway. The thought of the nurse and how those d-cups would only make him stay at the hospital brought a smile to his face.

"Excuse me Miss," Pete said in an attempt to grab their attention.

"The phone rang, "excuse me sir," said the brunette. Pete pulled out his billfold opened it flash his badge, "Excuse me Miss.

The brunette glared at him finished her conversation then hung up the phone. She looked at him for a moment the spoke.

"Now how can I help you sir." "I am detective Rodriquez."

She opened her eyes wide and tilted her head back as if surprised, "you're a detective?"

"I am sorry lady I did not mean to be rude. But I need to speak to a Nurse Gamble," he told her without raising his voice.

He knew that it would be easier with a little honey than vinegar he then smiled. The brunette pushed a button on computer keyboard the screen quickly came to life. The screen filled with a line of names. She then reached down for the phone to the right side of the computer. She dial then talked to the person on the other end then hung up the phone.

"Detective nurse Gamble is off for the night. After last night and all plus the reporters she took off sick for a couple days."

"I need to get in contact with her. Can I have her number I need to speak to her it is very important."

"I am not allowed to give out her number without the proper authorization."

"What the police department does not have any authority?" "Look you have your orders detective I have mine."

"Look this is very important."

"Hold up detective," she told Pete then made another call.

Her conversation on the phone was short. She turned and faced Pete.

"The director is coming to talk to you."

By the time Pete had turned around a man turned the corner and spoke.

"Hello Detective, I am the chief of staff. Now how can I help you?"

Pete looked at the man then read the man's name from the name tag. Pete stuck out his hand and greeted the man. "Mr. Blake."

The man studied Pete for a moment then spoke, "I heard good things about you detective," he said the added, "by the way how did you know my name?"

"I have to say it was the name tag that gave it away." "Yes, I can see why you are a detective I caught a glimpse of you last night as I made my way up to the I. C. U. You are one of those people who stick out like a sore thumb in a good way. It is kind of hard to forget your face. I spoke to Doctor Samuel the man talks very highly of you. He said you were the best and if anyone could catch whoever was responsible for the horrendous crime you were the one that could do it.

"I need to speak to a nurse Gamble. The nurse that was on duty last night."

"Yes, I know you are pressed for time detective," he told Pete turned and faced the receptionist, "Give him what he needs, " He said then faces Pete, "Detective I hope you catch him soon," he shook Pete's hand and turned and walked away.

Half an hour later Pete found himself in front of a white house with blue trim around the windows and doors. Surrounding the house was a white picket fence that framed in the boundaries of the home. The yard was well kept. The lawn nicely trimmed. In the center of the yard stood a large pecan tree with and old tire that hung from a worn frayed rope barely supporting the tires weight. This must be where she was raised. Post card house Pete thought to himself. Pete parked the car shut the engine off then stared at the house for a moment. Picture perfect that is what it was picture perfect he thought to himself again. He studied the house a few more minutes then climbed out of the car. He walked up to the fence. He open the small gate then walked up to the front door. He rang the doorbell. Pete found himself to be somewhat nervous. Okay, so questioning her was only part of it. The truth be told he wanted to see her again. Nancy opened the door and was surprised to see Pete.

"Detective Rodriquez right?" "That is right Miss Gamble." "I see you remembered my name."

Nancy had as well been attracted to Pete and this was the making for a somewhat uneasy moment. They stared at each other their minds telling them to speak to break the silence. Nancy spoke first breaking the awkwardness of the moment.

"Excuse my manners detective. Please come in you must have many questions to ask me."

"Please call me Pete," he said stepping inside.

"And you can call me Nancy," she said showing him a smile. "I hope I am not imposing at a bad time."

"No, Pete I am glad in a way that you showed up. I have not been able to sleep well lately. I haven't been able to do much of anything without thinking of what happen last night in the I. C. U."

"That is why I am here Nancy."

Pete felt a twinge of guilt knowing that it was only half the reason the other half was her. He wanted to see her again from that very night. He could not erase her from his mind. It was the worst of circumstances to meet in. But yet somehow their meeting had awakened something in him. Something that Pete thought had died with his wife. He looked at her not realizing he was staring.

"Pete would you like some tea? I just started a pot when I heard you knock. Wait was it the doorbell I heard," she felt her stomach feel with butterflies all of a sudden.

Frighten by the images of last night and something about Pete. Stranger thing did happen last night she thought to herself. He made the images go away for a moment. She was acting like a teenager when first meeting her date that she had a crush on. But she had not even lay eyes on Pete before until last night. She smiled as the thought ran through her head.

"Sure, I'd love some tea," Pete replied.

He wonder why he had said yes. Sense he did not really like tea. Hell, he hated tea. Tea gave him the runs if he drank more than a glass. Pete watched her walk out of the room. She returned with a tray that held a pitcher of tea and two glasses. A few minutes later she placed the tray down on the coffee table. She motion Pete to sit down next to her on the couch. She poured him a glass and handed it to him. Pete noticed for the first time Nancy's eyes where a beautiful green. She lifted her glass off the tray and took a sip. She held the glass between her hands on her lap.

"Tell, me what can I help you with," she said her hands shaking a little for she now had to recall the massacre.

"Are you all right with this? We can do this later." "Go, ahead Pete ask your questions. I just need to calm down and get some sleep. Maybe if I talk about it, it will help."

"I understand what you saw last night was the worst thing anyone could have seen. I am sorry that I came at a bad time to ask questions of you."

"I," her voice broke then she continued as she tried to grab her composure, "I saw that sickly man that is the only person I saw."

"That man you saw is Bobby better known as Bobby the Slayer. He believes that God talks to him. He believes that the voices in his head are angels. Angels giving him orders to kill. He believes he is therefore God's own messenger of death."

It had been a bizarre occurrence that had brought them both together. It was even more bizarre that he felt the way he did about her. He could not let his feeling rule him not at this time. He wanted to reach out to her grab her and bring her into his arms. He wanted to tell her that everything would be all right. But he knew that it would not be the truth. He knew that what she had seen would remain with her as part of her life from that time on. This made Pete more determine. He needed to catch Bobby and not let this happen again to anyone.

That night back at the precinct. Pete walked down the second-floor corridor to Gold's office. He was late, not a few minutes but a few hours late. Sgt. Gloria Morales ran up to him calling his name out. Pete stopped turned around. Seeing her he greeted her. Pete liked her and most of the time when he saw her, he wondered why she had become a cop instead of doctor or beauty queen. She was at least a D cup and a perfect 36 24 36. But she was a cop and a good one at that.

"Hey! Gloria baby what is ah, happening?"

"Your, ass is what is happening fool. The Chief is madder than fire and brimstone. Just thought you would like to know before you enter his office."

"Thanks my love for taking care of my back."

"And I have to say that is a fine ass, Pete. Oh, honey one more thing you are in for one hell of a surprise," she said then smiled.

She stood in the corridor and watched Pete walk down the corridor into the office. Pete noticed a man as he entered into the office. Who in the hell is this up tight ass hole he thought to himself. That was the first impression Pete got about the man. This man was wound up so tight that he would soon pop like a coiled spring Pete smiled at the thought then entered the office.

"Well, well look who is here," Chief Golds said in a raspy sarcastic tone.

"Chief buddy how are you today?"

"I am honored that you could take time out of your schedule to show up."

Pete turned and looked out into the hallway. He could see his fellow officers straining to hear him get reamed out by the Chief. He looked at Gloria. She shrugged her shoulders at him then threw him a kiss. You wicked bitch Pete thought to himself then chuckled softly.

"What do you find so funny Pete?"

Pete turned back around and faced the Chief.

"Chief I know you said A. S. A. P., but I remembered something important. I had to follow up on a hunch."

"You had to follow up on a hunch? Guess what Pete. "What?"

"Good that you asked Pete. I do not give a damn about your hunch. I don't need this shit from you Pete," Golds face reddening as his temper flared.

Pete knew the signs all too well. He knew that the Chief would soon explode, and the ass chewing would soon begin.

"Hell, I do not give a damn if Jesus Christ came down and wanted you to follow him. When I say get your ass down here Pete. That is exactly what the fuck I mean. That is what I expect of my detective got that. This is my precinct the last time I looked not Pete Rodriquez precinct."

"You're the boss."

"That is right detective."

The man against the wall had his hands crossed across his chest looking on. He just stood in silence just looking.

"Now that we got that figured out what did you want me for?"

"You definitely got a pair of balls to ask what I wanted." "You did call me in."

"That was about eight hours ago," Golds barked his temper rising.

But he was not going to let Pete have the last word. He would do this calmly.

"Pete this man has been waiting patiently for you. Now I'll tell you what I wanted. I wanted you here hours ago."

The room became a dead silent. Pete mind raced as he figured out what was coming next. He just stood in the center of the room and waited.

"Pete I would like to sugar coat it for you. But I just don't have the time. Meet your new partner."

A smile broke at the corner of Golds mouth. Pete looked at Golds for a moment then looked at the man then back at the Chief.

"You sly fox.   Pay back is a bitch," Pete said under his breath.

Golds began to count down from five that was about the span of Pete's temper. Golds knew him well. He had been in his platoon in Vietnam. He had sent Pete out on many missions as well as having him next to him on patrol. That time bomb of a temper that he kept locked up inside was the only thing that got him in trouble. The Chief knew Pete preferred to work alone. It was unusual but he did work better by himself. Pete's eyebrows furrowed here it comes thought Golds as he began to count quietly one, two, three. His thoughts jump back to the war. He recalled when his major had requested Pete personally. He wanted the best tunnel rat available and that was Pete. It was one of the worst jobs there was except for probing. Golds had asked him once why he did it. Pete had just said.

"It gives me a fucking rush 1st Sgt."

His thoughts jumped back this wasn't the bush. He would have to work with a partner.

"Come on Chief," Pete said.

"Not, this time you work with a partner."

"God Damn it I do not need to baby sit anyone."

"Pete I am not asking you if you want a partner. I am telling you what you are going to do."

You old dog Pete thought to himself. That was one way to get back at him, but he also knew that the Chief did not play that kind of game. He did what was best for his men.

"What's your name?"?

"Chet. Sir the name is Chet."

Pete looked back at the Chief then back at his new partner.

"Okay, Chet do you have a cigarette?"

"No, sir I don't smoke," he replied back in a New York accent.

"You don't smoke. I bet you are going to tell me you are some kind of whiz kid.

"No, sir."

"Chief I like to talk to you alone for one moment." "I'll step outside sir and leave you to whatever it is."

Pete waited for Chet to walk outside and close the door behind him.

"Chief the kid is going to get me killed."

"You know Pete that is the same thing that I told the Major about you. You were good at what you did but I saw it differently. I saw a young kid. I told the Major you were going to get me killed. He just looked at you then me and said, "Give the man a chance. He is young, the youngest Sgt., in this outfit. He is also good at what he does that is why I requested him here. I kept on thinking he's fucking green. I don't need a hot shot in my platoon. Things were dangerous enough as they were. But you showed me wrong. You took to the bush like a bush tiger and had returned with the news of the tunnel being clear.

I went in after that with several men and you. Seeing the bodies you left dead it made sense then to me what the Major said. The tunnel was clear, and you had cleared it and I was wrong. I had judged you in haste. What I am trying to say Pete is to give the man a chance before you judge him."

"If it is an order then I guess I have no choice." "It is an order, and I am glad you can see it my way." Pete turned and was about to walk out of the office.

Golds stopped him and told him to send the kid in. Pete opened the door the popped his head out the opening.

"Kid the Chief wants to see you Shet." "Sir the name is Chet."

"Okay, kid but lose the sir bit."

Golds went back around his desk and sat down. He waited for Chet to enter the office.

"You want to talk to me Chief?"

"Yes!" Seeing the look of concern on Chet's face he continued, "I just called you in here to tell you to ignore Pete's sarcastic remarks.

Pete is one of the best detectives in this city. Stay close to him listen to him carefully. His bark is louder than his bite. You can learn a lot from this man."

"Yes, sir I'll do just that."

"Chet before you leave this office lose the sir. One more thing why did you volunteer to work with Pete? No one else did. I know you must have heard the scuttle butt on him and his rep and all.

"I heard others say that he is too crazy to work with. That he takes too many chances. I also know he has one of the highest arrest records ever for this precinct. Like you said I can learn from him."

"I think you two will get along just fine now get out of here and get to work."

Chet stepped out of the office and made his way up to Pete. They walked out of the building. Chief Golds leaned back in his chair then said as he looked up at the ceiling.

"Yes, I think it well be just fine."

CHAPTER 13

Night fell rapidly over the city cloaking it with invisibility like a, plague consuming the entire city below. Cloaking what would come out and hunt this night. The small creatures scurried to their safety as Two Souls began to awaken from his sleep. The snakes coiled around its body others slithered off and others quickly moved out of its way. Several dropped off its body as it stood.

"I will return with food my children," it said in a low raspy tone.

It began a fast trot out of the dome and into the tunnel that would lead it out into the open. When it reached the opening, it paused flicking its tongue in and out for a moment. It steps out of the pipe and stood at the entrance. Again, it stood still then suddenly it began to walk around in a circle flicking its tongue in and out rapidly. Picking up the molecules in the air. It stopped abruptly tilted its head and looked up.

It flapped its wings several times as if to wipe off the sleep from them. It then walked around in half a circle looked up again. It flapped its wings and in one powerful stroke of its wings it sprang off its legs and took to the air. With each powerful stroke of its wings, it ascended higher into the night sky. Its wing made a sucking sound as they caught the wind underneath. With the gracefulness of a large bird it flew. Its deformed hideous silhouette shot across the moon. The ground below illuminated with the moonlight. Above the stars twinkled like a million eyes peering down watching the movement of the city below. Two Souls circled several times above the power plant then shot east, then to the south, over the congress bridge. Its radar like sensors picked up two bodies below running off the bridge onto the hike and bike below trail running west. It tucked in one wing to its side and shifted direction.

It tilted its head back and shot straight up and across the face of the moon. It seemed to stop in flight as it spread its wings out to their full extensions. Like a glider it hovered above with its sixteen feet wingspan. It hovered for several minutes then picked up the movement below. It hovered for a few more seconds then tucked in both its wings. Like a missile it would pounce upon its attended prey below. One of the runners stopped feeling his hairs on his neck tingle.

"Jeff," he called out to the other man as he felt a strange eeriness to the night.

Todd slowly ran back up to Jeff jogging in place then asked, "What's wrong?"

"I don't quite know. It is as if I felt something watching us."

"Jesus Christ, Jeff you should stop seeing all those damn horror flicks," as his words spewed from his mouth Todd caught a glimpse of a dark shadow shoot by above.

It was just probably the fact that Jeff had mentioned something and the fact that they decided to run at midnight. He erased it from his mind quickly. Fear was like a running spring. Once fear set in it would consume one's mind.

"You see now you got me thinking the weird."

They both saw the shadow shoot by again. The hairs on both their backs took life of their own. They looked up catching sight of something shooting straight down at them.

"Run!" Todd shouted at Jeff frantically.

Jeff stumbled over his feet. Instantly fear consumed his brain. He fought to gain control of his limbs. Maybe it was just a big bird he told himself. He tried to shake the thought from his mind. Todd ran back to helped him up. They saw the creature circling for another attack.

"Come on Jeff, come on, Todd shouted as he helped him up.

They ran as fast as they could but the thing above was faster, and it was gaining on them. There was nowhere to hide. Todd looked back over his shoulder. He could see his friend was exhausted by the look on his face.

"Come on Jeff just a half mile and we will be at the Y. M. C. A."

"I'm fine. I am right behind you now Todd."

Todd caught sight of the shadow shooting down at them again. He turned and began to run as fast as he could. All of a sudden, he felt the demons claws pierce deep into his flesh. The claws ripping through his flesh as he fell to the ground. Jeff did not look back he had to keep going. Inside he knew he had to help Todd. He looked up there was nothing in sight. He quickly jogged back to his friend. He reached down grabbed hold of his friend's arm and helped him to stand. In the dim lit area Jeff could see where his scalp had been severed through in several places where the flesh had parted. The blood only made possible to be seen by the moon above. The blood covered Todd's face.

This time it was Jeff that told his friend not to give in. "Come on Todd do not stop on me now."

Jeff pushed Todd to one side and jump to the right as the demon shot between them just missing them by a few inches. Seeing the demon coming at them again Jeff began to run. He ran under the 1st Street Bridge, leaving his friend behind.

"Don't leave me! Don't leave me!" Todd shouted seeing the demon with its claws stretched out.

It was like seeing an eagle with its claws stretched out just seconds before grasping a rodent in its clutches. Todd closed his eyes just as the demon's claws closed around his face. It dug in its claws and ripped the flesh apart. Todd felt the sting of the wounds of the gouges now opened. The fresh air hit the wounds causing a horrible sting as well as pain. The white of the bone showed through. The shredded flesh seem no more than shredded meat. It was no more than pulp just dangling. The demon circled flapped its wings rapidly as it suspended itself off the ground over Todd. The demon studied him for a moment then opens its claws. It grabbed him by the shoulders. It flapped its wing lifting both of them up higher and higher up into the night sky. It drew back its head its fangs positioned in to the forty five degree angle. It lowered its head and bit down injecting its poison into Todd. It released it right hand and brought it up to Todd's head. It cradled the head in its hand then crushed. It opened its hand and Todd's body plummeted to the ground like a limp piece of clay. Brain matter mixed with blood oozed on to the hike and bike trail. Jeff ran he was only a half mile away from the Y. Now where had he parked the black 2003 Mercedes? He could not remember. It was the fear he had to calm down he had to think. After a moment thought he remembered.

All he had to do was make it under the Lamar Bridge. He had to shoot across Chavez and make it to his car. He stumbled seeing the evil lunging at him again. He rolled to one side the demon missed, but it was too fast. It maneuvered like a bird moving with ease. It shift direction in a matter of seconds. Jeff hurried desperately to get away from it. The fear deadened his mind like a splash of freezing water thrown on his face as he watched it kill Todd. And now it was going to kill him. Death from above turned and it came swooping down at him. Its large fangs exposed with the many jagged teeth that filled its mouth. Its eyes leered at him as it manifested death. It flapped its wings several time just a few feet away from him and landed on the ground. Jeff scrambled to his feet. He ran with all his might.

The demon trotted picking up speed. Jeff side hurt from exhaustion. There was just about ten feet of total darkness under the bridge. If he made it through he was scout free. He did not care if anyone was at the Y, or not. He would crash through the glass door if he had to get away from it. His legs heavy with fatigue. They seemed like two five pound weights had been tied to them weighing him down. He had to fight the feeling if he wanted to stay alive. He ran looking over his shoulder continuously. He could not see it but he knew it was coming. He hoped it had left but no sooner had he thought it he felt the pain of its claws cut through his skin.

It was playing cat and mouse. It struck then vanished for a moment then returned. He had no time to feel the pain. He prayed the demon tired of him. He hoped it found him to be no challenge and would leave. All I have to do is make it under the bridge he thought to himself. But there was that ten feet of darkness he had to go through. Where the night lamps lit the hike and bike trail again. Time had stood still. It seemed but in reality, only a few seconds had passed. He picked up his speed hitting the first patch of darkness. Suddenly from the other side the demon hit him like a freight train. The impact of the force shocked Jeff's brain. Jeff's body fell like a limp sack of potatoes. It reached down lifted him up looked into his eyes. It snarled then flapped its wings rapidly. It lifted them up into the night like an owl lifting a rodent in its claws. It carrier him high suspending them in midair. It glided for a moment the released its grasp. Jeff's body plummeted fast to the ground like a ton of bricks. A dull loud thump and a puff of dust. The breaking of bones was heard as his body made impact with the ground. A soft moan escaped from Jeff's lips as his head rolled to one side. His broken and mangled body lay sprawled out with his limbs bent back in unnatural positions. A broken bone protruded from one of his legs. Two Souls landed beside him flapping its wings then in a slow trot moved around him. It studied the broken body. Jeff moaned again in agony.

Blood spewed from his mouth. It reached down and lifted him up once again it shot into the night. It flapped its wings and took flight again into the sky. Again, it released its grasp it had on Jeff's. The body plummet to the ground below. It then flew down and landed next to the body. It reached down lifted him up then injected its poison into his neck. It had been more of an animal instinct to inject the poison into the dead body than to kill Jeff. It lifted the body with one hand and threw Jeff's body against the concrete pillar. Blood ran down the corners of Jeff's eyes though there was no life to the broken mangled body. It walked up to Jeff reached down ripped his right arm off pulling it off at the shoulder. It dislocated its lower jaw and placed the arm into its mouth inching it slowly into its mouth.

Inching it down its throat devouring the sweet human flesh. It then thrust its hand deep into Jeff's chest. It pulled out the heart and placed it into its mouth. Blood overflowed from its mouth as it closed down its powerful jaws around the red muscle that pumped life. A lump formed on its neck then disappeared. It's tongue flicker in and out of its mouth covered in red liquid. It reached down and ripped the other hand off its victim then both legs off at the hips only leaving the torso behind. It flung the limbs over its shoulder like a butcher at a slaughterhouse would do. It began a slow trot the limbs bouncing up and down before it took flight into the night. Like a glider it stretched out its wings and hovered overhead for a moment. It changed direction heading back to the drain pipe pulling in its wings. Moments later it descended landing with a thump as the weight of the limbs it held weighed it down. It looked over its shoulder scanned the area making sure it had not been seen. It made sure it was clear to enter into the maze of tunnels. It entered the pipe and moved through the maze. Reaching the platform Two Souls could see that there had been many new arrivals to his world below the city. The swarm of snakes had tripled from the previous night. The large cotton mouth hissed at the other snakes as if to order them to be quiet. It faced their new master. Two Souls forked tongue flicked in and out of its mouth as it looked around his domain. It then began to tear small pieces of flesh off the limbs and tossed them out in all directions. It was as if one were seeing a man pulling bread crumbs off a loaf of bread he held in a bag to feed a flock of pigeons at the park.

"Eat my children you will not hunger any longer as long as I live."

It then tossed the human remains into the swarm and sat down in the midst of it all the snakes. Quickly the reptiles devoured the flesh resembling thousands of maggots on rotting meat. Two Souls reached down and caressed the moccasin's head and handed it a large piece of meat.

"My friend I saved this for you," it said in a raspy voice to the snake then caressed its head again.

Steam vapors rose from the waters of Town Lake as the heat of the morning sun beamed down eating away at the coolness of the night. It was as if the horror of the present night had not happen. Small splashes in the water indicated that the aquatic life was alive and thriving. The smell of the lakes water hitting your nose. Up ahead on the hike and bike trail a white and brown Pit Bull roamed down the trail heading west in the direction of the Y.M.C.A. It stopped then walked up to the bank of the river and began to lap up some water quenching its thirst. But there was still the matter of hunger. Its insides rumbled it needed to eat and anything at the time would do. It sniffed the air then look up ahead. It spotted something. It moved quickly hoping that it could be food and it did not matter what kind. It scampered up the trail stopped at the pile of breadcrumbs. It crouched down and began to eat away at the crumbs left behind by people who had fed the birds the previous day. Sniffing the air its nose worked wildly picking up a new scent more appealing to its taste buds. It began to run faster and faster making its way up to the First St., bridge. It studied the mangled body then licked the encrusted blood on the dead body or what remained of what was once a man. With ravishing hunger it began to tug away at the man's flesh and on several occasions lapped up some of the gray brain matter from the head. Its teeth making scraping sounds on the skull as it gorged away filling its pallet. A million flies seemed to fly off Todd's body as it moved the body with every tug it gave the flesh with its teeth. The flies flew but where back in a matter of seconds landing back taking their share of the morsel of the raw meat. The dead body had been called in by someone. The person had been running early that morning and called from the Y.M.C.A. Hysterically telling the person on the receiving end of the call the horrid details of the scene. The A.P.D, Austin police department had responded and had arrived on the scene of the crime. Pete and Chet had arrived on the scene and had walked up to the body. Just a few feet away from the corpse they watched the grotesqueness of the Pit Bull gorging its belly full. The dog turned its head and snarled viciously. Its lips curling up and exposing the large canine dripping with blood. A large piece of meat hung dangling freely from its mouth. Chet inched his way up to closer to the dog.

"If I were you Chet I would step back." "I'll be all right Pete."

"Get the proper equipment before you attempt anything," Pete told him. Pete noticed that the dog lowered its head and its ears had gone back.

"Get away from the dog it's going to attack."

"Get dog, get the hell away from that body. Scoot you mangy dog."

"Get away from the dog Chet."

"Scat, get the fuck away from the damn corpse you sick dog."

"Blendez get several of the men and comb the area up and down this trail. I have a bad feeling there might be more and get the humane society out here a.s.a.p."

Pete turned his attention back to Chet just in time to see the dog crouch down lower on its front legs. Its ears flattened back further they lay flat against its neck. It snarled and growled.

"Move Chet move," Pete shouted.

He knew that the breed of Pit's had a rep but that did not matter at the moment. Rep or no rep a dog was a dog no matter what breed it was. And a hungry dog made things even worst.

Chet was interrupting this dog's meal for the day. And it would attack to preserve the kill whether it had killed it, or some other creature had. It would protect like any animal that had not eaten for several days.

"It is not going to do anything don't have a cow. I have everything under control."

As Chet faced the dog it lunged forward for his throat. Chet raised his arm just in the nick of time. The dog's mouth closed around his forearm then began to thrash violently. Pete knew if he did not act quickly the dog could and would rip the muscle from Chet's arm. There was no time to think or to analyze. Time, time was the essence. He had to save his partner or let the dog ruin his career not to

"Get this fucking dog off me," Chet shouted.

The dog let loose of his arm and that had been just luck. As the dog landed on the ground Chet tried to kick it but it was ineffective. The dog crouched down and leaped for his throat again. This time Chet had managed to catch the dog by the neck. The Pitt Bull lashed out at him slashing his arms with its canines. Chet began to stumble backward. Pete knew if he lost control of the dog now it would manage to get to his throat. There was only one thing to do now. He would have to explain his action later to the Chief. Without hesitation or a blink of his eyes he reached into his coat and withdrew Baby Blue. It seemed to come to life in his hand. He lifted the Springfield without aiming at the target he shot off a round hitting the dog with a clean shot through the temple. Brain matter spewed out of the small hole. While on the other side a hole the side of the top of a coke can appeared. Chet held on stumbling back. Chet lost his balance as Pete had predicted. He stumbled further and fell in to the lake still holding on to the dog for dear life.

"Holly shit did you see that?" One of the officers in the background asked another as they witness the whole ordeal.

Pete was glad he hit the dog and not Chet in the process. He looked up towards the street Pete's face contorted with anger seeing the pedestrians that began to arrive on their morning walk. Not to mention traffic stopping to a slow craw as the curious wondered what happened below.

"Johnson!" "Yes, sir."

"Get this fucking area barricaded off like right now."

Chet slowly climbed out of the lake holding his gouged arm as water dripped from his clothing onto the ground. Chet faced the lake and stared at the dead dog now floating motionless on top of the water. He faced Pete and looked at him in silence.

"I have everything in control huh," Pete said then chuckled for a second.

Chet just looked at him still in a daze. "Let me see the arms partner," he says.

Chet smiled for it had been the first time Pete had called him partner. Maybe he had gotten his battle wounds deserving his trust now. Pete looked at his arms then told him that the wounds could have been worse. He then told him when the paramedics arrived to get his wounds attended to. Pete turned to walk up to the dead dog then turned back to his partner.

"One more thing when the paramedics tend to your wound call Franks and tell him we need the dogs down her. Oh! And don't forget to get the dog out of the water you need to check it to see if it was rabid as well. I thought I saw some white foamy shit coming from its mouth."

Chet was just about to tell Pete to fuck off when they were interrupted by Blendez voice.

"Pete."

"Save the thought Chet you may have a chance to use it later, Pete said and smiled then turned to face Blendez.

"What's up?" Pete said knowing what he was about tell him.

"As you suspected Pete there is another body up by the

Lamar Bridge and it makes this one look like amateur work." "Shit! Pete exclaimed then paused for a moment then spoke, "Blendez catch up with Chet and tell him to tell Franks to send one of the dogs down to the Lamar Bridge. By the looks of the blood trail on the ground this man had to be the first victim and maybe between here and the Lamar Bridge we can find some kind of clue."

Pete waited patiently by the water's edge looking out over the water as he waited for Blendez to return. Pete scanned the area up and down. His detective mind quickly taking everything in. That's funny he thought to himself. Why had the blood trail stopped? And why did it appear that the ground had been scrapped instead of having foot prints? As far as he could tell there was hardly a scuffle to begin with.

"Okay! Take me to the other body let's take us a look at body number two. I just hope there is not a number three."

"Why is that?" ask Blendez.

"If there is another body out here. I'll feel as if I am on the price is right. What is behind door number three?"

Blendez laughed then said, "I get it that is kind of warped detective.

"No, what this killer is doing is warped."

About three feet away from the first body, the blood trail ended.

"Detective Rodriquez the blood trail ends."

"I noticed that. But what now? We have a killer that can fly. What he probably wiped the blood off in the water after noticing the trail he was leaving behind."

They both look towards the Lamar Bridge. Fifteen minutes later they reached the Lamar Bridge. Pete and Blendez stood in silence and stared for a long time just looking at the dead corpse. Why had the body been dismembered? What were the voices telling Bobby to do now? What was the motive? Pete looked up and noticed that two other cops had arrived on the scene.

"Franks, Sikes, get a small team and comb the area from Congress up to the Barton Springs area. Anything, any kind of clue. Any droplet of blood you come and tell me."

From Chavez, street above White Cloud and the forensic team walked down the incline to the crime scene. The men and women of the team quickly dispersed in different directions. White Cloud stepped up to the body knelt down next to it. He set down the black briefcase opened it up the small black briefcase. He took out a pair of latex glove and put them on. He took out what seemed to be some kind of small brush. He expertly began to go over the body. He was puzzled Pete could see this by the look on White Clouds face. The sound of dogs howling in the distance reached them.

"Looks like our friend from the capitol struck again Pete." "Are you positive White Cloud?"

"I would have to say yes Pete. Tell me what you notice or see," White Cloud pointed to the man's chest."

"Several gouges against the wall where it looks like fingers dug into the meat."

"Good observation and this makes number three. I know there are other dead bodies but only three had their hearts ripped out. Three with perfect marks like that of an instrument perhaps. A tool of some sort that can extract the heart perfectly.

"The good side of it is that so far it looks like man is doing the killings."

"How long did you say the body had been dead?"

"I would have to say at least twelve hours. Body is frozen with full body rigor mortis Pete."

"Have you seen the other body yet White Cloud?"

"Yes, Pete and I know what you are thinking. You are thinking that a man could not have crushed the man's head in like that without a vise."

"Exactly, the only thing strong enough that walks with that kind of strength here on earth to crush a man's head like that is a gorilla. One more thing White Cloud what about the puncture marks on the man's neck? What was that yellowish shit that came out of the puncture wounds? I knelt down and probed at the punctures. I saw that yellow crap ooze out of the small holes in the man's neck White Cloud."

The dogs continued to bark in the distance. White Cloud stood up pulled off the latex gloves off and tossed them on the corpse. Pete looked at him for a moment then asked him of the excretion found on the victim's wounds again.

"Step over here for a moment Pete."

White Cloud and Pete stepped away from the body and away from Blendez for a moment.

"The lab has identified the excretion, Pete. The excretion is poison. You want to hear the rest"

"Okay! You have my attention."

"The poison found in each victim is snake venom. But for right now Pete I wouldn't worry about the poison. I'd worry where the man's limbs went. And off the record I think we are dealing with some kind of animal."

"The only thing we are dealing with is one sick fucking puppy. Not an animal but Bobby. I don't know how. Or why but he is using some kind of tool he rigged up to throw us off his trail James," Pete told White Cloud then looked over towards the lake. White Cloud looked at Blendez then back at Pete.

"Have you noticed that the dogs only went out so far then kept coming back to the corpse each time?"

"Yes."

"Well Pete, that means that whomever it is, is very intelligent. He or what has been erasing his trail all along somehow."

"No, James, Bobby just became smarter for the time being." "So, Pete what are you going to do now?"

Suddenly out of nowhere flashes of light bombarded the area as the reporter and their cameras took pictures. A news crew had begun to set up their equipment.

"What the hell are these ass holes doing here?" Pete said to no one in particular.

Blendez moved quickly as if the words from Pete's mouth had been a cue to step in. He began to move the reporters back up the incline. The reporter Blendez was pushing back stopped abruptly and violently shrugged his shoulder warding off Blendez hand.

"Do, not touch me again butt hole. I have authorization to be here, and it is straight from the mayor himself."

Two unmark cars stopped on Chavez heading east. The D. A. climbed out of one of the vehicles and made his way down the incline.

"Let him through Sgt., he has permission from the mayor to be on all the crime scenes without any harassment."

Pete thought for a moment then realized that he could use the reporter to his advantage. What better way to get the killer out in the open. And that was if he could get the psychopath angry enough that he would take a chance and show himself.

"Let him through Blendez."

"Yes, I have a few words for you," Pete said and waited for the reporter to put the microphone in position then added, "This killer is one sick individual we are dealing with. He may think he is evading us now but sooner or later he is going to make a mistake. They always do and I am going to be there to catch the sick fuck."

"Jesus, detective this is live T. V."

"Do, you want what I have to say, or not?"

The reported nodded then continues, "Detective do you have any clues, or a suspect as of this moment."

"Yes, we do have a clue, but I cannot disclose that at this time."

The reporter pointed his finger down to the dead corpse. The camera man quickly took his cue. He focused the camera on the dead corpse and began to take footage of the mutilated body. He then brought the microphone up to his mouth. The camera focused in on him.

"Public we are here live at Town Lake here under the Lamar Bridge at the hike and bike trail where something horrendous had taken place. People it looks like the beginning of another nightmare for our city. It appears that there is a serial killer out there. Or someone who thinks he is a wolf. Or better yet he thinks he is a vampire. He is loose out there, and no one knows who he is. There is a suspect to all these killings. And with our fine detective on the case, I believe this man will soon be caught and brought to justice. Perhaps we will find something out on the next murder. More at eleven tonight," the reporter then signed off.

Pete's face contoured at what the reporter said. His last words cutting sharply into his brain, "you may find out something on the next murder?" Pete could not hold in his words, "what do you think these people are just money in your pocket you condescending fart," Pete reached for his Springfield he withdrew if from the holster.

"You crazy son-of-bitch," the reporter said waving his crew back.

"Jesus all mighty Pete put the gun away," ordered the D. A., sometimes I think you're the one we have to watch. Don't you know who the reporter is?"

"No, and I don't give a damn either sir."

"Well let me tell you anyway. That man is the Mayor's brother-in-law. Damn Pete I will try and clear things up with the Mayor. I will tell him you were inspecting you gun, and he thought different. If you see this man again you will stay clear of him, got that Pete."

"Pete placed the Springfield back in his holster. Chet approached them holding onto his arm. The one that had been bandaged from the wrist up to the elbow."

"I saw what happen. Why do you hate reporters so much Pete."

Pete remained silent not answering his partner. He then turned and faced Blendez.

"Put two of you best men on each of the crime scenes and keep the runners away from this place."

"Pete," Chet called out.

Pete ignored the question Chet had asked and replied back, "Two fucking weird Chet and now I have to deal with the media as well."

CHAPTER 14

Pete and Chet returned to the precinct later that afternoon. They walked up the steps to the precinct building. Pete stopped abruptly at the top steps. He looked around taking in the aroma of a burger being broiled.

"What's wrong Pete," asked Chet.

"Damn the smell of a burger being broiled that just makes me hungry. Shit! It makes me want a hamburger."

"You know Pete I think, I will go over to the stand and order me one of those chili burgers," Chet said turned around and began to walk down the stairs.

"Hey, Chet order me one of those big Texas cheeseburgers with onions. Extra cheese, lots of lettuce, and mayonnaise.

Tell them to load it down with mayo. Hell, wait up I'm coming along."

As Pete was about to take a step down the stairs an officer came out of the building calling out to him.

"Detective, detective Rodriquez the Chief wants you in his office a.s.a.p."

Pete began to reach back to his back pocket for his wallet. "I got it Pete you better go and see what the Chief wants." "Thanks kid and make sure."

"I know. I know, lots of everything especially mayonnaise," Chet said cutting him off.

Pete smiled then turned around. He began to walk into the building wondering if Chief Golds had some kind of e.s.p. What did he wanted with him this time? Hell, all he knew was that in the last couple of days he was becoming popular all of a sudden. Reaching Golds office Pete looked in through the door window.

What the fuck he thought to himself. He noticed that the Chief was talking to a woman in a red dress. And he knew the woman well and he did not really care to see this woman at the moment.

"Damn it to hell that is all I need is the department quack breathing down my neck. I might as well take my ass rimming," he whispered to himself before knocking on the door.

Suddenly the thought of the reporter entered his mind. Downtown must have sent him a message like get therapy. The thought itself brought a smile to his face. He entered the office apprehensively thinking to himself that he would soon be on the chopping block. He walked up and stood in front of Golds desk as if he were still in the military standing at attention.

"Relax Pete," he told him then stood, "I think you already know Miss White."

"Why, yes I do," Pete replied back.

Miss White stood up from the brown leather couch.

"How have you been Pete?" she asked then reach out her hand and shook his hand.

"I've been better Miss White," Pete told her then waited for her to ask him if he still had the bad dreams.

"That's good Pete."

Chief Golds sat back down on the edge of his desk. He then told them to sit down. Pete sat down in a chair next to Golds desk.

"Are you here to break my brain open again Shirley?" Pete asked bluntly.

"No, Pete I am not here to break you brain as you like to call it."

"Good! I was kind of worried."

"But you know Pete it has been a good while since you been in my office."

"Yes, Shirley it has, and I'd like to keep it that way. So, if you are not here to see me then what are you here for?"

"Right to the point. Not holding back just straight forward that is what I like about you Pete. Honest and to the point."

"So, stop with the bullshit and just tell me."

Pete reached into his coat pocket pulled out a cigarette lit it and inhaled deeply.

"Should I tell him Chief or do you want the honor." "I'll take it from here Shirley.

"All yours Chief, she said as a smile grew on her face. "Pete, Miss White will be assisting you as well from now on the investigation."

Pete coughed in surprise as the smoke got caught in his throat. The smoke from the cigarette stung his throat as his throat muscles constricted.

"You got to be fucking kidding me right Chief?" he asked in a raspy voice and coughed several times then added, "Tell me you're just kidding."

"Before you put your foot in your mouth as always just listen to what I have to say. Miss White is highly qualified. Now just look at this as if you have two of the highest qualified people on you team."

"What do you mean two high qualified people? What I have is Chet. A rookie that was better than the rest and a brain probe."

"That is right Pete, Miss White is a brain probe. She might give us the edge we need on this damn investigation. Not to mention that because of your reputation no one else wants to be your partner and to boot because of you I get my ass rimmed out by the Mayor. So, Pete I do not care what you think. Finding who is responsible for these murders and catching him before more innocent people get killed is more important at this moment than what you think."

"Vengeance is my sayeth the Chief." "What was that?"

"Nothing Chief I didn't say a word."

Pete knew the decision the Chief had made, made sense. The way the investigation was going he needed all the help he could get. But he did not need an opinionated uptight quack on his back every minute. And it did not help that he had known her intimate. It was the right decision made, but he knew that she had been put with him to keep an eye on him as well.

"You are right the people come first Chief."

Pete stood up and walked up to Golds desk. A large black ashtray displaying the A. P. D., logo in bright white letters sat neatly at the edge of the desk. Its main purpose was for display and Pete knew this. Another smaller ashtray for the smokers sat at the other corner of the desk. Pete looked at Golds smiled then cut his cigarette off in the one that was for display. Golds face reddened with anger.

"God damn it Pete. I am beginning to think that you are fucking crazy and that you do need to see the shrink you psychopath. You asshole!"

"I love you too Chief," Pete said then smiled then added, "I guess I used the wrong one huh."

Shirley looked on. She had been Pete's analyst, slash lover, after his wife's death. She knew the hatred he held inside for Bobby and the guilt that ate away at him. He had blamed himself for her death. She had gotten deep in Pete's mind. Shirley knew that she would have to be accepted by him before he even would agree to be considered her to be a partner. She knew that as soon as he finished messing around with the Chief. She would be the next target.

"So, Miss White what are you going to do for the investigation? You think he is going to come up to you. So, you can break open his head? I don't think that is the way it is going to happen."

"What kind of off the wall question was that Pete," Golds snapped.

"You are absolutely right I had no right asking that kind of question. It is just that the mind we're dealing with is nothing like the ones she has dealt with before."

"I have to say that it may be true Pete. But at least give me a chance. Going into one's brain that is my specialty.

"You are right I should at least give you a chance." Shirley knew that Pete was accepting her at that moment. Not as a partner yet but for the fact that he was a fair man and he would wait. He would wait to see if she would fall on her face. Chet entered the office. He handed Pete his burger then looked at Shirley then whispered into Pete's ear.

"Isn't that the department quack?"

"Yes, that is right Chet. I don't know what the fuck you did. But she wants to crack open your head like an egg. She wants to see if the squirrels in your head are working as they should. You are in some deep shit!" Pete whispered.

"Oh!" Chet said then gave him his burger as he stared at Shirley. Pete opened the wrapping on the burger and took a bite. Chet looked at his partner with concern. Pete leaned forward and whispered it Chet's ear, "That is right you are a nut case. They are taking you off the case."

"If I can get an in depth view of his mind Chief," Shirley say to Golds. Pete looked at Chet and nodded then whispered, "you are fucked partner."

"If I can get an in depth view of his mind then maybe I can tell you where he might strike next. Or possibly where he might hang out."

Pete was about to take another bite of his burger. He stopped just inches away from his mouth then says, "Anything that you can do to get us closer to him Shirley. Chet take Miss White to the files pull Bobby's records so she can take a look at them."

"You still think it is Bobby doing the murders?" Chet asked. "I don't know but as it stands Bobby is the prime suspect.

This is getting crazy the murders do not fit his M. O. but he has killed all ready. We have to start somewhere and right now as I said Bobby is as good a place to look as any."

The phone rang Golds quickly answered it. He listened to the man on the other end then hung up the phone.

"You two hold up before you go anywhere. It looks like our friend has struck again at Sixth and Congress. The person on the phone related that the body he came across looked as if it had been dead for a while. Maybe several days, same M. O., the man said he saw a skinny man running from the scene."

"Before you leave for the crime scene take Shirley to the armory. Get her hooked up with a weapon she can handle Pete."

"This is unusual isn't it Chief?" Pete asked.

"It is Pete, but this is not your regular case and Miss White safety comes first. Oh! One more thing she did not tell you Pete. What you did not know of Shirley is that she was once a cop before she became the department's psychiatrist."

Pete knew a lot about Miss White that the Chief did not know. But it was their secret.

"Letting the skeletons out of the closet? Well I'll be damned," Pete said and took a bite of the burger.

Pete had known she was once a cop but he still cared for her. And hour later they had arrived on the scene. They climbed out of the vehicle and walked down the alley. An awful stench released from the decaying body reached them instantly.

"Jesus almighty that is horrible," Chet exclaimed. "Only if you inhale Chet."

Chet looked at him confused they had to breath there was no way around breathing. Pete smiled and nodded his head. Chet cracked a smile and nodded his head. They had to breath what Pete was telling him was to stomach it. Or don't but they had to investigate. Chet looked at the dumpster ahead as did Pete.

Pete knew the smell of death that was something he would never be able to forget. Vietnam had engraved the stench in his brain.

The Chief had mentioned that the caller had related that a thin sickly man was walking away from the scene. It had been a garbage collector that had spotted the dead body. He made his round to clean up the trash bends that were scheduled on his route. Pete thoughts ran wild as he approached the body. Well, Shirley wanted to get into Bobby's head. Well, it seemed the opportunity had arrived. She would see for the first time what a demented mind like Bobby's was capable of Pete thought to himself.

"Well! Miss White let's see what you can conclude from the corpse."

Shirley looked at the body that lay in a puddle of stagnant water. Flies buzzed around the corpse as several rats chewed away at the man's neck.

"God," the word escaped from Chet's mouth. He felt like puking as the word left his mouth, "I never knew a human body could smell this bad," he says to Pete.

Shirley looked up scanning the buildings walls then the alley way. She quickly took in that the bricks were laced with mildew. The metal staircase running up to the different levels on the foundation wall seemed intact. The silent emptiness of the alley gave her chills. Pete knelt down and studied the headless corpse.

"What do you make of it Shirley?"

Shirley knew whoever had done this atrocious deed had no kind of remorse. Or any human feeling left.

"Look at the body and carefully tell me what you think." "You, want to know what I think Pete?"

"Yes, enlighten me Shirley."

"Okay, I see that this man must have been drunk as a skunk. He had been looking straight into his killer's eyes when he died. The body has been dead for at least forty eight hours."

"How do you know?"

"See the spiders and the rest of the bugs these usually are the last to arrive. You want to see if I know my job detective."

Chet looked at them for a moment the turned and looked over his shoulder. He made his way up to the dumpster. He would let his partners fight it out in a way. He had his battle wounds and Pete had acknowledged him as his partner. That was good enough for him. He reached the dumpster and placed his hands on the lip of the dumpster. Flies flew out wildly from the inside in all direction.

"Oh! How I hate the fucking flies."

The thought of him wanting to be cremated and not to be worm or fly food ran though his thoughts. He moved the dumpster and stepped in back of it. He looked down. It was the missing piece. It was the transients head. He knelt down next to the head. He looked at the torn flesh around the man's neck. He knew not to touch anything before forensic came to do their job. He looked towards Pete and Shirley and tapped the head softly with his shoe. Several bugs crawled out of the ears and mouth.

"I think the time had to be night. The killer used the element of surprise," Shirley said as she looked up at Pete.

"See the way the flesh has been torn and gouge marks in the flesh. The gouges are made by either claws or a tool. It would make this body number four Pete.

"You are right Miss White. Now we have one more thing to do."

"Pete." "What? "Over here."

"We have to find the missing clue."

"Ah!   Yes the missing head," Shirley quickly replied. Chet looked around and then down at the head.

"I found the missing clue," he said proudly. Pete and Shirley walked up to the dumpster.

"I don't know what it was but look at the imprint of fright on his face."

They waited about twenty minutes before the forensic team had arrived. White Cloud climbed out of his vehicle. He walked directly to where Pete and his team where waiting. Without missing a beat he walked up to the head. He turned it over on its side. He inspected it carefully hoping to find something.

He moved the flesh from the neck where he was sure he would see puncture wounds. But he had been wrong. This head had been torn off the man. White Cloud stood and became pensive for a moment.

"Hum," he said.

"He turned and walk straight to the man's body. He looked it over. After the proper procedure for dusting the body had been done. The huge hole in the man's chest told them that the dead corpse was as the other bodies.

"Looks like the others," White Cloud said looking at Pete "Puts us back to square one," he told White Cloud. "White Cloud get me something anything to get closer to this killer."

"You said that as if you now expect there might be another person besides Bobby involved," Chet says.

"Search the area and see if there is something we might have missed Chet," Pete ordered ignoring Chet's remark.

A sanitation truck pulled into the opening of the alley off of Sixth Street. The man stopped the truck climbed out and began to walk in their direction.

"Well, Pete you did not answer Chet's question?" Shirley asked him.

"Bobby is strong but this I don't know. There have been times when serial killers join up."

Seeing several officers making their way up to him with their hands on their guns attached to their hips the man quickly spoke.

"I am the one who call in the dead body. I am the one who called the dead body in. I just came back to the dumpster to empty it. I was hoping the body would be gone by the time I returned. I was told that you wanted to see me as well for questioning. So, when I saw you here

I thought it would be just as good of a time as any and I am still on the clock."

"It's all right I'll take it from here," Pete said as he walked up to the man.

"You did the right thing. It is going to take a while to clean up here. The best thing for you to do is to come back in a couple days to empty the dumpster."

Shirley walked up to Pete. "Excuse me for a second here," she told the man then whispered into Pete's ear, "White Could has something to show you Pete and I think you need to see it."

Pete nodded his head then turned his attention back to the man, "sir what I need you to do right now is to go to the precinct. Fill out a report for us and make it on the clock."

"But I have other dumpsters."

"It is all right just tell your boss the police department ordered you to do it. You can do your regular rounds tomorrow."

"Okay, Miss White lets go see what White Cloud has for us."

Pete walked back to the corpse where White Cloud was busy taking something out of the man's chest.

"Ah! Presto change-o I got it," White Cloud said as he pulled out the object with large tweezers then added, "look at this magnificent piece of evidence Pete.

"Just tell me what it is before you give me ulcers." "I know. Suspense can kill," White Cloud said as he reached for a plastic bag to put the specimen into.

Pete knew it was not normal and he knew it was not going to be good news. He was beginning to have doubts about it just being Bobby doing the killing. But the abnormal kept sneaking in somehow.

"It looks like a claw but this is not form a dog or cat. It is more like one off a bear by the size of the claw," White Cloud said as he stood and began to place it into the plastic bag for tagging.

CHAPTER 15

The following morning Bobby, "The Slayer," waited patiently behind a huge pecan tree. He looked at his watch 7:30 a. m. No, one had come out of the house that he had been watching. He knew that whoever remained inside would be alone. Bobby looked at his watch again. It was time he thought to himself. He needed a kill to rejuvenate himself. Suddenly he heard the door open and the faint sounds of footsteps on the front porch. He watched as an old man walked out onto the porch. He walked down the steps. He climbed into his car. He started it up and drove away. Bobby stood then quickly lowered back down on to one knee as he heard voices behind him. He looked over his shoulder it was runners on the hike and bike trail. They approached him as they ran by. He waited until the runners were out of view before standing back up. He quickly scanned the back door. He accessed the quickest way to enter the house. He looked at the windows the door then the second story. Fast entry would be the back door. His decision was made. He sized up the windowpane on the top part of the door.

It would be easy he thought to himself. And if someone were to be in the house. Well to bad for them his mind ran with the excitement of the possible kill. He scrutinized the door for a moment. In his head he began a counted, one, two, three and he began to run towards the house. He ran up the stairs and ran across the back porch. He leapt in a dive with his hands stretched out like a battering ram. He hit the window shattering it. He tucked in his head. He brought in his chin to his chest. He sailed in through the window. He hit the kitchen floor and rolled twice. He rapidly stood erect. The old woman inside the house sat on a flora, print couch in her living room reading the morning newspaper. At the sound of an intruder, she screamed out loud. She dropped the paper startled by the noise from the kitchen. She stood then slowly got up. Her fragile bones struggling to help her up. She walked into the kitchen and screamed again as she saw Bobby standing in front of her. Bobby tilted his head to one side. He walked up to her without a care.

"What's wrong?" Bobby asked her then added, "is the old lady scared? Is the old lady going to cry and piss all over herself?"

The old woman placed her trembling hands over her mouth to suppress in another scream. Bobby grabbed her by the neck. He shoved her all the way into the dinning, room.

"Don't cry lady."

"Please no, please do not hurt me. I will give you whatever it is you want. Just don't hurt me," pleaded the old woman.

"I'll give you anything you want just don't hurt me," Bobby mimicked sarcastically then added, "How about some snooch. Y o u know poon tang?"

Bobby looked into her fear filled eyes. The expression of fear seemed to give him pleasure. He grabbed himself then told the old woman she was making him cum on himself. He gave her another forceful shove then struck violently at a bowl of fruit on the dining table. It slid wobbling then crashed to the floor. The old woman screamed at the top of her lungs. Bobby lifted his hand and pointed one finger up and shook it in the jester to be quite. He moved his finger from one side to the other.

"Now, now, lady you don't want anyone to hear you now do you?"

Bobby grabbed her by the neck again and forced her to her knees. He was about to strike her with a violent blow to the face when she began to pray. He paused for a moment. It was as if seeing her there praying on her knees had brought back some humanity back into him for a second. Suddenly the backdoor slammed open then shut.

"Expecting someone well let's go and take a look," he told her grabbing her by the hair.

He dragged her along on the floor behind him. It was like seeing a child dragging a doll on the ground behind them reaching the kitchen. Then let go of the old woman's hair. He took everything in the kitchen in. His eyes scanned everything quickly. His eyes shifted to the backdoor as he notice, something move slightly by the wind. Bobby looked down at the woman.

"Must have been the wind cause it sure in hell wasn't God answering your prayers now, was it?" Bobby said and began to laugh.

He stopped laughing as he caught sight of the broken door. It had been broken at the doorknob. Had he broken it when he had crashed through, he could not recall. He must have he thought to himself. He turned around in time to see a black cat hissing and jumping towards him. The cat hit his chest clawing violently. His chest stung from the sharp claws entering the skin as it tried to get away from him. The cat hurried out through the small opening through the backdoor and out into the yard.

Suddenly Bobby felt something behind him. Something that made the hairs on his back stand up. He turned but there was nothing but what appeared to be a shadow too big, to be that of man. His mind was playing tricks on him. He needed to kill to please the voices in his head.

"You some kind of witch lady? Did you tell that cat to do that? It doesn't really matter soon you will be saved from your pain old witch."

Bobby reached into his trouser pocket. He pulled out the surgical knife that he had taken from the hospital. He used it to cut across in a straight line. He cut deep into the old woman's forehead. The woman began to scream. Bobby punched her in the jaw momentarily knocking her out for several minutes. A blood trail followed them into the living room as he dragged her into the room. Bobby reached down and lifted her up. He placed her on to the table. The old woman begin to wake up. She felt the pain of the knife dig deep into her flesh again.

"No! God, please don't," she begged her words being cut off as Bobby cut her across the jugular vein. She grabbed her neck as a gurgling sound escaped. Bobby watched pleased as the life ran out of his victim.

"Sleep now my sweet for parting is such sweet sorrow," Bobby said then soaked his fingers in her blood and wrote, "The Slayer," on the east wall.

Hearing several loud thumps on the wood oak floor he exclaimed out loud, "What the fuck." Bobby felt the strong foul breath of something behind him.

The breath on his back made his hair tingle. Then he heard a voice. The voice of the demon as none he had listened to before.

"Turn around," Two Souls said in its raspy voice then added, "I want you to cut her heart out and hand it to me,"

Bobby stumbled back knocking over one of the chairs. Bobby stopped it was his god that had come to release him from his torment. He looked at the demon.

"The heart cut it out and hand it to me," it demanded.

Bobby did its bidding as if the demon had taken control of his mind. Two Souls grabbed the heart from Bobby's hand. Then like a phantom in the night it vanished leaving no trace of it ever being there. It could have killed Bobby where he stood.

But like all animals something about the crazy mind and the horrendous crime that Bobby had committed kept him alive. That small part of being animal that Bobby allowed to come to life.

Thirty minutes later sirens, flashing lights, surrounded the house. The sound of cop car and their tires screeching to a halt sounded though the air. Rifles being slapped into the palms of the officer's hands as they took the weapons and aimed at the house filled the air. Four officers rushed the house and positioned themselves against the wall of the house. Four others rushed to the back of the house and positioned themselves. Here they would wait for instructions or the perpetrator to come out running. Pete, Chet, and Shirley, arrived at the scene. They climbed out of the car and made their way up to Blendez. "Blendez what do we have?"

"Don't quite know as of yet Pete. As far as I know it may be a prank."

A bald heavy-set man came running across the street. He was about five, five and weighed about two fifty. It seemed he waddled more that he ran.

"I called ya'll. I heard a woman scream. I hear a woman screaming and thought it might be Mrs. Willis's"

"This, woman lives by herself," Pete asked.

"No! But I saw her husband leave when I was putting out the trash.

"Did you see anyone enter the house or leave after Mr.

Willis," Pete asked him.

"I think I saw a large man leave the house just minutes before ya'll arrive here."

"Heavy set man," Chet questioned.

"No, not like me tall, taller than most men. He had a tremendously strong build. He went around the tree and then vanished."

It was the second time someone had mention that the perpetrator vanished. What the fuck was this man fucking Hudini? His mine continued trying to put two and two together.

"What do you mean vanished?" Shirley asked.

"Yes, just what I said. He just vanished and was gone. It was as if the tree had swallowed him up."

"Are you sure you saw someone leave?" Pete asked the man. "I am sure but I do not know if anyone else is still in there."

The officers that had positioned themselves around the perimeters of the house waited for a signal to move in. Blendez looked at Pete. Pete nodded his head. Blendez made a motion with his hand waving the men in. They moved in as they had trained cautiously. Blendez looked at the men at the door. He then moved towards the back where one of the officers waited to relate his orders to the two men at the back of the house. Blendez lifted two fingers and motioned forward giving the men the cue to move into the house. At the okay it was to be a three count before charging in. They did not use the two way radios they did not want to give the man inside any clue when they would enter. It was just a precaution that might save a cop or two. On the back lawn a sniper had placed himself in the mist, of a small bush blending in with the environment. The man remained motionless as he looked through the scope of his rifle. He pointed it straight at the backdoor. The teams had entered.

They were now making their way through the doors. They entered into the living room only to find Bobby sitting in a chair mumbling words to himself in a daze. Pete entered the room then stumbled over the woman's body. Pete looked at one of the officers that had entered through the back into the living room. He stared at the writing on the wall. Another cop quickly approached Bobby and cuffed him without any resistance.

"Jesus Christ," exclaimed Blendez.

"No! Not Jesus Christ," Bobby said in a soft muffled tone as he continued to stare out into space.

Pete hated Bobby with a purple passion but there was something wrong. Wrong from the word go. Bobby would do anything to keep from being captured. And that meant that if he had to chew his own hand off like a wolf when captured by a trap he would. The stare in his eyes was different. Pete noticed that it was a stare of fear. Fear of what Bobby had seen. Or had it been that he had snapped back to reality, and he knows he had done something horrible.

"Please kill me. The voice in my head was not an angle but the devil."

Chet moved into the other rooms. Shirley studied Bobby but remained silent. Like Pete, she as well knew now that the killer they were dealing with was not Bobby but someone stronger. Someone that might have gotten into Bobby's head. Getting into his head and cause him to do its bidding. It frightens her some to think that whatever they were dealing with was not of the human origin.

"Want to question him?" Pete asked Shirley. Shirley shook her head no.

"Get him out of this place," Pete ordered.

Chet walked outside and walked up to a group of cops looking down at the ground at something. Shirley walked up to the wall in the dinning, room and studied the writing. One thing for sure whether he had been manipulated or not Bobby was sick, real sick mentally.

"Pete, I think you better come and take a look at what they found outside," Chet shouted out to him.

Outside next to one of the big pecan trees Chet moved the remains of a half an eaten heart. With a twig he poked the heart several times. The heart rolled over and exposed a large bite mark that had removed half of the muscle.

"Look at the size of the bite," Chet exclaimed.

"Chet get White Cloud out here like now," Pete said then added, "do not touch or move anything out here until forensic does its job.

Pete made his way to the back to the front of the house. He noticed the property was well kept. It had rose bushes running down the side of the house. It had several others in the backyard where a small gazebo had been placed in the center of the yard. The grounds had been landscaped immaculate. He stopped at the front steps of the house and lit up a cigarette. Shirley walked out of the house. She stared at Bobby for a moment.

"You have another smoke Pete."

"I thought you stopped Shirley," he told her seeing the forlorn look in her eyes.

"I did Pete, but I need a smoke believe me."

Pete handed her one as White Cloud and his team arrived. White Cloud climbed out of the vehicle and made his way up to Pete.

"In the back," Pete told him waving his hand in a gesture to go to the back of the house.

Pete and Shirley made their way to the back after their smoke giving White Cloud time to examine whatever it was, they had found. Chet looked at Pete and Shirley as they made their way up to them.

"Bet you can't eat just one," White Cloud said humorously. "It looks like are friend has a craving for the pumping machine," Pete replied.

"I think the killer needs it in a way like a junkie needs his drugs. It gives him that one rush of exhilarating life," says looking at White Cloud.

"No, it is more like a ritual killing.

"So, that is why the heart has been removed from all the bodies?" Chet asked.

"More likely than not," Shirley answered back. "Pete." Blendez said.

"What is it Blendez."

Blendez pointed up to the tree. Pete stared at it for a moment before his attention was brought back by Shirley.

"What are you looking at up in the tree?" "Up and to the left," Blendez says.

"Ah! I see it," Shirley replied. "Bring it down," Pete ordered.

"Looks like some kind of layer of skin," Shirley says. Next to the tree Blendez looked up then at Chet.

"Give me a boost up."

Chet cradled his hands under Blendez foot then told him to spring out for the limb above on the count of three.

"I'm ready," Blendez told him.

"One, two, three and as Chet pushed up with his hands. Blendez sprung up off his leg catching the limb. He quickly climbed up the tree.

He grabbed the skin like material that had been snagged off whatever creature it had come from.

"Watch out below," Blendez shouted then dropped the material to the ground.

White Cloud stood and his eyes widen. He knew the tales of the old ones. He kept the thought to himself. The story of the evil one. Two Souls he did not mention. He had only related to them that the skin seemed to be that of a snake and that further test would determine what it was.

"It is snake skin."

"Snakes do not have a pair of arms White Cloud," Shirley exclaimed.

Pete studied it carefully then shook his head. He ran his hand through his hair as he always did when puzzled. What the hell was happening? Why was the hearts of the victims being removed? And what in hell sheds its skin like a reptile? And it had been twice they had found this thin rubber like material at one of the crime scenes.

"What do you think White Cloud," Pete asked seeing the look on his friends face when he had seen the skin.

"I can tell you what I think. I can tell you of what it is. I can tell you, but you will not believe me. I can tell you that you will need help. We all will soon if it is not stopped. For now, I will tell you as a forensic expert that the test will tell you that the skin is that of a snake."

"Now what Pete?" ask Chet.

"We go back to the beginning."

"We have done that twice Pete," Shirley replied back. "Correct that is where we are going again for the third

time, and the fourth, and fifth if we have to. We will do this until I find out what is missing to this investigation."

"You're the boss!" Chet exclaimed.

"Right now, before they send my friend back to the asylum, we need to interrogate him. I want you to try and get into his head Shirley fine out what he saw. Then we go back to the hospital."

Pete noticed that the cops where already in the process of barricading the place off with the yellow tape that read, "Police do not cross."

"I am going to take one last look in the house. I'll be right back," Pete told his partners.

He walked into the house to the back looked out the door. He watched as forensic and White Cloud moved about. What did his friend know? Why did he say he would not understand? Pete turned back around. He began to walk out of the living room when he looked down at the dead woman.

"Dead people don't talk," he thought to himself.

He regretted that the woman was not alive and able to tell him what it was she had seen. He made his way back out of the house. Seeing Pete, Bobby made his way out of the cop car. He butted the cop with his head that was trying to restrain him. He broke free and ran up to Pete. In pure instinct Pete reached for Baby Blue his Springfield and drew it and began to squeeze the trigger. Gloria jumped out of her cop car and ran and tackled Bobby to the ground. They rolled on the ground and in an instant, they were both on their feet. Bobby tried to turn around. Gloria kicked the back of his knees from under him. Bobby's face contorted with pain. He looked up at Pete then shouted.

"Please take your gun squeeze the trigger and kill me."

Pete watch as Gloria took Bobby back to the car. She placed him into the vehicle. The look on Bobby's face puzzled Pete. What had been so horrible that had made him want to die? It wasn't in his character to give up so easily. He had seen something but what? Pete watched Gloria drive out of sight. He needed answers to something that was becoming too weird even for him.

"Gomez take to men and wait until everything has been wrapped up. Wait for the husband. Relate the incident and find out if he has any relatives he can stay with.

"Yes, sir I'll do just that."

"Chet, Shirley lets go talk to Bobby."

Back at the county jail house in the interrogation room Shirley paced around the table asking Bobby questions hoping to reach him somehow. Bobby laid his head on the table with his hands stretched out in front of him. Chet sat across the table from Bobby. He watched and studied the man carefully. Pete watched them through the large viewing window in an adjacent room. Bobby slowly lifted his head and stared into the window. He knows I'm here Pete thought to himself. Bobby looked at the window and whispered knowing that Pete would see him and read his lips.

"Detective you should have killed me."

"Bobby, look at me. I can help you if you just let me," Shirley tells him as she placed her hands down on the table next to him.

She looked at him. Chet sprung up from the chair he sat in like a coiled spring that had just been released. Swiftly he moved around the table and grabbed Bobby by the hair assisting his head up.

"Look at the lady she is trying to help you," Chet snapped impatiently.

Chief Golds entered the viewing room and stood next to Pete watching the scenario.

"What do you think Pete?"

"I don't really know what to make of it." "Seem bewildered Pete."

"To a point Chief yes I am," Pete replied.

"I would say you have a hunch. You know something and you're not telling."

"I cannot disclose anything I think I know Chief. Not without proof. I will tell you not on the record that I am beginning to think that something subhuman is out there. It is out there watching and waiting to kill. I have to find out what it is that Bobby saw."

"You mean a creature of sorts?"

"I am just saying that, that is what it is beginning to look like. It almost looks like another Jack the Ripper. Now you see him know, you don't. And only the dead victims know his identity. And dead people can't talk."

"Pete, I think it is time for you to take a vacation." "When we entered the house Chief, Bobby was sitting down in a chair mumbling words incoherently. He then requested I kill him on the spot. It just doesn't add up. Crazy as hell, yes he is, but that does not bother me. We caught him and he is here. It's the words he used to describe what he saw. He said it was the devil Chief. Not man but the devil."

Shirley opened his folder up in front of Bobby. She pointed to the pictures inside.

"Now come on Bobby. Tell me how it felt to kill all these innocent people," she pressed then showed him the photos.

She spread them out on the table for him to see. "Now tell me what you see."

"I only killed the lady in the recovery room and cut some tubes in the I. C. U. That was all. I am telling you the truth," he shouted.

"Calm down," Chet orders him.

"The voices in your head are not the angle of mercy Bobby," Shirley continued.

"Yes! I help to kill the weak. I kill because I am told to do so by God."

"God!"

"That is what I thought until I saw it." "Saw what?"

"It was the devil that ordered me to kill." "You talk to God personally?"

"I thought I did?"

"So, it was the devil." "Yes!"

Bobby looked straight into Shirley's eyes then spoke, "I know what I saw.

"Okay, Bobby you talked to the devil and the rest of the time you killed.

"I thought they were angles. I thought they were angles," he pounded his hands down on the table frustrated.

"Does God, I mean, the devil tells you to mutilate these bodies and take out their hearts?"

"I kill the weak yes, but I am not given permission by the lord to take their hearts. The Devil is amongst us. The Devil ordered me to take the heart," Bobby shouted angrily.

"Tell me Bobby what do you feel like when you kill someone?" Shirley pressed on.

"I don't know what you mean?" Bobby said looking at her. "You know what she means Bobby," Chet said out loud.

Bobby leaned forward in his chair. They could see the change in Bobby's demeanor as if another person had taken his place. He leered at Chet then spoke.

"You want to know what it felt like to kill the innocent. Well it felt good. It brought a peaceful feeling over me," Bobby said coldly then laughed wickedly and stared at Chet for a moment then spoke again, "Yes I will have to say it feels good to help the weak and the helpless. Is it not what love is all about?"

"Do you not feel any remorse for what you did? Any regret the slightest bit for killing in cold blood?"

"No! I do not. But you know what? "What? Chet says.

"I did not mutilate anyone," Bobby said this time lying as if again his personality had changed.

"Okay! You did not. So, who did?"

"I have told you it was the Devil, and you don't believe me. Okay! Then how about a monster a real live fucking monster. Don't you get it with all the fucking diplomas you have. It is a real live fucking monster," Bobby shouted in despair.

"Chief I am going to go in there and see if I can make him elaborate more on this creature, demon, devil, whatever the fuck it is."

Moments later Pete walked into the room and walked up to the table.

"You know Bobby I think you are full of shit," Pete said sarcastically then slammed his fist down on the table and added, "It is all bull shit. You kill innocent people for the pleasure for no other apparent reason. It is in black and white Bobby."

"No! I help the supreme power by letting the weak and the sick go to the light a lot sooner. I kill but not like that monster," in a boyish tone again changing personality.

"Bobby some say what you do is the work of a monster." "I am telling you the truth detective. I thought I was getting my orders from the supreme power. I did not know it was the Devil."

"Describe him for me in more detail Bobby."

"Okay detective, he says then continues," It stand as least seven feet or more. It has characteristics of a reptilian. One of its eyes is human the other seems to be of a snake.

At several minutes of Bobby's description and taking it all in Pete remained pensive for a moment then spoke.

"Guard get him out of here and take him back to his cell."

The guard took Bobby by his elbow and escorted him out of the room.

"I am telling you the truth it is the Devil. It stood just inches away from me," Bobby shouted out as he looked over his shoulder.

"Well Shirley, tell me what you have if you got anything out of this interrogation."

"As you can see, he has multiple personalities. That means that as a child he could have suffered a very horrible trauma. I think he is experiencing a mental delusion. A delusion where he can experience seeing this monster as he. He himself commits these horrible crimes therefore eluding the fact that he is in actuality doing the killing."

"So, what it amounts to is that he is one sick puppy. Hell, I could have told you that, "Chet exclaimed.

"In a way yes in a way no. You see the personalities he possesses range from a child to that of a genius. That is one of the reasons he is able to elude the police."

"So, he is crazy," Pete exclaimed then added, "They actually pay you money to come up with these evaluations."

Shirley felt the sting of his sarcasm, but knew if she showed any sign of weakness now, she would lose his respect. She knew he was under a lot of stress as well. She had to come up with something to stay on his team.

"Yes, they do pay me for my professionalism. Do you have a better answer? I believe not with what we have it could very well be the leprechaun in those sick movies."

"Yeah, I seen those movies fucking awesome." Chet said enthusiastically.

Pete stopped as he stepped out of the room turned around, "take it easy you are right. I just could not help myself from saying it," Pete said then smiled.

"You can be a cold bastard at times," she told him.

Pete's eyes seemed to come to life with surprise. He chuckled at her remark for he never thought he would have ever heard her use such language. I think I am growing on her he thought to himself. He thought then spoke.

"Okay! Let us look at all this in perspective." "Okay!" Shirley agreed.

"Chet," Pete said. "I'm with you."

Pete walked back into the room.

"Bobby said it was a Devil. A monster. Now let us look at the possibilities."

"You are kidding right Pete," Chet said looking at him. "Okay, let's say it is of an unknown origin for argument sake," Pete continued.

"That will work for me it will make things easier," Chet said in a sarcastic tone.

"Be open here Chet," Pete says.

"I think I know where you are going with this Pete," Shirley said.

"All I know is if it is a creature that means we have the upper hand. It cannot think like a human," Chet said.

"Here's one for you genius. What if it can think, and it is intelligent, and its intelligence surpasses that of a human," Shirley interjected.

Pete knew that Shirley could very well indeed be right.

That part scared the hell out of him. He also knew if it wasn't Bobby then the killings would continue to go on but to a higher scale. The room became silent the frustrations of their toils weighed heavily on their shoulders. Pete looked at them both.

"You know what let's go and get a cup of coffee, and some doughnuts. We can try to figure out what it is real and what is not."

"Doughnuts," exclaimed Chet.

"Doughnuts sound good about now let's get the hell out of here," Shirley says.

Pete smiled, two times in one day she has potential he thought as they walked out of the interrogation room.

CHAPTER 16

Down at Tom Miller dam the following morning a couple enjoyed the warmth of the new day in their boat. The man checked his wife's water-skiing gear. He made sure that all the equipment was functioning properly. Everything seemed safe he gave the thumbs up. She prepared herself for entry into the water. She lowered herself slowly into the water. She released her grip from the small latter that ran down the back of the boat next to the motor.

"Okay! Bill hand me my skis." "You sure your ready go solo."

"Yep! Let's do it," she said enthusiastically.

He handed her the skis. She grabbed the skis from him and put them on then gave him the thumbs up. Above undetected by Mary and her husband the hideous monster glided undetected above. Two Souls flew above like a giant condor as its sensors home in on its prey. It flapped its wings then brought them in to its side. Then swiftly lowered down a few feet it then abruptly spread its wings allowing it to glide and circled above. It flapped its wings then brought them in to its side shooting down like a missile. Mary looked up and as soon as she had seen the creature she began to scream frantically. Two Souls moved in rapidly. Her husband turned around and stared in disbelief at what was descending from sky. It could not be there was no such animal known to man like what was coming at them. In a matter of seconds, it had landed on the boat and was upon them. It grabbed the man's head in its hands. It then ripped the man's throat out. It worked its jaws back and forth in a sawing motion as a lump of flesh and bone slid down its neck. Blood spewed from its mouth as its black forked tongue flickering in and out. It let go of its grasp. The man body fell limply to the floor lifeless. It squatted down and sprung from its legs up into the air.

The boat went out of control maneuvering itself. It swayed from side to side moving towards the dam on a collision course of no return. The boat hit the dam and exploded into flames on impact. The woman moved her hands and legs as never before. Moving them in that final attempt to get away from the flying predator from above. She moved her hands and kicked with all she had hoping that if she just made it to the shore she could get away. Two Souls flew low just inches above the water. It reached out its claws. The menacing claws of death that would soon fall upon her. In a fraction of a second, she went under barely evading its grasp. Two Souls shot up like a missile moving upward into the sky flapping its wings. It stopped in midflight its body turned and its head pointed down. There was a moment of pause as if time had stood still. Two Souls descended with incredible speed. It knew she would have to come up for air soon. It would time its approach. It raised its head and shot parallel just inches above the water. Its bat like wings sucking away at the water causing it to splash upward like a curtain of water hanging down the span of each wing. Mary struggled with the remaining breath of air she had in her lungs. But she knew she had to surface to for air soon. She kicked her feet and shot to the surface popping her head out of the water.

She gasped for a breath of air. But at that split second the demon swung its razor-sharp claws gouging the flesh of her face from the nose to her forehead. Before the demon could sink in its claws deep, she dove under the water. Her mind was in a daze from the pain. Mary again felt the panic that came with needing air. She needed air she would need to surface again. It was the only thing she could do. It was a chance, but it meant staying alive and not drowning. She counted in her head one, two, three, she kicked and surfaced. She took in air into her lungs as quickly as she could. She began to go under the water. Two Souls shifted when it saw the ripples of the water circulate outward as she surfaced. It shifted circling and shot across the water in her direction.

Just as her head was in the process of going under its claws went slightly under the water grabbing her at the throat.

Her scream suppressed by the claws that dug into her flesh. She kicked and struck at the demon's hands for dear life. It took flight upward a few feet above the water. In a forceful jerk it ripped her throat out. Her body hit the water feet first. Her body began to move down into the water. Quick and forceful it flapped its wings. The demon shot down just as her head was about submerge. It grabbed her by the hair. It flapped its wings in swift fast motions lifting her out of the water. It suspended them in air. Her blood fell into the water mixing with the water below. The blood in the water looking like red die from above. It held her by her hair then slowly it begins to lose its grip. She broke free and her body plummeted to the water again. With incredible speed it dove down. In a matter of seconds, it caught her before her entire body was submerged in the water. It did not bother to lift her body out of the water this time. Her shoulder and head remained above the water as it flew dragging her body to shore. On the bank of the lake, it mutilated her body tearing, ripping limbs, and flesh, off with brute strength. It ate what it put into its mouth, flesh, blood, nerves, veins, bones, devouring the woman. Just as Pete was about to parked in front of the precinct the two-way radio came alive.

"Pete, Pete."

"This is Pete over."

"Chet is on the way down." "Got it chief over and out.

"Pete there has been another murder. It struck again Pete," Chet shouted as he ran down the stairs to the car.

He opened the door and climbed in then added, "been waiting for you a couple of minutes. Looks like our friends just struck again. I think we just got our break for today."

"Looks like it, Chet, looks like it."

Thirty minutes later they had arrived at the Tom Miller damn. Why the dam? Was it because it was more secluded? Or was it expanding its hunting grounds. Pete parked the car looked out at the calm water. He caught a glimpse of the woman's body. Her body lay just a few feet from the bank of the river. Pete climbed out of the vehicle. He walked up to the body. Mary's remains or what was left of her lay on the ground covered with the bugs of our world. Eating away at the flesh. Pete brought his attention to the man speaking to one of the officers rambling on. Chet climbed out of the car and walked up to the officer and the man. Chet listened for a while then headed in Pete's direction. He approached the body he stepped on the slime like substance.

"Search the area, Chet."

Chet left and Pete head towards the officer and the man. He then listened as the man spoke.

"I was about to go fishing here when I decided to get a better spot. You know in the shade out of the sun rays. Well any way I walked up to this spot here and there she was. Or what remains of what looks like a woman. At first I thought it might have been a wild animal then I saw something moving."

"Did you get a good look at what it was?"

"I did and I wish I hadn't. Well I kept my eyes on it.

It started to run as I approached it. It ran like a man and what it did next is not possible. It jumped off its feet and took flight."

"Are you sure it was a man?" Pete questioned.

"Why of course it was a man it ran upright. I do not know of any other creature that can do that except an ape. As I said it leaped off its legs like superman. It looked like it had a cape as well that spread out like wings is the best way to describe it.

"Like I said I saw something kept my eyes glued to it. It jumped up in the air and took flight. Hell, I was not going to stay in this place to find out either. So, I did the next best thing. I did the only thing I could do and that was to call the cops. I returned because I figured that you might need directions to where the woman was. I could not believe what had been done to that poor lady."

"Tell him to tell you the story again from the beginning.

Take his statement down," Pete told the officer.

This is the third time they had mention that it had taken to the air. What are they up against this time?

Pete walked up to the corpse looking down at the body. He studied the remains of the body. He knew that this was not going to be an everyday of the mill investigation at this point. Bobby was a killer and he had killed several people and he was safely put away. But the killings where the bodies were mutilated, and the hearts removed was done by this thing. Person, animal, whatever it was there was the question of how it was possible for anyone to have done this to this woman. It would have been impossible to lift her out of the water. She would have had to put up one hell of a flight. It would not matter how strong her assailant had been. She would have dragged them both underwater with her. They both would have drowned. Maybe she had made it to the bank of the lake where he waited. It or who attacked her, but then there was the question of a tool. Or how he managed to tear her limbs off like a butcher. Like a butcher at a meat market Pete thought to himself.

"Looks like a bad one huh Pete," White Cloud said as he walked up.

Chet checked out the surroundings. Especially the area where the man had stated he had seen a man vanish. He walked around the tree looking around the trunk looking down he saw something strange running down the trunk of the tree. It was the same slime like substance that lead from the dead body.

"Pete, you need to come and see this," Chet called out. Pete and White Cloud made their way up to the tree. "Look at that," Chet told them as he pointed to the globs of excretion running down the tree then added, "it starts over by the dead body and ends here."

"Snake spit," White Cloud said bluntly then added, "It seems to be part of all the murders."

"Chet get a crew out here to recover what they can of the boat."

"There is nothing left out there Pete," Chet tells him. "There is always something just have to look closer. Right now, every clue is valuable."

Chet walked up to the vehicle grabbed the two-way radio to call in a cleanup crew.

"That is the second time you said it had to do with a snake White Cloud."

"Seen lots of snake spit up in the hills as a small child."

"How can you be so sure?"

"I just know it is Pete. The result of the test will be in today sometime to verify what I tell you."

Pete looked down at the remains of the dead corpse. His face showed the frustration and the bewilderment. He looked up towards the dam then walked back up to the river. He stared into the void of the water. At that moment it was as if his mind floated and enter the realm of space and time. There was something out there amongst us something that was not normal.

Where was it hiding? Why aren't there any clues except that several people had seen it disappear? Here it is now its not. Not to mention the slime indicating it just ate something. Pete looked back down at the remains then back over the water.

"The answers will soon, come Pete," White Cloud reassured him.

"What else do you know?"

"I can only tell you that if it is this fable character that the old ones believed it to be. Then the person to kill it will come to you. This person is protected by Montezuma. He is called an eagle warrior."

"You're Indian."

"Yes, but it has to be a direct descended of Two Souls, I am Navaho."

"This Two Souls you mention what or where does he come from?"

"I do not really know Pete. I do know what I have heard from some of the old Indians. It is believed that this thing or person is the Devil on earth. I believe that if it gets the power it needs to complete its stay here. It will then release six other demons loose on this world."

"Do you have anything for a headache?"

"I believe I do Pete. Let me go to the truck and I'll get you one."

Pete returned back to the bank of the water and just looked out over the lake. This man, creature it had attacked during the day light hours. It had only killed during the night. It has gotten braver. It will make a mistake soon.

CHAPTER 17

Night began to fall. The clouds above shifted changing taking shape to one's own imagination. Images of all kinds were quickly absorbed by the mind. Fish, saints, dragons, whatever one wanted to see they were up there. Slowly they vanished like the day as night set in. Lightning shot violently across the sky like gigantic spears of energy falling to the earth below. The wind blew intensely as the storm came in over the city of Austin. The trees swayed back and forth with the wind whistling through their limbs. The branches creating a swooshing sound as they rubbed against one another. Rain began to fall to the ground.

The sound of thunder roared out like giant drums in the distance. It was like hearing drums being pounded as a battalion of Roman soldiers prepared for battle. Downtown in the heart of Austin on top of the N. C. B., building a silhouette moved about undetected. It came to life with every electrical charge above that shot across the sky. A shadow moved trotting on the building top. It leapt up on the ledge of the building. It sat and watched everything below. Its figure resembled that of an ancient gargoyle as it remained without movement perched on the ledge like a statue. It would wait and strike out like a phantom without warning. Two Souls silhouette came to life for several seconds as another flash of lightning shot above illuminated the night. Sam walked out of the corner bar unaware of the danger that lurked outside. He had parked his car at the corner of sixth and congress directly under the streetlamp. He walked up to his car got a cigarette pack out of the glove compartment. He lit a cigarette he closed the glove compartment then climbed out of the vehicle. He closed the passenger side door. He looked up at the drizzling rain. He enjoyed the feeling of the cool droplets on his face. He took in a deep breathed of smoke the exhaled. He pushed his tongue out as far as it allowed.

He took in another deep breath smelling the dampness of the earth in the air. He loved the smell effect of the rain mixing with dry earth. He loved the smell. The demon stirred then shifted its head as its sensors homed in, on Sam. Its large black forked tongue collected the molecules in the air. Its heat sensors located at the side of its nose felt every movement Sam made. Sam began to walk east back to the corner bar. Two Souls leapt off the ledge ran across the building's roof top. Two Souls jumped up on east ledge then jumped across to the adjacent building. Two Souls perched itself on the ledge ready to spring down on Sam. Out of nowhere a police car turned the corner. Two Souls squatted back down on its hunches and watched the car passed below with its siren wailing away. Sam turned and watched the cop car then turned back around. He pulled his coat lapel up over his neck. He shrugged his shoulders as a tingling sensation like that of a thousand ants were crawling up his back. He stopped and looked all around. It was weird but he felt something watching him. Though he did not see anyone he still felt as if a pair of eyes watched him from the roof top.

"Ah, maybe I am just getting old and being paranoia is a side effect," he told himself.

He turned and faced the building across the street. Lightning struck across the sky and with the illumination of each electrical charge. Sam thought he had seen something crouched down on the ledge of the building leering down.

"My mind is playing games with me tonight," he told himself then added, "too many beers tonight."

He took a second look but whatever it had been had vanished. Sam shrugged it off and entered back into the tavern. He was greeted by several of the regulars. Sam greeted them and headed back to the bar. At the bar Sam looked around at the people. He shook his head almost in disgust. It appeared that the same people were still in the tavern including himself.

"Hey! Sammy thought you were leaving," Vic said as he strolled up to the bar.

"No, I just went outside to get a smoke and some fresh air."

"So, in those few minutes what's new?" "Not much just you Vic., just you." "Ball and chain mad at you again Sam?"

"Up yours Vic," Sam retorted then laughed then said,

"Talking about the ball and chain see you are missing the boss." "You are right. The old bat threw me out of the house again," he leaned against the bar and added, "to bad, it wasn't sooner."

"Why did she go and do a thing like that for Vic." "Well, it's like this you really want to know why?" "Yeah! I like to know. Don't want to make the same mistake."

Vic walked to the jukebox put in a couple of quarters, worth of songs and returned to the bar. He took a sip of his beer placed it back on the bar counter and looked at Sam.

"Okay! Here it goes. This is what happened are you listening?" He looked around then continued, "Sue told me that her mother was arriving late in the afternoon around seven p.m. She told me to make sure to pick her up at the train station. Well, I went and forgot."

"You what?

"I forgot!

"Shit! Vic how could you forget something like that?"

"Hell! Sammy I didn't mean to forget. I came down here and time passed so fast by the time I remembered it was too late. Anyway when I got to the station she had already gotten a cab. I went home and tried to make things right. I asked Sue where her mom was. No, sooner did I spit out the words Sue jumped me like some angry alley cat. I swear her fingernails looked like claws coming at me. She read me the riot act up, down, sideways, every which way you could imagine. Meanwhile my dear mother in law was smiling at me from the corner of the room. So, I said screw it and came back here. The bitch, never like me anyway."

"Sue!"

"No! My mother in law." Both men laughed out loud.

"Yeah! I can see you are upset Vic," retorted Lisa a woman that had more than her share of booze.

"Better watch that one tonight Sammy she is in one of her better moods," Vic warned him.

Vic., walked around to the other side of Sam pulled out the stool and sat down and ordered himself and Pete another round. Sam sat down turned and faced Lisa. He contemplated if he should talk to her. Seeing that Lisa's glass was almost empty he asked Jim the bartender and owner of the place to give her another beer. He took a beer from one of the coolers opened it and walked down a few feet and placed it on the counter. He told her that it was from Sam. Sam smiled at her then asked.

"What's new Lisa?"

"Life sucks, doesn't it?"

Sam was taken aback by her remark not quite understanding the meaning of what she had said. He had asked a totally different question. But by looking into her glassy eyes he knew he was going to regret asking her anything.

"You, know what is new? Not a damn thing Sam. I like sitting here for hours in a room filled with smoke as thick as a fucking cloud. Not to mention the foul language and the jerks that try to pick me up,"

Lisa said then looked at the beer bottle in front of her then added, "I guess there is nothing new Sam," she then took a drink of the beer.

Sam looked at her wondering what had gone wrong with her. She was a young woman. Lisa was in her mid-twenties and she was what one would call a looker. He noticed her head wobble loosely from side to side indicating she was drunk.

"So, Lisa how was work today," Sam said trying to keep her mind off of drinking.

Mary, Sam's fiancé entered the tavern her eyes focusing on him as he talked to Lisa. Mary's face flushed with jealousy. Mary felt the heat of her anger rising to her face. She sauntered over to the bar next to him.

"Hi Mary," Vic greeted her loudly hoping to get Sam's attention.

Mary ignored Vic and stared coldly at Lisa. Everyone in the place brought their attention up to the bar.

"Oh! Shit there is going to be fireworks tonight," Vic said softly.

The place went silent. Sam turned around and met Mary's cold stare. His mouth seemed to fall open with surprise.

"So, this is what I have to look forward to Sam?" Mary asked then went around to the other side and placed herself between Sam and Lisa.

Sam noticed or maybe it was his imagination, but he saw Mary's fingers curl as she face Lisa. He knew if he did not act quickly Mary would lunge out and tear Lisa's eyes out at that moment. Lisa must have noticed as well for her eyes widened noticing the expression on Mary's face. The last thing on her mind was to take her man from her.

"Mary, Mary look, at me it is not what you think."

"Oh! It's not. Well, why don't you tell me what it looks like and it better be good Sam.

"Jim, give me an orange cooler for Mary."

"Let's sit down Mary," Sam told her as he grabbed the wine cooler from Jim's hand, "let's see how about over there in the corner."

Sam wrinkled up his nose and let out a light chuckle as he passed Vic. Vic smiled back not wanting to bring the woman's scorn upon himself. That is all he needed was to have the wrath of two women come down on him for another possible mistake of saying just one wrong word. Sam placed the drinks down on the table. He went around and scooted out a chair for her to sit down on. He then assisted her in pulling if forward. He sat down then placed his arms on the table as he held his beer. He leaned forward to talk to Mary. The table wobbled from one uneven legs. He reached down and placed a coaster underneath it making it level. The tabletop was black Formica the edge framed in chrome. The chairs were mismatched two had black pads the other two had red padded seats. It reminded Mary of a large checkerboard. Mary looked back at the bar at Lisa. Lisa mumbled to her beer bottle or to herself while Vic stared at her. Vic shrugged his shoulders. Sam reached over and grabbed Mary's hand.

"Mary!"

Mary looked at Sam with her light brown eyes that melted his heart like butter.

"Mary, I want you to be my wife," he said as he grabbed her softly by the chin and lifted her head up slightly.

"What did you say?"

"I said will you be my wife."

"Oh! Yes, yes, yes, yes," she shouted out happily.

She stood and quickly went up to him and hugged him so tight that she almost toppled him and the chair over. Tears ran down her cheeks as her head sunk softly into his shoulder. Vic stood up and went to the jukebox and put on the anniversary waltz. Al Jolson began to croon. Sam took Mary by the arm.

They made their way to the center of the room. They began to dance as if only the two of them existed in the entire world. He looked into her eyes as she did. Sam leaned forward and kissed her passionately on the lips.

"Lest get out of her Sam." "I'm I going to get lucky?"

"Oh! Lucky is an understatement."

"You got it babe let's get the hell out of here."

"But first let me go to the lady's room to freshen up a bit," Mary told him then kissed him softly on the lip.

She turn and left to the women's rest room. She turned to leave and tripped losing her balance. Sam reached out and grabbed her holding her up by the waist. She stood up right and smooth out her dress.

"You okay?"

"Yes, I am fine. It is just that I am so happy my head is spinning."

"I'll wait for you outside," he told her thinking if all the women in the world when it was time to leave somewhere. If they all had to go to the lady's room at that particular moment.

Sam made it to the car. He stopped then opened the door and climbed in. He leaned over and reached over to the glove compartment. He pulled up on the small latch reached in took the cigarette pack out. He sat up straight then pulled out a smoke and lit it. He felt something watching him again. He looked up across the street to the other buildings. This time he had seen the shadow take flight from the adjacent building from the N. C. B., building. Lightning shot through the sky. I must be going crazy he thought to himself. Then out of nowhere like a falling rock. Out of the sky the demon landed solidly on the hood of the 1965 Plymouth he had restored from scratch. Two Souls bent down and looked in through the windshield.

"My God! What in God's name," he asked in a tone of disbelief.

Sam attempted to escape from the creature but with a flap of its wing. The force of wind created by its wing caused the door to slam shut on to Sam's legs. Sam cried out in agony as the pain reached his brain. Two Souls placed its hand on the windshield and scrapped slowly with its claws. The screeching, sound its claws scrapping the glass penetrated into the depth of Sam's ears. It peered through the glass at him. It was playing with him. Playing like a cat would do with a mouse before eating it. It swayed its head back then rammed its fist through the windshield and grabbed Sam by the face. Two Souls release its grasp and withdrew its hand. Large gouges and oozing blood appeared instantly as the flesh separated across Sam's forehead, cheek, and jaw line. The blood covered the right side of his face. Two Souls jumped off the hood of the car. It moved around to the drive side in a slow gate. Then with the swiftness of a jungle cat with a powerful tug it yanked the car door off its hinges. Then as if it were a toy, it tossed the door into the middle of the street. One of its claws remained embedded into the metal frame.

Sam reached up and grabbed his face in bewilderment and fear. He felt his flesh that was now no more than shredded pulp. Through the blood-stained hands, he saw the demon fly into the night. Why had it attacked? Where did it come from? And what on earth was it? The thought ran through Sam's head. Hopefully it had gone at least this is what he hoped. Please leave. Sam did not notice that the demon had circled back as he relaxed back in the car seat with relief. The demon hit the car like a battering ram. It hit with a tremendous force crushing in the top of the car. Sam moved out of the car as quick as he could with panic in every inch of his body.

Somehow, he had managed to get out of the car before the top caved in. The demon shifted and flapped its wings several times sending Sam to his knees. It leaped down and walked up to him. Sam stood and ran west up six street. The demon watched him without concern for it knew Sam would not get away. It continued its slow trot after him again playing the cat and mouth game. Its dragon like feet echoed out as it approached Sam. It swung out its clawed hand cutting off Sam's right ear. Sam's ear fell to the street like a leaf from a tree hitting the running water in the cutter. The ear floated away with the rain water down into the drain. Sam grabbed where his ear had once been in horror. He turned around and stared at the demon.

"Oh! God no," he shouted out in fear as the demon stood in front of him leering down.

Two Souls shot its hand out sending it into Sam's stomach. Sam grabbed his stomach in a helpless attempt to hold in his intestines. His hands filled with his guts. Looking down at his hands he fell down to his knees. Two Souls bent forward shifting its head from side to side then reached down grabbed Sam up by the neck. Sam held his intestines in with one hand and the other he swung with the little life that remained in him. The demon struck out again severing his hand at the shoulder. Sam looked at his arm dangling by a thread of flesh. The demon clawed his face leaving it no more than a pulpy flesh remains. Sam left eye hung out only by the muscle of the eye socket. It just hung freely just dangling. It moved from side to side with every movement he made. Two Souls brought Sam closer to its face. It studied him for a moment then began to dislocate its jaw. It fangs shifted into forty-five degree angles. Saliva dripped from its mouth falling to the street. It lowered Sam down and looked straight into his eyes as if it were trying to read his thoughts. It shifted its head to one side like a pet confused or curious at his master's movements. It watched Sam's body twitched twice as the last breath of life escaped from his lips.

Mary step out of the tavern sing happily without a care as she made her way up to the car still in a daze. She turned the corner. She stopped abruptly as she saw the demon and Sam. The fear of what she was looking at overwhelmed her very soul. She saw the car and seeing the creature with Sam standing in the middle of congress. Mary began to run her face a blank less expression of fright. It was as if she had not seen the demon. She stopped and looked up at it then as if awakened by a bad nightmare she began to scream. She looked at the thing before her. The creature before her resembled some kind of reptile. Its skin was a pinkish brown with a black diamond patterns over its body. The marks resembling the marks of the eastern diamondback rattler. Its midsection was a yellowish white. Its eyebrows stuck out at the edge of its face. Its nose flattened as if only having two holes on a protruding jaw. Its entire body was covered with scales. Its muscular arms and frame stronger than that of man but yet it stood as man. Its dragon like feet added to its hideous existence. Mary looked on as the demon held Sam up and bit down with its fangs. It sunk them deep into his neck as it injected its poison into him. Sam's neck ballooned as the poison was being pumped in at a rapid speed. It withdrew its teeth then as it held him up with its left hand it ripped Sam's heart out then released its grasp. Sam's body fell with a thump to the asphalt. It looked at Mary and let out a horrifying growling sound. It fangs stained with Sam's blood. Blood ran like a river into the rain gutter. The demon's wings sucked at the air as it lifted itself off the ground and to flight into the night sky. Mary plopped down in a daze in the middle of the street staring out into oblivion. Moments later Pete had arrived at the scene of the crime.

Blendez gave his team orders to tape off the area. Pete looked down and up sixth street then walked east in front of the alley between the Driskill Hotel. He looked back at the crowd that had gathered and at Mary. Its wings sucked at the air as it lifted itself off the ground and to flight into the night sky. Mary plopped down in a daze in the middle of the street staring out into oblivion.

"Blendez get half the men into the alley and the other, half have them comb the entire area."

Shirley walked up to Mary and grabbed her softly by the shoulder. Shirley knew Mary had withdrawn herself from reality. She just hopes she did not withdraw too far to the point of no return.

"Did anyone of you see anything," Chet asked the crowd that had gathered.

"We heard a horrible sound like a growling noise. We quickly rushed out of the tavern. When we reached Mary all we saw was her just standing there like a zombie. You know it is kind of strange."

"What do you mean?" Shirley asked.

"Well one minute he was laughing and getting ready to get married an all. The next time we see him he is dead," Vic says.

"I see," Shirley said nodding her head several times.

Pete walked into the alley he stopped and looked around then felt something looking at him. He knew he would come across Sam's killer that night. Chet knelt down next to the corpse and turned Sam's head to one side. He noticed the yellow excretion coming out of the puncture wounds on the neck. Same as the rest he whispered to himself.

"Detective I just saw something moving up ahead," Gloria called out.

Pete caught a movement behind the dumpster. His gut feeling was on the money it was there waiting. His thoughts where disturbed as he heard noises behind him. He turned around to look who it might be. It was the news crew running into the alley. They stopped and positioned themselves. The reporter looked into the camera as the camera man began his count five, four, three, two, one, then pointed at him to go.

"Tonight, as you can see it appears that our vampire has struck again in our fine city."

The camera light focused in on the reporter.

"Can the police capture this fiend? Let us walk in further to see our police force at work."

The camera hone in on Pete then again into the alley then back to the reporter.

"People I do not know if they can capture this man.

Somehow, he has eluded them by being one step ahead of the police. I hope they can catch him before our vampire kills again. People of Austin lock your doors and hope to God that this killer can be stopped. Remember lock your doors and pray tonight that it is caught."

Pete heard noise coming for the dumpster he knelt down on one knee and withdrew his Springfield. Again, the camera light shinned on him the light capturing the lower torso of the demon. Pete could not see the demon's face but what he saw he could not believe. Its frame was muscular. It was impossible the man had to be wearing some kind of costume.

"Move the camera up slowly," Pete told the camera man.

The light barely shone on the demon's face when it leap off its powerful legs as if they had been coils of springs. The gust of wind created by its wings blew dust in all directions. Pete eyes focused on the demon's wingspan. Then all of a sudden, round from his weapon began to sing out. Then other guns began to sound off. The burst of bullets echoed out in the night.

"Stop your fire," Pete shouted after several minutes then stood.

"What was it you saw?" ask the reporter. "What is your name?" Pete asked him.

"James now tell, me what you saw." "I saw what you saw?"

"How about did you did you see anything?" he asked Chet. "No, I was a little late showing up."

"I know you saw something and you're not telling us," the reporter told Pete.

"What I saw, and the camera saw are in the camera." "That is right?"

"But before you get to excited, we need it as evidence," Pete tells the man then motion Chet with his head to confiscate the camera.

"You can't do this I will have your badge detective."

"You can have it when we're done with it James," Pete told him then stormed through the camera crew and walk out of the alley and up to the dead man.

White Cloud was in the process of making a chalk outline of the dead corpse. White Cloud lifted Sam's arm up slightly to mark around it the arm came loose in his hand. Chet walked up to were Pete stood.

"Oops looks like he is giving me a hand," White Cloud quipped.

"Damn man how can you joke about something like this," Chet said angrily out of nowhere.

"Take it easy cowboy no disrespect intended to the dead especially from an Indian. We take these things serious I see dead people all the time. I have to lighten up the moment at hand a little refraining from using the line again that he saw dead people. You know cowboy there are times I can't believe another human being can do this to another. I just want to go into the mountains and stay up there. But I can't do that and do my job properly now can I cowboy."

"I am going to take a look at the car Pete." "Cowboy, look but don't touch. Rookie!"

Pete waited until Chet was far enough away before he spoke.

"Good story but I think you spoke with a forked tongue White Cloud my friend."

"Yeah but it was a good story."

"Yeah the new ones are so sensitive these days," Pete said.

"I KNOW. The boy is going to get ulcers mighty quick if he doesn't lighten up some," then added as he took off his gloves, " I don't think I have to tell you anything you don't already know on this one Pete."

"Hum!"

Chet studied the door on the ground. He was not sure but what he saw lodged in the door looked like it might have come from the demon.

"Pete, White Cloud, I think you better take a look at this."

They both walked up to Chet and looked at the door. White Cloud left and returned moments later with what appeared to be large tweezers. He grabbed the object firmly with the instrument and wiggled the object until it was free. He opened a plastic bag and placed the claw into it then laid it across his palm.

"Holy Great Ones it is at least two inches long and at least an inch in diameter at the base."

Bobby had been telling the truth something was out there and it was killing. The question of what ran through his head. He could feel it, this thing, this man genius, or whatever it was. He also knew after today that it was not scared, and it was playing a cat and mouse game now. Pete began to recall back. It was like his days in Vietnam waiting for the enemy to jump out at any given time. The raindrops reminded him of the sweat that ran down his forehead into his face in the humid climate. He began to recall the dark damp tunnels where he would lean against the earth waiting in the dark for the enemy. Waiting for the enemy to return. Or to pop out of a crevice knowing that they were in the dark waiting for him to make one wrong move. He felt a weapon pointed at his head. He fought the fear and waited and hunted the enemy down. He recalled his men giving him the name Raton meaning rat in Latin. In a strange way that was what he was a rat in a tunnel. Pete knew it was out there watching him but why what was the reason. It was as if it wanted Pete to see it and only Pete. What was the reason? Why, why did it want him? The camera's light focused in on

Mary's face. The sound of the reporter's voice brought Pete thoughts back to the present. Back to the reality of the horror of death.

"Miss, can you tell us what or who killed this man," James asked Mary.

Shirley moved out from the back of the ambulance like a wild cat ready to attack. She pushed the reporter back into his crew.

"Hold up lady what the fuck is wrong with you?" James exclaimed.

Without thinking Shirley's hand formed into a fist and she struck out punching the reporter square in the nose. The reporter fell back still holding the microphone in his hand. He looked at her for a moment in a daze then grabbed his nose with his other hand as he lay on the ground.

"What the hell did you do that for?" asked James as he grabbed his bloody nose.

"What the hell is wrong with you people can't you see that she in a state of shock? Don't you have any kind of compassion don't you give a fuck about people's feelings," Shirley said angrily.

Pete walked up to her and, whispered, "reversed psychology ha," Pete said knowing the frustration she was feeling at that moment was what he felt for years. It was Shirley's first case on homicide. Her first case away from her desk. He waited for a moment then spoke.

"It goes with the job Shirley it goes with the job."

Blendez stepped in quickly, "You want me to get them out of here Pete?"?

"No, I will take care of it he has orders from downtown and I think our friend is in trouble."

Shirley looked at Pete knowing that he was right.

Striking the reporter was not the ideal thing to do. "You'll pay for this lady?"

"Listen mister," Pete said. "James, my name is James."

"Okay! James we have to come to some kind of agreement.

Walk with me to the corner," Pete told him and held out his hand. James looked at him apprehensive for a moment then grabbed Pete's hand. Pete helped him up off the ground. James brushed himself off then both men began to walk. James looked back once at his crew and shrugged his shoulders.

"James let us say we start over and try to help one another. You want the news and I just want to catch this sick puppy."

"It sounds reasonable go on," James agreed.

Pete stopped at the corner under the night lamp. Both men agreed that it was now more than possible that the killer was some kind of animal.

"Animal I do not think it was?"

"Look I can't really say what I saw but I do know this it was subhuman."

"Maybe an alien," James said. "Perhaps," Pete acknowledged.

"Now that would make a perfect headline."

"Agreed but there is one thing you have to do for us." "And what may that be?"

"We need to work together on this James."

"Okay! So, tell me what it is I must do for you?"

"I need you, not question anyone that has been a victim of our killer until Shirley gives you the okay."

James looked at her then grabbed his nose then looked at Pete and said, "I think the bitch broke my nose."

"Hazards of the job," Pete told him. "I think she broke my nose."

"James, we can fight each other on and on and neither of us is going to give in. We can work together just let it go."

James looked at Pete for a moment then spoke, "sounds reasonable enough just keep your goons away from me. Pete smiled then agreed and walked back to the ambulance. James grabbed his nose and looked up as if he might see the creature flying across the sky.

CHAPTER 18

The following day down at the precinct Pete paced up and down the cubical. He ran his hand through his hair. He stopped bent down and placed his hands on his desk then looked up at both of his partners.

"We have to figure out where this crazy son-of-a-bitch came from and where it is going to strike next."

"But yesterday I overheard you tell the reporter it was some kind of alien," Chet says.

"I did say it appeared we might be dealing with some kind of unknown origin."

"But I heard you say."

"No! Chet I said what he wanted to hear. And what I saw well was from the waist down. I couldn't see its face but what I did see was from the torso down and what I saw was not possible. As far as I know it could have been a man in a costume on a glider. But the only thing with this theory is that it was ascending from the ground up. It was just too dark to tell. I can't go bursting in on the Chief saying I saw something with wings. Do you have any ideal, how crazy that sounds I need proof," Pete said as a transient walked in.

The man wore a ragged wool coat walked into the corridor of the second floor. Pete's eyes stayed glued on the transient.

Pete watched as the officer spoke to him and sat him down on the bench in the hallway. The transient turned his head and stared at Pete as if he had known Pete was there watching him. He just stared at him in silence. The officer walked up to the cubical that was Pete's office. He stopped at the doorway and said a few words to Pete's.

"So, it is possible it could be an alien."

"Possible!" Pete says and focuses on the officer's voice." "Detective the man out on the bench wants to speak to you and only to you,"

Just as the words left the officers mouth the transient barged into the office.

"I told you to stay put," snapped he officer firmly.

Pete instantly recognized the Marine wool coat on the transient for it was the same he had worn so proudly in the Corps. The man looked worn and tired as the coat he wore. The elements of our world had made him look older than what he was. Pete studied the man then spoke.

"Chet, give the man your seat," Pete ordered him.

The transient scanned the room his eyes froze on Pete's military picture. He studied the picture for a moment then brought his attention to the other picture that stood next to it.

"Pretty woman," the transient said. "Yes, she was," Pete replied.

"I am sorry."

"It is okay it has been a few years since she died."

Pete noticed the gold double bars on the man's lapel. He had seen the face sitting in front of him many times before on the battlefield. Different people but yet the same in many ways. No one was immune to the war to any war. The war had reached many, white, black, poor, rich, it did not matter it did not discriminate. Who knew why this man had given up on life? Pete knew he was an officer by the double gold bars on the lapel. The ribbons on his coat told the story of this man's life especially the "medal of honor." The man was no coward but why this life he choose?

"The thing you are looking for is Two Souls," the transient says.

Pete remembered what White Cloud had told him. Who ever knew of this demon would come looking for him.

"Tell me about this Two Souls," Pete said.

The transient began relating the story of the demon. The stories of the old ones and of his relation to it, and of the evil Witchdoctor. He told him of the Witchdoctor and of his death and of how he was reborn as Two Souls.

"You're shit-n us right?" Chet bellowed out?

"No! On the contrary Two Souls is real and I am not shit- n you."

"Relax Chet let's hear what this man has to say. Please continue,"

Pete told the man.

This thing is real, and it is not human. I myself of Meso American parents did not want to believe this story. This story or belief of such evil. It is unheard of. I like you believed Two Souls was just something conjured up. Like I said I was like all the rest of the young believing that these stories were made up to keep us in line. But a few nights ago, I saw it. I saw it as clear as day just a foot away from me.

I looked into the demon's eyes."

"There are no real monsters in this world," Chet exclaimed.

"It is as real as you and I."

"How can you see anything you are wasted most of the time out of your mind? Hell. I can smell the booze on you from here," Chet snapped.

"I know what you think of me but what I saw I did not make up."

"Then why did it not kill you as well," Shirley asked. "I do not really know. I closed my eyes and began to chant the prayer of the old ones taught to me by my grandmother." "So! Now you are saying that a prayer passed down to you saved your life?" Chet questioned?

"Cool your jets Chet," Pete said then leaned back in his chair and listened to the transient speak.

The phone rang Pete picked it up and answered it, "hello!" "Pete this is Sally I think I have something for you."

"Be right down Sally," Pete replied and hung up the phone the said, "Chet, get someone to watch our friend here until we get back. I might need his assistance with the history of this Two Souls."

"Tell me you are not believing this mumble, jumble Pete," Chet says.

"Do you have a better explanation, Chet? "No, not at this moment."

"Shirley?" "No, I don't Pete."

" Well of yet I do not know what we are really dealing with. But I do know that in folklores there is always a way to destroy the demon." Pete replied. He stood and walked to the coat rack grabbed the holster with his Springfield. He returned to the desk took a drink of his coffee then looked at both of his partners.

"Let's go see what Sally has for us," he said as he put on his shoulder holster.

Down in the morgue Sally sat with her back toward them looking into the microscope as they walked into the room.

"Be right with you Pete," she said hearing them enter the room as she was writing something down on a piece of paper.

She turned around on the stool stood and walked up to a metal cart and took an instrument off of it. The object resembled a small hand saw. She clicked the switch on, and it began to hum. The motor came to life in her hand. The sound generating from it made Shirley's stomach uneasy for she knew what was coming next.

"Be right with you I just need to finish this up," she said and walked up to the metal table.

Sally placed the saw on the man's cranium that lay on the table. She began to saw into the man's head. The blade hit the skull with a sharp thump. The humming from the saw seemed to strain as it cut through the bone. Sally then took a different instrument for what she was doing. She began to take different parts of anatomy then placing the organs into a jar with formaldehyde. Shirley pretended to be interested in one of the microscopes pulling her eyes away from all the gore. Chet felt his stomach churn. Sally took small tissue samples and put them onto a Petri dish. She walked up to the desk and scribbled down some words on a note pad. She returned to the corpse and pulled out the man's liver. The liver seemed to quiver in her hand. She smiled at Chet and sat down on the metal stood at her desk. The liver quivered in her hand. She lost her grip and it slipped from her hand to the floor like a glob of Jell-O making a sick wet plopping sound as it hit the floor.

"Shit I hate when that happens," Sally said in a joking tone.

"Oh my God," Shirley exclaimed as she turned to see Sally pick it up off the floor. "Damn!" Chet exclaimed.

"The young," Sally said again in a joking tone.

Pete chuckled then said, "Sally, there is no way in hell I could do your job."

"Pete, I look at it this way at least I don't have to worry much about my job security ha."

"You know Sally I think you might have something there."

Sally smiled and placed a tissue sample under the microscope. She looked into the microscope focused in on what she was looking at. She turned and looked at Pete.

"Take a look at this."

Pete bent down looked into the eye piece of the scope not knowing what it was Sally wanted him to see. Sally took out the small dish and placed another into the view port. She did this several times.

"What am I supposed to have seen Sally?" Pete asked puzzled.

"Hold on to your pants," Sally said as she placed yet another dish into place.

She turned around, "it looks all the same under the viewer doesn't it Pete. Cells are cells."

"No, wait a minute there was something different in one of the dishes. It appeared the cells were shaped slightly different and moving faster."

"Correct! Sally said then reached for the large book on the table and opened it to one of the pages then pointed her finger sharply to the picture then said, "Here Pete."

Pete studied the picture Sally pointed to. It was a picture of a snake at the top of the page. He read the bold letters under the reptile. Pete studied the picture Sally pointed to.

"Diamondback Rattler," the rest of the words where in small letters under it that read from the "Crotalus family." Pete looked at Sally.

"Sally, tell me you are not trying to tell me it was a snake that kill that man."

Pete's thoughts where back to the alley and what he had seen that night. Pete looked around at his surroundings. The place reminded him of some whacked out scientist's lab where the scientist had gone mad doing his experiments. The small vials, with the tubes running out of them into larger ones with boiling fluids at least that is what it looked like to him. The residue flowed from one vial to another through the winding tubes.

Organs of the dead were in large containers filled with formaldehyde. It seemed like something one would see on the movie screen in a horror flick and not in real life. Pete's mind raced on as he told himself he was not in a horror movie. I just hope she does not tell me that it is a real live vampire and that it is out there stalking Austin his mind raced on.

"Pete."

"Oh! Here it comes."

"Pete what you are dealing with," she said then pointed her pencil at him then continued, "What you are dealing with is a large venomous reptile. There is a lot more than I can't explain. I made every test possible. Each of the test came up with the same finding. Whatever it is it belongs to the snake family. But then to make it more confusing there was also human traces of D. N. A. I ran the fang that White Cloud gave me and the claw through strenuous test. I stayed over last night and ran the test several times more plus some just to be positive before I gave you an answer. The cells I showed you under the scope are those of a poison snake but the human D. N. A.? The mucus like substance found also had human qualities. I guess what I am trying to say without going overboard and sounding like I lost a few marbles is," there was a small pause then she continued, "Pete whatever you are up against could indeed be half human and half reptile. I do not think one could rig something like that up. There is no way it could be made as perfect as what we have found Pete."

"Jesus, Sally," Pete exclaimed.

"I am not one to believe in aliens from outer space but this time I would have to say it could be. The tests do not lie Pete."

"Maybe there is something to this Two Souls character the transient was telling us about," Pete said out loud.

"What transient?"

The phone rang Sally reached into her smock pocket and withdrew her cell phone, "Hello."

Sally listened to the voice on the other end then handed Pete the phone.

"Pete, Bobby escaped from the county jail last night." "How, Chief how did he escape?"

"Appears someone or something broke him out several of the officers were killed as well. There was another body and by the description Blendez gave I believe he thinks its Bobby."

"Blendez would know if it is or not."

"Technically yes but the body was headless, and the head can, not be found," Chief Golds tells him.

"Let's say it is Bobby but why break him out then turn around and kill him?   Doesn't make any sense."

"White Cloud is out there with the forensic team, the D. A. is on his way."

"Thanks Chief I will be out there as soon as I can," Pete said then hung up the phone and handed it back to Sally.

"What is wrong Pete?"

"Seems someone broke Bobby out of jail then decapitated him," Pete told her then told her as he was walking out of the morgue, "Sally tell me what else you come up with."

"Why, yes I will Pete," Sally said then mumbled to herself, "decapitated Bobby."

Pete paced back and forth in his office cubical. He stopped and looked at Chet with his hands crossed looking at him from the corner of the room. He then looked at Shirley that sat with her legs cross at the desk.

"Okay! Meeting of the mines let's see what we have. We have a mutilated body at the hospital. Another at the capitol. A transient in the alley.   We have a live transient that says that it was Two Souls that is a myth.   We have Sam and the two bodies at the hike and bike trail off of Lamar blvd. The old woman Bobby killed. Bobby or a body made to look like his. But why go through all that trouble? We have reports of missing people. We have reports of people seeing something strange. We have reports that it flies. Bobby said that he saw the devil.

And Sally says that we may indeed be dealing with a half human, half reptile life form to boot. Did I leave anything out?"

"I think you covered everything Pete," Shirley agrees. "True Shirley but we forgot to ask the most important question during our own toils on this investigation." "And what could that have been Pete?" Chet asked.

"We forgot to ask ourselves why the young officer's body at the hospital vanished without a trace. We forgot to ask why there was only what appeared to be rotted human remains let behind. We forgot to ask where, did the kid vanish too?"

Shirley stood up then said, "I see what you are saying Pete. What you are thinking is that maybe there is some kind of connection between the two.

"Damn this is like a dream. No, it is more like a fucking nightmare, and I am caught up in it. Can't be. Are we are all a sleep and these murders, and this Two Souls is real," Chet exclaimed.

"Hell! I feel the say way Chet. But these killings are real and this thing I don't know," Pete said.

"So, now what," Chet asked.

"Now! You get the transient," Pete said.

Chet picked up the phone and dial the front desk. He asked for the transient.

"What!" Chet exclaimed out loud then hung up the phone. "You are not going to be like this Pete."

"Let's me guess the transient gave them the slip." "How did you?"

"Lucky guess Chet," Pete says then continues, "Put an A. P. B., out on him. I need the transient and I need answers. He might be the sword in the dragons back."

The investigation dragged on making the months seem more like years and there had been no sign of the transient. Their faces began to show signs of fatigue. But one thing continued to grow and that was death. It was as if this thing was gathering up a food supply for the winter. Pete's thoughts were cluttered with the many faces of the dead. There was still one thing in the midst of this turmoil that he considered to be beautiful. He had only seen her several times since it all began something about being with her put a new perspective on things. Nancy and he had somehow stumbled upon one another by fate. It was as if he had known her all his life. It was as if they were linked for some unknown reason. Dejavu! Perhaps. It was inevitable that they should meet. Pete fumbled through the paperwork on the desk.

"What time is it?"

"Five p. m. on the money," Shirley replies.

"Ah! Here it is," he told himself then reached for the phone and dialed the number on the paper.

Pete pulled out his cell phone and began to dial. Hell, things were not getting any better at the moment. Besides what did he have to loose. It was a strange time that called for strange measures he thought to himself.

"Hello!" Nancy answered.

"Nancy this is Pete," he said as he felt the palms of his hands began to sweat like a teenager's trying to get his first date.

"Yes, detective. Tell me what can, I help you with.

"I would like to know," there was a short paused and he repeated what he said then continued on with the question, "I would like to know if you would like to have dinner with me."

There was a pause that seemed slightly longer than it was or at least this is what Pete felt.

"Pete I would love to have dinner with you." "Then how about, eight?"

"Eight sounds good Pete."

"Then eight it is," he said then hung up the phone then said to himself, "yes I think this is going to be a good day for once."

Pete stood went to the coat rack pulled Baby Blue his Springfield from its holster and checked it as he always did before putting on the holster. He popped out the clip examined it thoroughly. He placed it back into the housing slapped it secure into place. He put the Springfield back into the holster and put it on then put on his coat.

"I do not know about you two but I am going to take a break from all this before it drives me crazy."

"Well! Don't we look all handsome Pete," Shirley said. "Whoa! Looking sharp buddy looking sharp. Things between you and the nurse getting hot and heavy," Chet says. "Get off it, Chet," Pete said.

"Whoa," both Chet and Shirley said at the same time.

Pete's mine raced on he knew his partners needed a little time off as well. He thought for a moment and came up with the ideal that it would be a good move to invite them to have dinner with them. Just in case something went wrong with his date.

"I need you two to meet me at the new restaurant off of Lamar around eight tonight."

"What about the reporter? You know he is waiting out there like a hawk," Chet said.

"That is right Pete. He had been hanging around like a vulture waiting for food scraps," Shirley added.

"Well! Give him a biscuit the man wants a story well then give him a story. I know you two can figure something out. For now get rid of the bastard. Keep an eye on him and don't let him out of your sight until you know you can make a clean break."

As they walked out of the building and began to walk down the stairs Pete spotted the news van parked at the corner.

"Do! You see the news van." "Why, yes indeed I do," Chet said.

"Yes, to the left about ninety degrees," Shirley replied. "Man if I was a sniper I could have blown that son of a bitch away easily," Chet exclaimed.

"Check it out Pete he is trying to hide behind the newspaper," Shirley added then chuckled then added, "I can't believe that crap."

"You two go and take care of the reporter so I can get out of here without a tail."

Pete watched his partners turn the corner as he remained at the bottom stairs of the precinct building. He lit a cigarette and waited. He watched Chet sneak up around the news van. He watched Shirley making her way to the driver side of the van. She was as good as any soldier he had seen in Nam. He smiled and threw his cigarette away and walked up to his car and drove off. Just as James put down the newspaper Chet tapped on passenger window then squatted down out of sight. Then like a jack-in the box he sprung up. The reporter and his assistant were taken aback startled jumping back.

"What the hell do you think you are doing," James snapped.

At that moment Shirley opened the driver side door and pushed the man as she pointed her gun at the man. She climbed in sandwiching James between her and his assistant.

"Don't even say a word just sit there and listen." "Listen to the lady," Chet added hoping she had something

good up her sleeve.

"You want a story. Well, we want to give you one," Shirley said.

"This some kind of sick joke you two are playing for your boss?" James questioned.

"Look do you want a story or not?" Shirley asked. "Yes," James replied and just looked at her.

"You, what is your name?" Chet asked the assistant. "Tom."

"Get your ass in the back like right now."

The man hurried into the back of the van and Chet climbed in.

"Well! Let's go get you that story," Chet exclaimed. James thought the matter over for a moment before Shirley broke his train of thought. "Well?

"Okay! Let's go get the story." Shirley and Chet climbed out of the van.

"Get your camera and follow us," Shirley said as she closed the door to the driver side of the van.

"Tom, do you have your cell phone?" "Yeah! I do."

"Good get out call Sandy to come and pick you up from here."

"Well! Big guy you coming," Chet told him as he began to cross the street to their car.

"It better to be good," James shouted out to Chet. Moments later Chet pulled up to the capitol and parked.

James pulled up climbed out of the van with the camera and walked up to Chet and Shirley as they climbed out of the car.

"What the hell are we doing here?" James asked a little miffed.

"Look you want a story, and we want to give you one. What better way to start off the story than the look at the criminal's mind," Shirley told him.

"That is a crock of shit! James shouted angrily. "No, I just want to go over some of the things and I thought they would prove valuable to you on your documentary. Then later tonight we meet up with Pete and you get the rest of the story."

Chet looked at her then leaned forward and whispered into her ear, "you are crazy."

"Pete told us to give him a story," Shirley tells Chet as they walked back to the car then added, "he said to keep an eye on the man and what better way to do just that than to have the man at our side where we can see him.

"So, I gather you are going to tell Pete look who's coming to dinner. Did you forget he said to make, a clean break."

"Look he is not buying, and I don't think we are going to get a clean break we just have to keep him at our side."

"James bring your camera we're going to dinner." "What about the story?"

"James the best place to get a story is to be right there when it happens right," Shirley says.

"True," James agreed then said, "what about my van?"

The van will be fine just leave it parked and we will bring you back to get the vehicle later. James walked to their car and put his camera into the back seat then climbed in.

Twenty minutes later they had arrived at the restaurant. I n s i d e found a table then waited for Pete. Eight p.m., came around then fifteen more minutes passed.

"Do we wait, or do we order," Shirley asked. "I am thinking the same as you," Chet said.

They ordered and waited. The reporter was beginning to annoy Chet if he asked just one more time about his story he would kick him.

"Ah! The food is here," Shirley said as she saw Pete walk in then added, "look at mister Don Juan."

Pete strolled in with Nancy holding on to his arm. Chet looked at his watch he would have to razz, Pete for making them wait thirty minutes longer than what he had said. Pete turned and looked in their direction. Chet looked at him then shrugged his shoulders he then pointed to Shirley. Shirley continued to look at the couple as they were being seated then thanked Chet for pointing the finger at her.

"Just throw men under the bus Chet."

"Nancy looks good in her red evening gown don't you think."

Pete must of went and bought himself a new suit. They looked good together Shirley thought to herself.

"Excuse me for a sec," Chet said as he scooted his chair back then stood.

He walked up to Pete's table. "Pete, Miss Gamble," Chet greeted.

"What the hell is the reporter doing here?" Pete asked. "You said keep an eye on him. What better way to do just that than to have him here us."

"You know Chet it makes sense you and Shirley enjoy each other's company. Oh, one more thing, keep that scab away from me tonight."

Chet returned to his table and sat down then said, "I guess we dine alone."?

"So, what about my story?" ask the reporter.

"You are going to get a story and it is going to say "officer beats the crap out of reporter and leaves him for dead.

Now ease up and enjoy the meal and the atmosphere," Chet said as he began to cut a piece of his steak. Pete reached over and grabbed Nancy's hand in to his. One of the waitresses walked up to the table to take their order.

CHAPTER 19

Suddenly the nightmare became a reality. Screams echoed out. People frantically moved back away from the large windows in front of the restaurant. They screamed as they saw the demon diving down like a missile at the window. The sound of shattering glass echoed out through the restaurant. Glass fell like a million rain drops of crystal to the floor below.

"Nancy, get under the table. Stay there until I tell you to come out."

"Pete, Pete," Nancy cried out.

"It's going to be all right just stay under the table and don't come out until I tell you to."

Two Souls landed on one of the tables. Its demon head swayed back and forth quickly scanning the inside of the place. Blood splattered on several people from the table as it bent forward and shot its razor-sharp claws across a man's face severing his flesh like paper. Pete's nightmare was unraveling right before his eyes. The subhuman life form jumped off the table and landed on its dragon like feet firmly on the ground. Its reptilian tongue whipped in and out of its mouth like a black whip. Pete's mind began to swim with confusion. He did not want to grasp it as reality. It had to be an illusion of his own mind. No, it was no illusion it was as real as anything that breathed air. One of the waiter rushing to safety stumbled over one of the chairs. Two Souls lunged forward shooting out its hand. The sharp claws shot across just inches above the waiter's head. A woman screamed in horror. Then like

216

a shadow the demon disappeared when the lights came on. It moved and was upon a man that was trying to exit through the entrance doors. It spoke in a gruff raspy tone.

"Not today."

In a blink of an eye it was in front of the man. There was no time for the man to react. Like a piston moving in and out of a motor its hand sunk into the, man's stomach. And as it moved bring back its hand it brought with it the man's intestines in its grasp. It held them up high above its head as if in victory. Another woman began to scream in horror. Her screams were futile. In that instant the demon struck across her back as she ran toward the broken window to escape. It wasn't like she felt pain but more like she became frozen in place as fear sunk in. Suddenly like one closing a book after reading it her body bent forward. Her dress stained with blood then as her body bent further the flesh opened like a large mouth exposing the red meat then exposing her insides. Her body folded in half and toppled over. Screams of panic and horror filled the night.

"God what is that?"

A man's voice shouted out in disbelief. "The window," a woman cried out.

More screams echoed through the restaurant and many more found their demise at the hands of Two Souls. Children cried helplessly for a mother or father to come to their side. The demon honed in on one of the children. It did not discriminate on who it was to kill. It trotted up to the child that held tightly to her mother. The mother tried to hold her daughter in her arms. The demon grabbed her by the arm and pulled her out of her mother's hands. The girl's mother reached out and grabbed desperately at the daughter. The demon leered at the mother then severed her arm at the elbow. She screamed in horror seeing her own hand dangle from the child's shoulder as it still held on.

Two Souls brought the girl up to its face. It looked into her eyes as it studied the girl. After a moment as if it had put thought in to is decision its fangs tilted into the forty five degree angle. Its fangs dripped of human blood. For a flash of a second the demon's eyes changed back to that of Jesse's. It lowered the girl back to the floor and released her. The girl rushed to her mother side. She tugged at her crying out to awaken but the life had flown out of her body. She looked up at the demon as it turned. It began to move towards Chet and Shirley's table. Chet moved instantly his reflexes quickly taking over. He tumbled over the table then knocked it over on its side. Chet and Shirley positioned themselves behind it. James stood grabbed his camera. He switched on the camera light and moved up towards the demon.

"Get back here, you crazy son of a bitch," Chet shouted urgently.

Shirley fired at the demon as it trotted towards them. "Chet forget about the asshole and help me get it away from us before it is too late and we become its dinner."

Shirley reloaded and aimed then released the tension on the trigger as James got in her way. Can't the dumb fool see it is getting to close to him? Pete thought to himself as he aimed at the demon's back. Pete's gun echoed out like a giant firecracker and Two Souls let out a horrifying screeching sound. It turned and closed its wings around its torso deflecting the oncoming assault of bullets. The bullets lodged safety into the thick hide of its wings.

"This is going to be the best footage ever on tape," James excitedly said out loud.

"You dumb shit!" Pete shouted.

The demon turned and glared with a hatred for James. Shirley fired in hope of saving the overly zealous reporter but it was no use. Two Souls shifted the bullet missed by a fraction of an inch.

"Stay under the table Shirley," Pete said as he moved forward and used another of the tables for cover.

As the demon moved towards James a waitress panicked and began to run for the doors. Chet saw the demon shift and its eyes focused on the girl.

"Fuck! Shirley cover me," Chet shouted.

As Chet began to run and just by a mere second as the demon lifted its hand to strike out at the girl he dove. He grabbed the girl by the waist and plummeted to the ground. A second later and she would have died by the demons hand. They looked at the demon as it turned.

"Look at me not at the demon," Chet tells her then continues, "on the count of three we run towards the entrance door."

The demon moved rapidly in their direction.

"Jump," Chet shouted as he grabbed her hand, and they dove over a table.

They rolled to a stop he aimed his gun and fired several rounds. The demon covered its torso with one of its wings. It looked at the people moving towards the windows. It shifted and headed for the windows as people got up off the floor to make a desperate attempt to escape. It was too fast. Before the people knew it was upon them. As they reached the windows it cut them down. A man sprung for freedom it lashed out ripping the man's back open. As the man leaned back from the searing pain it struck out again cutting across the man's neck. It watched as the man's head folded backwards and hung from a strand of flesh. It was like slow motion his body wobbled several times and he fell to the ground. It thrust its hand out and caught another holding the woman up by her neck with its fingers protruding through her throat. With its other hand it lunged out and severed a man's thigh. The man fell to the ground in agonizing pain. The woman in its grasp grabbed frantically at its hand.

Her eyes opened wide with fear as she tried to breathe. Her cry for help muffled out by the demon's fingers running from the front of her neck to the back. Several people did manage to jump out of the window but landed hard on the ground below. Their bones broke and fractured from the force of pressure on the limbs at impact. Two Souls looked at the woman then threw her out of the window again letting out the screeching sound. It had tossed her out like a child throwing a rag doll. People scrambled on the ground like chickens with their heads cut off. Some in fact did have their heads cut off. Two Souls reached out and picked another victim. It lifted him up and injected its poison into his neck like a baker filling a jelly doughnut with cream.

"I need to get a better shot at this damn thing," Pete said to himself.

The demon sensed his movement and it shifted and headed toward Pete. Pete dove and rolled and shot hitting the demon in the neck. The demon let out its horrifying screech and a yellowish glow appeared where the bullet had hit. It illuminated the puncture wound of the bullet. In a matter of seconds, it had healed itself. This was not good Pete mind raced. Shirley stood and fired emptying her revolver into the demon's back. The demon moved its wing her bullets lodging into them as it shield itself.

"Come on just a little closer," Pete said then squeezed another round off.

It let out the screeching sound again. One thing Pete knew was that it did feel pain and if it felt pain there had to be a way to kill it. A glow appeared again from the puncture wounds and again it had healed itself as before. It swayed its head back and forth studying Pete. It then began to move toward him.

"Oh God no," Pete thought to himself as he saw the demon stop in front of the table where Nancy hid under.

It sniffed the air and had honed in on her scent. It looked at Pete as if it knew she was his girl. Revenge but it was impossible Pete thought but he knew different. It had spoken this was a human quality. When the demon reached down and tossed the table away. Pete knew there was no time to think. He reacted quickly he began to call to the demon.

"Over here, you ugly shit," Pete shouted waving his hands back and forth.

Two Souls grabbed Nancy by one of her arms and drug her behind it like a rag doll moving towards Pete.

"That's it come on come on just a little more."

Pete lifted the Springfield from his side. Two Souls was too swift its hand moved in to quick. Pete had aimed and had begun to squeeze the trigger. Two Souls knocked the gun out of his hand. The metallic sound of the gun echoed out as it moved across the floor. Pete scrambled for his weapon. Two Souls stepped in front of him it flapped its wings then stood there leering down at him. Its wings spread out halfway. It shifted its head from one side to the other as it studied him. Its radar sensors picked up on the three bullet wounds on his back. Pete rolled over and looked up at the same time James had moved in for a better angle. The camera's light focused in on the demon. Two Souls moved toward James. James moved back and stumbled over a dead body. He quickly stood and moved back until his back had hit the wall. The light switch of the restaurant sticking into his back. The demon struck out its hand crushing through the wall. It clenched its hand around the electrical wires yanking them out. Electrical sparks and fire shot out of the wall. How had it known that the wires were back there? Could it indeed think was it intelligent Pete thought to himself. Suddenly the lights went out.

"Chet, Shirley," Pete called out.

"I'm still here Pete," Chet replied back as he held his gun out in front.

"I'm doing Pete," Shirley answered as she held her gun out in front with both hands.

Her eyes searching for any movement. Sparks from the light switch came to life somehow. The wires must have fused themselves together enough to allow the lights to come back to life. The flickering, lights gave the place a strobe light effect. The scenario below played out in slow motion. The grotesque form of the demon shifted its head from side to side. Its red and yellow eyes reflecting the light off of them. James continued to take his footage. The demon flapped its wings throwing James off balance. In a matter of a seconds, it was upon him. It severed his head. James head fell to the floor with a thud his mouth still open in surprise. The camera fell out of his hand and the light went wild in all directions as it rolled to a stop. The camera stopped landing in perfect aim towards James head. Chet loaded his weapon and aimed at anything that moved. The strobe light effect caused confusion his wits thrown off by the flickering of the lights. Pete dove for his gun as he grabbed it Two Souls moved in front of him. It leered down at him.

"Chet cover me," Shirley said as she moved around to take a shot at the demon.

She fired and hit the demon in the abdomen it screeched out in pain. Again, the wound began to glow and healed in front of their eyes.

"I have him in sight I have a shot," Chet called out. "Hold your fire Chet you might hit Pete," Shirley replied back.

"The hell you say," Chet exclaimed and let loose of several rounds echoed out.

Two Souls flapped its wings deflecting the bullets. Pete took this opportunity he rolled to his right and fired hitting the demon several times in the neck. But it had been like a mosquito bite to the demon it turned and rushed Chet and Shirley.

"Move Shirley move," Chet shouted.

"Where to," Shirley said as she looked around.

"To the kitchen," Chet said as he past her running as fast as he could.

Shirley did not question him this time she just followed running after him. Two souls just feet away from them and it was gaining on them fast.

"Dive," Chet cried out.

Chet and Shirley dove at the same time sailing through the double doors leading into the kitchen. Shirley hit the floor and rolled. Chet had been stopped in midflight and midway through the double doors. The demon had grabbed him by one of his legs. Shirley positioned herself by the stove and aimed at the door. Chet's body fell to the floor like a sack of potatoes. Chet kick in desperation his pant leg ripped and he was freed. Chet moved quickly into the kitchen. Two Souls stopped momentarily at the double door. It then walked through but for some reason it turned back around. It then walked back out into the restaurant. It walked up to Pete in a slow trot. Its dragon like feet echoing out with each step on the wood floor. Pete reloaded and aimed the demon reached down and lifted him up by the neck. It looked at him as if it had found interest in him. It snarled at him viciously its intense hate had grown. Its jaws began to protrude its fangs shifted into position. Its excretion dripped rapidly from its fangs as it opened its mouth wide.

"No. Leave him alone," Nancy shouted pleading with the demon.

The hate from the demon vanished as he looked down at Nancy. It was as if one were seeing a dog look at his master faithfully. It lowered Pete back down to the floor. It was like beauty and the beast. It was as Nancy had put a spell on the demon at least for the moment. Pete took Baby Blue and aimed he squeezed the trigger. Click!

"Shit! Pete said out loud looking at the demon The sound of his weapon being empty was the most horrifying sound for him or any officer when in a conflict that depended on life or death. Pete reached down to his belt to retrieve another clip. Two Souls swung its arm sending Pete over a table. The abomination walked forward and hunched down over him. Its lips pressed back in a snarl. Pete looked into the demon's eyes. At that moment he knew in a way what the demon wanted. Somehow, he knew that the only reason he was still alive was because of Nancy. Pete ejected the empty clip from his gun to the floor then dropped his weapon. Two Souls opened its mouth exposing its fangs. Chet and Shirley opened the kitchen door and stared at what was playing out. If they fired the weapons at the demon it would cut Pete down.

There was no need to think it was just what would happen. Pete remained on his knees and turned towards the kitchen. He could see Shirley supporting her weapon on Chet's shoulder ready to fire on the demon. Shirley's mind raced on as she asked herself if she should take the shot. Maybe she should pinch herself before she attempted it. Maybe she would wake up from this terrible nightmare. She knew it wasn't a dream in a way she was just hoping. When she had hit the kitchen floor and rolled it hurt too much for her to be dreaming. Right now, she had to be in hell, and it was her punishment to do battle with this winged demon. A battle of good against the Devil her mind continued on.

"Don't fire that weapon," Pete shouted bringing her back to the present.

"What? That thing is about to kill you."

"Just put the weapon down slowly and just wait."

"You are crazier than I thought," She told Pete then did what he wanted.

"Chet do the same and don't ask any question just do as I say."

Chet did as he was told apprehensively. Two Souls stepped forward and kicked Pete's gun further away from his reach. Pete stared at his gun. His good luck. He had even given it the name Baby Blue. The gun scrapped along the floor then stopped. Pete felt helpless not having his gun at his side. It made him feel as if he were naked and at the mercy of the demon. Two Souls looked down at Nancy. Its snarl had vanished it tilted its head and looked towards Chet and Shirley. It looked at them letting them know that if they made a foolish move, it would kill Pete.

It would kill him and not hesitate to do so. It then crouched down almost touching Pete's face with its hand. Then abruptly it stood erect and began a quick trot towards the windows. It flapped its wings and darted out into the night. Pete stood retrieved his gun and placed it back into his shoulder holster. Nancy hugged him tightly Pete could feel Nancy's body quivering next to his. Chet and Shirley made their way to them making their way around the many dead. The place looked like a battlefield with wounded waiting to be transported to a hospital. Or waiting for then medic to come. Through the whole ordeal the camera had continued to take footage of James' decapitated head. Chet picked up the camera and used the light to scan inside the restaurant.

"Jesus! Chet exclaimed then added, "What the fuck was that thing?"

Shirley closed James' eyes shut at the same time trying to keep her own sanity in tack, "only in the movies," she told herself as she walked up to Pete.

Moans of despair could be heard as the loved ones of the dead caught sight of their family members mutilated bodies. A woman cried out as she held her boyfriend tightly rocking him back and forth in her arms.

"I love you Laura," the man said as the last gasp of breath escaped from his dying lips.

Somehow the lights in the restaurant managed to come back on. Pete brushed himself off then looked at the living before him walking around no more than zombies in a daze. He was now more determined than ever to kill this Two Souls. Or was this demon actually the devil himself either way he was going to find a way to kill it or it would kill him. Was this thing following him now and if so, why? Why did it want him? From the very beginning nothing made any sense. Nothing added up. Where had it come from? It was something that had been released from hell or was it from the heavens his mind raced on. Wherever it had come from it definitely was not a friendly E. T. There were no answers for him at the time for his questions. The only thing he had an answer for was that it was indeed intelligent. Its cunning made it that much harder to capture and that was if it wanted to be captured. It managed to elude them and evaded capture. It tracked them down and it just looked at Nancy but why? What would be its next maneuver? Sirens filled the air and moments later cops rushed into the restaurant at the ready to do battle.

"What the hell happened here?" Frazier asked.

"Frazier if I were to tell you, you wouldn't believe it," Pete answered back.

"Looks like the reporter got his story," Blendez quipped.

"Hell of a way to get a story don't you think," Chet replied.

"I'll go ahead and take care of things here Pete." Frazier told Pete.

"Thanks Frazier," Pete said and put his arm around Nancy's waist and began to walk out then stopped and turned around, "if anyone has any questions? I'll be in the office bright and early tomorrow," he said and continued out of the building.

Frazier began to bark out orders then turned to Chet and Shirley and told them to go home and to get some sleep. Frazier knew they probably would not get any sleep that night. But the rest away from the scene would do them good.

"Pete, I don't want to stay alone tonight," Nancy pleads to Pete. Pete opened the passenger side door for her to get in before he could say he was taking her home.

"Where is it you would like for me to take you to?" "I'd like to stay with you tonight if you don't mind." "Okay," Pete said then waited for her to be seated and buckled her in then climbed into the vehicle. He made his way around the fire trucks, the police cars with their lights blinking on and off. He past the vehicles drove away.

CHAPTER 20

Pete stared at the ceiling sleep tugging away at his eyelids as he fought to stay awake. He lifted his hand up to his face and pushed the light button on his wristwatch. Four a.m. in the morning. He rolled over grabbed the remote off the coffee table and turned on the television. He listened for a while then rolled over on his side. His hand falling upon a fleshy substance that was Nancy's buttock. Pete was surprised and moved his hand back quickly. He then smiled he had forgotten for a moment that Nancy had spent the night with him and was about to jump off the couch. His hand went into a search mode as he slowly investigated the smoothness of her body. He jokingly poked at her buttocks. They had spent an intimate moment of passion as they forgot the rest of the world for a short period of time. The evil had brought them together in a way it was a good thing. And in another way, it would be something they would both remember for the rest of their lives. He just hoped that the good would outweigh the bad and that they would learn to beat the horrible memory that had brought them together. Perplexing as it was their affection for one another was flourishing in the midst of the ugliness. Nancy suddenly stirred under his touch awakening. Pete kissed her behind the neck and lay back.

On occasions he looked at the clock ticking away. Six fifteen a.m. Pete stared at the clock he felt that something was not quite right. Something had gone wrong something he could not think of. What was it? There was no answer his mind was a blank. He had a gut feeling and it was gnawing at his insides. Pete picked up the remote clicked on the on button and the television came to life again. He pushed the channel button to change channels. A woman reporter sat behind a large desk in the center of the screen. She began to speak.

"I will be filling in for James," she said.

The words cutting deep into Pete brain. The horror of the previous night hit him like a sledge hammer. Last night James was killed in a brutal way just for news. One of the crew walked up to her and handed her a piece of paper and whispered into her ear.

"Read what is written on the sheet of paper," he said then walked back off the set.

She looked straight into the camera.

"Here is an update. Last night a massacre was due to our serial killer and James was one of the victims," her voice betraying her bewilderment.

On the left corner of the television live footage of the demon and the massacre came on. It was James last news footage and in a way he had been right it would have won him an award. Pete watched as the demon lifted his hand and decapitated James head off on live air. The camera focusing on Two Souls hideous face then focusing back to James body as it plummeted to the floor without his head.

"Is this a savage act of crime committed by one man or an attack of some kind of animal?" she asked then said, "Or is it just another sick joke mastered up by some demented mind to cause fear and panic in this city for his own deranged amusement? Will they catch him before there is another person killed?" The rest of the story at eleven. Now for the weather."

Pete cut the television off. He was glad that Nancy had not seen the news footage. He climbed off the couch and went into the kitchen and put on a pot of coffee. He needed to get something inside him that would help him stay awake. He went into the bathroom and washed the sleep away from his eyes. He could already smell the aroma of the freshly brewed coffee. The smell of coffee quickly spread through the house. Nancy stirred underneath the blankets. The smell wakened the senses of her nose. She turned over onto her back and yawned. Pete entered the room with two cups in his hand. She looked at him then smile and reached out her hand. Pete handed her the coffee and was in awe of her perfect body. At least this is what he thought. Round were round should be and flat where flat should be he thought then smiled. Pete cut the television off. He was glad that Nancy had not seen the news.

"Smells good Pete."?

"Why yes it does," he replied and sat down on the couch next to her.

The feeling of something that was wrong came back and no sooner did think of it when the phone rang. Pete stood and went to the phone on the kitchen wall.

"Hello."?

"Pete," Chet shouted excitedly. "What's wrong Chet," Pete asked?

"Pete, it came back. The thing came back." "What do you mean it came back?"

"Last night this Two Souls, demon, devil, whatever you wish to call it came back to the restaurant."

"Okay relax and back up and start from the beginning."

Chet took a couple of deep breath then began to speak, "we had driven about half a mile Shirley began to analyze what had happen and said it was impossible that such a thing could even exist. She argued that with all the special equipment today one could create the same special effects. Such as monsters, demons, and things that fly. Or in fact they could make whatever they wanted to create. I kept telling her it was real as you and I.

I told her that it was just too real to have been concocted up by some man. I asked about the bullets of course she came out with he probably wore a bullet proof vest. Then it hit her she said drive back I just remembered something. I asked her what it was. I saw everything she had seen. She said in that doctor tone blood doesn't glow. I said yeah so. She then insisted that I turn the car around and head back. She said that it was the only way she could explain it. I did as she requested and no sooner had I turned around, boom. It was like a dark hole in the universe had opened. It shot across the windshield at an amazing speed. It was like a blur when it shot past the front of the car. It circled around then dove in closer scraping the windshield with its claws as if to torment us. As if to scare us shitless. It stayed ahead of us then it disappeared. We figured it flew the coop and that it had probably gotten tired of the game and left. I told Shirley we should go to the precinct and think about it some more. I told her we could come back in the morning. And that we could think it out. But she insisted that the evidence probably would not be any good then. That's when it landed on the hood of the car and peered in through the windshield at us snarling viciously. I thought I had seen it up close before. But shit not like this though. Hideous Pete there are no words to explain what we saw up close. I looked into its red and yellow eyes and its human eye.

My hands seemed to become paralyzed I couldn't move them. Shirley took several shots at it. It pushed off and it was gone that quick. Never in all my life have I ever experienced such evil Pete. This thing is a thing from hell," Chet's voice broke in despair. He regained his composure then continued to speak. This thing landed back on the hood. I floored it and swerved the car to see if I could knock it off the car. But it managed to stay on as if its feet had been glued to the vehicle. Moments later it smashed in the windshield breaking it like a thin piece of glass. I can still hear Shirley's scream. I lost control of the car for a few seconds as I tried to help Shirley fight the demon off. It tried repeatedly to grab her I made a fast turn and headed up Fifth Street heading east. I managed to get rid of it for a few seconds. But again, it was no use it landed on the back of the car. Shirley pointed her gun blindly over her shoulder and just squeezed of rounds. It screeched out in pain I guess that made it madder. It broke the back window and grabbed her by the hair. Shirley shot again blindly hitting it again and again. It flew away I don't think it was because it was hit. But because it was playing its cat and mouse game with us. It was as if it was having fun at are expense. It seemed to find pleasure in its game of torment. I stepped on the accelerator and went under the I-5 over pass.It hit us broadside sending the car up on two tires.

I held on firmly to the steering wheel then remembered to move the wheel back to the left slowly. Somehow, I made it up to Seventh Street I turned left to head into the parking lot under the bridge. It hit us hard sending us in a spin. I lost control as the front tire hit the curb. My head hit the steering wheel and the world went black. When I came to Shirley was screaming urgently for me to help her. I managed to open my eyes focusing them on Two Souls as it approached the car. I could see the look on its face, and it was not good. It had tired of the game. It was going to make sure we did not get away alive. We were trapped inside the car we were no more than half a block away from the precinct. Officers came out of the building running to our aid. Others pulled up in their vehicles screeching to a halt. They climbed out of their cars ready to do battle with the demon. The battle was futile they had only walked into their own demise. It took their lives one by one tearing their bodies apart like small rag dolls. It turned and looked straight at us then vanished. Sgt. Johnson swung around and tried to get to us. I tried to get out of the car, but the door was jammed shut where it had crashed into it. As soon as it saw Johnson trying to get out of his vehicle it vanished and was upon him. He was all most out. You know he is a big man. He had his right hand on the seat as he pushed his three hundred and thirty pounds up right.

Its speed was incredible Pete there was no time. The door shut Pete. It shut as if there had been no one standing in front of it. His head fell to one side. It rolled hit the side mirror and bounced to the ground his jugular pumping away. Blood spew everywhere. His ankles were cut off his head had popped off and his torso remained inside the car. It was held in position by the door as it held on to his flesh. I don't even think he had enough time to scream. Blendez would have been next, but he managed to hit the demon in the neck throwing him off balance for a second. It gave him enough time to dive under one of the trucks parked in the parking lot. It reached Blendez and it tried time and time to get him. It reached down and searched with his hand for Blendez. It then got tired it lifted the truck from the front. The men let out with gunfire from their positions. From behind the concrete pillars, cars, some just out in the open. They fired emptying their weapons at it. It flapped its wings with a tremendous force the bullets seemed to be persuaded by the force of air. The bullets fell to the ground while others went around it. The men had to cease fire afraid that a stray bullet would hit their partners or them. A few of the larger caliber rounds just lodged in its leather like wings. Shirley began to make a break for it. She began to climb out the passenger window. She was halfway out when it landed next to my door. Shirley stopped in her tracks not wanting to make a sudden move and draw attention to herself. As I said before it did not matter. Nothing mattered it was gunning for us Pete. You can say the others killed to night were just freebies. I unbuckled my safety belt and dove into the back seat. It did not seem to care at this time it just moved in a slow trot knowing I was looking on.

One of Shirley's legs was completely out touching the ground. Suddenly the screams that I dreaded to hear came. I knew it had killed her. It swung its arm and ripped open Shirley's thigh to the bone. Pete. Chet's voice broke he paused for a moment then continues, "She screamed out in such pain then fell backwards out of the car. The next thing happened so quickly. I moved to the window she was standing with her intestines coming out. She tried to put them back in. There was nothing I could do Pete but just look on. It moved forward bent down slightly and glared at me. I knew I was next but then I realized it was not the same look it had given us before. It tuned and vanished. All it left was death and its destruction. I think it was leaving a message for you Pete."

"Calm down Chet," Pete said then asked, "where are you right now?"

"I'm here at the hospital waiting for the doctor to come out of the I. C. U. with some word on how she's doing." "I'll call the Chief and I'll be right down."

"The Chief has been here with me since she was admitted to the hospital."

"All right I'll be there in about fifteen minutes."

Eighteen minutes later Pete arrived at the hospital and walked down the corridor to the I. C. U. He could see Chet pacing back and forth down the corridor in front of the double doors to the care unit. It was like seeing a nervous cat about to go crazy. Chet was in a distraught state. He rubbed his hands together feeling guilty for what happened to Shirley. He knew there was nothing he could have done. If he had tried Two Souls would have cut him down instantly as well. But still it was guilt for the feeling that he was lucky to have gotten away without a scratch. Chet stopped suddenly then looked up.

"Don't you lose it now Chet calm yourself down we have much work ahead of us yet."

"I'll be all right Pete."

"Good, now grab one of these cups of coffee off my hands."

Chet took one of the cups then sipped at the black liquid inside.

"Everything is going to be all right."

"Pete all I want to do is to go out and find that damnation and kill it."

"I know Chet. I know I'm kind of fond of her to."

Chief Golds walked up to them holding to cups of coffee. "Well I guess you beat me to the punch."

"I guess I did Chief. Here I'll take the extra caffeine I need the boost," Pete told him as he reached out his hand.

"Here you go. I must have just missed you." "Any word on Shirley as of yet?"

"None as of yet Pete," Golds replied back then faced Chet, "why don't you go downstairs and lay down on one of the sofas in the waiting room Chet."

"I did nothing to help her Chief."

"Chet, you did all you could do. If you had tried to help here, you would probably not be standing there right now. Now stay focus because what we have to do is capture this thing before it is too late. And if you give me any inclination that you are going bananas I will pull you off this case so fast your head will spin got it."

"Understood Chief," Chet said looking straight into the man's eyes letting the Chief know he was still with them.

"Okay, now do you have something to say Pete," said Golds as he saw the look on Pete's face.

"No, not really Chief."

"Good. Now whatever you need as fire power goes. I will approve it."

"What about downtown?"

"The hell with downtown let me worry about the stuck-up ties."

Doctor Samuel's walked out of the I. C. U. He walked up to the group of men looked at them studying their faces. He could see the concern on them like writing on paper.

"How is she doc.?"

"With a little rest she will be just as good as ever Pete.

The cuts were clean lacerations none of the vital organs were damaged. Thank God for that. It was luck. You know that fine tissue that holds your guts in before you cut completely through it must have barely been cut through. Gravity assisted in pushing her guts out making it seem worse. She will have some nasty scars, but she will be fine. The laceration to her thigh was bad but again no real damage to the nerves like I said she will be as good as ever. She is a fighter that one."

"Why yes she is doc."

"Pete if I could, I would like to see you in my office for a moment."

"What is it doc?" "In my office."

Pete nodded his head turn toward Golds then says, "Chief I will be right back."

Pete and the doctor walked down the corridor. They waited for the elevator door to open then entered. Jack pushed the first-floor button and moments later the door open and the two men walked out onto the first floor. They passed several door, then stopped in front of the door that had Doctor Jack Samuel name in bold letters. He opened the door and they walked into the office.

"Sit down Pete," Jack motioned with his hand at the chair in front of his desk.

Jack walked up to one of the shelves and retrieved a video. He then walked up to the VCR. He put the tape in then faced Pete.

"Before I push the play button, I want you to know that I am very sorry. I do not know how it was misplaced. No one picked up the tape Pete. I handed it to one of the officers to give to White Cloud. Somehow it was forgotten. I founded it this morning someone had placed it on my desk. I do know this Pete it is going to tell you what you need to know without a doubt Pete."

"What the hell are you talking about?"

"Just sit there and watch what is on this tape I think you will see."

"Okay doc.," Pete said then sat back in the chair.

Pete watched the T.V. with curiosity as it came to life. What took place next was unbelievable. It was just too hard for his mind to take in. Pete mouth fell open as he saw Jesse climb out of the hospital bed covered with bandages. He watched as Jesse reached over to his arm and pulled out the intravenous feeding tube. He began to rip parts of the bandages covering his body. He tore them off like a larva in a cocoon breaking through as it metamorphosis was completed. It, Jesse, Two Souls had become whole. The metamorphosis was complete but there was no butterfly being born into the world with its beauty. Instead, what was born was the most horrifying creature man would ever lay eyes on. Jesse now was no more. Jesse had become a demon.

A demon that flapped its wings trying them out for the first time. The mucus like substance flung out into the air as the rotted human flesh gave way to what lay underneath the human flesh. It shook the skin free form its frame. How, was this possible in the twenty first century Pete's thought to himself it was just to baffling. Suddenly the name, Two Souls echoed like firecrackers going off in his head. He sighed then whispered to himself, "Goblins, Vampires, and Snakes," he reframed from say the words, "oh my," he had heard from one of the scientist fiction movies he had seen. He fought with the ideal of the legend of this Two Souls. Na! He said out softly just a legend but yet there it was staring him in the eyes from the television.

"What was that you said Pete?" "It was nothing Jack."

The knock on the door startled Pete. Jack told the person at the door to come in. A nurse entered the office she looked at Pete then at the doctor.

"Doctor the woman has awakened and refuses to take any of her medication until she talks to some Detective Rodriquez."

"Tell her we will be right there," Samuel told her. The woman turned and left the room.

"We don't make it a habit for the patient to have visitors right after they have been emitted into the I. C. U. Unless the person is about to get the last rites. In any case I don't think we should keep her waiting, Pete."

Moments later in the intensive care unit Pete walked up to the side of the hospital bed. Shirley managed to raise her hand up weakly. She placed it on top of Pete's and smiled. Her voice was in a faint whisper.

"The demon looked down at your back as if to study something on it Pete."

"What?"

"In the restaurant Pete that is why it did not kill you." "Nurse," doctor, Samuel nodded.

The nurse walked up to the other side of the bed and handed Shirley several pills in a small paper cup. This time Shirley did not hesitate she took the medicine.

"Shirley all I have on my back is three bullet wounds." "I don't know what it is Pete? But there is some kind of correlation with you and the monster and the map." "The map," Pete said.

"Triangle, the map Pete," her voice trailed off as the medicine finally took hold taking her to a deep sleep.

"What about a map Pete?"

"I will tell you what we believe Chief. First I need the team in the briefing room early tomorrow morning. I will explain everything Chief."

Back at the precinct in the briefing room Pete explained what the video contained. He explained that what was on it would be too hard to grasp as reality. The mind would tell them it was man. A movie, he told them to keep an opened mind. That the tape he was about to insert was not made but captured live on cam.

"Chet cut the lights off," he told Chet then reiterated,

"What you are about to see is something you would never have imagined even in a dream state. It is something that will stay with you even after we kill it. And I hope that we can kill it."

"Hell of a pep talk Pete," Shirley interjected.

Pete smiled then pushed the play button. When the tape was over, he stopped the video and cut the T.V., off then told Chet to put the lights back on. He walked up to the middle of room in front of all the officers.

"Any questions?" Pete said.

"Un-fucking believable," exclaimed a voice from the back of the room.

"Took the word right out of my mouth," Pete agreed. "Damn! It was better than the movies," another officer

bellowed out the added, "the special effects great."

"This is not a joke. This thing as I said before is real and it can rip out your heart and show it to you while it is still pulsating in its hand officer Williams. It's as real as you and I. You see it was the kid at the hospital all along.

Somehow, he turned into this thing. How who knows? But it is as real as you and I.

"Do you see any cameras any faces that are new in here.

This is not that fucking program where they scare people this is real life. If someone would have told me, Chet, or Shirley a week ago we would have probably thought the same. But my fellow cops we have seen it up front as well as some of your brothers in arms."

"Hell, if someone would have told me that a couple of days ago I would have told them I was having a nervous breakdown," Chief Golds tells them.

"You are right about one thing Pete." "What is that Blendez?"

"It is hard to believe even after you have seen it up close as you and I have. But still, it is out there, and we now have to believe that it exists."

"Blendez I will give you the rest of the orders to give to each of the team. And yes, it is hard to grasp but what or where it came from does not matter now. We need to find a way to kill the son of bitch."

Just as Pete and Chet where about to walk out of the briefing room Frasier and another officer came in with news.

"Detective we came across the transient we asked him if he would help us on this matter. He was reluctant at first just said that a Witchdoctor sold his soul to the devil for immortality. I was going to pull him in on a vagrant charge.

Then get this you know what the shit head said? He said that if I brought him in on some trumped up charge, he would sue the hell out of the police department. He started to ramble on some legal term and gave the number of the article and all that. Hell, this was coming from a drunken bum. I don't even know all the mumble jumble. So I thought it was better to leave him alone."

"Sometimes Frazier those bums are in that drunken stupor to try to forget who knows what. To forget whatever is eating away at them like a cancer. The bum we are talking about was an officer in the U.S. Marine Corps at one time. The man is well educated.

"Officer you say well I'll be damned."

"Yes! Indeed this case has many surprises," Pete said then added, "Sally had said that it was a sub human. The transient said it was a reptile man. It stared down at my back as if to study the bullet marks. Shirley said triangle on the map. Why did it not kill me? I have a slight idea why it won't kill Nancy for the moment."

"What reason?" ask Frazier.

"Nancy was the one who took care of it while it was still in its human state as Jesse," Pete said then as he rushed away, he told Chet to follow him into Chief Golds, office.

In Golds office Pete quickly removed his shirt as if a thousand ants where crawling on his back. He leaned over Golds desk as the man looked at him bewildered.

"Don't ask any questions Chet just grab a pen." "Now what," Chet asked.

"See the bullet wounds on my back?" "Yes."

"Well now let's play connect the dots Chet." "Damn it is a perfect triangle," Golds exclaimed.

"No, not a triangle Chief a damn pyramid Pete replied. "I know I am going to regret asking this but what does a pyramid have to do with what we are dealing with Pete?" "I don't really know I just know it has to do with mythical powers," Pete remained silent for a moment as if thinking about what he had just said then added," Chief I am going to need a lot of fire power."

"Pete, I said I would approve whatever you needed as long as you kill it."

Pete put his shirt back on then told Chet to follow him. They walked out into the corridor and began to walk to the stairs. Gloria walked up to them. Pete could see the excitement as well as determination on her face.

"You are getting closer to capturing this killer aren't you?" Gloria asked.

"I think we might just have something to go on."

"Let me be on one of the teams Pete I have the training." "Gloria we are not dealing with a human here," Pete told her.

But he knew Gloria and he knew it would not be a good enough of an answer. And besides she had been at his side in some hell of situations.

"Tell Blendez that you are on his team."

"Thanks Pete," she said and watched them walk away. "You are letting her on one of the teams after what happened to Shirley."

"I know what happen to Shirley and I also know that she is an officer and a damn good one Chet. I prefer her on one of the teams. More than I do some of the men. She's coming along Chet."

As they made it to the ground floor Pete walked up to the map on the wall by the entrance to the precinct.

"Chet grab that fire extinguisher."

Chet grabbed the extinguisher off the wall by the map. "We can ask for the key at the front desk Pete."

"We can do a lot of things Chet. Just break the glass."

Chet shook his head then lifted the extinguisher high above his head. He hit the glass with the butt end of the extinguisher breaking the glass on impact. Everyone entering or leaving the area looked on not knowing whether to run or stay put. Several officers at the front desk rushed out from behind the counter and up to the two men. Seeing the detective and recognizing him the officer stepped back.

"I have a good reason I have orders from the Chief," Pete told them knowing that the Chief would get a hold of him later on the matter, "don't have time to explain just talk to the Chief," Pete told them then grabbed the map and began to walk out of the precinct. He attempted to fold the map as he walked out of the building.

Chet turned around and handed the extinguisher to one of the officer, then followed Pete out of the building.

"Where are we heading to in such a hurry?" Chet asked. "We are going to see a friend of mine," then added,

"Here," he said as he handed him the map, "find all the murders on the map and all the missing people that you can remember off hand and mark them down on the map.

CHAPTER 21

They arrived at Herb's house one of Pete's friend minutes later. Pete faced Chet and told him to study the map and when he came up with something valuable to come and get him. Pete parked the car climbed out and walked up the stairs leading up to the house. He knocked on the door and waited patiently. A short heavy-set man with blonde hair and a piggish nose and thin lips answered the door. He opened the door seeing that it was Pete standing there he chuckled joyfully.

"Pete old man," he exclaimed.

"Herb how have you been," Pete replied greeting the man. "Herb who is it?" Herb's wife Julie called out her voice trailing through the house.

"It is the old man," Herb replied. "The old man," she asked.

"Pete, Julie its Pete." "You mean Pete, Herb?" "Yes, sir one in the same." "Tell him hi for me honey."

"As you just heard Pete, Julie says hi. Now tell me what brings you out this way Pete. Oh please forgive me. Come on in Pete."

Pete stepped inside and scanned the place it was a habit of the trade. A thief scooping out the area to rob the next day would probably have thought the same thing. Pete mine bounced back on the reason he had come to see his friend. He wondered why Herb always called him old man. The odd thing was he should be calling Herb the same thing. Herb was three years older than him. One thing about Herb that

Pete respected the most was that Herb had put himself through college without help of scholar ships or his parents. And to boot he had made a name for himself in the architect business. The house he lived in was proof enough on how Herb had done well for himself. Maybe one day I will buy myself a house up here on the west side. But first I better have a rich relative in the wood pile he thought to himself. A smile grew on his face. Herb stopped and faced Pete.

"So, tell me what is it that brought you up this way?" "I need your expert advice in a matter that pertains to saving lives," Pete told him not wanting to drop what he had to say on him like a bomb.

"Here let's step into my study old man," Herb said as he held the door open then swung his other hand in a gesture for Pete to enter the room.

"Old man, close the door behind you and tell me what, is your poison of choice. Is it still bourbon on the rocks?"

"Don't touch the stuff any longer."

Herb fixed himself a drink then stepped back around to the front of the bar and looked at Pete.

"That is great Pete that is really great."

Herb leaned against the bar putting one of his feet on the bar stool on the part that braced the rest of the chair at the bottom.

"This here is all about the thing out there doing the terrible killings."

"You heard about it all ready." "Pete it is called the news."

Suddenly the doorbell rang. The ringing became erratic. Julie, Herbs wife ran downstairs and opened the door. Chet could tell by the look on her face that she was surprised and a little miffed.

"Sorry but I need to talk to detective Rodriquez." "Come on in," she told him and walked him to the study where she knew Herb would be entertaining Pete.

Julie knocked on the door first and waited for a reply. "Come in."

Julie then opened the door. She popped her head in and looked around until she saw Herb.

"Herb someone is here to see, Pete."

Herb faced the door and saw Chet standing in the doorway holding on to a map that he seemed to be fighting with.

"Come in young man."

Chet entered the room holding on to the map by the edges. He stopped then asked Herb if he could use the bar to place the map on.

"By all means young man, do what you have to."

Placing the map on the bar top Chet pointed to the area on the map that he believed that was the place that Two Souls inhabited.

"I think you better finish telling me what I can do for you Pete," Herb says.

"Good! I was just going to get to that. The reason I appeared unannounced at your doorsteps is that I remembered reading something about the mythical powers of the pyramids. I believe that this thing did not kill me because the bullet pattern on my back resembled the triangular structure of the pyramid. Shirley believed the same. She whispered into my ear the word triangle. Then it came to me what she was trying to say Herb. She was trying to say that the connection between myself the demon and dead victims it has murdered is that they should form a triangle pattern on the map."

"I see what you are trying to picture here. So, you think it has set itself a border that limits it from killing outside of this pyramids triangle whatever you want to call it."

"Correct! Pete replied.

"I can see why you became a detective, Pete."

Herb walked up to a cabinet in back of the bar and brought back with him what appeared to be a ruler. The numbers and other signs on it would be weird enough to an ordinary person. But to Herb it was a way of making money. He had done well by making calculations. Herb placed the ruler on top of the map and began to do the numbers. Calculating would be a better word. He took the measurements multiplied this with that. He measured the inside of the triangle writing down the map's scale and multiplying more numbers. After about an hour he faced Pete.

"I might have calculated off a few centimeters thus throwing off the polygonal base and the triangular face that meets in the common vortex."

"Now! What the hell does all that mumble jumble mean?" Pete questioned.

Chet watched and just stood holding the map open in silence.

"What it means old man is that this triangle on this map could indeed be the basic form of a pyramid. This is old and could have been used in the Egyptian or the Inca time."

"I thought you said that you might be off on your calculations."

"Pete, Pete, old man when have I ever made a mistake?" Pete smiled he had to agree with the man he was a genius.

And as far as he knew Herb had never been caught or been known to have made a mistake and especially a mathematical error.

"You got all that from the map?" Chet asked puzzled. "I understand the pessimism young man. You see this triangle if it had just been a coincidence, it would have been off by a long shot. But this is perfect from angle to angle. This thing gave itself a border for a reason."

"What do you know about the Aztecs?"

"I know this. I know that they were one of the most magnificent people that ever-walked earth. These people are off springs of the Inca and the Olmecs. These Meso Americans gave us some of the most important things in the world, numbers, time, and structure for our cities and they built pyramids as well.

Whether they have powers that I cannot really say? I did read once that they had mazes inside these pyramids. Whoever went in to steal found himself lost and died within the confines of the pyramid. Now that is something you might want to look into.

"What do you mean?"

"Pete the possibility of whatever you are looking for could be lying in a place probably dead center of the triangle.

A place that could have a maze-like structure to it. A place it could call home."

"Herb thanks you've been a great help."

"One more, small bit of advice Pete this thing has to be killed with in the range of the power of the base," Herb chuckle then spoke again, "I forgot to tell you this base holds its power. How can I put it? It holds it power like a fulcrum. But this fulcrum does not pivot like a tool. It pivots its power.

In this case equalizes it out as far as the border. And that is if the stories of the pyramids are true."

"Okay, so how much distance do we have?" Chet asked. "Calculating in my head you have about two miles in each

direction. The bad news is that it can relocate. You know what they say, location, location, location."

"Now all we have to do is figure out where it will kill next." Pete said out loud.

The power lies with in Chet told himself his finger stopping abruptly on the map.

"I got it Pete."

Pete looked down where Chet was pointing. It was the old power plant.

"The old power plant," Herb said out loud then added; "you did mention that it was some kind of animal."?

"Yes, the transient said this Two Souls was half man and half serpent. See this thing you would have say the man was right."

"Yes, that would work perfect for this thing. What better you see the old power is a cool and damp place with mazes in this case tunnels. Drained pipes running in all directions underneath the city. Don't you remember walking through those damn things when we were kids Pete?

Remember how big they were. One could drive a fucking full-size car through without having any problems."

"I do remember, and you are right as always and thank you again Herb."

"Hey! Pete have I ever been wrong?"

"Guess not buddy guess not," Pete replied back.

Herb walked them out to the door he watched them go down the steps then called out.

"Door's open whenever you want Pete."

Pete turned back around, "I know Herb and thanks."

As they drove off Pete began to get a migraine again as his thoughts ran on. The dead flashed in his mind like an old movie footage repeating itself over and over. The demon tormented his very soul. Pete hated the demon, but he also knew that the kid was in there somewhere. It somehow managed to take control of him and turn him into this hideous monster. The kid was innocent with no fault in what had happened to him or what he had become. The only thing he was at the wrong place at the right time.

Pete and Chet parked in front of the precinct quickly got out of the car and ran up the stairs entered the building and ran down the stairs into the precinct armory. The man behind the wire cage greeted Pete.

"Detective Rodriquez I have been waiting for you to sho up."

"Joe," Pete greeted.

"I wish I was going on the hunting case with you," he said as he fumbled with the lock as he inserted the key into the lock to open up the door.

He let them in and then closed the door behind them as if someone would come down and rob the place. Chet looked at all the guns in different racks as they made their way down the aisles. He stopped and pulled out what appeared to be an oversized shotgun.

"Holly shit! Look at this fucking tank stopper."

Pete stopped and turned around. He noticed the look on Chet's face. It reminded him of some child in a candy store with all the different candies before him and choosing the one that caught his fancy the most.

"How about this one Pete," Chet asked.

"That one makes an elephant gun look like a B.B gun," Pete replied.

"That is no lie the rounds in that can penetrate through five inches of concrete with ease," said Joe.

"That's right Chet we can't use that God only know what would happen if someone got in the way. This Two Souls is a clever opponent. It could use the weapon against us.

"But you and I know that this thing can take a slug and rejuvenate itself," Chet interjected.

Joe reached out his hands. Chet handed over the weapon and watched the man as he began to talk as he inspected the weapon.

"I gather you have never seen a demonstration of this weapons fire power sir?" asked Joe then added, "Being, in charge of the armory and having to take details to make sure these weapons fire properly that is when this job come to life. It is fucking awesome. This weapon can definitely make a mess of things. If one of us got in the crossfire or was just near the blast there could be severe repercussions."

"Then why have them," Chet asked.

"The proper use comes up on occasions."

"What do you have that we can use Joe?" Pete asked.

"The National Guard dropped these off today matter of fact they just arrived about thirty minutes before you arrived Pete.

The Chief said you were going to need some heavy fire power I guess the Chief wanted to make sure. I put these aside for you. The fire power these have sends a rush through your body. Come with me," Joe said and took them around the corner where he had placed several of the guns on the cleaning table to be inspected.

Pete walked up to the table and picked up the weapon and slid back the loading chamber handle. He lifted the weapon up eye level and looked into the ejection port and up the firing chamber.

"M-60's good call Joe."

Pete grabbed several boxes of ammo walked up to the mesh door and place the ammo boxes down then returned and grabbed two more boxes.

"Chet," Pete said.

Chet turned and looked at him. Pete turned around without saying a word and started to walk with the ammo. Chet new what Pete had wanted without him having to say a thing, he turned back around and grabbed two more boxes of ammo then followed behind Pete. After several trips to the door Pete walked back up to the M-60 and began to field strip the weapon.

"Detective the weapons come inspected to us."

"Joe always inspects the weapon you are going to use in combat it could mean your life or theirs."

"I understand Pete I'll give you a hand."

Chet walked down the aisles and returned with a two grenade.

"How about some of these," Chet asked.

"Put the grenades back and come and help me clean this weapon," Pete said.

Chet placed the two grenades into his pockets as the guard walked back around the corner for another M-60.

"I never field stripped an M-60 before."

"No, shit!" Pete retorted as he ran the long rod with a cleaning cloth through the bore of the weapon repeating the process several times.

He lifted the weapon and inspected the bore by placing his eye next to the ejection port and looking up the barrel. After cleaning the weapon he placed it down in back of them. Joe brought another M-60 out to them.

Chet learned to inspect and clean the weapon in a matter of minutes. The phone rang several minutes later Joe went to answer it then returned with a message for Pete.

"Detective they just saw the demon in the vicinity of Town Lake."

"Well looks like are demon doesn't give a shit if someone sees it or not," Pete exclaimed.

"Pete the Chief said that it looked as if it was carrying a woman."

"Shit! It has Nancy."

"How do you know that Pete," Chet asked. "Gut feeling that is all I can tell you."

Pete hurried up front and grabbed the phone and dialed. A busy tone reached his ears. He hung up the phone and quickly returned to the weapons. He lifted the M-60 off the table and cradled it in his arms.

"Joe, open the door up and do not lock it. I am giving you the direct order. Put one of the ammo boxes in front of the door so it will not close then help us load the weapons and ammo into the car."

They reached the door. Joe stopped then stood in front of it.

"Sir, I can't open it until you sign for the weapons." "Forget my name Joe?"

"Good after we loaded the weapons in to the car Joe." "Pete I have to follow procedures."

"Joe if you don't open the damn door now son you won't have to worry who the hell is going to sign for the weapons." Pete stopped place the M-60 down and withdrew his

Springfield, he pointed the gun at the lock and slowly moved the trigger back with his thumb.

"Okay, okay I'm opening the door," Joe says as he opened the door wondering if Pete would have really shot the lock off.

They made several trips from the armory to the vehicle.

On the last trip Pete asked where he had to sign. "At the bottom Pete."

Pete signed the paper then said "there," out loud.

"I'll be right back have to have the Chief's signature as well."

"No, time to waist. Look don't worry just tell the Chief I had to leave. I am pretty sure he will sign for all the weapons. He did tell you to give me the fire power I needed. "Right!"

"Now let's not waste any more time."

Pete and Chet walked out of the back entrance to the building. As they walked to the car they spotted the news van.

"Looks like another reporter on our tail Pete."

"Don't they ever learn," Pete said then open the car door and climbed in.

He waited until Chet had climbed in turned the car on. He sighed Chet looked into the rearview mirror.

"Red head doesn't look half bad from here."

"For now, keep the rocket in the pocket partner. I hope she threw you a kiss because that is all the time you have for."

"Why don't you stop and tell her not to follow us?"

"It wouldn't do us any good besides we don't have time. I just hope she does not get in the way. Or better yet loose her pretty little head," Pete said then floored the throttle pedal.

The car's tires squealed smoke rising from the back tires as they grabbed at the pavement. Time was the essence and time was running out especially for Nancy. Her life was hanging on by every second. Pete knew it had not killed her. Whatever the reason was or the connection between them was did not matter along as she was still alive. But it might have changed its mind. All Pete knew was that this Two Souls was becoming more and more dangerous. Pete swerved around the corner coming to close for comfort to a telephone pole on the passengers, side.

"What the hell are you trying to do kill us? Aren't we supposed to kill the demon first?"

Pete's mind continued to race on had Nancy found her demise at the hands of this demon. No, she is still alive he told himself. The thought ate away at him why had it carried her off in broad daylight? It was strange it had eluded them all along and now it did not matter. Was this its challenge to him? Pete swerved around another corner the vehicle jumping the curve. Again, the car was in a collision course but this time it was with a streetlamp.

"The street lamp," Chet cried out as he held onto the dash with both hands.

Pete cut the wheel to the right missing the streetlamp just by an inch.

"What the fuck are you trying to do kill us?"

"Don't worry you have a seat belt on, don't you? Hell, you are in good hands with Pete I'll get you l get you there in one piece."

"Shit! You are crazy you know that?"

"Damn everybody cusses around me," Pete retorted. "Yeah! And I wonder why Pete."

Pete drove past the South First Bridge, then suddenly in the midst of all the traffic he put on the brakes and turned the wheel right making an abrupt U-turn in front of the east bound traffic. All one could hear were the squeals of tires and horns blasting out. Pete jumped the curb on the other side and the car remained half on the street and half on the grass. Pete threw the car into park. It seemed he was out and standing looking out over the lake before the engine had completely stopped running.

By the time Chet had climbed out Pete was already taking out the weapons.

"Chet get on the radio and get Blendez out here. Tell him to bring the rest of our team."

Night would soon come down over the city of Austin. The air began to cool down Pete took out a large black case that held flares and two large flashlights. He took the flashlights and laid them on the ground. Chet walked up to him and pulled the two grenades out of his pocket and showed them to Pete. Pete recognized what they were instantly.

"You didn't tell me, you did not tell me I could not bring one." Would you believe sticky finger run in the family."

"How many did you take?"

"Just the two," Chet replied and waited for Pete to say something else.

"Well give one of them to me," Pete said and reached out his hand.

He took the grenade and fastened it to his shoulder holster. Chet grabbed the two bullet proof vest out of the car while Pete loaded the M-60's. The belt of rounds seemed like giant firecrackers running down and coiling on the ground.

"Here Pete," Chet said handing him one of the vest. "We need all the protection we can get."

Pete took off the shoulder holster with the grenade and his Springfield and placed them on the M-60. He put on the vest then strapped his shoulder holster back over the vest. He took the Springfield out of the holster and quickly inspected it as he always did. Pete looked at Chet as he placed his finger on the grenade release.

"This is for last resort."

"If you don't get this Two Souls, I'll be damned if I am going to let it kill me. With this here I feel invincible.

"That's good Chet. If it makes one mistake, I will be able to put it in its place and it will take its last flight and boom that will be all, the end.

"And if it doesn't make a mistake," Chet asked. "You had to ask."

"Well!"

"Well, if it doesn't make a mistake then we both go boom and you kill it while it is wounded."

"Hold up a minute you mean you are going to be the bait?" "You got it Einstein besides without the bait we can't set the trap but whatever you do. Do not wait to see the red of its eyes. If you can see it shoot its freaking eyes out and don't miss."

Darkness moved in and it was coming with death. "Pete we have visitors."

Pete turned his eyes focusing on the woman reporter making her way down the small incline down to the bike and hike trail below from Chavez St. She and her camera crew hid behind one of the small shrubs as if to be cloaked from Pete and Chet's eyes. Pete shifted to the left as if he were waiting to see the woman come out from behind the shrub. His eyes caught the reflection of the night lamp. Light bounced off the camera lens the man held.

"Barney could have hidden better?" "Barney?" Chet asked.

"You know that purple hippo or whatever it is that comes out in the morning for kids."

"You watch Barney."

"No, comment," Pete said and continued to set the trap ignoring the visitors.

"What are we going to do about the reporter?"

"Nothing, not a damn thing. I just hope she does not get in the way."

A deadening silence filled the night air. Pete had heard this silence before in Nam. It was as if the animals as well as the insects of the world could feel evil approaching. The deadening quiet of a mortar before it hits. Pete hair on his back tingled he knew Two Souls was near. Pete stared up into the sky then spoke.

"Chet get ready I think it is time for our friend to show its face."

Pete took his position under the night lamp on the hiking trail. He looked up again into the night but this time he could see a shadow swooping across the sky. It was as if the adrenaline running through his veins had brought a new prospective to his senses heightening their level. The smell of fish became stronger in the air from the lake. He could feel the branches move. He could feel the air caress his body. He was ready to do battle. The demon's wings sounded like blades on a helicopter as it was getting ready to land on the ground as the blades shopped through the air. The sound took him back to Viet Nam, but Pete knew it was the demon he would be battling. Two Souls wings sucked away at the air as it stopped suspending itself above as it looked down on them. Pete saw the camera light pop on. With thought of what he had to say the words just came out.

"Cut the fucking light off," he shouted.

It was too late the demon shifted straightening its body. It flapped its wings several times then pressed its wings next to its body and it dove down. In a matter of seconds, it had attacked and severed, the woman's head from her body. Her head rolled down the incline onto the bike trail landing next to Chet as he lay still on the ground waiting for a sign from Pete. The woman's head rolled to a stop. Her blue eye's stared back at Chet. Her mouth gapped open as if her scream had been caught in her throat. Chet shifted his glance up to the woman. Her body was still erect for a few more seconds. He could see the blood pumping from her jugular veins as if it were oil pumping from an oil well gushing up out of the ground. Her blood seemed black in the night. Suddenly her body fell over to the ground. Two Souls took flight and circled then landed by the head.

"Don't fucking move a hair on your body," Pete told Chet. Chet tucked his chin in. He begin to, breath in slowly.

Two Souls reached down and grabbed the reporters then paused and looked towards Chet. It was about to release its grasp on the, woman's head when it heard movement behind it. It turned its head and leered at the camera man squirming for dear life. Its lips drew back for a moment then turned back around and lifted the head off the ground lifting it high above its head. It held it high like Persues holding up the head of Medusa in victory. Two Souls sprung off its legs and ascended into the night then hovered over them like a vulture waiting for a meal.

"Is it gone?" Chet asked as he lifted his head to look around.

"It's up there just hold on I do not think it is over quite yet."

No, sooner had Pete said the words when the demon tucked in its wings and began to descend towards Pete.

"Here it comes," Pete said out loud as he pointed his Springfield at the approaching shadow.

His fingers tightened around the stock as he began to squeeze the trigger. Chet counted to ten then stood up yelling as the adrenaline shot through him.

"Ahhhhhhhh, Ahhhhhhh, Ahhhhhhh," he shouted as he let loose with the M-60. The machine gun echoed out rat-tat-tat-tat- tat, as it ejected each round out of the chamber. Two Souls opened its wings wide and arched its back as it pointed its head upward then flapped its wings rapidly. The wind created by its wings brushed over Chet as he stood clicking away with an empty M-60. The demon released the woman's head dropping it at their feet then vanished.

"You all right Pete?" Chet asked as he placed the M-60 back on its tripod.

Pete reached down grabbed the woman's head then walked up the incline.   He noticed the camera light was still on next to the two dead men on the ground. He stood there for a moment then walked up to the decapitated woman and placed her head back in place. The head half rolled stopping itself on its nose.

"Hell of a price to pay for the news lady," Pete said then walked back down the incline."

"This kind of shit only happens in nightmares," Chet exclaimed as he looked around again.

"You're right Chet the hell with all this get the teams all of them out here A.S.A.P. Tell them to meet us up at the old power plant."

Pete walked up to the car with Chet he took the other M-60 as Chet made the call for the s. w. a. t., teams. Pete cradled the M-60 in his arms and began to walk west down the trail to the power plant. Chet quickly scrambled down the incline grabbed the other M-60 and flung the rounds over his shoulder and made his way up to Pete. As they walked down the trail, they could see fish jumping out of the lake on occasion. The evil had gone for the moment, but it was coming back Pete thought to himself. The water rippled as the fish enter back into the water. They reached the drainpipe that they believed was Two Souls haven.

The dark opening that lead into the lair of this demon made Pete think back to the Marine Corps. In Viet-Nam he had been the best tunnel rat the Corps had produced. Maybe it was his will to survive under such adverse conditions that made him the best. Or maybe it was his fear of the dark and the unknown that lurked within that pushed him into the tunnels after the enemy. Or maybe it was the pitch-black blanket of darkness that made everything in the tunnels invisible that made him so determined to live. His mission had been only one and that had been to seek out and destroy even if it meant his life.

"Seems like you are in another world," Chet told Pete. "Just thinking of what I have to do."

Pete knew what he had to do and the thought of entering the tunnel brought sweat beads to his forehead. There was no way around it. He wanted to kill this thing and he wanted to get Nancy out alive. That was if she was still alive. They did not move from the opening. Morning came quickly and the s.w.a.t., team arrived plus extra back up which Pete was glad to see. The men climbed down the incline like blue ants in hunt for food, but their hunt would be for Two Souls. The lights from their vehicles flashed on like beacons. The red and blue light flashing on and off like lights from a Christmas tree.

"What do you want me to do boss?" Blendez said as he approached them.

"Make sure everyone has plenty of rounds we do not want anyone going dry on us not with this thing."

"Understood Pete," Blendez said and began to bark the orders to the men to check their weapons and to make sure they had plenty of ammo.

CHAPTER 22

Inside the winding abyss of tunnels below the water plant Nancy sat on a platform next to the demon. Nancy's fears surpassed that of anything one could ever comprehend. She scooted herself back against the concrete wall. The reptiles slithered around her legs as if she wasn't even there. The stench of decaying flesh numbed her sense of smell. The hoard of snakes gathered at the demon's feet as if they were his servants and it the king. Two Souls stood and walked to the edge of the platform.

"Soon my children you will have to guard our domain from intruders," Two souls tell the creatures of his domain.

It opened its wings then crouched down slightly and growled. Its voice echoed through the tunnels. The thousands of snakes lifted their heads up off the ground. It was as if to reply back acknowledging its words as a soldier would salute their officer in command ready to do battle for them. Two Souls reached down and lifted the largest of the water Moccasins up out of the water.

"The rest of you my friends guard this lady for me," it said as it looked at Nancy and over at the other snakes.

The snakes slithered and squirmed up on to the platform and coiled around its legs while others opened their mouth and hissed back at the demon. Their thin black tongues whipping out and in like tiny whips. Nancy began to panic and just began to shout.

"What do you want with me? What is it you want with me?"
"You? I want for food. I want you for my children there is no true

reason other than that," it says in its raspy tone. "It is Pete that you want?"

"Yes! Two Soul said the added, "I want the man I want the power he holds he is from the family of my enemies," it tells as it crouched down next to Nancy. Its venomous excretion seeping from its mouth as it spoke in its horse raspy tone. It leaned forward almost touching her face as it exposed its deadly fangs.

"I want his heart."

The reality of the evil as well as her fear combine penetrated deep into her mind. Her head swayed to one side as she fainted. Two Souls stood and screeched out its deafening screaming sound and took flight jetting straight up hitting the manhole cover above and shot out onto the street above. The asphalt broke like clay at impact sending the manhole cover flying sailing out like a Frisbee. The manhole cover crashed into the Starbucks Coffee Shop window on sixth and congress. The sun rose on the horizon police car lights continued to flash on and off like a choreographed light show. Two cops remained with the vehicles up top on Chavez ST. Each of the men wore protective gear ready for whatever it was.

"Blendez are the men ready?" Pete shouted.

"They are ready as they can be sir. We are just waiting for the word from you."

"Good! Now gather the teams around the entrance for a quick briefing and get the dogs."

Blendez gathered the men quickly and then walked up to Pete's side.

"All the men are here and the dogs are ready to go Pete." "Chet let me use your back for a brief second."

Pete lay the map of the maze of tunnels they would be going in on to Chet's back as best that he could. He studied the map carefully after a moment he pointed his finger almost center of the map.

"Here dead center is where we have to be. No matter what we have to get there."

Pete turned around and walked up to the group of men.

"Okay! Listen up check your flashlights it is critical that they work. Make sure the two-way radios are working. Inside the drainpipes the radios will be only means of communications. Blendez find me another set of the two-ways and let's do it."

Frazier walked up with one of the dogs as Blendez returned and handed Pete the two-way radio. Pete turned and handed Chet the two-way radio then brought his attention back to the group of men.

"Team one you will enter first. Kane keep the dog at the lead make sure that you hold on to the dog's leash tightly. Once they pick up its scent, they will be going crazy. Do not let go of the dogs. Team two, Frazier your team will follow. Gloria you take the third team. Move in carefully and slow Pete said and looked at the group of men, "one more thing good luck. Chet, Blendez, let's go do what we get paid for let's go hunting."

"Kane, you and your dog's are lead. The black and brown Doberman entered the drain pipe first then Kane. Pete and team, one followed behind. The huge drain pipe lead deep into the center below the city of Austin like catacombs. They slowly made their way into the tunnel each minute seeming like an hour. Kane held on to the dog leash as the dog begged to be released. If it had not been for the muzzle, they had put on each dog they would have drowned the tunnels with their barking. They reached the first intersection of pipes. If left unattended the demon could circle around undetected. Pete stopped. He lifted the M-60 supporting it on his hip.

"Belendez, post two men at this intersection."

"Smith, take you post here make sure it does not leave from this entrance no matter at what cost. Grab the last man from Gloria's team to help you," related Pete's orders to him then turned and began his ascent further into the pipe with the rest of the team.

Pete knew if the demon made it that far one man could not hold it and, in that fact, they had probably failed as well. Each step they took echoed as the water splashed out from underneath their feet. The lights from the flashlights moved around in all directions like small orbs of energy in space. The dogs began to get more and more restless. They began to growl as if they sensed something in the air. Thirty minutes into the drain pipe had brought them in about two hundred yards the ascent was difficult. The sound of trickling water made a distinctive sounds up ahead. The lights glistened on top of the water that ran down from the rain gutters above that ran back into the lake. As they moved in further, they began to smell a stench.

"What the hell is that God awful smell," Chet said.

"That is rotted human flesh," Pete said without having any doubt.

The repugnant smell made them nauseous the saliva in their mouths hard to swallow. Then abruptly a sound echoed through the maze of tunnels.

"Hold it did you hear that?" Pete asked.

"I did not hear anything," Blendez and Chet replied as well as some of the officers.

They did not hear anything, but each man stood fast. The adrenaline in their veins moving in like a quick drug fix.

Several of the men knelt down and aimed their weapons in anticipation of something coming at them. And others held their weapons at shoulder level as they watched through their sights. Pete held the flashlight in one hand and the machine gun in the other as he balanced it under his arm pit.

"Okay! False alarm keep your ears open and let's move in."

Moments, later they began to approach another set of pipes that intersected into the main artery. These were in from above. The dogs Kane held onto began to growl with such a hate that they began to foam slightly at the mouth. Pete ordered for Kane to take their muzzles off. The Dobermans began to bark frantically. Kane yelled out for the dogs to stop as he pulled back on the leash. The leash broke and the dogs were free from his hold. They ran into the tunnel their barking becoming faint as they went in deeper into the maze of pipes.

"Kane take another man and get those fucking dogs back," Pete shouted.

No, sooner had he given the order when they heard a loud yelping then silence. Each of the men knew that what it had encountered had killed the dog. Then came another then another yelp and then silence. They had a job to do and there was no pulling back now.

"Okay! We have no dogs. Keep your guard up let's finish what we have started.

They continued to move in passing yet another set of intersecting pipes. Pete placed another two cops to guard that position. Pete raised his hand, Chet gave the order to halt. The order was pasted down to the other teams. Pete made his way through the men up to team two.

"Frazier you take your team into the south tunnel and good luck."

Pete made his way back up to the third team.

"Gloria, take your team into the north tunnel and let's flank the fucker and do not try to be a fucking hero." "You're the boss."

Pete turned back around and made his way up to the front again. The ideal is to get the demon out into the open. This would have been the time the teams would release the dogs. But now it would be human instinct and the will to survive. They reached another set of intersecting pipes. Pete would continue straight ahead. Pete moved forward with team one then gave the sign to stop. He watched the two teams disappear into the tunnels. The place became silent lifeless only the trickling of the water could now be heard. A few faint words from some of the cops as they vanished further into the pipes. The quietness was too eerie. Something ate away at Pete's stomach. Intuition perhaps or was it just him thinking the worst of things to come. There was a sound that reached their ears. Something was plopping down into the water. This gave Pete even a worst feeling. Bats flew frantically some bumping into them in their frantic flight out of the huge drain pipe.

"Shit! I could have been a damn lawyer but no I had to choose this occupation shit," Chet said out loud.

"Oh, God look up," one of the officers said as he saw rats running overhead on the piping over their heads.

The rats began to fall like giant black rain drops upon them. They could not believe the size of these rats. They were in awe of the size.

"Must have been the rats we heard plopping into the water up ahead," Blendez said then added, "Whoever is taking care of these rats must be feeding them pretty good."

"Keep your guard up or you might be their next meal," Pete said for he knew that if it had been the rats that had fell into the water, the sound they heard would have been louder.

Pete was not sure what had fallen into the water maybe it had been the rats, but he was not going to take any chances. Pete motioned with his hand and they began to move in deeper. Pete's eyes caught a glimmer of something in the water then again, he quickly raised his hand and the team stopped.

"Did you hear that?" Chet said.

They all listened to the sound of thousands of things plopping into the water. It was like hearing small pebbles falling into the water at once.

"Shine your lights into the water," Pete ordered. "Oh fuck," Blendez said out loud.

It had not been rats that had fallen into the water from above but snakes the size of which Pete or his men had seen before.

"Okay! Let's back up," Pete said then realized it would not matter for the snakes where moving in to fast, "pick a spot Chet and take aim no time for us to run. The rest of you men position yourselves the best you can it's going to be somewhat crowded in here. Aim down and away from anyone in the way."

Chet dropped onto one knee positioned the M-60 on to a tripod on the floor. He then placed the machine gun in place. It had been a good thing the machine gun weigh what it did. If not, the running water entering from the gutters above would have washed it out into the lake. Pete braced his legs solid on the pipe and kept the M-60 at his hip John Wayne style is what he called it.

"Look at the size of these fucking snakes. They need to be in the record book of Guinness," Chet exclaimed.

"The only book they are going to be entered into is the dead book of dead," Blendez boasted.

Pete's machine gun exploded to life then Chet's then Blendez's thirty-eight. Then the rest of the weapons came to life. A flash of light bursting out of the muzzles as each round shot out of the weapons chambers. The casings from the machine guns ejecting less than a second apart. The water exploded as each round tried to fine a target still somehow several of the snakes made their way undetected. An officer's cry filled the tunnel as the fangs of one of the snakes entered deep into his flesh like two ivory nails without any resistance. The man reached down grabbed it by the back of its head and pulled until it released its grasp. He then brought it up to his face and started to yell then brought it up closer to his face and bit down on the snake. He bit down right in back of the head until he had killed it. It had been an act of frustration and fear and the remaining of his adrenaline rush. The man began to stumble back then fell to the floor. The reptiles continued to move in some climbing onto the dry part of the concrete pipe. Others hissing moving their heads from one side to the other halting for a moment and just looking at them. Pete leaned back supported himself on the pipes wall and let loose. The rounds hitting the reptiles splattering them into a thousand pieces other projectiles ricocheted off the wall causing small sparks of light. Several snakes floated past them with their heads split open. Pete knew now that Two Souls was the hunter and they were the hunted. Pete lifted his flashlight and searched the water.

"What are you searching for Pete we got them all?" Chet said.

"Oh! You fucking shit," Blendez cried out as he let loose with the thirty eight.

"What's wrong Blendez," Pete asked.

"The damn thing bit me can you believe that. Half of its side was blown off," he said then leaned against the pipe as he felt the poison rushing through his body. Pete's eyes caught something moving it was one remaining snake and it wasn't going to get away.

"Stay still. Don't move," Pete said as he reached for the Springfield. He aimed and fired.

The snakes head exploded sending its brain and water in every direction. Another snake popped its head out between Pete's and Chet's leg and swam about a yard away and made its way onto the dry part of the concrete pipes wall. It slithered into position looking at them.

"You the last one? Pete says.

It hissed at them as if to tell them something. Had the snakes grown in intelligence Pete mind raced with the thought of somehow Two Souls had managed to send in scouts and snipers in a figure of speech. Had Two Souls been able to teach them the way man had done with the dolphins? If so, the human race was in for a deep kind of hurt in the coming years. Pete followed the snake out of sight as it turned and left.

"You going to let it go Pete?" Chet asked confused.

"It will go back to the creature, and it will tell it where we are," Pete said as he watch the snake.

"You and you get Blendez and Gomez out of here and get some help for them immediately," Chet order two of the officers.

The remaining cops on the outside positioned at the entrance watched as dead snakes and rats floated out and rolled into the lake.

"What the hell is going on in there," Smith called on the two-way radio.

"Don't have time to explain right now just make sure Blendez and Gomez get help they are on their way out," Chet replied then said, "Over and out."

He cut the volume down on the two-way and placed the radio back in the side pouch attached to his belt. The snakes had intelligence and had indeed attacked as soldiers. They served their master well that meant they would be waiting for them Pete thought to himself. They would have to take more caution and react to any sound if they wanted to stay alive. A dark shadow flashed across their path then vanished out of view as quickly as it had appeared in the south tunnel. Phobia was setting in not knowing what was lurking in the dark cloaked by the pitch blackness was beginning to get to them all. Pete leaned against the cool concrete. The two-way radio came to life.

"This is team two to team one come in."

"Team one what is it team two."

"What the fuck is going on heard lot of gun fire." "Frazier it will have to wait. Everything seems to be all right for now. Frazier any sound you hear act on it."

"Tell Pete there is day light up ahead. Will stop in position until I hear from you to move in over and out."

The radio came on this time it was Gloria and her team asking what had happen. She as well ended with they would hold up and wait for us to give the order to move in.

"Teams are at the main intersection of pipe that go into the main dome."??

"Good!" Pete said as his mind began to go back in time.

The Vietnam War entered his thoughts he recalled leaning against the cool earth where he would wait until it was time to move in on the enemy using the element of surprise. Not this time the enemy knew that he was there. It knew he would go in after Nancy. He had to, he could not live with himself if he did not. He had to get to her to stop Two Souls from taking her. Bobby had taken Karen's life. He could not let that happen to Nancy at the demon's hands. For now, he would have to keep his mind clear if he wanted to save her. The putrid stench was getting stronger and more nauseating than it had been. Up ahead they could see the large opening at the end of the pipe as they approached it. At the edge of the pipe, they stopped and looked into the large dome area. A platform had been built straight ahead from the main artery that Pete and his team now stood in.

A light dimly glowed overhead illuminating the place vaguely illuminating the metal steps along the wall heading up to a manhole cover above. Pete eyes could see Nancy lying down on the platform. Snakes slithered between her limbs. She had to be unconscious, and it was a good thing she was Pete thought to himself. Pete put the M-60 down on the ground and pulled the Springfield out of its holster. As Pete was about to step forward a snake slithered out from behind Nancy's neck. Pete stopped he recognized the snake as being the same one in the tunnel that had attacked them. It was the largest of the snakes Two Souls was feeding its pets well. It stopped and lifted its head and hissed exposing its white venomous fangs.

"Shit!" Pete said to himself.

There was no time to analyze the situation he just aimed his gun and fired. The Moccasin seemed to know what his intention was. It hissed and almost instantly another snake squirmed out from behind Nancy and lifted its head and hissed. Pete looked at both the snake it was a gut call, but he figured Two Souls needed the girl for the moment and must have given specific orders not to harm Nancy. Fuck it! There was no time to waste he would have to take a chance. A chance that the snakes slithering over Nancy would not attack. Abruptly the Springfield echoed out as it recoiled ejecting a bullet at a time. The Moccasin's head exploded splattering against the wall of the tunnel.

"Team one this is team two."

"This is team one."

"I don't know what you did but the snakes that were heading our way just made a one eighty and they are heading your way."

"Thanks Frazier."

"Team one this is team three same thing is occurring." "Let's see the snakes heading your way turned around and are making their way to us," Chet replied.

"That's right! We are moving in heading towards you. Good luck!" Gloria said and signed out.

Pete scanned the three large pipes heading into the dome area. He saw snakes crawling out of the main artery they had just come out of. The snakes had executed a military tactic. They had sent in the front line and had sent another to flank them through the small pipes connecting into the large ones. He then caught sight of the snakes coming out of the other two pipes making their way in.

"Watch the snakes." Pete shouted.

It had been a trap they had been waiting for us to get to the center of the dome for the slaughter. Pete's eyes followed the steps leading upward against the wall up to the manhole cover above. The climb would be too arduous of a task for all of them. All it would cause would be a cluster fuck. Panic did that to people there was only one way out and that would be the same way they came in. The other two teams arrived and stared in awe. Pete was caught between a rock and a hard place. It was going to be hard to get out of there alive.

"Pick a tunnel Pete," Gloria said.

"The main artery leading out. Clear me a path Gloria. Frazier move your men back into the tunnel until I can make it to the tunnel. I don't want any of your men hit with stray bullets. Frazier pulled back his men. Gloria noticed that two of Kane's men were missing. There was no time to plan.

"Must be thousands of them," Chet said as he looked at the swarm squirming in.

"Will count them later Blendez," Gloria replied then smiled,

"Okay on the count of three," Gloria shouted the order and started to count.

On the count of three the weapons opened up from their sleep the blast from each gun sounding three times its strength. The guns fired and the bullets hitting the snakes making them jump up in the air on impact. The bullets entered their bodies. For the first time in the dome area Pete noticed the dead bodies that lay sprawled out decapitated, mutilated, as well as being cut up like cattle at the market. Their flesh rotting away like useless garbage. He especially noticed one in particular it was Bobby's head. The body they had found decapitated was Bobby's there was no more questions to be asked about if Bobby got away. All questions had been answered. The hideous scenario before them was the work of a dark force there was no other explanation needed. Pete caught sight of rats as they gorged their fill as well as the insects and maggots on the bodies. All the missing lay before him. A scream broke out abruptly from one of Gloria's team.

"I've been bit," the man shouted and in anger began to shoot at any snake he could.

Chet opened up with the M-60 making an opening straight to the tunnel.

"Nancy, Nancy, wake up, wake up," Pete said over and over. "Come on Pete it's now or never."

Nancy stirred awake and looked at him and began to cry. "Nancy listen to me. Get up very slow and I mean get up now."

"I can't Pete, I can't the snakes."

"Listen to me. Do as I say. The snakes will not harm you. You have to trust me on this Nancy."

Nancy began to stand slowly then stepped over the snakes as she made her way to the edge of the platform. The sound of bullets echoed out.

"That's it just a few more steps," Pete urged her as Nancy stepped over the snakes.

Nancy made it to the edge and stepped off falling into Pete's arms. She wanted to hold onto him forever. She began to cry. Pete pushed her back softly but firmly. She wanted to hold onto him forever. She began to cry.

"Cry if you must but we are going to have to walk out of here now. Take this flashlight and stay close to me.

Pete followed the steps leading upward to the street above again. Two souls had access to other openings into the main tunnel he thought then looked back at the decaying bodies that lay at the opening of the other tunnels. This demon this Two Souls had to be stopped. But first they had to get Nancy out of there.

"Gloria get your men and let's get the fuck out of here before they regroup."

Gloria and her team made it safely into the main tunnel. Kane and his men made it into the tunnel then Nancy, Chet, Blendez, and Pete. Frazier's team followed. Again, they had entered the abyss of pitch black and the flashlights their only eyes.

"Team one this is team three." "What's up?"

"Reaching the intersection of pipes seems clear."

"Stay focus, over and out," Chet replied as they moved on.

Team one passed the intersection of the tunnels making sure that it was clear for the other teams to continue.

"Okay Nancy, Chet says as he reaches out his hand for her to grab." She looked over at Pete."

"Go ahead Nancy I will be right behind you."

She turned back around and as she stepped into the center of the intersecting pipes Two Souls shot through in an attempt to grab Nancy and disappeared into the drainpipe.

"Ahhhhhhhhh, ahhhhhhhh, ahhhhhhhh," the Chet screamed out.

He reached out and grabbed his elbow where Two Souls had clawed his arm. Chet had managed to pull quickly enough to get Nancy across in the main tunnel heading out. He then moved forward and lifted the M-60 and began to fire into the south tunnel. As quickly as it had ascended on them it had disappeared.

"You okay Chet? Pete asked.

No sooner he said the words Two Souls had circled around. It came from the north tunnel but before Chet could react it clawed lashing out cutting deep into Chet's face. It claws making deep lacerations into his flesh. Blood ran down his face. Chet ignored the wound and shouted angrily into the tunnel as Two Souls vanished.

"I'll kill you so help me God."

"Here Blendez," Pete said as he gave him the M-60. "Shit! Do I look like Arnold," he quipped as he grabbed the weapon and pointed the muzzle into the south tunnel.

Pete took the M-60 from Chet.

"Okay! Now move when we began to fire," Pete told them as he pointed the weapon into the north tunnel.

Kane finished bandaging Chet's face the best he could with the cloth from one of the officer's shirt that lay dead next to them. Pete opened fire then Blendez. Kane then helped Chet and headed for the opening. Nancy followed and crossed then the screams from Frazier's team reached them.

"Team one this is team two."

Kane took the two-way radio from Chet. "Go ahead."

"Snakes are moving in and their moving fast."

Blendez saw thousands of snakes moving in from the south tunnel. Pete saw the same and began to shout.

"Move, move, move," he shouted the order.

Blendez moved across the men from Frazier's team and Frazier then Pete. He moved back and let loose with the M-60. Meanwhile the first team had crossed another intersection of pipes then Nancy. Two Souls had been waiting and watching like an invisible ghost. Nancy stepped into the tunnel and pointed the flashlight into the south tunnel. The sound of water splashing reached her ears. She lifted the light up slightly only to shine on the demon's face. She screamed and in that split second it vanished with Nancy into the north tunnel leaving no trace except the cries for help from Nancy. The teams crossed Chet waited for Pete to approach.

"Get the men out of here," Pete said then added, "I'm going back in alone. This is between me and, Two Souls."

"You're nuts," Chet said.

"No! This thing wants me that's why it is playing this fucking cat and mouse game."

"Well, I am coming along partner."

Pete looked at him and knew there were no words to change his mind.

"Okay! Let's go hunting," Pete said

Pete and Chet made their way back into the domed area. Suddenly gunfire echoed out throughout the maze of tunnels as well as screams. Horrifying scream that reached them and sent chills down their spine. Pete saw movement out of the north tunnel. Quickly Chet and he aimed in the direction of the screams. They could see the opening to the main intersection of pipes the dome area Carefully they entered and made their way over the decaying bodies. They climbed over several of the fallen officers.

"Over their Chet, Pete called out.

Chet moved up to them and helped them into the opening. "I have never been so happy to see someone in all my life as I do now," said one of officer then looked at Pete and said, "It got them we could not see it. It was just too fast. It was just too fast."

"What about the rest," Pete asked.

"Gloria and several of her team moved into the south tunnel. Frazier and his team just moved back into main artery. They heard scraping noises and footsteps. They all aimed at the opening then saw who it was. Speak of the devil there they come. Frazier made his way out of the pipe into the dome area as well as his men. Gloria and her team came out of the south tunnel back into the dome. She looked around then spoke.

"I guess there is no way out of here."

Chet noticed one of the snakes moving up next to Blendez. He lifted his revolver.

"Don't move," he said then broke out with gun fired.

He fired at the snake as if a hundred snakes where moving in. He fired upon the creature filling it with rounds from his gun. The snake exploded, it remains where left like ground beef.

"Get ready boys there back and by the hundreds," Gloria shout as she saw more snakes coming out of the south tunnel into the dome.

Frazier and his men pointed their weapons at the main tunnel while Pete, Blendez, and Chet aimed at the north tunnel with Kane and his team. Chet took the grenade from his side as the snakes squirmed up to the edge of the pipe.

"No, not yet," Pete told him as he placed his hand over Chet's then added, "we may need them in a few. This has been a trap well set."

"So, now these snakes have a purpose," said Gloria.

"I mean these snakes will be waiting for us no matter where we go. But still, you need to get out of here. I will go in alone after Nancy. Something it will not be anticipating. Meanwhile you and your men get out through the main tunnel. Kill the snakes first of course."

"We have tried that all ready," Frazier answered back. "Get on the two-way and call for back up and get your men out of here Frazier," Pete side with conviction.

"What about the snakes?" said one of the, officers. "Blast the hell out of them then. Blast them some more until you make your way out of here."

"I don't like spiders our snakes," Chet sang to himself as the rest of them looked on.

The sound of the manhole cover being moved reached them. The place went dead with silence. Two Souls dropped down from above on its way down it struck at the light. The tunnel as well as the dome area they stood in became pitch black. Everyone lifted their flashlights. The light shone on the demons eye the sign that it was in there with them.

"Fire," Pete shouted.

Cries echoed out as they found their fate at the hands of Two Souls. The demon claws ripped through the darkness like lethal blades. Again, after its attack it vanished.

"The snakes are moving in," Chet said as he shone his light at the openings of the pipes.

"Gloria," Pete called out. "I'm still standing."

"Chet," Pete called out.

"Here and running low on the M-60's rounds." "Frazier."

"One man down," he replied back moving his flashlight along the edge of the domed area.

"Kane."

"Four down and they need medical attention badly."

Again, gun fire echoed out through the dome. Flashes from the guns illuminating the dome.

"Fucking snake are getting on my nerves," Blendez shouted pointing his gun down at the dead snake.

Pete scanned himself with the flashlight and the area around his legs. He noticed his grenade was missing. Somehow the demon had managed to take the grenade in the darkness. It had been close enough to have kill him if it had wanted. But it was not time it was just playing with them. The grenade had been fastened to his shoulder holster.

"What's that?" Gloria said.

They became silent as they listened to the metallic sound moving down to the main tunnel. Chet shinned his flashlight up into the pipe.

"It's the grenade take cover," he yelled and dove to the ground.

There, was no time to think about the snakes. They did what they had to do. They dove to the ground. Boom! The blast from the grenade caused them a momentary loss of hearing. The ringing in their ears slowly subdued after several minutes. A snake sprung from its perch striking at Blendez leg. Blendez moved and fired killing it. He had fire so quick without aiming that one of the bullets before he hit the snake past through his pant leg.

"I think the snakes has the hot's for you Blendez," Chet said.

One, gun then two, three, four, echoed out as the men blasted away at the snakes by them. Pete waited for a moment before giving them orders to carry out.

"Gloria you, Brown, Kane, and Frazier get these men out of here. Either of these tunnels south or north. They have to lead to another dome. Reach it and climb up the latter to the manhole cover above to safety.

"What about you and Chet?" Gloria asked concern.

"This thing has closed us in there is only one way to get it out in the open and that is to go after Nancy. It has outsmarted us it has kept just one step ahead of us. It wants me I don't know why but I know it does. So, it will have a chance to do what it wants. Now get the men out of here."

CHAPTER 23

Pete watched as Gloria and her team and those that could still walk moved into the south tunnel.

"Okay! Chet, we go north."

"How do you know it will be waiting at the end of the north tunnel?" Chet asked.

"I know this Chet gut feeling and just because Gloria and her team went into the south tunnel.

"I don't understand your reasoning, Pete."

"Look it wants me there is no doubt there. I know it has scouts moving to it as we speak to tell it which way we are going. Just think how, was it possible that it kept one foot in front of us.

"Look we don't speak snake, but it does."

" I understand. But do you know how absurd that sounds?" Chet states and then nods his head a few times in agreement.

Pete pointed his flashlight illuminated their way. Pete began to sweat he hated tunnels. And it did not matter which of the tunnels he had, chose Pete knew it would be waiting for them. It had used Nancy as one would cleverly move a pawn on a chess match. She had just been bait and that was all. Why hadn't he known? Fifteen minutes into the tunnel there was still no sign of the demon. Pete spotted something up ahead. They moved slow and careful. At first his heart missed a beat then he calmed his thoughts ran wild then he rationalized the situation. He stopped and scrutinized the leg they had come across. It was a woman's leg and part of Nancy's dress was wrapped around it. It had given him a sign letting Pete know that he was on the right track. But was this Nancy's leg had the demon severed her leg. Pete thought for a second then looked at his partner.

"Okay! Let's play your game," Pete said under his breath.

Pete hoped it was not Nancy's leg. It was a cat and mouse game, but he was not the lead actor. Pete kicked the leg to one side and continued to move in.

"Pete," Chet called out bewildered as he recognized part of the dress as he bent forward to pick up the leg.

His flashlight falling out of his hand. The flashlight hit the concrete and the light went off.

"Leave it alone Chet it is not Nancy's," Pete said as he looked over his should then continue.

Pete followed the pipe as it curved around and headed in another direction. Another pipe entered the tunnel at the bend. Pete scanned the pipe and continued on.

"Don't fall too far behind Chet," Pete said as he made his way around the bend.

Two Souls appeared out of nowhere at the opening. It watched as Pete moved around the bend. It began to move toward Chet.

Somehow even in the pitch back tunnel he knew something was coming he felt a tingle at the base of his neck. The hairs on his back literally stood up. He hit the flashlight several times before it came on. And as the light flashed on it shone on Two Souls hideous face. Its face was to close for comfort. Chet knew his only hope to survive would be to escape. Escape to where? His eyes scanned the pipe in urgency. Up ahead he notices two smaller pipes coming in, in an angle into the tunnel. Maybe three feet before the bend in the tunnel where Pete had vanished. He just hoped it was not his imagination playing tricks on him. He began to move backward keeping an eye on the demon. Two Souls trotted forward slowly as to play with him. It was an attempt to scare him and at this point it was working.

Chet stopped turned and tried to look into the smaller pipe. He tried to focus his eyes the best he the darkness allowed. He sized up the opening quick. Two Souls stopped and tilted its head as if it knew what Chet was up to. Chet's eyes quickly measured the opening. It would be a tight squeeze, but it was his only hope of getting away alive. One, two, three, he counted then ran with all he had. Hell at that moment he did not care if it went up or down or sideways. All he knew at that moment was if it kept him alive it was good enough. He saw Two Souls lips turn up in a snarl. Chet kept an eye on the demon. Two Souls moved his foot forward as he got ready to attack. It had been the sign for Chet to move. He jumped into the pipe and with his elbows he began to crawl up the pipe until his feet were in. His elbow began to bleed as the concrete rubbed his flesh raw. The M-60 had managed to free itself and drop to the pipe below.

Chet stopped momentarily and looked down then turned back and began to climb upward. Abruptly he felt a grip like a vise around his ankle. He was jolted back an inch. He felt the burning sensation as his flesh became even more, raw as he was being dragged down. Bracing, himself with his other leg as best he could. He had a second or two before Two Souls yanked him into the tunnel with it. Chet reached over with one of his hands and grabbed the grenade from his side. He placed the pin of the grenade in his mouth and pulled as hard as he could. At that moment he did not care if he lost a tooth pulling the pin as long as his ideal worked. He let go of the prime handle and let it drop to the pipe below. The grenade fell at the demon's feet with a metallic clank. Instantly he felt the pressure subside from his ankle. He was released and he did not need time to think of what to do. He began to move upward as fast as he could. The blast came and it echoed out tenfold. The blast reached his ears and ruptured his eardrums. He was safe he thought to himself then fell unconscious from the searing pain. Pete was forced down to the ground from back lash of the blast. The demon had set his trap well. He was alone now the hunter now the hunted. Pete knew he had to move on to where Two Souls wanted him go. Gloria and her team had finally reached the dome area. She moved her flashlight around the dome only to see that team two had been massacred. Two Souls had been waiting and had surprised them slaughtering the whole team. She began to hear footsteps coming quickly.

"Cut the lights, cut the light," she said urgently.

Then the sound of the demon's wings reached them as it entered the dome. It was dark and the only way it could see them would be the light and their body heat.

"Lie down, get one of the dead bodies and place their body over yourselves and keep the fucking lights off."

Each officer remaining did what she said. The inside of the dome went pitch black. Two Souls landed shifting his head from side to side scanning the area for life. It tilted its head as its sensors worked. Dead bodies were the only thing it could pick up. Gloria felt a snake crawling next to her face. She would not scream she told herself even if it bit her she would not give them away. Two Souls shifted its head again then began a slow trot then flapped its wings and shot straight up to the manhole cover above.

"It worked," Gomez exclaimed.

"Let's get the fuck out of here before it comes back, I do not think this trick will work again. Check for anyone that might be alive and let's make like the wind," Gloria barked.

"What about the dead?" Gomez asked.

"I don't think the dead will mind they can wait for us to return when it is the right time. Now move let's get the hell out of here."

Two Souls returned to where he had left Nancy. It perched its self on the ledge that ran around the top of the dome. It fixed its red eyes on Nancy. From below where Nancy was it looked like a dragon from the old folklores perched above. Pete saw alight ahead at the end of the tunnel. He knew it would be where Nancy was. He knew the demon would be waiting for him. He also knew the demon would have the advantage. It could see in the dark he couldn't. Still Pete would play its game he made his way into the dome and looked around. It looked abandoned except for Nancy. As Pete entered the dome it watched and scrutinized his every step. Pete felt its eyes on his back. He sensed the demon was there. He grabbed Nancy into his arms.

"Don't turn around. It is on the ledge looking at you," she told him.

She could see the demon start to get up. "It's getting up Pete."

"Do not panic just remain still and quite."

Like a bird of prey, it swooped down as if pouncing upon a fish jumping out of the water with its claws stretched out.

Pete face contorted as he felt its razor-sharp claws clamped sinking deep into his flesh. It closed its hands firmly around Pete's shoulders and lifted him up into the air. Chet moaned as he stirred awake his head hurting like the dickens, but he had to find Pete. His eyes focused in and out. He had to find Pete if he was still alive. He made his way back down into the pipe. He bent down and searched through the rubbish for the M-60. He lifted it up or what remained of the weapon.

"Can't fire this," he said to himself the dropped it to the ground and retrieved his revolver. He stumbled forward as he made his way down the tunnel and around the bend. Chet cupped his ear as the pain shot through, but he did not stop. Light up head let's hope he is still alive his mind raced. He reached the edge of the tunnel only to see Pete dangling in the air from the demon's feet. He fell to one knee for support aimed and began to fire holding on to the revolver with both his hands. Two Souls released his grasp. Pete was dropped to the ground like a sack of potatoes. Pete stood and went to Nancy and grabbed her hand.

"This way Pete," Chet called out.

"That leads back to the tunnel we just came from." "I know Pete but there is a smaller pipe that leads upward. It is the only chance we have. It can't follow us in there its wings make it impossible for to follow us."

Chet moved in front of the tunnel holding his revolver out in front. Nancy entered then Pete. He waited for a moment. He fired two rounds then two more rounds at the demon. "Eat this you fucking snake," Chet shouted.

The sound of the gun firing pin hitting dead steel reached his ears. He squeezed the trigger again, click, he tried again, click, he looked over his shoulder.

Pete looked at the two tunnels leading upward. Chet looked back and shouted.

"Fuck! Hurry up Pete I'm out of bullets. Take the one on the left."

Chet looked over his shoulder again. Pete was out of sight he just hoped the demon would continue to fly until he could make it to the opening. He counted one, two, three; he turned and rushed through the tunnel to the opening. He could see the light from Pete's flashlight up ahead. Chet had managed to make it to safety as he looked back, he could see the demon's red eyes leering into the tunnel after him. He stopped and reloaded his weapon. He looked at Two Souls as it growled at him in anger. He discharged the complete six rounds into the demon. Two Souls cried out in agony. The screeching sound sounding like a siren through the tunnel. Chet knew he could not kill the demon but at least he could cause it pain.

It had been about an hour. Gloria had come to an opening the dim light exposing the opening to freedom. They stopped at the edge and looked in only to see it had been where they had just came from. The tunnel had led them back to Two Souls domain. The dead lay on the ground like that of the civil war. Men lay dead over their comrades in arms. Heads missing, legs, arms, scattered.

Pete handed Nancy his Springfield.

"Take this Nancy, you will need it soon."

"Let's do it," Pete said as he made his way up and out of the small drain pipe.

Gloria and her team entered the dome area looked around Two Souls was nowhere to be found.

"Follow me," Gloria said as he reached down to picked up a revolver from one of the fallen.

She pride it free from the arm that lay away from the cop it belonged too. They made their way through the north tunnel making their way into another domed area. The domed area that Gloria and what remained of her team where in. Hearing the approaching footsteps Gloria shouted the order to fire. They fired blindly in the dark.

"Hold your fire it is us," Pete shouted urgently. The gun fire stopped.

"You are alive," Gloria exclaimed happily as she rushed up to them.

"Glad to see some of you made," Pete said.

"Thanks to Gloria's quick thinking the few you see standing here made it. If she had not told us to lie under the dead and to wait for the demon to scan the place and leave, we would all be dead."

"I studied up a little on snakes and the reading paid off.

It has a radar like sensor, and it picks up on heat. So, I just thought that if the dead were not generating warmth maybe it would not detect us. It was a long shot but it worked."

"We are not out of trouble as of yet," Pete reminded them.

From above Two Souls descended down. It had fooled them again it had known that Pete would find his way to this dome. It landed and flapped its wings several times then leered at them as its head swayed back and forth from side to side. Its black tongue flicking in and out of its mouth as the cops flashlights shone on its face.

"Where does that thing come from?" asked Gomez. "From hell! It comes from hell." Chet replied.

Two Souls began to flap its wing fast then faster as if he had read their minds. The force of its wings sucking and discharging the air in the dome made it hard for them to aim and fire. Some of the rounds managed to get threw and hit their target. The demon screeched out in pain. Blood oozed out of its wounds. But it was like seeing a movie being on rewind as the bullets were forced out of its flesh and its blood and wound healing right before them. It leaped up it flew around several times then flew low and as they aimed it knocked the flashlights out of their hands leaving them to fend in the dark.

"Nancy."

"Right beside you Pete," Nancy said as she pointed the weapon out in front of her.

"Gloria."

" I'm still here."

The rest of the men answered out in the same manner they were all safe for the time being. It had left them in the dark. The dark would now play a game on their minds. The fear of the dark and what monsters lay in its depth would eat away at them.

"Pick up the lights do it nice and slow," Pete said for he knew it had not left it was playing its favorite game and that was fear.

"I can barely see just a few inches in front of my eyes," Gloria says.

"Use your hands."

They searched blindly for several minutes then the silence was broken.

"I found one," said one of the men then another then Gloria.

Gloria scanned the area and picked up another flashlight off one of the dead body, she repeated the process two more times then said out loud.

"Three flashlights that work the rest busted."

"Okay! There are twelve of us left we are going to have to fend like the blind to get out of these mazes. One of you will be point Gloria. Gomez take the tail and you take the middle and the rest of you just follow. Now grab on to the person in front of you and let

"I don't think Williams can make it Detective," said Brown. "I can do it just help me get out of here," Williams said desperately.

"You heard him Brown now let's get the hell out of here," Pete said and faces Nancy.

She nodded her head and that was the sign to go. It was a slow tedious effort for each step they took. They would have to restrain their fears as well as the anxiety of having to travel through the tunnels. They made their way with hardly any light knowing that the demon could attack and would attack them at any time. The only thing in their minds at that precise moment was to stay alive. None of them could believe that it had taken place. Or that they had lost so many men and that a creature like Two Souls even existed. It had taken them three hours to penetrate the tunnel out to freedom. But they had endured the arduous task by pure determination. They were free their insides exhaling a sigh of relief as they stepped out into the open air. At the entrance the paramedics waited anxiously. As soon as they saw the wounded, they rushed over to them and quickly put them onto gurneys and transported them to the hospital to be looked at.

"Detective, Detective, look up there," said one of the paramedics as he pointed up to the sky.

Two Souls let out its horrible screeching then tuck its wings in and dove down like a missile. Pete looked up and knew what was going to happen next. He began to run to the ambulance where Nancy stood. But the demons speed had been too fast. Before Pete could reach her it was too late. The others looked on dumbfounded. Before they realized what was happening it had grabbed Nancy by her shoulders sinking in its razor claws into her flesh. Nancy screamed out in agonizing as Two Souls spread its wings and flapped then hard and fast. In a matter of seconds it was high in the sky and it spread is wings out wide and glided suspending them in midair.

"I don't think it is taking Nancy to see the Oz," Chet said out loud.

"Please whatever you are let me go," Nancy plead.

Two Souls brought her up eye level to his. He glared at her then in a flash no more than a second Nancy noticed the demon's eyes had turned back to their human state for a few seconds then turn back to the horrible snake eye and the soul's human eye. The eyes peer into her soul. A round was fired by one of the officer Chet rushed the man like a fullback reaching the man. He reached out and brought the man's hand down then both men fell to the ground with a hard thud.

"You crazy, you might hit the lady," Chet told him then rolled over and looked up at the demon.

Two Souls tucked its wings in and descended from above like a falling rock then before reaching the ground it began to flap its wings rapidly then landed with a dull thump as its feet hit the ground. It began a slow trot. The demon leered at all the officers as it turned its head from side to side. It gave them a vicious snarl. It flapped open its wings and spread his wings showing its enormous wingspan. Nancy fell to her knees next to its feet as if praising a God. One of the men still wearing his riot gear moved in. But the riot gear was no threat to the demon. As the man moved in close enough Two Souls lashed out its vengeance. Its claws slashing out cutting into the bullet proof vest as if it were just mere paper. The man moaned once and fell back like a falling tree.

"Everyone remain still and wait for my orders," Pete says out loud firmly.

He then looked towards Two Souls.

"I have a shot Pete I can hit it right between its freaking eyes right where it hurts," Chet told him as he aimed his revolver.

"No, we may not be able to kill it. We may not be far enough from the base of its power source," Pete replied and motioned with his hand for Chet to put the gun away then added, "We do not want to make it any angrier than it is. Nancy's is too close for comfort besides it wants me."

"You are nuts that thing will kill you as soon as you get in arms reach of it," Chet told him.

"That is the ideal but hopefully I can buy myself a little time."

"How can you do that it is an animal there is no reasoning with it."

"If that is true Chet then it will kill me. But it is intelligent therefore it will reply to my questions. It will hopefully give me enough time to think of something."

"I hope you are right Pete and good luck."

Pete began to walk slowly up to the demon then stopped just about an arm length away from its reach. Two Souls studied Pete's every move. Pete moved just a little closer. He then began to reach for his Springfield as he withdrew the weapon halfway out of the holster the demon lips moved back into a snarl to expose its teeth. Pete walked to his left the demon's head turned following his movement then the clanking of the many rifles as the officers slapped them down hard into their hands and aimed filled the air. Gomez attempted to move in and reached out to take Nancy's hand. In a twinkle of a starlight, it came to life swinging its arm and catching Gomez by his. It brought Gomez up to its side. It then grabbed his head into its reptile hands and before everyone's eyes it crushed the man's head as if where a melon. Brain matter spattered and oozed out between its fingers. Where there had once been Gomez's face now there was no more than shredded meat and eyeballs that hung freely from his eye sockets. The white of bone shone through like broken porcelain chips. It lifted Gomez up then thrust its hand into the man's chest and pulled out the heart. Gomez's heart still pulsating in the demon's hand. It released its grasp Gomez' body plummeted to the ground. Two Souls tilted its head upward and screeched out as if in victory. It then looked at the crowd of officers paused for a moment then threw the heart at them. Its head moving forward as its black tongue flick in and out of its snarling face.

"Okay you ugly shit! You want me, then take me just to stop killing them," Pete shouted out in frustration.

"No, please, no please don't kill him," Nancy begged the demon.

Two Souls reached down lifted Nancy up by her neck then looked at Pete as it caressed her cheek with its razor sharp claw. It scrutinized Pete face it was as if it wanted him to act without reason as if it wanted him to become primal, primal, in a rage like an animal for the battle between man and demon began.

CHAPTER 24

From out of nowhere the transient that knew the story of Two Souls appeared. The one person of Two Souls blood line that Pete had been searching for came running up to them. The demon looked on as the man quickly untied two leather pouches. Two Souls tilted its head and watch as the transient immediately began to make a circle around the demon. He moved rapidly with two different colored powders as he made the circle around Two Souls, he began to chant words out loud.

"Move back detective," ordered the transient.

Pete did as he was told. The transient completed the circle then looked back at Pete then said the remaining words to finish the ritual to keep the demon at bay.

"Will that hold him?" Pete asked.

"For now, yes, but not for long my words are not strong enough. You have to complete the ritual. My word will only give you more times."

"What do I know about this ritual you speak of?" "Detective you have to trust me it will come to you. Two things you need to know detective. One you are an Eagle Warrior. Second you are from his blood line as well. That is the reality and the reason it wants your heart more so than the others."

"Fuck, I need to wake up from this fucking nightmare is what I need. I need this like a bullet to the head."

"You may just want that by the end. As crazy as it sound detective, you are an Eagle Warrior."

"Okay! For argument sake just explain what the fuck is an Eagle Warrior so we can understand what the hell you are babbling about," Pete said.

"An Eagle Warrior is a guardian for the Gods. It protects the God's from evil that tries to enter into their world."

"And you think that I am one of these so call guardians." "You were born and raised here in Texas, Tex-Mex! But

detective your blood line is from the Aztec origin."

"Yes, my grandmother did speak of such roots, but she never mentioned that I was some Eagle Warrior."

"One is not told that he is such. One must first defeat death in a way where the odds are stacked against him. And if he lives then he is chosen by the Great One to be a guardian. At this time when your spirit refused to leave this world it becomes strong. This is the time the Eagle Warrior is born within you and intertwines with your spirit. So now you must either help me defeat this demon or die at its hands. Just repeat the words as they sound if you are truly a chosen one the Aztec words of the old ones will come to you automatically."

Pete nodded his head agreeing with the transient. "What the hell it's worth a try. The transient began to chant the words of the Old Ones.

"Two Souls you have called upon the dark forces for you evil deeds. You have called the God of hell to give you immortal powers," chanted the transient.

Pete followed and as the transient stopped Pete continued to chant the words of the old ones as if he had always known the words. The word spewing from his mouth in the Aztec dialect.

"Now I call upon the Eagle God the spirit of life to fight this evil power of hell. Spirit God; defeat this demon take its powers away and send it to the fires below form which it dwells."

As Pete chanted the transient pulled out a dagger from his side. He lifted it above his head and chanted several words then spoke.

"Detective this is the same dagger Two Souls was said to have used that night. That night he sold his soul to the Devil. It is the only thing that can kill the evil. It must be driven straight through its heart when the circle of life burst into flames.

"You sure this will work?" Pete questioned.

"I am like you detective I only know what I am told or taught. But if you ask me again if it will work? I can only say I do not really know. If it doesn't it might buy you enough time to get the girl away. After that, I guess I would have to say kiss your ass goodbye."

"Okay! Do whatever it is you have to do?"

"No, detective you do what you have to do. You and you alone can do this. You have about thirty seconds when the circle becomes flames to thrust that dagger in your hand into its heart. Now you must raise the dagger above your head. You must now ask for the power of the Great One to enter into the blade. Sink it deep into the demon's heart. Now the tricky part is in order to take the lady out of the circle you must be very careful. If the circle is broken at any time the dagger will be useless and all will be just a futile cause. You must tell her to believe in you. You must tell here the flame will not harm her or you when you go through the fire. When you are ready to enter the circle just raise the dagger up high. Waste little time entering the circle and remember do not break the lines. Walk through the flame thrust the dagger in the creature and walk out of the circle."

The demon's head swayed back and forth. It moved its foot forward it screeched out in pain as the force field of the fire kept it from moving out of the circle.

"Nancy, Nancy look at me. I love you very much so do as I say," Pete told her as she remained kneeling at the demon's feet.

"I'm scared Pete."

"I am to Nancy. I am to."

Everyone looked on in bewilderment it was something that was not real. Or that could never happen in this world. But it was happening in their world.

"I know you are scared baby I know," Pete acknowledged.

Pete knew the circle kept the demon in, but he did not know if it kept the demon from killing Nancy. From above a raven and an eagle appeared in the sky at the same time. Both birds cawed and vanished from sight.

"Now Pete now," the transient shouted, "the sign has appeared now."

Pete stood in front of Two Souls standing at the edge of the circle of fire. Somehow Pete knew what to say as he lifted the dagger up above his head.

"Great One, release your powers into this blade. I, call upon thee to come to us on the wings of the eagle your brother."

Pete opened his shirt and ran the dagger twice over his heart the dagger dripped of his blood. As his blood trickled down onto the circle of fire at that instant it burst into flames. It radiated like a rainbow of different colors. He ran the blade in the aura of the flames and lifted the dagger again over his head.

"Great One, we have now opened the gates to the two worlds. Grant me the power Old Wise One, grant me the power to bring this human back. Bring him back from the dark side and send the evil that holds him captive back to hell."

As Pete chanted the flames rose with more brilliance of its energy. The demon's eyes began to change back. The once red evil piercing eyes with the yellow oval slowly returned to their human state. It was as if the last words Pete spoke were making Jesse fight for control of his soul. Jesse was trying but the demon was still too strong, and Two Souls was not ready to give up his fight of as yet. Two Souls growled and in that instant the eyes returned to their previous stated back to the demon's eyes. It moved its head forward and leered at the transient.

"Why do you help this man against me I can give you what you want," Two Souls growled in its raspy voice.

"You know as well as I Two Souls why I help him."

"No, matter fool if he is an Eagle Warrior it will do no good. I will get stronger with every minute. The Great One has lost this battle my brother. The Wise One cannot help you or this man. He has grown old even in the mystical world. It is too late."

"You lie as the devil you are."

Pete continued, "The power of the earth is the same as the universe. You created the rivers that flow. You created the wind that allows the eagle to fly amongst your stars. And in the heavens, you live Great One. Release your vengeance against this evil spirit. Lightning shot across the sky as never before in broad daylight. Lightning struck zigzagging its way down. A branch of the lightning broke off making its way to the tip of the dagger. The electrical charge bouncing off the dagger onto the demon. Its devil eyes turned back to human eyes. A strained voice from within the demon spoke. It was Jesse's voice.

"Kill me you must kill me please."

"Show me the face of the evil that dwells within," Pete called out."

From behind the demon the evil Witchdoctor, Two Souls face appeared as well as the amulet Jesse had found as a child appeared around his neck.

"You have no power over me," Two Souls growled.

The amulet sprouted needle like legs and clawed at the Jesse" flesh for reentry into Jesse's heart into his soul. Chet saw the amulet he figured what the hell he had one chance to help Pete either he would do what he set out to do. Or the demon would cut him down right in front of everyone's eyes and he would look like a big dope. What the hell he told himself and began to run. The transient saw Chet and knew what he was about to do.

"The circle, do not break the circle," the transient yelled as Chet threw himself through the air.

Chet closed his eyes and reached out with his hand. He felt the amulet in his hand quickly he wrapped his fingers around it. Two Souls swung his arm in an attempt to ward off the advance, but he began to lose power moving slower. Its claw scraped across Chet's side tearing his shirt just scratching the surface of his flesh. Chet hit the ground and rolled managing to land out of the ring of fire.

"I got the amulet I got it," Chet shouted.

The raven they had seen up in the sky before reappeared. It swooped down taking the amulet out of Chet's hand. Suddenly the eagle appeared in the sky with its talons out in an attack mode. The eagle dove at the raven sinking its talons deep into the ravens back. The bird cried out in pain releasing the amulet. As the amulet fell a door seemed to open up in this universe from a different dimension. An old Aztec Indian walked out of the opening slowly. It was Montezuma, he looked at the eagle reached out his hand and the amulet fell into the palm of his hand. The transient spoke in the old tongue.

"Montezuma," He exclaimed.

The transient and Montezuma exchanged words as Pete listened understanding every word. Montezuma looked at Pete and spoke. But his words were in English.

"You have done well Eagle Warrior. I will save a place for you at my side for now you have many years to live still. Learn the old ways for it is part of you. For now, do what you have to do to kill the demon," Montezuma said and vanished through the doorway into the dimension he had come.

Pete wasted no further time he quickly stepped into the circle. He hesitated for a moment as he lifted the dagger as Jesse's face appeared pleading with him to stop. Pete knew it was the creature trying to trick him. He paused for a second dwhat if he was wrong. Then abruptly he shouted.

"No!" Pete cried out and sunk the dagger deep into Two Souls heart.

As the demon screeched out a horrible cry Pete grabbed Nancy and helped her out of the circle. No, sooner had they stepped out of the circle of fire when the guns fired out like a thousand firecrackers going off at once. They filled the demon with bullets. The glow of its power ceased, and the demon fell to the ground into a fetus position. In stages in slow motion, it began to change separating into two spirit like bodies one of Two Souls the Witchdoctor and the other of Jesse. From Two Souls a giant serpent crawled out as the earth began to open up. Smoke escaped from Two Souls body as the serpent slithered into the crack back into the earth. From the smoke a pair of hands were created. It moved under Two Souls body lifted it and brought it to the crack in the earth and vanished into its depth. Only the stench of strong sulfur remained. As they looked up into the sky as the eagle cawed a shooting star shot across the sky. Pete wondered if it were possible for a star to shoot across the sky during the daytime hours. It probably did happen it just went unnoticed. Who really knew? They continued to look up at the sky.

They wondered if it had all taken place at all. Nobody really knew what had happen all they knew was that the story of the Ancient Ones of Two Souls and his evil powers. Of his desire for immortality and his need to call upon the evil power of the God from below. Pete was just glad that the powers of the Great One, to us in this time and age better known as God, was all they had needed. The eagle appeared in the sky screeched several times then flew straight up into the heavens and vanished from sight. There was no way to explain what happen. With all the intelligence and professional opinions, they would still refuse of such an entity as the Devil or evil at its best. A shooting star shot through the sky again and the eagle cawed out and vanished into thin air.

www.ingramcontent.com/pod-product-compliance
Lightning Source LLC
Chambersburg PA
CBHW061220310726
48971CB00007B/1891